I0748575

PRAISE FOR EMISSARY

Immersive. Engaging. Thrilling.

Brooks promises action, adventure, and a little love to boot in the first book of his quintet, and *Emissary* certainly delivers.

Emissary is the first GameLit novel which truly feels unique in its genre.

The concepts of various video games are so seamlessly integrated into the story in ways that I'd never considered and that seem completely natural for the setting. It's really quite brilliant, and I've never read anything like it!

The writing style is absolutely beautiful and really blew me away.

The attention to world-building, the character relationships, the emotions on display across many different scenes and moments, the climax at the end - it was all a part of a single ride which I'd very gladly jump on again.

SANDSTORM

EMISSARY QUINTET, BOOK 2

E. B. BROOKS

First Edition: May 2021

ISBN 978-1-7347398-5-5 (ebook)

ISBN 978-1-7347398-3-1 (Paperback)

ISBN 978-1-7347398-4-8 (Hardcover)

Cover art by Julisa Basak

Maps by Soraya Corcoran

Sheet music written with MuseScore v3.6.2

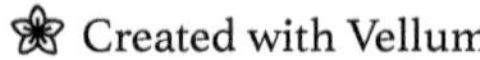
Created with Vellum

To my daughter cats, Freya and Tifa, my brother cat Spartacus, and to parents of all stripes

CONTENTS

It is the knife you cannot see which ends up in your back.

— Caitsid'h Proverb

PROLOGUE

THE SETTLERS WERE DEAD THE MOMENT THEY LEFT THEIR vehicles.

The large transport, what these soft people called a camel, emerged from the curtain of dust, its engine audible from far away. It was flanked by two smaller ones, the kind that preferred to come first and alert the settlers to another resource to plunder. The kind that flipped so easily.

The vehicles came to a stop and shut down, the sudden silence even louder than their roar. Moments later, a stream of settlers emerged, their black armor betraying their movements against the pale sand and rubble.

Kellan laughed in his mind, though his face remained as impassive as the rest of his body. So much treachery these settlers suffered! Awa's informant had been true again, giving the Lynx clan more than enough time to prepare their ambush.

The intruders fanned out, spreading themselves thin. Through the gaps in his woven hood, Kellan saw two kinds. The settlers were predictably furtive: skittish, glancing up from their scanning devices as though they already scented the Lynx in the sands around them. But these were escorted by others, the new kind. Loud men brandishing heavy blades and shields, while foolishly leaving their real weapons strapped over their backs. Warriors, as bold as they were careless.

A mixed party drew near, almost to arm's reach, but Kellan waited. He let his breath become the desert wind, one with the Great Mother's. The Twice-Forsaken were Her favored children, not these thieving, fat cowards who plundered the world their ancestors had broken. *His* people had faced Her wrath, and in so doing, had earned Her forgiveness.

There would be none for these settlers. Kellan was the Huntmaster, and they were prey.

The party passed him by, but he marked their position by the scrape of their boots. He listened as they took inventory. He cast his senses out, feeling the mood of his pack. They were disciplined, controlling their eagerness until he gave the signal. Already, his skirmishers were creeping toward the settlers' camel, cutting off escape—

A lone settler came rushing down the transport's ramp, tugging his mask on. He stumbled, and through careless misfortune he fell with a curse on top of one of Kellan's hunters. For one instant the two regarded each other; then the settler cried out.

"Locusts!"

Kellan responded with a feral roar of his own, and his pack sprang up with him. He flung his cloak aside, opening fire as he whirled about to face the party that had passed him. Two men fell as their blood took to the wind, but one, their warrior, crouched behind his shield.

Staccato gunfire pierced the air, followed by the screams of the dying. Kellan kept his enemy pinned until one of his fellow hunters, Nali, slipped behind the warrior and slit his throat. She laughed as the body fell, glancing up at Kellan with bright, hungry eyes before sprinting off to her next target.

Kellan followed her, but inwardly he was cursing their luck. The intruders hadn't gone far enough afield, and now a group of warriors had set up a barricade, finally using their own guns to cover their allies' retreat. The Lynx hunters shot many as they fled up the camel's ramp, but not all. Not enough. The camel's engines roared to life again and the great beast tore away, out of reach.

The remaining warriors held their ground, unafraid, as two sprinted for one of the smaller vehicles.

"Pin and stagger!" Kellan commanded, joining his pack. "Turn them to dust."

His hunters moved with perfect coordination. One group laid cover fire as the next slipped forward, alternating until they were close enough to fling grenades into the warriors' midst.

Half the enemy died in a flash of light and fire, but the survivors drew their swords and rushed forward in a doomed charge. The hunters' next grenades flew too far, and the warriors began cutting them down in melee.

It was knife work from there. The small vehicle escaped, while the remaining warriors carved a bloody cairn for themselves before they were finally overwhelmed.

The pack gave a triumphant cry as the last warrior fell, and all eyes turned to Kellan. He stepped up to the fallen man, clutching his sword as though death was only a temporary setback. There was still a fire in his glazed eyes, a resilience as troubling as it was impressive.

The Huntmaster pried the blade free, but he did so respectfully. These new settlers, these warriors, were no mere prey. They didn't belong here any more than their weakling allies, but they at least had something of the heart of the Twice-Forsaken.

"Take what you need," Kellan told his pack. "We move at dark."

Three hunters moved to the lone remaining vehicle, but as

they opened its hatch, a ball of fire rushed out, consuming them and searing Kellan's face. His pack roared and raised weapons, but the hiss of snipers' fire killed two more hunters, silencing the rest.

A man's voice called out from nowhere. "Congratulations on your victory."

Kellan whirled about, but there was no one. No one but the Lynx, injured yet alert. "Show yourself, prey," he growled.

The voice turned cold, thin. "The Diamond Lord is no one's prey."

Curses drifted through the pack, but Kellan raised a hand. "Diamond Lord. You are the traitor, the one who spoke to Awa?"

"It is enough that I speak to you," answered the voice, seeming to come from behind the vehicle's wreckage. "I have an errand for you."

Kellan scowled, twisting his clan markings into a death mask, but without a target, the gesture was meaningless. "The Twice-Forsaken do not perform errands."

Now the voice seemed to come from behind him, and its pitch was changed. Higher, female. Harsh. "You do now, if you value your miserable lives. Tell me, what is your assessment of the war?"

The Huntmaster silently directed two people to the voice's new source. "We have advanced on your settlement. None have stopped us."

The voice scoffed. "You measure success differently. Discounting the benefit of our information, your combined nation hasn't successfully attacked a single Central scouting mission for a month." Two more bullets sliced the air to drop the searching hunters, and the voice resumed from a third location, now a scornful bass. "Surely even you have noticed the change in our personnel."

"We have seen the difference." Kellan struggled to keep his voice level. *The arrogance of this creature!* he thought. He counted his remaining hunters, noting with pride that they stood unafraid, then scanned the nearby roofs for the snipers. "What can you tell us about these new warriors?"

"I can tell you they are many," the voice said, a hard edge honing the words. "Over a hundred million."

"Million?" Kellan repeated, uncertain. "Many tens? Hundreds, even?"

"Yes, savage. Many, many tens, just waiting to be roused and sent to annihilate you. Already, the few which have emerged have changed everything. It is they who build our new weapons, and they who die so nobly for their homes and delusions." Two more hunters fell to the invisible predator, and the voice shifted yet again, to a lilting alto. "At present, the rest are as helpless as you are. I would prefer they remain in that state."

Kellan snarled, then dismissed the remainder of his pack. If he died, they would tell Awa how it happened. "What is your errand?"

The voice chuckled. "So you do learn. Here's your next lesson. Every advantage the Centre possesses is rooted in electronic technology. We're completely dependent on it, for everything from life support to transportation. Disrupt it, and we are vulnerable. Remove it, and we are defenseless."

Kellan's eyes narrowed, but he waited until he heard the engines as his pack reached their trucks. "Why do you not disrupt it yourself?"

"Because our numbers are as yet insufficient for a full mutiny," the voice replied, obviously frustrated. "Thus, what we cannot produce, we must scavenge. Fortunately, our ancestors were adept at creating the kind of device we require."

Something beeped, less than thirty paces from Kellan.

"Go on," said the voice, now seeming to come from the same position as it returned to its original quality.

Kellan glanced at the rooftops once more, and this time he saw a man standing. A hundred paces away, but near enough to see long black hair and settlers' armor. And a rifle, trained on him. Cursing under his breath, Kellan moved to the sound and picked up a device not unlike the settlers' scanners. It was thin and flat, with a glowing screen that currently showed a man.

The man was also thin: not a warrior or hunter. His face bore a prominent crooked nose under dark hair and narrowed eyes. His frail body wore gray, with a silver pin on the left breast in the shape of a circle behind a vertical line.

"At last, we meet face to face," the man jeered. "Take this tablet. On it, you will find the description for a weapon capable of crippling every electronic device in the Centre, as well as a map detailing the most likely places to find it."

Kellan lifted the tablet, turning it over in his hands. "You slit your own throat, with this. What is to stop us from using this great weapon to kill you all?"

"Aside from your technical incompetence?" The man smirked. "Because unless my people repair the broken systems after our coup, the Centre would be merely one more ruin."

This time Kellan laughed. "We are comfortable with ruins."

The man glared murderously, impotently, from his screen. "You are fools! Parasites, living a miserable existence on the bleached bones of your ancestors. Help us take the Centre, and you will have a reliable, permanent source of food and shelter."

As the man spoke, the hunters' truck approached, with two gunmen riding the top.

Kellan crossed his arms, concealing his hand from the settlers as he silently indicated the sniper's roof. "We will consider your offer," he said to the tablet man. "But finding this new weapon will require much in time and resources. The clans have heard the call, and we have many mouths."

Kellan saw the man tap another device, then heard a shout as his hunters opened fire. He looked up just in time to see a rocket streak toward his pack, and he barely took cover before the explosion.

"Do not attempt to haggle with me," the man said coldly, unmarred by the blast. "You have your orders. Contact me when you have the weapon; use the frequency on the tablet. I'll be waiting."

The tablet's screen darkened. Kellan cast it aside to search for survivors among his pack, but there were none. Nali's scorched body was behind the steering wheel, her face grimacing in a final snarl.

As he pressed his brow to hers and pledged revenge, a third small vehicle tore out of the sniper's building, taking the structure down in its wake as it raced into the desert.

Growling, Kellan retrieved the accursed device, smearing his people's blood across its screen as he activated it. It rewarded him with a map of ancient military outposts, where this Diamond Lord's weapon might be found.

But where one weapon was, surely there were others that could be put to better, more immediate use. These settlers were arrogant but weak, hiding behind their devices and electronics. Their continued existence, especially the traitor's, was an insult to the Great Mother.

Kellan put the tablet in his pocket. He would take it back to his alpha. Awa would find the weapon, and the Lynx would lead all the Twice-Forsaken to conquer the Centre. Then, once the devils in the walls had repaired their damage, they would be eliminated as well. All of them, settlers and their pet warriors alike, were caught up in the storm of vengeance, just like the ancients who'd driven the Twice-Forsaken from the promised land of old. Each death, each injury, each offense was a grain of sand blown in the eye, to be repaid in kind when the winds inevitably shifted.

And the Diamond Lord would bleed for the hunters that died today. Kellan would ensure that.

He flicked his hood up, then began the long walk north to rejoin his clan.

PART I

SAND

Sa'diya
Ch'ira
Each Rajj's Assessment of Her Sisters
Friendly
Neutral
Hostile
Allied
Deferential
Indebted
Ransomed
Pliable
Vulnerable
Disappointing
Belligerent
Grasping
Unmannered
Suspect
Adversarial

The South and
East of Sah'rassa
As the 32349th
Moon sees it
Qa'ya
J'unai
JAB'ATTAN
The Mountains

1

DIFFICULT TERRAIN

"MASTER O'MEARA, THE REST OF US DO NOT HAVE THE LUXURY of turning a blind eye to reality."

Ewan glowered at Director Carmine Rothchild across the ancient wooden desk that dominated the circular room, a lot more effectively than the bald man himself. Idly, he wondered if the Director's throbbing temple veins would actually pop—and if they did, whether that would be enough to finally end this meeting. Or would he keep on lecturing Ewan in front of the other chiefs, telling death to wait its turn until he'd finished his point?

How Veridian, Ewan thought wryly.

"Sir," he said through clenched teeth, "You made it my job to get players to fight your battles. How am I supposed to do that if you won't let me log any more out?"

"The ones already here are consuming too many resources," argued Alice Spencer, the Chief of Nutrition. She turned to the Director. "Just this morning, the dining hall ran out of food half an hour before the breakfast period was over."

Ewan shifted his glare to her. "Just because my people have something worth getting up for—"

"Love, please," Tree whispered, squeezing her husband's hand under the desk to make him back down. Unlike him, she actually belonged here, with the little black epaulets on her shoulders proclaiming her status as Chief Emissary. Addressing the other chiefs, she said, "We all knew the incoming players would require a considerable amount of nourishment to restore their bodies."

Robert Nichols of Medical sighed and straightened his glasses. "We've tried to mitigate the impact through use of concentrated supplements during the electro-muscular stimulation therapies."

"But they come out hungrier than ever!" Spencer snapped.

"That's because they need to bulk up," Ewan said, scoffing. "You can't expect them to fight the Locusts on civilian rations."

"And you can't expect them to eat like they did in their simulations," she countered.

"Enough," Rothchild muttered, rubbing his face. "Alice, you know as well as I do that the players constitute an essential military resource, safeguarding our transports from Locust raiders. Integrating them into our hierarchy, into the world as it is, is an expensive but necessary task."

Spencer's face tightened. "But we're already using every square inch of hydroponics, including the auxiliary bay we installed on the observation level three months ago. Carmine, we can't grow food without space."

"Then see to it that non-military personnel are placed on tighter portions," the Director ordered. Taking a deep breath, he looked around the room before locking onto Ewan again. "As for you and your people, Master O'Meara, we cannot add any more than we already have."

"You could assign more staff into rotation on the game floors—"

"This is not negotiable!" Rothchild thundered. "The Central staff are highly specialized and essential to their stations.

Whom would you have me send to the simulations? The kitchen staff? The caretakers? That would harm your fellow players even more."

This time Ewan rubbed his own temples, tangling his fingers in his curly hair as he gazed up through the ring of short, broad windows lining the office's high, domed walls. The sky outside was brown, thick with blown sand and dust the way it had been every day since he'd come to Earth. The way it had been for two and a half millennia, since the Centre was founded and the game worlds were created to ride out the storms. Long enough that no one from his home of Veridor even remembered the real world, much less that the skeletal Central staff had been keeping millions of players alive the whole time. If Tree hadn't come to Veridor last year with dire warnings about the Locust Nation, Ewan's people would still be blissfully ignorant of Earth's problems.

And they would have died—permanently—without ever getting the chance to defend themselves.

"Stupid frapping world," Ewan grumbled. "There'd be plenty to go around if we could just grow our food outside."

"Master O'Meara, you are more than welcome to try," the Director said.

Maura Pell of Caretaking coughed politely, breaking the tension. "Food resources aside, the emissaries were originally talking about recruiting from an entirely different simulation."

"As if the first wave weren't trouble enough," Shane Powell of Security muttered. "Every day, I'm processing another one of your precious Ether Swords for disorderly conduct."

Ewan snorted. "That's rich, considering your goons start half of those fights."

"We've been going through an adjustment period," Tree conceded, crushing Ewan's fingers in the way that said if she'd had access to Veridian-style private messaging, she'd have told him to shut up already. "The cultural differences alone are challenging, but from the players' point of view they are being asked to risk their lives for people who, frankly, have treated them as less than human." She looked around the desk, her brown eyes hard and defensive. "And more than a few of them have died."

"Isn't that a reason not to log any more of them out?" Spencer asked.

"It's the reason that my section began looking for... supplements," Tree replied. "The Veridian warriors have already proven themselves to be capable against the Locusts, but they've been plunged into a conflict that requires a lot of re-specking, as they would say."

Nathan Sanderson, at 14 years old the Centre's youngest chief thanks to his new Defense section, leaned forward with a frown. "Treanna's right. The players don't know the first thing about the Wastes, or about guns. They rush into combat with no regard for how little our armors protect us."

Ewan noticed how the boy's hand moved automatically to his own shoulder—the one he'd had shot up by the Locusts the previous winter, when Ewan had been in charge of Defense.

Rothchild nodded. "Are the players ineffective?"

"Oh, no, sir," Nathan replied, catching Ewan's eye and stiffening. "If nothing else, they're perfect for sacrifice tactics. Just last week, a squad bought the retreat for one of our scouting parties."

Ewan shot his former student a reproachful look. "We lost seven good people."

"They volunteered," Nathan answered simply.

"In fairness, my people feel much safer with a player escort," Ben Root of Scouting commented. "Even though they're not familiar with our world or its weapons, the players have a presence that can't be trained in a matter of months." He glanced at Powell. "Out in the field, at least, their behavior is quite professional."

"So, you think it is worth continuing to recruit Veridian players for our military needs?" Rothchild asked.

"Yes, sir," Ben replied. "Nathan's done a good job with our own volunteers, but they're just that."

Nathan frowned at his old chief, but the Director spoke before he could reply. "Very well. Chief O'Meara, please—Annie, are you all right?" he asked, his voice suddenly taking on a grandfatherly concern.

All eyes turned to Tree, but hers were closed, scrunching as she winced in pain.

Ewan leaned toward her. "Stomach cramps again?" he whispered.

She nodded, face reddening at showing weakness in front of the most powerful people on Earth. "Yes, I'm fine," she said in response to the Director, but she did squeeze Ewan's hand again.

She took a steadying breath, then plugged her tablet into the computer hidden in the desk. An image appeared over the worn wooden surface, an image of windswept dunes under a blue sky utterly unlike the real one outside. "This is Sah'rassa," she said, her voice returning to firm and controlled. "It's a small world, both in population and area, consisting of a desert ringed by impassable mountains. Its inhabitants primarily live around the oases which dot the landscape, although some of them are nomadic."

She panned the camera, then zoomed in on a small party of figures walking just under the dune's ridgeline, out of the wind. Figures with long, fur-covered tails swishing out from under their white robes.

"What are those?" Spencer asked, her disgust obvious.

"Those are the players," Tree replied calmly.

The nutrition chief's scowl deepened. "But...they're not human."

"No more or less than any other player," Gabe Reid of

Programming said wryly. "I wouldn't expect you to realize it, but the players' avatars take a wide variety of forms, depending on the simulation in question. During the Founding, the initial staff researched their world's most popular games and stories for inspiration." His eyes lingered on the image. "This particular style must have appealed to a small subset of the first players, and so here they are, these...what did you call them, Annie?"

"That's Treanna to you," she said irritably. "They call themselves Caitsid'h. Cat people."

"They're revolting," Powell muttered.

"They're experts in desert warfare," Tree insisted. "From what we've seen, the Caitsid'h have a tribal society, with frequent skirmishes and shifting alliances as they raid each other."

The figures on the image suddenly leaped to combat stances, drawing curved swords as a set of others sprang up from their hiding places in the sands.

"They fight like Locusts," Nathan said quietly.

"Not entirely," Tree said, watching the scuffle play out. After a few moments—in which no one was killed—the traveling party was escorted away as captives. "They have more restraint, and a strong sense of family, from what we've seen. If we can appeal to them, convince them they're part of our larger family, then they could be valuable as allies."

"Director, I object," Powell said. "It's difficult enough to keep order with the first kind of player roaming the halls as if they own them. But at least O'Meara's kind are human!"

"The Caitsid'h are human, too!" Ewan shot back.

"They may not see it that way," Nichols pointed out. "I must admit, I have concerns about whether such a race would be able to assimilate into the Centre. There's potential here for severe psychological strain."

"Then I suggest that you recruit only the most well-adjusted players first," Rothchild said firmly to Tree. "You have authorization to explore the world and make contact, but the fact remains that we are at the population limit already. For every one of these, er, people you bring to the Centre, you will be required to retire a Veridian player."

Ewan clenched his fists. "But—"

"But nothing!" Rothchild snapped, trying to flatten Ewan to the chair with his eyes. "The laws of this world do not bend to your whim, young man."

Tree kicked Ewan under the desk. "We'll communicate this to the Veridian Ether Corps."

Her grandfather nodded curtly. "Thank you, Chief O'Meara. Now, if no one objects, let us proceed with an update from the *other* sections."

Ewan only half listened as the civilian chiefs gave their reports, but even he could tell that almost all of them were feeling the pressure of having fifty-odd players out and about. Medical had already converted an entire ward into an incubation area for incoming players, with Engineering tearing it apart to route enough power to the dozen "shockies" that cut player rehabilitation from months to weeks. Programming was helping the emissaries by providing information and bridge personnel, but Gabe said there was still a lot of ill will between the sections, thanks to Ewan's claims that James Frasier had used the avatar of the ancient Diamond Lord to murder a hundred Veridians, five months ago. Gabe was still the chief programmer, but his new duties in gathering intelligence against the Locusts had left him delegating more to his section. Alice Spencer noted that the Veridians were complaining that Central food was bland and lifeless, though her tone said she couldn't have cared less. Caretaking wasn't affected too directly, although Chief Pell warned that the nurseries were reducing the adoption quota to ease pressure in the long run. Scouting was struggling to keep up with the new focus on ammunition and weapons-grade materials, sending out recon parties in the small kangaroo rat transports, while teaming up with Engineering to build a more combat-oriented vehicle. The engineers were also hard at work improving the fighters' gear, with Karl Taylor reporting that Ewan's kid sister, Kate, had been instrumental.

"She's still learning the ropes, but that young lady's got a lot of imagination," Karl finished, eyes twinkling under bushy gray brows. "You know, she's even started working on a flying machine in her spare time."

Ewan smiled; Kate had been nursing that dream ever since she was a little girl.

"Improved armor would be a considerable asset," Gabe said, plugging his tablet in to replace Sah'rassa's image with a map of the Wastes surrounding the Centre. "Thus far, the Locusts have only staged raids on our scouting parties, but they're clearly after something more." A series of colored orbs appeared over the map. "These icons represent the locations of all encounters since the conflict began. Blue represents Central victories, whereas red indicates that we retreated. If we filter the encounters by date of occurrence, there is a clear pattern."

The dots all blinked out, then slowly reappeared, one after another.

"They're getting closer," Spencer murmured.

"Precisely," Gabe agreed, his voice grim. "We haven't seen any large parties in the Wastes so far, but it appears that the various clans are coordinating, searching for our location."

Ben Root nodded. "So far, we've followed Chief Reid's advice and varied our approaches to the north, to try to confound their triangulation, but there's only so much we can do there. The Locusts are coming for us."

"How long?" Rothchild asked.

"I estimate three months from now, maybe half a year if we're lucky," Gabe answered. "Of course, if we were to prioritize attacking them in force, we could end the conflict before it can escalate further."

"Is such a thing possible?" the Director asked, stroking his white beard.

"I'm certain it is," Gabe replied, shooting Ewan a quick look. "And I expect it would appeal to almost everyone, although some sections would, of course, become obsolete upon victory."

Ewan glanced over to Nathan in sympathy, then colored as he realized the other chiefs were watching him. "What? No. You can't just tell us to go back to the tubes."

"Why not?" Spencer said.

"It's where you belong," Powell added.

"No!" Ewan half shouted. "We're making a difference out here!"

"Like what?" Spencer challenged. "Starving the rest of us?"

"Of course not! But we've got, um—"

"There is more singing in the dining hall," Gabe offered.

"Yeah!" Ewan said, ignoring his friend's glib tone. "And entertainment, like the combat tournament, and Kate's got a ton more she can offer!"

"Be that as it may, such things are not essential," Rothchild said wearily. "Your priority is to successfully resolve the conflict with the Locusts, not to 'enliven' the Centre. To that point, is it possible to mount a decisive attack on the Locust Nation?"

Ewan glowered at the old man. "We'd need a lot more players, wouldn't we?"

Rothchild's face darkened, but he didn't take the bait. "Very well. Perhaps these cat people of yours will give us a new opportunity. Unless anyone has anything further to contribute," he added, clearly hoping otherwise, "I call this general staff meeting to an end. You may address any further concerns to me in private."

The chiefs stood, frustration pouring off them as they crowded into the elevator and jostled for room. As usual, Ewan did his best to shield Tree from the other Centrals and vice versa, fighting off a claustrophobic pang as the doors slid shut.

It's like we're all stuck in one tube together, on the game floors.

"Sorry to step on your toes, O'Meara," Gabe commented from his left.

"No worries," Ewan said halfheartedly. "You still on for our session later?"

"Unfortunately, my afternoon's filled up," Gabe replied, blue eyes glittering with amusement as the doors opened onto the hangar level and Ben Root stepped out. "It's so easy to forget I'm the chief of two de facto sections, these days."

"Doubtless, your constantly reminding us all helps you," Tree said acidly. "Make sure Alex is on the bridge Friday morning."

"As you like," Gabe answered, unruffled as usual by Tree's habitual aggro toward him—or almost anyone who wasn't her husband.

She took Ewan's hand as they stepped out onto the main residential floor, leading him back to their apartment. Ewan smiled, watching her face relax as the other chiefs split off to their offices. One of the best perks of their tiny section was that whenever they weren't logging into Veridor, they got to work from home.

"I'm sorry," he murmured to her as they walked. "I didn't mean to get in a shouting match again."

She lifted his hand and kissed it. "It could have been worse."

He chuckled, returning the kiss. She was right, of course. The chiefs might be a bunch of grumpy old jerks, but they didn't speak for everyone else. Ewan and Tree still got dirty looks as they walked hand in hand, but at this point he figured that was more because they kept their marriage exclusive than because she'd chosen a player. More than a few Centrals now sported Veridian-style jewelry, and Gabe's jibes aside, Ewan still got the odd call to sing the birthday song he'd introduced last year. Someone had even taken the trouble to update the old, yellowed signs at the hallway corners, just to help the players find their way around.

He grinned as they walked the last few feet. Rothchild could be nerfed, along with the others. Putting some life back in this old ruin was just as important as defending it.

Then Tree gripped his hand, her sharp inhalation bringing him to a quick stop, and he saw the message scrawled in red paint across their door.

Player Go Home.

She cursed under her breath, but he merely sighed and pressed his thumb against the scanner. "Good thing we locked up, huh?"

The graffiti whooshed aside, but the emissaries had both lost whatever verve they'd recovered. Tree silently retrieved a wet cloth and went back out to clean the mess, the hardness in her eyes warning Ewan to leave her be as she dealt with a Central problem.

Funny, how many Central problems turn into Veridian problems, Ewan thought darkly.

He flopped back on the bed in the dark, wondering who'd done it this time. He imagined catching the vandal and fixing things with an old-fashioned beatdown, but he decided Powell just would've thrown him in the detention cells, instead. Weren't players supposed to inspire art, after all?

Huffing to himself, Ewan reached for his tablet to see what else was wrong in the world today.

There was an update from Ben about the next week's scouting runs, asking if Ewan had anyone fresh from the shockies to cover their recent losses. The next message was from Paul Castel in Whitehaven, confirming the casualties and warning him the Veridian Patriarch wanted to see them about a change to recruitment policies. There was an invite from Gabe, no message included, for a rescheduled session later that week. And last, half an hour ago, was a tense note from his mom, letting him know that Kate hadn't been replying to her recent messages—again—and was she all right?

Ewan sighed again as he hauled himself off the bed, then made for the door to see if he could at least get his little sister to listen to him.

2

HEAD IN THE CLOUDS

Despite its nickname being the Hole, Engineering was actually situated above the residential levels. A quick ride up on the main elevator, and Ewan stepped into the broad cave of a room that housed the Centre's great foundries. As always, the place felt like the inside of a volcano. Not for the first time, he suspected the people here didn't notice on account of the grease they wore like armor.

He walked the familiar route to Sam's workshop—Kate's workshop, now. Sam had been more than willing to let Kate move in up here, apparently literally. In a few months' time she'd given the whole place an overhaul, filling it to bursting in an odd mix of her tidy forge and the ocean of laundry and clutter her room had been back home.

Ewan smiled to himself, wondering how Sam put up with it, then stepped through the door. "Hey, guys."

"Gems!" Kate swore, half diving, half falling off the table—and off Sam? "Learn to knock, E!"

Whatever he'd planned to say flew away as quickly as his sister's hands, smoothing her clothing back into decency. "What do you think you're doing?!"

"None of your business," she said, her face still flushed and almost as red as the rumpled hair smeared around it.

"Of course it's my business! Kate, you're not old enough—"

"I'm fifteen!" she snapped, reaching out to grab Sam's huge brown arm as he tried to slink off. "Just a year younger than you were when you started up with your Tree-elf, and it's not like I'm running off and getting married."

"Running...does Mom know?"

"Frap no, and you're not telling!"

"Want to bet?" he growled. "I came up here because you've been ignoring her messages. When I tell her why—"

"No!" The color drained from Kate's face. "It's not what it looked like. I'm no Central."

Ewan glared at her. "No, you're just fooling around with one."

"Like you're one to talk," she shot back. "Look, I'll talk to Mom, okay? Tell her that we're a thing?"

"You'd better," he warned, closing his eyes to try and delete the image. He knew Sam had been crushing on Kate ever since she'd made his metal leg, but since when had she started caring what boys thought? *These Centrals are a bad influence*, he thought, but his own face heated as he thought about Tree moving him straight to her room after he'd logged out. *She and I are married now, though. That makes it okay! Doesn't it?*

"So," Kate grumbled, "you came up here to check up on me?"

"Not just that," Ewan lied. "I also wanted to give you two the gist of the morning's staff meeting."

Sam tilted his head like a baffled puppy. "Won't Chief Taylor do that?"

"I'm sure he will, but my kid sister's still in the Emissary section. Tree's, um, busy, so I thought I'd come by."

"Fine." Kate sighed. "Mule, how about you find us a chair?"

Sam quickly lumbered off, metal leg clunking. Kate's eyes

followed him, but then she caught Ewan looking and glowered at him again. "I already told you, we're not going all the way. And he swore up and down he'd keep it to just me. His idea."

Ewan shook his head before the image could take root again. "Great. No offense, but...Sam?"

"Yeah, Sam," she said defensively. "He's sweet, and big, like a tamed aurochs. I feel at home around him, and I know he's got my back."

Ewan tried to wrench his face into a smile. "He's a good guy, I'll grant that. I just...I didn't know you were into that kind of thing."

"Yeah, well, a lot's changed since March," she said quietly, closing her eyes. "Dad's gone, and I'm out here. Sam's been there for me, you know?"

Her sudden gentleness tripped a guilty pang in Ewan's heart. In an instant, he was replaying the battle in Whitehaven in his mind as clearly as she probably was, as clearly as if it had happened yesterday. His family in shackles in the main square, under arrest to flush him back into Veridor. The Diamond Lord —or at least, the Central posing as the ancient Gem—coming down like a meteor and deleting the other O'Mearas. Kate and his mom had pulled through the ordeal of logging, but his dad...he'd been taken first, sticking up for Kate. She'd refused to talk about it, wearing her gruff face and bossing Sam around, but Ewan knew she'd been totally freaked out by the whole thing.

Gems of old, who wouldn't be? he thought. *Maybe Sam really is what she needs.*

"Well, I'm happy for you," he said, trying to mean it, "but please keep me in the loop? I don't like getting caught between you and Mom. I'm not Dad, you know."

"You got that right," she agreed, reequipping the tough-girl armor as she leaned against the wall and crossed her arms. "How's the great Gem hunt going, anyway?"

"Nowhere," he answered, face heating for a new reason now. "Gabe and I keep looking, but he's long gone from the logs. The bastard's probably laughing his butt off right behind my back, but since Rothchild won't go for arrests without frapping 'concrete evidence,' there's not much I can do but wait for him to screw up."

"That's your plan?" she asked, surprised. "Sit and wait?"

Ewan sighed. "Pretty much. I'd been kind of hoping that I'd get his goat by logging more players out, but there's only so much room for them," he replied, shuffling aside as Sam came back in with a folding chair. "Rothchild's put a cap on us."

"What for?" Kate asked.

"Probably because we're at the population limit," Sam said, clearing a space for himself on the workbench. "I asked Lisa why the meals had been light recently," he added by way of explanation.

"You're dead on," Ewan said, mentally chiding himself for downplaying his friend's intelligence. "Without more food, we can't get more players."

"Fair enough, but do we really need more? Ow! No offense!" Sam added quickly when Kate slugged him. "But we've already got enough to guard the scouts, and we're making better weapons all the time, like the armadillo."

"Rothchild wants to bring the fight to the Locusts," Ewan said, half-truthfully. "For that, we'll need hundreds more."

Sam's dark eyebrows furrowed. "Hundreds? They won't be getting my dinner."

"Yeah, I know!" Ewan snapped, sick and tired of hearing the Centrals whine about losing meals to their defenders. *And they have the gall to say the players aren't realistic!* "Isn't there any way to add more hydroponics? What about the game floors?"

"That wouldn't work," Sam replied slowly, scratching his head and oiling his short curls up even more. "The plants would need light, and the players do best in the dark. There's plenty of space in the residential area, though, what with all the vacant rooms."

"What's the deal with those?" Kate asked.

"Oh." Sam smiled, looking pleased to be useful. "A long time ago, the Centre had a lot more people on the staff. But the Directors streamlined everyone's roles, kind of like how Outfitting is technically part of Engineering. We got really efficient, so, um, fewer people had to come to Earth."

Something about his tone left Ewan's skin prickling. Over the past year, he'd had it beaten into him—literally—that while the Centrals resented players for a lot of things, their biggest beef was the fact that every last one of them had been 'adopted' from the game worlds, stranded on the broken Earth instead of living the good life on the game floors.

"So, could that work?" Ewan asked after a moment.

Sam shrugged. "We could maybe cram some stuff in there, but those rooms are tiny compared to the bays we're using now. Unless you want to try knocking out every wall in the level, I think we're stuck with what we have."

Ewan sighed. "Yeah, and it's not like you guys have a lot of free time right now, what with the Locusts. It was all so much easier back home."

"Yeah, well, Veridor has big fields, not little cramped rooms," Kate huffed. "We've got all this ground around us outside, and nothing to do with it."

"What use is it?" Sam said. "It's not like we could just plant anything out there; there's no sunlight."

"Now that would be an epic project," Kate said, grinning at him.

"Huh?"

"Clearing the sky, you big dummy." She laughed, thumping him on the head. "I'd kill for a good bright day out here. I look all pale."

"Not with all that soot on you," Ewan teased, his spirits

lifting with Kate's grin. "So all we need is a way to clear the storms out."

"All?" Sam asked, looking more dumbfounded by the second. "The only place anyone's ever seen blue sky is down at the coast!"

"Really?" Kate asked, surprised. "Well, there you go. We'll just go to the beach for a vacation."

"That's even crazier than your idea for an ornithopter! What's wrong with good, solid, ground?"

"Um, the fact that it's not solid?" Kate replied, obviously enjoying getting a rise from her boyfriend. "There's more sand in the sky."

"I wonder why they didn't build the Centre on the beach," Ewan mused.

"The hurricanes would have flooded it out ages ago if they had," Sam said. "The archives say the coasts were the first regions to become uninhabitable, even before the Rapture."

"Rapture?" Kate asked. "What's that?"

"Oh, that was way back before the Founding," Sam replied.

But Ewan closed his eyes, an old, familiar anger stirring in his heart as he recalled the sorry tale from his own time with the Central archives. "The Rapture was what the survivors called it when Earth's elites bailed from the planet as it collapsed," he said quietly. His jaw tightened. "They ditched everyone else, left them to rot in the mess they could've fixed. Should've fixed."

"That's the one!" Sam said with jarring cheerfulness. "Though the resource wars afterward probably did more damage."

Ewan sighed. *Why should he be upset by it? That's ancient history, now.* "Well, it's not like we're going to up and move the Centre, anyway. Has there ever been a break in the clouds here?" he asked, looking at Sam.

Sam shook his head. "Not that I've heard of, not since the

Founding. There's nothing out there that would hold soil down, so it just gets blown around all the time."

Ewan scrubbed his hair. "So, we can't plant anything without light, we can't get the light unless we get the ground to hold still, and that will only happen when we can grow plants in it. Did I miss anything?"

"Nope," Sam said with a little shrug. "That's about the size of it."

"Well, it'll give me something to think about once the armor's in production," Kate said, before shooting Ewan a pointed look. "Are you happy, now?"

No, he thought. He had a sinking feeling that Rothchild wasn't going to be on board for adding more hydroponics; there were already enough players running wild in the halls, to hear people like Shane Powell say it. The Director wanted to drive the Locusts off, but if he did that before Ewan could sort out players' rights, they could all find themselves locked back in the tubes for their trouble. Ditched by the people in power, just like all their ancestors had been in the Rapture.

Why is everything so complicated in the real world?

"Yeah, sure," Ewan muttered. "Enjoy the rest of your break."

Trying not to think about exactly how they would, he turned and headed back for the elevator.

3

BREAKING IN

THREE DAYS LATER, ANOTHER FIGHT BROKE OUT IN THE GYM.

Ewan heard it from the hallway. He'd been headed for the training area anyway, hoping to warm up a little before his sparring session with Gabe and maybe see how the new batch of Ether Sword recruits was doing.

About as well as the rest, he thought irritably, slinging his swords over his shoulder and breaking into a run.

He rushed through the sliding double doors to see a brawl in progress. A good dozen people were pummeling each other, thankfully still keeping it to fists only, while at least twice that many gawked and jeered to encourage their teammates.

"Break it up!" came Nathan's voice, barely audible over the hubbub. The boy stalked around to the front, face blood-red. "As your chief, I order you to stand—" he bellowed before getting knocked onto his back by a rogue elbow.

Ewan ran to him and offered a hand up, but Nathan swatted it away angrily, then reached for his tablet. "That's it," he snarled, stabbing the glass.

Ewan grimaced. "Nathan, hang on—"

"Players, I'm calling Security! You're all going to the brig!"

"Ether Cadets, fall in!" barked a deep voice from the far side of the scrum.

Half the brawlers—the Veridian half—snapped into a stiff line on the left side of the room, trading only a few punches back as the other half took their parting shots. As they cleared, an imposing man with dark skin and a pencil beard strode forward, with a scowl forbidding enough to make even the Centrals take a step back.

Nathan lowered his tablet, but his glare was fixed on Captain Al'Dashan.

"Explain yourselves!" the captain boomed.

"It was my fault, sir," squeaked a young man with close-cropped black hair. "That Gem called us meat shields."

Ewan sighed as the cadet pointed at one of his least favorite people: a Central man with a dark ponytail, a huge scar in place of his left ear, and an attitude to match. "Vincent Coley's just a bully," Ewan said, as the scout flashed him a smug grin. "He's certainly no Gem. None of the Centrals are."

At least, none of them will own up to it.

At his words, the Veridians only just seemed to realize who had walked in on their fight. "Hero!" the young man yelped as his voice broke again. "I didn't know you would be here!"

"Where else would I be?" Ewan grumbled as he moved to face the new recruit. "What's your name?"

"Patrick Lee," the boy answered quickly. The color had drained from his face, highlighting the patchwork of red spots left over from the shocky. "From Fen's Retreat, sir."

Ewan took a calming breath as Al'Dashan sidled behind him. "Well, Patrick, the first thing you've got to learn about Earth is that it's got no room for screwing up."

"But Hero, he said—"

"It doesn't matter what he said!" Ewan snapped, before taking another calming breath. "Patrick, this isn't Veridor. There's no Logos. No menus. No respawning. You get maimed out here, you're done. You die out here, there's no limbo, no bind for you to return to." He glanced back at Coley, who was smirking as Nathan tried pointlessly to dress him down. "And in case you haven't noticed, we're not exactly welcome here."

Patrick followed the glance. "But don't they need us?"

"Yeah, they do," Ewan said, raising his voice for the Centrals' benefit. "It's Veridian warriors who escort every transport through the Wastes. It's Veridian warriors who battle the Locusts without fear."

"And it's you players who jump in front of their bullets, so we can come home to the women," Coley jeered.

"That's enough!" Al'Dashan ordered as the cadets gave another outraged cry. He stepped forward, moving in quickly to keep the brawl from restarting. "Ether Cadets, fall out to the hallway for a pack run—"

"Belay that!" Nathan shouted. "Central Corps, reassemble on game floor alpha-one in five minutes. Full gear. Unless you object?" he asked angrily, turning to Ewan and Al'Dashan.

The captain spoke calmly, but his eyes blazed. "It's your command. Sir."

Nathan led his group out in silence. Coley tried to check into Ewan as he passed, but Ewan had already taken a wide stance that tripped him up. The scout stumbled, then whirled about with fists raised and a glare that nearly had Ewan reaching for his swords.

"You're going to be late," Ewan said. "Wouldn't want to make your commander mad."

Coley hesitated, then stood down with a huffed laugh. "My commander's fine with it. We'll be seeing you, O'Meara."

"What did he mean by that?" Al'Dashan asked quietly as Coley exited.

Ewan realized his hands had found his swords on their own, after all. "Nothing good, I'm sure." Slowly, he let go of the weapons. "Al, from now on I want you to break the cadets in for a week before mixing them with the Centrals. We're losing enough of them to the Locusts without the likes of Coley piling on."

"Consider it done," the captain replied, his own eyes darkening. Turning to the greenhorns, he ordered, "Warm up, then pair off."

The unmolested Veridians formed up without incident, and Al'Dashan directed them through a series of stretches. "You're on your first day out of the shockies," the captain explained, grinning as they bent and groaned. "They're wickedly effective little twinkers, but they can't loosen your sinews for you. Every morning you will devote at least fifteen minutes to leveling your flexibility, or you will find yourself back in the tubes and squinting at the sun again by day's end. Do you get me?"

"Yes, sir!" they shouted, somehow looking more afraid than ever.

Ewan chuckled and joined them. They all gave him big-eyed stares, unable to believe that their Hero of Veridor could be touching his toes next to them.

"Did you see those iron maidens they had us in this morning?" one of the young men whispered, swaying as he bent forward.

"Scariest frapping thing I ever saw," another agreed. "These Centrals are glitching if you ask me. Who'd make something like that?"

"Actually," Ewan said, "the Lil' Shockies were my sister's idea."

The cadets tripped over themselves to apologize, but Ewan waved them off with a smile. He let his mind wander as his body finally relaxed, working through the stretches. *What would these noobs think of my three-month rehab, last year?*

"That's good enough," Al'Dashan said eventually. "For the rest of the day, if you're going to get yourselves hurt, do it the old-fashioned way." He walked over to a cabinet and flung it open, revealing an assortment of melee weapons and shields. "Lieutenant Castel says you're proficient in sword-and-board. Show me."

The cadets rushed to the locker, and in moments the gym echoed with the ring of steel on steel. Ewan went to stand by Al'Dashan, chuckling as now and then someone went off-balance.

"The gear always feels heavier, fresh from the shockies," the captain observed. "But they'll get back on curve soon enough."

"Yeah," Ewan said. "Thanks for handling them."

"Gladly."

Ewan smiled to himself, watching the greenhorns with the man he'd once killed. Al'Dashan had proven himself to be as capable a leader here as he'd been in the Veridian city of World's Edge, bringing a perfect mix of firm discipline and patient guidance to the Ether Corps this side of the game floors. Ewan had been more than happy to delegate training to the captain, hoping it would help show the Director there were plenty of good players just waiting to be logged out.

"So," Al'Dashan said after a while. "Did the Director approve Treanna's plan for your new world?"

"Yes and no," Ewan answered. "He okayed it, but he's also maintaining our overall limit."

The captain scoffed. "And who does he expect to guard his transports? The Centrals?"

"He just might," Ewan said. "Al, we've got to keep our people in line. Robert Nichols and Ben Root are sticking up for us, but the others are just begging for an excuse to get us logged back in."

"They'd be dooming themselves," Al'Dashan said, pausing to scold one of the sparring pairs to keep it clean. "If anything, we need more of us to take the fight to the Locusts."

"We could get hosed that way, too." Ewan dropped his voice to a whisper. "If we drive the Locusts off before securing our place, then the Centrals might decide they don't need us out here anymore."

"Lucia wouldn't like that," Al'Dashan muttered, frowning. "Do you want me to pace our efforts, then?"

"Lucia Howe?" Ewan said, startled. Did his capable leader just offer to throw the war, and for the Centre's brazen nursemaid, at that? "Um, no, I don't think we need to. I just thought you should know that the idea got floated around the chiefs the other day."

"I'll keep it in mind. In the meantime, we'll keep protecting our people."

"Agreed. And Al? Let me know if any more foolishness comes up. I'd rather hear it from you than from Powell."

The captain pointed with his dark eyes to the double doors, toward a gray-haired man in white robes striding in. "In that case, here comes more, now."

"Frapping hell," Ewan muttered. "I wish the Patriarch would let us send *him* back home and free up another slot."

Al'Dashan gave Ewan a humoring, cautioning look, then thundered, "Weapons sheathed! Father Brian," he added by way of greeting as the older man joined them.

"Captain," the priest replied, smiling broadly when he turned to Ewan. "And Hero. I've missed you at services."

"Yeah," Ewan said evasively. "But I've got to run, so—"

"Patience, child," Brian said magnanimously, holding up a hand to block the doors. "Stay for the welcoming blessing. It would doubtless encourage our brave soldiers."

Ewan glanced at the clock. *Come on, Gabe! Where are you?* "All right."

The cadets gathered round in a half circle. "I didn't know there was a priest in the other world!" whispered one, her eyes wide.

"Oh, yes," Brian said, smiling warmly as he folded his hands in front of his waist. "I was in Whitehaven when our

Hero fought the evil Gem. I was one of the deleted ones, but foreseeing the spiritual needs of Veridians like yourselves, I chose to remain in this desolate place. Truly, the Logos works in mysterious ways."

Patrick's head tilted, and his eyes drifted toward Ewan. "But I thought the Logos wasn't out here."

"Of course it is," the priest said firmly, also following Patrick's gaze. "Be seated, my children."

Ewan barely kept his sigh inside as he took a seat on the end beside Al'Dashan. The priests' attitudes had always annoyed him, even as a kid. He couldn't count the times he'd been censured for some heresy or other, or been scolded by his parents for planning cave dives with Kate during sermons. Being the Hero of Veridor meant that the Church couldn't punish him outright anymore, but it also meant he had to play nice to keep their support.

"O great system that pervades our lives," Brian intoned, raising his arms in benediction. "That provides us with comfort, health, and rebirth. I call upon you to guide these bold young men and women as they venture forth to defend our world from the demonic hordes—"

"The Locusts are human," Ewan cut in. "Scary nomads, but still human."

The cadets gasped. Al'Dashan nudged Ewan in the ribs. Brian's smile tightened, and his voice became slightly less magnanimous. "The unwashed barbarian hordes which threaten our peace. Preserve their skills and faith in this world of thankless heathens, and see to their needs, that they may safely respawn in their homes one bright day."

"Amen," the others answered.

Brian lowered his arms. "Welcome to the Earth, holy warriors. As the representative of the Church and Logos, I am here to alleviate the stress of your transition."

"And as the first player to actually be here," Ewan added, "I'll tell you what it's really like."

Brian's face twitched. "Naturally, Hero. Now, have any of you questions or concerns about this place or its people?"

The cadets looked uncertainly between Ewan and Brian, and one of them raised a hand. "Father, is it true that food doesn't absorb perfectly out here?"

"Unfortunately, yes." The older man wrinkled his nose. "But the people here use 'bathrooms' to allow the rest of their interactions to be civilized. I would be happy to offer what help I can, as you adjust."

Ewan bit back a laugh, but lacking a message box—or Kate—he kept his thought to himself.

"Is the world outside really a desert?" another cadet asked.

"Oh, yes," Brian answered, as though he'd been out in the Wastes at all. "The husks of a once-mighty civilization are all that remain, buffeted relentlessly by scouring winds."

"Are our ancestors really from here?" a man asked.

"That is what the Centrals would have us believe, yes," Brian said ruefully. "But as with all things, let us apply the lens of faith. The Logos foresaw this world's plight. It led our ancestors, the wisest of their generation, to Veridor and prosperity."

"Fat frapping chance," Ewan muttered. Al'Dashan nudged him again.

"But don't the people here worship a goddess?" asked a woman, hopefully.

Brian gave her an indulgent smile. "In a manner of speaking. The people of this world chose to treat the Earth as their 'Mother.' You'll hear it in their expressions, but this Mother's influence is so weak as to be nonexistent. Pity these Centrals, my children. They worship a false goddess who cannot answer their prayers, and so they have given up on praying. They live only to keep breathing, and so they do not grasp life."

"Is that why they hate us?" asked Patrick.

"Actually," Ewan said, "it's simpler than that. If you would stop and think about it."

Brian sighed audibly this time. "Please enlighten us, Hero."

Al'Dashan nudged Ewan again, but he ignored the captain. *Am I the only one who ever talks back to the priests?* "They hate us because we got to live in a beautiful place like Veridor. We had no idea how bad it was out here, but they've slaved away for centuries, keeping our world running with no reward whatsoever."

"A good deed pays for itself," Brian countered.

Ewan shook his head. "It hasn't for them. Especially since they know full well they would've been players."

Murmurs spread around the group. "What do you mean?" the woman asked.

Ewan closed his eyes. "Brian says the Mother's dead, but he doesn't know how right he is. I have it on good authority that every last Central was adopted as a reject from the game worlds. The only divine intervention they ever got was getting kicked out here. To them, we're a living, breathing, and now walking reminder of how good they could've had it." He shot Brian a warning look. "And the *last* thing they want is to depend on a bunch of smarmy players who won't shut up about how much frapping better they are."

It wasn't until he'd finished speaking that Ewan realized how quiet everyone else had gotten. Brian's face was growing little red splotches of its own. The cadets were paler than ever, casting furtive glances between their hero and their priest. Al'Dashan's expression was stoic, but Ewan could easily imagine the reproachful private message from the captain.

Then the gym's doors opened, and Gabe strode through.

Speaking of interventions, Ewan thought. "Well, guys, my

partner's here, so I've got to go." He stood, giving the greenhorns his best bracing smile. "Just save your fighting for the Locusts, okay?"

They mumbled something like an affirmative, and Ewan jogged over to meet his friend. "Hey! What kept you?"

"Work, as usual," Gabe replied. "I trust you found something to occupy yourself in the meantime?"

Ewan gestured toward the Veridians. "Yeah. Father Brian's already starting in on the new blood."

"So I see." Gabe watched with mild amusement as the priest exchanged words with Al'Dashan. "Remind me, why is he still here?"

"Aside from being deleted?" Ewan asked.

The programmer arched an eyebrow. "It would be simple enough for me to reinstate him with a proxy."

"Oh, yeah. Well, there's a bit of anti-GM sentiment going around just now."

"That man's helping it to spread," Gabe said, voice turning grim as Brian touched each new cadet before departing. "He disrupted breakfast this morning, ranting about the Logos speaking to him through his tablet. I'd hack it myself for the fun of it, but I'm certain it would only encourage him."

"Probably," Ewan agreed, deciding not to mention the brawl. "Oh, I ran into Coley earlier. He said something suspicious."

"Vincent Coley?"

"Yeah. He was in here causing trouble as usual, but he said his commander was fine with it."

"So?"

"So, maybe he's working for the Diamond Lord. Oh, come on!" Ewan complained when Gabe started chuckling. "The guy's a player-hater."

"So are most of the Centrals," Gabe replied easily. "It's not exactly damning evidence."

"I know, but we haven't had a lead in ages! Can't we just question him or something?"

"Not without going through the Director. But if you like, I'll put a trace on his communications," Gabe said as Ewan opened his mouth again. "Coley will never notice, so he won't complain."

"Thanks." Ewan grinned. "Now, you ready to get your butt whipped?"

"Hardly," Gabe replied, drawing his long, thin rapier from its sheath. "I've been practicing."

The two of them stepped out onto a vacant mat, a safe distance away from the Veridians, then saluted each other before leaping into combat. In no time, Ewan was feeling more like himself again, putting it all out there to max his abilities.

He had to, just to stay ahead of Gabe.

Even in the early days, when Ewan founded the Central Corps, the programmer had been a sharp student: quick to learn and hungry for more. After their tournament-ending duel last winter, Gabe had taken it as a challenge to beat Ewan at his own game. It was a challenge Ewan was happy to accept, and the two of them had quickly moved their regular Gem-hunting sessions to the mat when it became obvious they weren't getting anywhere with searching the logs. Ewan loved getting to spar with a motivated opponent, and it felt good to take out his frustrations about not finding the Diamond Lord yet, but he also had a secret reason for pushing the other man so hard. Of all his Central friends who'd gone to the Wastes with him last winter, Gabe was the only one who hadn't been injured—or worse—by the Locusts. Ewan intended to keep it that way.

Gabe kicked out at Ewan's ankle, drawing his attention to his feet, and only the light glinting off the polished rapier warned him what the real tactic was. Grunting as his toes got stomped, Ewan parried the thin blade, then leaped back.

"Nerf it all, no head shots!"

Gabe smiled in reply. "Why not? You do have a head, or at least you pretend to."

"Don't whine because you can't make me lose it," Ewan teased back. "The rules are there for safety; you know that. It's either follow them, or we have to start wearing helmets."

"I doubt that would do much to improve either of our images," the chief agreed. "Very well."

He lunged for Ewan again, still aiming high, but this time Ewan was ready for the cheap shot. Dropping to a quick crouch, he reversed his grips and punched with both pommels into Gabe's belly.

Gabe grunted, doubling over. Ewan spun as he leaped up, pretending that he had mobs on his back as well, before delivering a slap to Gabe's side. The programmer toppled forward, landing on his face, and Ewan lightly pressed a sword tip into the back of his neck.

"Do you yield?"

"For now," Gabe said, still gasping. He let go of his rapier, and Ewan gave him a hand back up. "For someone who acts concerned about his pretty face, that was a foolish risk. What if you hadn't ducked quickly enough?"

Ewan shrugged, surprised at how little he'd thought of it at the time. Back home, it was perfectly normal to lose eyes, limbs, or even lives to a sparring buddy. "I know my own speed, and yours. Besides, we're just using practice swords, and Nichols is a pretty good medic."

Gabe stared at him, then shook his head. "Unbelievable."

"Well, maybe you should play by the rules, so that it's not a problem," Ewan retorted. "Want to try again?"

After a few more rounds that left them both with some healthy bruises, they took a bench by the wall, watching as the Veridians marched out like militant little goslings behind Al'Dashan.

"There seems to be no end to them," Gabe observed, following them with his blue eyes.

"No...just ends for them, out here," Ewan said quietly, thinking of the Swords this batch was replacing. "Has Rothchild said anything more about your idea for an all-out attack?"

Gabe leaned back and took a long drink from his water bottle. "I've told you before, O'Meara. I don't have the Director's ear like you think I do. Much less the way Annie does."

"But surely you've heard something."

"Rothchild's quite adept at implying promises," Gabe said irritably. "There's a diplomatic art in bringing people to heel by letting them think you've given them what they want, and he's a master. If I were you, I would be prepared to compromise."

Ewan sighed, wondering what form that compromise would take, other than crappy. "We're never going to drive the Locusts off without shaking things up."

"I quite agree," Gabe said, standing with a wince. "But frankly, you're lucky Rothchild's let as many of you out as he already has. He's only ever been interested in maintaining the status quo."

Ewan scowled. That luck had come in the form of a hundred Veridians—including his dad—killed by the Diamond Lord. "Yeah, well, the status quo sucks," he called as the chief headed for the door.

Gabe glanced over his shoulder, expression humorless. "I know."

4

NEW GROUND

THE REST OF THE WEEK PASSED WITHOUT FURTHER INCIDENT, AND Ewan woke on Friday in good spirits. After breakfast—thankfully without Father Brian's preaching, this time—he walked to the bridge with Tree.

"Hi!" said the thin, curly-haired woman standing in the room's center. She beamed at them, her smile as bright as her skin was dark. "Gabe says you might be logging into a new world, is that right?"

"That's right," Tree said, not returning the smile.

Ewan couldn't blame his wife: Alex Johansen had been one of the least sensitive, most infuriating Centrals when he'd met her. He didn't know if she'd simply gotten used to dealing with players over the past eight months, or whether something clicked during her brief tour of Veridor in May, but now the programmer finally seemed to get that players were people, too. This had helped Ewan realize much the same thing about the programmers, so he'd done his best to make his new friend feel more welcome.

He joined her at the rail, a console that allowed the game master on duty to do pretty much whatever she liked in the virtual galaxy. Unlike some people Ewan had tried to name, Alex preferred using it for friendly purposes, like exploring the dozens of simulations with the emissaries using the bridge's flying camera program or—her personal favorite—making rainbows appear after thunderstorms.

"We have Grandfather's approval to make contact in Sah'rassa," Tree said, pulling out her tablet with the official order from the Director. "Would you bring it up?"

"Sure thing," Alex replied. Her hands flew over the console, and a moment later, a world map of Sah'rassa appeared on the huge bank of monitors covering the front wall. "Hmm," she murmured, zooming in. "There's no green."

Ewan smiled; half a year ago, no Central would've thought anything of that. "It's a desert game. If you zero in on one of the oasis villages, I bet you'll see some."

She nodded, the motion drawing his attention to a pretty bronze clip in the hair behind her ear. *Kate's work*, he realized as his smile broadened.

She grinned back at him instead of working the controls.

Tree jabbed him in the kidney.

"Ow!"

"I'm right here!" she hissed in his ear.

Ewan blushed in sudden understanding. It wasn't his fault that the Centrals treated friendliness as an open invitation to, well, more friendliness, but Tree still acted like he thought so, too.

Alex also caught the hint. She quickly returned to her work and zoomed in on one of the central villages. "This is An'jar," she commented, glancing up as the camera settled. Buildings clustered around an oasis of startling blue, split by a wiggly network of paths. "It's apparently one of the bigger settlements, population three thousand."

"Ugh." Tree lurched forward, clutching the rail.

Alex looked at her in confusion.

"Not the town," Ewan explained, rubbing his wife's shoulders. "Tree's just been feeling off the past few days."

"I have not," Tree grumbled, closing her eyes as she leaned into him. "And if I am, then it's got to be the new food Lisa's serving." She stifled a burp. "I can't believe Tina showed her how to make that pepper sauce."

"You mean that red stuff on the breakfast scramble?" Alex asked. "I liked it. Was that a Veridian idea?"

"Yeah." Ewan gave her what he hoped was a more Tree-approved smile. "Our friend at the local tavern uses it to spike the drinks at last call, to make sure everyone's fit to go home."

"It ought to be a weapon," Tree muttered, actually starting to turn green.

"I'll mention it to Kate," Ewan teased, but he brushed a hand across her sweating brow. "Tree, we can do this later—"

"I'm fine!" she snapped, wrenching away to prove she could stand on her own. "Alex, tell me about An'jar."

Alex exchanged a glance and a shrug with Ewan, then turned back to the rail's miniature screen. "Well...it seems like a fairly typical village. I'm not seeing anything about a world capital, but there's something—someone, I mean—called a 'Rajj' that seems to be in charge."

Ewan pondered the map on the wall, frowning. "I don't know."

"Know what?" Tree asked, moving beside him again.

"Sah'rassa's ringed by mountains on all sides, right?"

"So?"

Ewan shrugged. "If we just pop up out of nowhere in the middle of their world, wouldn't that seem a little, well, odd?"

"No more than it did in Veridor—" Tree's face colored. "That's not fair!"

Ewan grinned. "Are there any decent-sized towns near the edge?" he asked Alex.

"Sure. Which direction?"

He scanned the map but couldn't pick out much in the sand. "How about southeast?"

The camera swept away from An'jar, hurtling over dune after dune, but eventually it slowed, then settled on a village that might as well have been the same one, for all Ewan could tell. "This is...J'unai," Alex said, looking up from the console. "At least, I think it is. Did the camera move?"

"Yeah." Ewan chuckled, leaving the rail to get closer to the screens. "Can you pull up the local quests?"

"Sure. Looks like this one's at war with a couple of its neighbors."

"Nothing new there," Tree said. "As far as we can tell, the settlements are almost always raiding each other. Who are their allies and enemies?"

Ewan blinked as the little white dots on the screen transformed into mixtures of reds, blues, greens, yellows...and more. "What do those mean?"

"Current diplomatic status of the other villages with respect to J'unai," Alex replied. "I've got a key, here."

She started explained the colors' meanings, but Ewan tuned her out, reaching up to touch the dots instead. Constant conflict, wide open spaces. Adventure. Had Veridor looked this complex before the unification? *The Caitsid'h may be the perfect counter for the Locusts*, he thought, sheepishly. *If Tree had gone here first, would she have even needed to come to Veridor?*

"There's also a bounty for the capture of 'Nightpaws,' whatever those are," Alex said. "And it looks like there's some kind of ritual hunt, scheduled for three days from now."

"That sounds perfect!" Ewan said. "We could log in, help them bring down some epic mobs—"

"Using what?" Tree cut in. "I don't think our Veridian avatars are going to help us keep a low profile among the Caitsid'h."

"Oh. Um, yeah. Alex?"

"Sah'rassa and Veridor run on compatible engines," the programmer said, her eyes scanning the rail for details. "Leveling frameworks, core mechanics...there are some linguistic differences, but we do our best to make the Logos standardize the essentials across each world. The menus help with that quite a bit, teaching even babies how to read common English. I've often wondered whether it was worth incorporating other subliminal lessons, maybe as the players fall asleep. What do you think, Ewan?" she asked.

She was in her element, working with the Logos and now getting feedback from a player. *I guess I know it as well as she does, in my own way*, Ewan thought with a grin that he quickly deflected when Tree huffed. "I don't see why not, as long as it's benign," he said to be polite.

"Thanks! Anyway, I should be able to adjust your profiles, give you local names, that kind of thing. We'd want to add cosmetic changes to your avatars too, of course, so you won't stand out."

"You can do all that in three days?" Ewan asked, stunned.

Alex laughed, her eyes bright. "We can do that now, if you want."

"But what about my old body—avatar?"

"What about it?" Alex asked.

"Well, it's kind of personal," he admitted, running a hand through his hair. "I put seventeen years into it. Can you put it back the way it was, after?"

"I could always make a backup profile," Alex said, half to herself. "But indexing it could get tricky, especially if you start logging into more new simulations. I could start you out fresh with a new profile and assign your current stats. Better yet, we could augment them to suit your needs and tastes. I could even disable damage and fatigue parameters—"

"Hey, wait," Ewan said quickly. "We can't do that. It would be cheating."

Alex looked up at him, puzzled. "Cheating?"

"You're talking about making us invincible."

Tree touched his arm. "Love, it would make things easier."

Ewan frowned at her. "No, it won't. We can't just log in and start swaggering around like Gems. What kind of first impression would that make?"

"The kind that keeps us from getting arrested and losing months," she answered bluntly. "Had I done so last year, I never would've needed to flee your Church."

"You never would've met me, either," he countered.

She stiffened, face darkening as she fingered her ring. "Love, I—"

"We're not going to force these people into an alliance by acting high and mighty," he insisted. "At best, they'll log out for fear, but then they'll realize we're just as vulnerable as they are in the real world. You talk about fleeing the Church, but would they have allied with us if I'd come back overpowered?" He flashed her his best rakish grin as a peace offering. "Besides, I could use a good challenge."

Tree gave him a long, measuring look, then sighed. "Fine. Alex, no modifications beyond whatever it takes to keep us innocuous."

"Okay," Alex said uncertainly. "Do you want to get started now, then? I can put you in the ready room, but I can't guarantee there won't be some glitches in the adjustment."

Tree nodded, and Ewan helped her into one of the special tubes installed for their relative convenience. "You sure you'll be up for a dive?" he asked, checking her eyes for lingering sickness as she reclined on the foam pad inside. "It's not like you to back down so quickly."

"I told you, I'm fine," she muttered, but she did return his quick kiss.

A moment later, he was in his own tube, thumbing the release lever Sam had thoughtfully installed on the inside. *It's too bad the game floors don't have these—not that the players would be strong enough to use them.*

"Ready room set up," Alex said, her voice muffled through the casing. "Commencing in five."

Ewan felt the now-familiar pinpricks as the tube's wires slipped into his neck and face, somehow seeking out the right nerves. They were eerily painless, especially compared to the bone injections of his rehabilitation. Alex's countdown faded along with the rest of the world, and Ewan heard a chime in his mind as the Logos acknowledged his returned presence, followed by a brief message, flashed across his vision by the wires behind his eyes.

Ea'win Omi'ra: Logging into the Ready Room.

Then he was standing in an empty room, wearing a plain tunic and pants. The walls and ceiling looked to be made of the same stuff he'd seen on buildings in the monitors, and the cool, gritty pressure under his bare feet spoke of a dirt floor.

He turned, taking it in, and Tree appeared beside him, her unbound virtual hair whipping around her shoulders the way it always did when she logged in. As always, she looked magical to Ewan, even though she'd been equipped with garb as common as his.

"Don't you look rakish," she teased, looking him up and down.

"You too." He grinned as she playfully flicked her long skirt at him, obviously feeling better in the game.

"I've recalibrated the audio channels," Alex's voice announced, from somewhere near the ceiling. "Can you hear me?"

"Loud and clear," Ewan answered.

"Okay. First things first, let's adjust your physical features. This may feel a little weird."

Weird wasn't the half of it. Ewan's ears seemed to turn into jelly, slipping and trickling up toward the top of his head, while his nose sank out and forward, as though someone was molding his face like soft clay. His whole body tickled and tingled, and his fingers felt like they were being gently pinched to points. When something especially peculiar happened to his backside, he decided to just close his eyes and wait it out.

Eventually, the feelings subsided, but he knew it had worked when Tree giggled. "Look at you," she said, her voice suddenly raspy.

"I can't," Ewan replied, eyes widening as he turned to see the lioness wearing his wife's clothes. "But you'll fit in just fine." The honey blond of her hair now stretched into a fine golden fur over her body, even to the luxurious tail flicking randomly out from behind her. Her eyes were still the same rich brown, but now they looked larger, with half-moon pupils soaking in the light reaching past her whiskers.

"Alex, can we get a mirror in here?" he asked.

A rough dressing mirror materialized by the wall, and the emissaries took turns looking into it. Ewan hardly recognized himself: green eyes with those huge pupils looked back at him, blinking in surprise from under a sleek black coat of fur. His whiskers twitched as he pulled his lips back to reveal large, pointed fangs. His ears were almost as big as his hands—or were they paws now? He tried flexing his fingers, then gave a yelp when his claws extended.

"Your tail's all frizzy!" Tree laughed, grabbing at it.

"Hey—yah!" he yowled when she caught it. "Alex is watching!"

That made her own fur stand out, but she didn't let go. "I…I wouldn't think the Caitsid'h see it that way."

"I'd rather not find out," he chuckled. "Alex, any tips on how to use all this stuff?"

"Sorry, you'll have to work that out for yourselves," the programmer said. "I'm taking an image. You two look adorable."

The emissaries spent a while, working out how to move their tails and other various new bits and pieces. It was a blast, getting to play and explore with Tree, although Alex's constant chatter kept Ewan behaving himself. He hadn't expected to find his wife so alluring in this form, but it really did accentuate her natural grace, and the blond fur felt wonderfully soft under his fingers. *Hey, we're still the same species, right? It's not that weird,* he told himself when she nipped his ear.

They were wiggling their tails and flexing their claws as comfortably as any cat when Alex spoke again. "You two are welcome to stay in there if you like, but I need to get some dinner."

Ewan blinked. "Dinner? Already?"

"That's right," Alex replied. "It's six o'clock in the Centre."

"We'd better be getting out as well, then," Tree said reluctantly.

A few seconds later, Ewan was letting himself out of the tube, working his jaw bemusedly.

"Don't worry, you still look human here," Alex reassured him.

"Thanks," he said, swaying slightly as he stepped out. "Funny, how easy it is to get used to the tail."

"Perhaps Robert's right about needing to anticipate challenges for the Caitsid'h," Tree said, her human eyes seeming to narrow to slits as well. "I'll discuss our options with him tomorrow."

The O'Mearas bid the game master a good night, then headed back to their apartment. "Sure you don't want to eat something?" Ewan asked hopefully, as his stomach reminded him they'd already skipped lunch.

Tree shook her head. "I'd rather not. To be honest, I'm still feeling a little queasy. Maybe we should take metabolic inhibitors before we log in on Monday. We could be in there for a while."

"After all that practice?" Ewan grinned at her. "We'll blend right in with the natives."

She returned the smile and wove her fingers through his. "There's still so much we don't know about them. But I'm sure that with your help, we'll have a much more productive first contact, this time."

5

THE HUNT

EWAN SPENT A MISERABLE NEXT DAY LOGGED INTO VERIDOR, offering his Hero's condolences to the families of this month's fallen. He hated it more than anything else in his job, but as he was the reason they'd come to Earth in the first place, it was the least he could do. It didn't help that they never understood what he was telling them at first. So what if their loved ones were dead? And they were already logged out, so what did that matter to them? But it would always click, eventually. Then there was dumb grief, followed by the blank, hollow look that meant Ewan had done his part and that it was Paul's turn, as an official Church rep, to console them.

As they transferred back to Whitehaven, materializing beside one of the twinned yews at the base of the cathedral steps on the edge of the city square, Ewan and Paul received a joint message from the Patriarch.

To Hero Ewan O'Meara, Lieutenant Paul Castel and Captain Al'Dashan of the Ether Swords, and Reverend Brian Graham of the Church of Veridor:

Let me begin by extending my thanks to you for continuing to protect our world and its people. The names of those who gave their lives shall be added to the memorial in the square, with the usual honors.

I am concerned, however, with the rumors spawned by our returning soldiers. They tell of a bleak, hopeless world, where the Logos has no reach and their efforts are unwelcome —and meaningless. These rumors have already begun to undermine our people's faith, which in turn undermines their will and, ultimately, our defense efforts.

Therefore, I have determined that all future volunteers for the world beyond must be possessed of unshakable faith, in addition to the other crucial qualities befitting such work. The Church's liaison, Father Graham, will review each candidate soldier before transfer, in coordination with the military advisors.

May the Logos guide us all.

Ewan and Paul stood there, staring at each other through the words.

"Frapping hell," Ewan muttered. *Was this because I talked back to Brian the other day?*

"He's not wrong," Paul said carefully. He shook his head, dismissing the message. "Almost everyone comes back shaken, depressed. We call it getting Wasted. A little extra faith might be just what we need to send out there."

He turned and started for the steps, but Ewan grabbed his arm. "Hey! All the faith in Veridor won't change the real world. We need people who can handle the hard truths, not zealots who ignore them."

"We need some good news," Paul said grimly. "Has Kate had any luck building armor that can stop these arrows of theirs?"

Ewan sighed and released his friend. “Not yet. She’s working on it, though. In the meantime, I’ll see if I can’t lighten our load by recruiting from the other world.”

Paul gave a small shrug. “Good luck with that. I’ll keep doing what I can here.”

Things in the Centre weren’t much better, though. Ewan hadn’t spoken two words to Al’Dashan in the dining hall before Father Brian interrupted, handing them both a list of Ether Swords he wanted to send home. Leaving the captain to deal with it, Ewan stormed off to get some food—and saw James Frasier, watching him from an isolated table.

Fists clenching as the fires of Whitehaven burned in his mind, Ewan changed course for the Gem in plain sight. “What are you doing?” he snarled.

Frasier smirked up past his crooked nose, which Ewan had broken for him last spring. “Surely even you comprehend eating by this point, player.”

Ewan pressed his hands down onto the table, one on each side of Frasier’s tray, to loom over the dark-haired man. “All by yourself? Not very sociable of you.”

Frasier spoke quietly, but his voice was hard. Dangerous. “What choice do I have, player? I’ve eaten alone at every meal since you killed my wife.”

Ewan froze as the memory of his dad’s deletion switched to one of a terrified scout, bleeding out in his arms. “I—I didn’t kill her. The Locusts did.”

Frasier’s eyes burned with hate, so much so that Ewan half expected the man to sprout angelic wings right there at the table. “Don’t waste my air to ease your conscience. Be grateful instead that your own woman is so well-positioned.”

The chill in Ewan’s blood shot through his heart. “What do you—”

“Unless you intend to make my life even more miserable, leave!”

Shaken, Ewan retreated to the main door. But when he glanced back, Vincent Coley had taken the seat across from Frasier.

I should report this, Ewan thought. *But to whom? Gabe won't believe me, and Tree's already got enough on her plate, getting ready for Sah'rassa.*

Eventually, the day of the hunt came, and Ewan woke feeling more upbeat, shaking off the week's stress with a touch of his old eagerness. How many times had he dreamed of exploring wild new places as a kid? Veridor didn't have deserts, much less ones filled with cat people.

When the alarm sounded, he hopped out of bed.

Tree groaned as he dislodged the blankets. "I only just got to sleep!"

"Then you shouldn't have kept me up all night," he joked, playing a little tug-of-war with her over the sheets until she smacked him and fled for the warmth of the shower.

They skipped the Central grays, choosing soft gym clothing instead on the chance they'd be logged in for a while. Tree shot Ewan a mischievous wink as she bent to slip her shoes on, but she also bunned up her hair, jabbing a burnished stick through it as a warning to everyone else that she was still on duty—and not to be trifled with.

When they were ready, they locked their apartment and went to Medical, where Robert Nichols was waiting for them with a pair of syringes and his usual dour expression. "I've loaded a moderate dosage of the standard inhibitors," he informed them without preamble. "It should be enough to offset your base metabolism and give you a week without food, provided you don't place any normal demands on your bodies."

"At least you won't have to eat any more hot sauce," Ewan said lightly to Tree as Nichols slid the first needle into her shoulder.

"We might as well simply drill permanent IV ports into

your bodies," the doctor muttered, ignoring them. "It would save your skin the trouble of regrowing each time."

"No thanks," Ewan said, wincing as Nichols added his own little spot to the collection dotting his arms and neck. "Are you ready for these new players?"

"As ready as any of us," the doctor replied. "The Centre clearly didn't have enough excitement with only your medieval horde roaming the halls."

Michael Patton was busily cleaning the tubes when they got to the bridge. "Good morning," the young man said in his soft voice, glancing up with a smile partially hidden by his abundant pimples. "I know you're only planning to be in for a day or two, but I wanted to sterilize the pads, just in case."

"Good idea," Ewan agreed. Michael was one of the most considerate, least Central-like people he'd met in the real world. Originally a caretaker for the players on the game floors, he'd since been reassigned to Tree's section to tend the bridge whenever the emissaries logged in.

"How are you, Tree?" Michael asked.

She opened her mouth, then belched and went pale as the sound rebounded off the walls.

"Are you okay?" Ewan asked, squatting down to face her as she doubled over.

"I'm fine," she said into her knees, but she didn't throw him off—which only convinced him she wasn't feeling well.

"Already warmed up, I see," Alex said as she entered the room behind them. "Breakfast still disagreeing with you, Tree?"

"She didn't have any," Ewan answered with concern, as Tree let loose another echoing blast that drove his hair back. "Love, you don't look well."

"I said I'm fine!" she snapped, but then she heaved, losing her balance—and her nonexistent breakfast, all over his shirt. Alex yelped, and Michael jogged over to help.

"Well, I still think you're beautiful," Ewan said bracingly, trying not to inhale the fumes wafting up from his shirt. "But something's wrong. We can try again another day."

"No," Tree rasped, her dark eyes burning with embarrassment as everyone stared at her. "We need to go; we need the Caitsid'h as allies. I'll be—"

She emptied herself on him again, then fell into his arms with a groan.

Ewan gave her a messy hug. "Love, it's okay, really. We can go another day."

"The hunt is today," she countered, her voice furiously muffled against his chest "And *you're* not vomiting. You go ahead, and I'll catch you up in a little while."

"But—"

"That's an order," she growled, pushing on his shoulders to stand with as much dignity as she had left.

"Yes, ma'am." Ewan gingerly stripped off his shirt and used a clean corner to wipe her face. "Now, will you please go to Medical?"

Tree pulled away, then sighed. "Yes. I'll be back soon."

"Thanks. I'll head for J'unai after the hunt, so meet me there if you're wrong?"

She gave him the glare that said she was never wrong. "Agreed. Good luck."

"You too," he said, leaning in to kiss her carefully on the cheek.

"I'm telling you, I feel fine," she muttered. "I'm just sick, that's all."

Ewan watched her go, then joined Alex and Michael in a sigh of relief. He walked to his tube, still fretting about his wife, but the shock of cold pads on his back brought him back to the moment. "Yah! So much for cleaning the tubes," he said apologetically.

"No worries," Michael replied, sealing him in. A moment later, the contacts slipped into his head again, giving him just enough time to give a quick thumbs-up before relaxing and letting the real world fade to nothing, leaving only a nagging concern about Tree.

Ewan stood at the base of a high dune with the sun at his back, blazing against the sand in the still air. Turning and squinting, he could make out the border mountains, a dozen miles away according to the minimap that popped up in response to his curiosity. He wasn't a stranger to mountains, not after last year, but the Argenones had at least offered passes. The wall of red stone in the distance looked uniform, unbroken, as though some great Gem had hollowed out the sandy world around him by pulverizing the innards of a great plain.

Some Gem probably did, Ewan thought darkly. He raised a furred hand and extended his claws. *If they can make humans look like this, then world building was probably child's play.*

[All right, I'm in,] he messaged the bridge as he started up the dune to get a view.

[I've got you on screen,] Alex confirmed silently.

[Can you tell me where this hunt is?]

[I've got a large party of Caitsid'h about three miles northeast of you, moving west.]

[Three miles? You couldn't put me closer?]

There was an awkward pause, then, [I thought you didn't want to appear in the middle of them.]

Ewan growled, low in the back of his throat. [Very funny.]

[Do you want me to transfer you?]

[No, thanks. I could use the time to get acclimated, anyway.] He was panting by the time he reached the peak, but either his new body couldn't sweat, or it had already dried up in the withering heat. [How hot is it out here?]

[I'm reading one hundred fourteen degrees at your position,] the game master replied.

One hundred fourteen?! Ewan called up his inventory, but he hadn't put anything in there since his last trip home. [Alex, I could use a change of gear. All I've got is night armor, and that's even blacker than my fur.]

[Sorry, Ewan. Tree gave me direct orders the other day to avoid 'cheating.']

Ewan grimaced. [Well, if I pass out, you'd better revive me!]

She didn't reply, so he started walking, pulling up the minimap and finding nothing but dunes. *Would it have killed her to put the Caitsid'h in my party?* he grumbled to himself as he worked his way down to the shaded side, where it might as well have been a hundred and fourteen below zero. *What kind of people live like this?*

He went on, striking generally northwest and hoping to intercept the hunters, but the temperature swings were doing a number on his stats. His stamina was already tanked out, and on the daylit sides—growing bigger by the minute as the sun rose—his health was starting to drop.

By the fifth dune he was chugging potions, watching his inventory shrink through grayed vision as he swore to get back at Tree for this. There was no way she'd have insisted on no supplies, not if she was there, too!

To take his mind off his imminent death by misadventure, Ewan pondered just what he was going to tell the Caitsid'h when he found them. Truth be told, he hadn't really put much effort into planning negotiations, seeing as how Tree was supposed to be there with him. She was the one with the political skills, not to mention the commanding presence.

Maybe we can just whack the mobs together? he thought hopefully, then swore again when he cleared the next dune to see nothing but more sand. *Or maybe I'll just beeline for J'unai, hunting be nerfed.*

He kept on, pausing to rest in a last bit of shade behind a curved dune. He wished that Sah'rassa was more like the clouded Wastes—then snarled as he realized what that meant. Drawing his behemoth-horn swords, he stabbed the dune. "I'm supposed to be having fun!" he shouted at the frapping sand pile. "This is a game, not an oven!"

The dune roared.

Ewan leaped back, tripping over his tail as the sand shook. He just had time to see a figure in white come sprinting over the crest above, before the whole dune exploded to his right. Sand flew everywhere, half burying him as the biggest mob he'd ever seen plowed through the hole, snapping at the white-clad player with teeth as long as Ewan's swords.

Spitting sand, Ewan watched in shock as the monster kept coming through the gap, brushing the dune aside like water. It was low to the ground, reptilian, with a long neck like a snake, but even then it was a good three times as tall as Ewan was at the shoulder, and moving faster than anything he had left in him.

[Alex! I need stamina!] he pleaded.

[That would be cheating,] she taunted back. [I thought you wanted to earn their respect on your own.]

Cursing enough to make Kate blush, Ewan did the only thing he could think to do. He clawed his way back to standing and took off, sprinting for all he was worth at the epic mob's belly. He nearly got clobbered when a massive leathery wing punched through the dune, but he had just enough presence of mind to grab one of the wicked barbs on its front and haul himself up.

Giddily pleased that the brute would do the legwork for him now, Ewan clambered up the wing to the shoulder, then worked his way up along the massive neck, grateful that he had claws to hang on with. Ahead, he could see the white runner sprinting like mad up the valley, staying ahead of the sandalanche the monster—the dragon, he realized with a panicked thrill—was making as it gave chase. *What in blazes are they doing?* he thought as he grabbed at a neck spine to keep from getting flung off.

Then he heard cries, fierce and keen, from either side. Looking up in amazement, he could see dozens more Caitsid'h on the dunes' crests, waiting for their prey to come within range. Realization dawned on him, and he whipped his gaze down to the fleeing figure, stunned by the runner's nerve.

They're kiting this thing!

The spears came, pouring down in a torrent from all sides. Ewan flinched as one struck home a few feet in front of him, sinking a foot-long blade deep in the beast's neck. The mob roared again, lifting its head to snap at a few of the Caitsid'h, but then the kite turned and threw something as well, something silver, that struck the monster in the face and drew its aggro firmly back to them.

Ewan let out a whoop of his own as he drew his own blades and gave the creature a few good stabs to be social. Some of the Caitsid'h seemed to notice him, pointing and rushing to each other as they shouted. Ewan waved back, riding it like some epic horse, but the players launched another volley of spears —at him.

"Hey!" he yelled, narrowly avoiding getting pincushioned as he dove forward. "Hey, I'm trying to help!"

Either they didn't hear him or they didn't care, because more spears flew at him than at the dragon. Dodging for his life, he sprinted for the beast's head, hoping to get a little cover behind its horned frill, but then he saw the kite stumble and fall.

The dragon bellowed in triumph, but Ewan rushed forward, swatting spears aside left and right as he sprinted the rest of the way, and drove his blades at angles into its skull.

It let loose an ear-splitting roar and shook its head wildly, but the swords held. Ewan barely managed to keep his grip as it tried to fling him off. He whipped around, the flailing giving him a break from the spears, and after a harrowing, weightless moment, he planted his feet between his blades. Wrenching hard to the right, he steered the monster, slamming its head into the dune's side and scattering sand everywhere.

The impact knocked him free and he half sailed, half tumbled forward along the dune, rolling to a stop beside the prone kite. Panting and near death, he looked up to see another barrage of spears sink into the dragon's neck and open mouth as it came for the two of them.

"Look out!" Ewan rasped. He grabbed the kite by the shoulders, then flinched back when they slashed at him with a dagger.

"Asst! Get off me, demon!" a young girl's voice hissed.

He grabbed her anyway and threw them both aside as the massive head slammed into the ground where they'd been. She yowled in shock, then scrabbled away from it.

Ewan lay there, staring in awe at the dead eye not a yard away from him, still glaring at him for ruining its owner's fun. "Gems of old," he whispered, coughing as a shout went up from the dune crests. "What *was* that thing?"

"It was my kill." The girl spat and came at him with the dagger again. He tried to seize her wrists, but she stabbed him in the arm and sprinted off down the valley.

A horn sounded from above, and a wall of silver light suddenly appeared. It shimmered like an aurora, curling around to corral them both, and the girl wailed in outrage. "I have drawn the D'jin's blood!" she shouted, waving her little knife as proof. "I am not allied with it!"

"We shall see," came another voice, seemingly from the light itself. The wall emitted a shrill, fur-raising sound that brought with it a wave of dizziness, and Ewan lost his balance and passed out.

6

FIRST CONTACT

EWAN OPENED HIS EYES AND WAS SURPRISED TO FIND DARKNESS.

Casting out with his other senses, the room began to take shape around him. He was seated on cold stone, with his back propped up against a rough wall. His wrists and ankles were shackled by chains that gave each limb only a foot of free play, as he discovered when he tried to stand up. A dull ache throbbed from the stab wound on his arm, though a firm pressure indicated someone had at least wrapped a bandage around it. The air still tasted dry on his rough tongue, but not nearly as dry as it had been outside.

Ewan called up the menus as he waited for his eyes to adjust to the now-dim light, coming from a small slot to his right. The minimap informed him he was underground, in a small room. When he tried to pan up to the ground floor, he found he couldn't, as though prisoners here could only see the extent of the cell by some special magic.

Uh oh, he thought. Was that kind of lockout normal for a cell? The Veridian Church had a lot of what amounted to programmers' privileges, but despite his rocky relationship with the priests as a kid, he'd never actually gotten jailed.

"Hey, Alex," he called out quietly, searching his inventory and finding it stripped clean. "Can you hear me?"

A moment later, her soundless reply appeared in the party menu. [Yes.]

"What's my status?"

[You've been in there for about two hours. The Caitsid'h dumped you both in that cell as soon as they returned to J'unai.]

Ewan frowned and checked his map again. "Both? I'm not alone?"

In answer, a second voice spoke from the far corner, making his own fur stand on end. "Why do you speak with the air? Did the sun take your mind?"

"I don't think so," he said dubiously, recognizing the voice but unable to see its owner. "You're the kite, aren't you?"

"I am Cerri'dah," the voice replied: wary, and a lot younger than he remembered.

Ewan tried to mimic her pronunciation. "Carry...dah?"

"Yes. Cerri'dah," she repeated impatiently. "What is this kite?"

"It's what you were doing in the desert. You were leading that epic mob to your party, just like flying a kite."

There was a pause, then a hiss. "Speak sense or be silent."

"Okay, okay," Ewan said quickly. *Why is she in here with me?* "Take it easy. It looked like you did a good job."

"What do you mean?"

Ewan sat up taller, as far as the chains would let him. "Well, your people got the mob, didn't they?"

"Mob," she repeated, sounding puzzled. "You speak of the *Ta'anin*?"

"I guess so," he answered, figuring there wasn't much chance they were talking about anything else.

"Yes, the tribe completed the kill," she said bitterly. "No thanks to you."

Ewan stiffened. "Hey, that's not fair. I think it would have gotten you if I hadn't—"

"You did not help me!" she shouted. "I was the one tasked with drawing the beast, but your interference has cost me everything!"

"Oh," Ewan said, feeling more stupid by the second. "I'm sorry. I was just trying to help with the hunt."

"*Sh'takh,*" she growled. "See what they do to reward you. I hope they cast you to the winds."

"Um, okay," he said lamely. [Alex, help!]

[But you can't cheat!] she shot back with a speed that told him she, at least, was having a blast. [Don't worry, you're not in danger yet. If things get hot, I'll log you out.]

[That'll go over really well,] he grumbled, still searching for his cellmate without luck. *How can she hide so well? There's not even a dot on my map!*

[There are plenty of other villages,] Alex pointed out. [Maybe if you irritate J'unai's people enough, they'll like you more.]

[Very funny. I'd rather save this one, thanks.]

"The Rajj has not decided whether you are a D'jin," Cerri'dah commented, her voice turning bored. "But I have."

Ewan sighed, jostling his chains as he leaned back against the wall. "I'm just a Caitsid'h, like you."

Cerri'dah hissed. "You lie, D'jin. Even the stupidest cub knows better than to walk under the sun in black!"

"Yeah, well, I didn't gear up very well before I came," he admitted. "But I'm not a D'jin, whatever that is. My name's Ewan. Ewan O'Meara."

"Ea'win Omi'ra," she said, working her voice around his name. "Perhaps the sun truly did rob you of your senses, if you do not know what the D'jini are."

"Maybe you could explain it to me," Ewan offered.

Cerri'dah said nothing for a moment, then huffed softly.

"You are as a kitten. The D'jini are the great spirits, the creators and former rulers of all Sah'rassa. The ancient songs say they rode the Ta'anin along the winds to hunt my people for their sport. Just as you did."

"I see," Ewan whispered, his hackles rising—literally—as he guessed at what she was talking about. "Did your people drive them out, then?"

Her young voice turned fierce, proud. "Yes, we drove them out. Long ago, the Moon cast its light at the feet of the first Rajji, and the Naza sprouted from the sand. My foremothers used the Moon's gift to pierce the cold hearts of the D'jini and sent them away. Every moon, we hunt and slay the Ta'anin which fly down from the mountains, to ensure that their masters cannot ride the winds ever again. From that day until this, no D'jin has dared to return to Sah'rassa."

Ewan closed his eyes, putting her words and his own memories together—and realizing how bad his entrance must have looked to the Caitsid'h. "For what it's worth, my people have similar legends. Our great Hero used an amulet to defeat them."

"Your mind is gone," she replied. "These are not legends; they are a threat. And the Naza are great silver spears, not some trinket."

"Maybe for you," Ewan retorted, more heatedly than he'd meant. "But I can tell you for a fact that ours was an amulet. I used it earlier this year, when I fought a Gem."

"Jem'ah?" she repeated.

Ewan scowled in the voice's direction. "Yeah, that's right. It's what my tribe calls them."

"You lie. None of the forty tribes call them by such a strange name."

"Well, I'm from a different tribe," he said, "from over the mountains."

"That is where the D'jini come from," she snarled. "Why did you return?"

"Nerf it all, I'm not a D'jin!" he shouted. "Believe it or not, I'm actually hunting one."

Silence answered him, but a moment later Cerri'dah's face emerged from the darkness: delicate and small, with large amber eyes framed by a pattern of dark spots that resembled pebbles in a creek's bed.

"What do you mean?" Cerri'dah asked, her ears flattened against her head and fangs bared.

Ewan took a deep breath, noting with concern that the girl wasn't wearing any chains. "Last year, one of them appeared and attacked my town. A lot of people got logged out, never to return."

She crouched lower, her body still mostly hidden so that he couldn't tell whether she was planning to strike. "You mean the winds took them?"

"Yeah, I guess so." His own claws were out now, as if he was back in Whitehaven yet again. "But the bastard got away, and I've been looking for him ever since. I'll admit that I'm not a Caitsid'h, but don't call me one of them."

Cerri'dah watched him glare at her, her eyes narrowing, but she did ease back a little. "But *if* you are not a D'jin and you are also not Caitsid'h, then what are you, Ea'win Omi'ra?"

"I'm a Veridian," Ewan said carefully, gambling that honesty would serve him better at this point. "A human, from the world of Veridor. I left it for another world, the Earth, because there was a danger there which threatened my home."

She stared flatly at him. "But the D'jini come from another world."

"Yeah, they do," he agreed. "From Earth. Their job was to make sure we all got settled into our worlds, but then they got abusive."

"Get settled?" Cerri'dah asked. "What do you mean?"

"My people, and yours, we originally came from Earth," Ewan replied, silently thanking the Logos that she was still listening.

"Then why did they come to Sah'rassa?"

"Because something really bad happened a long time ago, something that made it hard to live there anymore. Our ancestors moved into new worlds to escape that."

"You still speak nonsense. The Caitsid'h have been here since the Moon first rose."

"Technically, that may be true," Ewan agreed. "Sah'rassa wouldn't have existed before your people colonized it."

"You make less sense as you go!"

"Bear with me, okay?" Ewan said, straining to keep his tone patient. "Look...have you ever had a dream that was so real, you didn't know you were asleep?" When she said nothing, he continued. "That's what we're doing right now, Cerri'dah. We're sharing a dream right now, but our sleeping bodies are on Earth, just waiting to wake up."

She hissed softly, then crept close enough that he could see the rest of her, clad in worn leather armor. Close enough to rip his throat out. "You are saying that when the winds take us, that we go to this Earth?"

"More or less—" Ewan began, but then the door flew open, revealing bright torchlight from the hall beyond, despite the hulking cat-man in the way.

"Slipping your bonds again, Cerri'dah?" the man rumbled in a deep bass, his silhouetted tail swishing ominously behind him. "Come," he ordered, and Ewan's chains dematerialized, replaced by a simple set of handcuffs that locked his hands in front of him. "The Rajj will see you both now."

There wasn't much choice, especially when Ewan's eyes cleared well enough to see the wicked curved sword hanging at the guard's belt and a second, equally huge man behind him. Without a word, he stood up, shaking his stiff limbs awake again, and stepped between them. Behind him, Cerri'dah muttered as a soft metallic clink told him she'd been bound again.

Once they'd left the cell, Ewan's map expanded to reveal his position two floors underground, below the largest building in the town. His guards' positions blinked on, a dot on either side of him, but Cerri'dah remained invisible to his detection.

What kind of kid is this? he wondered, glancing back to see her padding sullenly behind him.

They climbed a stone stair, doubling back at landings on each floor, then emerged into a brightly lit hall. Long banks of high windows stretched down the length of it, with painted awnings blocking the harsh sun while letting the light rebound in from below. Columns fluted out from the walls at intervals, seemingly carved of the same pale stone he'd seen in the ready room, although a series of ornate jars and woven tapestries added plenty of color to complement the pale red-and-blue swirls of the polished stone floor.

As they went, Ewan saw dozens of Caitsid'h peering cautiously from the many rooms on the building's interior side. He smiled hopefully at them, but most of them drew back, evidently unwilling to risk returning a D'jin's greeting.

The guards took them up a series of stairs around the outer walls, and finally through a bead curtain that rattled loudly as it let them into the broad chamber in the building's center. Ewan whistled softly—or tried to, with his new mouth—as he looked around. The room was filled with plants he'd never seen before, their long, flat leaves stretching out to the light filtering in from more of the high windows. Above them, torches blazed from their sconces in a display of wasteful opulence, with the smoke curling out through a series of holes cut at angles into the domed ceiling.

Aside from the plants, it's kind of like the Director's office, Ewan thought.

There was a long stone table in the room's center, lavishly decorated with a cloth like spun gold. Half a dozen well-dressed Caitsid'h sat on the two long benches on either side of it, dining on fruit and meats laid out on silver dishes, but as Ewan's party passed near them, their ears flattened and they quickly stood to make their exits.

Cerri'dah growled behind Ewan, low in her throat but loud enough to make him fear for his tail, as they approached a woman reclining in a high-backed wooden chair set upon a dais at the room's far end. She was dressed in a silk gown, her long legs hanging lazily over one of the chair's arms. Her fur was gray around the muzzle, but her golden eyes were sharp, and her whiskers twitched as the guards brought Ewan and Cerri'dah front and center.

"Ahh," she purred, rising with fluid grace and opening her hands, palms up. "Our guests arrive. Ea'win Omi'ra, is it not?" she asked, narrowing her eyes slightly the way Veridians did when checking the menus. "As Rajj, I welcome you to J'unai."

Ewan's guard gave him a little nudge, opening his free hand, and Ewan followed suit. Cerri'dah resisted, keeping her right hand tightly closed, but the Rajj swept down faster than Ewan would have thought an old woman could. She swatted Cerri'dah's arm, hard, and the girl yowled indignantly as her hand opened to reveal some kind of lockpick.

The Rajj's ears drew back, but she said nothing as she took the pick and stashed it in her own inventory.

As covertly as he could, Ewan tried scanning the Rajj for more details, but the Logos wouldn't give him so much as her name, much less anything he could use to negotiate.

The woman moved to sit at the middle of her long table, and the guards moved their prisoners to seats on the opposite side.

"Though you have already met my Claw, allow me to introduce him," the Rajj said, indicating the first guard as blue-clad servants appeared to deposit fresh plates of grapes, figs, and smoked fish onto the table. "Rocco sees that my will is done, whatever and wherever that may be. It was his spear that slew the Ta'anin."

Rocco's massive chest swelled as he offered Ewan a toothy grin.

"I thought that Cerri'dah deserved the credit," Ewan replied.

"That remains to be seen," the Rajj said, ears flicking to the girl. "She is a troublesome cub, with a history of choosing disreputable company."

"No more so than the fate you would have me suffer," Cerri'dah hissed, her tail lashing from behind the chair.

"I must apologize for your rough quarters," the Rajj said to Ewan, ignoring Cerri'dah. "We were uncertain as to whether you were a friend or a foe."

She slid the plate of fish across to him, drawing a hungry growl from Cerri'dah. A moment later, a servant placed a silver cup of ice-cold water in front of Ewan, the dew on its side making his mouth ache with thirst.

"How do you know I'm a friend now?" he asked, not quite trusting the encounter's sudden good turn.

"I don't," the Rajj answered smoothly. "But after inspecting your belongings and recognizing your assistance in slaying the Ta'anin, I have decided to allow you the chance to explain yourself. Go on," she added, her ears flicking to the water. "Drink. It is not poisoned."

"Great," Ewan muttered, put off that she'd even suggest it. He scanned the food anyway, then took a long drink and a nibble. "It's delicious, thank you," he said politely. He started to slide the plate over to Cerri'dah, but Rocco's large hand grabbed his wrist.

"Not for her," the Claw warned, eyes gleaming.

"Ea'win Omi'ra," the Rajj said, "your intrusion into the Hunt has caused my people great unease." Her voice was controlled, but her ears twitched toward Rocco, drawing back just a little as she stared at her guest. "Many of those who saw you ride the Ta'anin believe you are one of the D'jini."

Ewan stalled by taking a bite of fruit, but his own unease grew as he guessed that the Caitsid'h had been communicating a lot more with their ear twitches and tail flicks than he'd realized. He glanced at Cerri'dah, but the girl ignored him, staring instead at the fish as though she could will it into her inventory. "Is that what you believe?" he asked, turning back to the Rajj.

"I am...undecided," she replied, baring her fangs in a subtle smile. "There has been no sign of the D'jini for thousands of moons, and the ease with which you bleed does not match the old stories. But then, you are obviously not Caitsid'h. No one as weak or foolish as you proved yourself to be would survive to your age, and there are no oases between J'unai and the mountains."

Without warning, she lunged forward. Ewan flinched back, but it was Cerri'dah who yowled as the Rajj's hand pinned hers —holding a piece of fish—to the table. "Young one," the woman said with odd warmth, only releasing her after Rocco had extracted the fish from Cerri'dah's grasp. "You have spoken with this creature. What do you believe he is?"

Cerri'dah licked the back of her hand as a couple bloody spots appeared on it. "He is a sun-blinded fool. He claims to be from the spirit world, but he is ignorant of Sah'rassa. I believe that if he is a D'jin, then he has forgotten himself, and his power."

"Thank you," the Rajj said. She glanced at Rocco, and the big man slid the plate of fish over to the girl. "In the end, Ea'win

Omi'ra, *what* you are is of less importance to me than *why* you have come."

She regarded Ewan expectantly, so he started from the beginning. "Right. My name is Ewan O'Meara," he said, stressing his name's usual pronunciation. "I'm a human, born in the world of Veridor but recently come to Earth, a desert world not unlike your own."

The Rajj's ears drew back sharply, and the answering shift from the guards made Ewan's fur rise. "Then you do ride the winds."

"You could say that, yes," Ewan agreed, mind racing to find the right balance of nonthreatening and informative. "I know my story's going to sound hard to believe, but please hear me out. I can offer proof afterward."

The old woman again looked at the cub beside him, but Cerri'dah snorted, still gobbling the meal as though she hadn't had a decent one in weeks. "Very well, Ea'win Omi'ra who still claims not to be of the D'jini. Tell me your story."

Ewan told her everything. About Earth, about how it was so bleak that almost no one lived on it in the usual sense. About how the Caitsid'h, as well as millions of other players, were the descendants of refugees who'd fled the disaster to wait it out in the game worlds. About the Locusts, how in the past year the nomads from the Wastes had taken notice of the Centre and begun moving with purpose to find it—and what that would mean for Centrals and players alike.

"So you see," he finished, "I'm here as an emissary from the Centre, to secure an alliance with the Caitsid'h." Going for a little diplomatic flair, he added, "The tales of your warriors' prowess have reached us over the mountains. We believe they can make a decisive difference in the Wastes."

He took a sip of water, watching the Rajj. Her face had gone from patient indulgence to flat disbelief as he spoke, but at the mention of warriors, her interest rekindled. "So, Ea'win Omi'ra.

Your story is incredible, and I must admit that I do not understand all of your words. What I do hear is that the spirit tribe across the mountains has need of us, and that you are willing to forge an alliance with J'unai if we will send our finest warriors on the winds, never to return."

"They could return," Ewan replied. "We've got a system in place; they'll be up and about in less than a month and can log in again at any time."

"How convenient for you," she said, ears flattening to match her tone. "You ask a high price for alliance, Ea'win Omi'ra, but you have not yet offered J'unai anything in return."

"Well, what would you like?"

He knew instantly he'd made a mistake. The Rajj's ears and whiskers shot forward, and she leaned on her arms with a hungry expression almost identical to Cerri'dah's as the girl inhaled the fish. "If we choose to ally with you, then your tribe is obligated to answer us in time of need, as are we to yours. Do you propose such an alliance?"

"Yes," Ewan said uneasily, searching for hidden meanings in her words but not finding any.

"You will protect J'unai's interests, as you would your own?"

"Um, sure...as long as you do the same for the Centre."

The Rajj's lips curled into a smile. "Of course. In this case, you can demonstrate your usefulness as an ally right now. This cub," she said, her ringed tail rising to indicate Cerri'dah, "was once my granddaughter, a noble member of our proud tribe. Unfortunately, she has disgraced herself by consorting with thieves."

Ewan glanced over at the girl, then back to the Rajj—*her grandma?* Cerri'dah spat, drawing her ears back and claws out, but Rocco gripped her shoulders, holding her fast.

"She was given a chance to redress her crimes by drawing the Ta'anin in the Hunt. However, she was unable to complete her task alone, and in the attempt brought you to our hall," the Rajj said firmly.

Ewan narrowly dodged Cerri'dah's lashing tail. "But I didn't do anything, other than save her at the end."

"That was enough," the Rajj said. "The Caitsid'h honor the traditions of our ancestors. The pariah must act alone, from start to finish, and none may interfere. Especially not the D'jini!"

"I told you, I'm not a D'jin!" Ewan snapped, even as his map flashed a warning that another two dozen warriors had entered the room and were now surrounding him.

"By intruding as you did, you have laid claim to Cerri'dah," the Rajj insisted, ignoring the cub's curses as she tried to lunge for her grandmother. "You have accepted responsibility for her life, and she now owes you that life."

"Hang on a second, now," Ewan spluttered, feeling more out of his depth by the moment. "I didn't claim—"

"If you wish to have the Caitsid'h as allies, then you will honor our traditions," the old woman growled. "Alliance with another tribe is through marriage. Your spirit tribe will be no different."

Oh, frap! "But—"

"Right now, Cerri'dah has no place in our tribe, and she cannot be allowed to run wild."

"You cannot do this to me!" Cerri'dah wailed, smacking into Ewan as she fought to break out of Rocco's grip.

"Be silent, child!" the Rajj snarled back, baring her fangs at the girl. "I am giving you one last chance to find your family again."

Inexplicably, this calmed Cerri'dah back down to seething —which only made Ewan panic more. "But I can't marry her!"

"You will, if you wish our aid," the Rajj growled. "She will see this Earth you speak of, and when she has returned to tell us of it, we will have the proof of your story." She smiled again, her ears high in triumph. "You will have your recruit, Cerri'dah will have her place again, and *we* will have peace and quiet in J'unai."

"Not through marriage!" Ewan shouted. "I'm not going to marry some kid I just met, and besides, I'm already married—"

A fierce wind swirled out from the dais, guttering the torches as a figure of light formed in the Rajj's seat. A moment later, it resolved into Tree's feline avatar, now geared up in clothing and jewelry as fine as any the old woman was wearing.

"To her," Ewan finished, though no one was paying him any attention now.

"Your terms are unacceptable, Rajj of J'unai," Tree said in her most forbidding voice, ignoring the way every last guard leveled weapons at her.

"It is another D'jin!" cried one. He flung his spear at her, but it glanced away, repelled by the energy shield she'd learned to cast in Veridor.

"Do not attack!" the Rajj commanded, already on her feet and moving to within a few feet of Tree. "You claim this man?"

"I do," Tree answered, the murder in her brown eyes telling Ewan just how furious she was. "I would forge an alliance with J'unai, but as the spirit tribe, we claim the right to bend tradition. Would you be so foolishly stubborn as to reject our *offer* and see us ally with one of your many rivals, instead?"

The two women glared at each other, making the room crackle with tension, but then the Rajj chuckled, raspy and low. "I recognize my young sister Rajj from the spirit tribe," she said at last, her nostrils flaring as she regarded the intruder sitting in her chair. "You would have done well to come here in the first place, Tri'ana Omi'ra, but under the circumstances, I suppose it could not be helped."

Tree nodded stiffly, but her golden tail lashed behind her. Making no move to vacate the seat, she said, "You will return my husband's equipment to him at once. In recognition of your need, we will accept responsibility for the cub, but there will be no marriage. The cub will have Ewan and I as guardians, and she will learn the ways of our world before returning here with us. When we do, we will request your finest desert scouts and warriors. In exchange, you may call on our tribe in your times of need, as an ally."

The old woman growled at her. "You make many demands, spirit Rajj. Your arrogance is equal to the stories of old."

"I'm not the one exiling a child to the real world to get peace and quiet," Tree growled. Her eyes narrowed to slits as she opened her hand, palm up, to reveal a ball of flame hovering inches over her claws. "These are my terms. You will either accept them, or declare war with us by your refusal."

The guards were on her in an instant, pressing their blades against Tree's energy shield. Ewan reached for his own swords, but all he found was empty air.

[Tree, don't act like a D'jin!] he messaged frantically.

[It's better than only *half* acting like one,] she snapped back, sparing him a glare before opening her other hand for a ball of lightning. [We've got thirty-nine other villages to try if this one won't cooperate.]

[But they won't listen if you destroy this one!] Ewan countered, calling up the submenu to log them both out.

"Lower your weapons!" the Rajj hissed, and a few seconds later, the warriors reluctantly obeyed. "In light of your circumstances, I will forgive your rudeness, Tri'ana Omi'ra. This once. I accept your terms, in the best interests of both our tribes."

Tree blinked. "Thank you—" she said, bemused, but then a silver spear blazed into being in the Rajj's hands, its gleaming blade cutting effortlessly through the shield to brush Tree's throat.

"But I add this term," the Rajj said, her voice forbidding. "Never again will you or your tribe threaten my people. My ancestors drove the D'jini out before, and I will do the same to you if you attempt to coerce us again."

Tree stared down the spear's ornate haft, the command in her eyes suddenly muted and replaced by something else... resignation? "Of course, Rajj. Please accept my apologies for overreacting," she said quietly, dispersing her magic and vacating the throne as soon as the spear—the Naza, Ewan realized—vanished back into the Rajj's inventory.

The older woman smiled triumphantly. "Then come, sister, and feast with us to celebrate our new alliance."

Ewan stood quickly, moving to escort his wife around the table as the guards grudgingly made room. [Are you okay?] he messaged, flinching when her hand found the wound on his arm.

[I keep telling you, I'm fine,] she answered, though her expression screamed the opposite, Caitsid'h ears or no.

[How was Medical?] Ewan tried.

Her grip tightened, breaking the wound open. [We have a job to do.]

Ewan sighed. [Fine, but promise to tell me later, okay?]

Tree nodded, mercifully letting go so he could help her over the bench and take a spot between her and Cerri'dah.

The mood around the room wasn't exactly celebratory, but at least it was civil again. The servants brought more bowls, with fruits and meats that Ewan didn't recognize but still enjoyed. He went out of his way to thank the Rajj, but the Caitsid'h leader waved him away, far more interested in Tree now.

"Already, she grasps for more," Cerri'dah muttered on his other side. "Even bringing a D'jin under her control is not enough for her greed."

"Tree's not under her control," Ewan answered quietly. "But what about you? Are you okay, coming to Earth with us? I could try to talk them into sending someone else."

The cub closed her eyes, taking a deep breath. “You would not succeed. Besides, my grandmother is correct, much as I would like to say otherwise. I owe you a life debt, Ea’win Omi’ra, and *I* honor my debts,” she said, shooting a death glare at the Rajj, only to be ignored as much as Ewan. “Bah. I am tired of Sah’rassa, and Sah’rassa is tired of me. Soon, I will see for myself where the winds take us.”

“Okay,” Ewan said, admiring her courage. *Just this morning, she’d never even heard of Earth, and now she’s about to log out.* “I was a player too, so I know what you’ll be going through. I promise to help you however I can.”

Cerri’dah nodded, accepting the invitation to join his party with a little smile. “Then I will hope that you are more competent over the mountains.”

“I would also hear more of your village,” Rocco said as he approached them. An item transfer confirmation appeared in Ewan’s vision, and a moment later his gear was back in his inventory. “It would be a fine test to meet the spirit Claws in battle.”

“I’m sure you’d be up to it,” Ewan said half to himself, watching the imposing man as he stepped back to observe the room with unblinking eyes. *If he was tough enough to take out that Ta’anin, then even just a dozen players like him could change everything.*

They ate for a while longer, but eventually Tree squeezed his hand. “Michael’s beside the girl’s tube, ready to bring her to Medical,” she murmured. More loudly, she said, “I thank you for your hospitality, Rajj, but it is time for us to depart.”

Beside Ewan, Cerri’dah began to tremble. “Grandmother,” she whispered, her voice shaking. “I—”

The Rajj smiled at her. “You are named well, Cerri’dah, my spirited wind. Let all present recognize you as my granddaughter again, and honor you as our emissary to the spirit world. But try not to get into too much trouble there," she added, her whiskers twitching humorously.

"No more than usual," the girl rasped, relaxing slightly before turning to Ewan. "Ea'win Omi'ra, I am ready."

"Okay," Ewan said quietly, glancing over at Tree before calling up the menus to log his party out. "I'll see you soon."

7

OUT OF NOWHERE

EWAN SIGHED IN WEARY RELIEF, FOGGING HIS TUBE'S GLASS AS THE bridge materialized around him. He worked his face a moment, relearning its human shape, then reached up with his furless hand and broke the seal.

"Nicely done," Alex called from the rail, her eyes laughing as he stumbled out. "And you didn't even need my help."

"Need? No," Ewan answered with a rueful smile. "But remind me to do my prep work better, next time."

He helped Tree out of her tube, hoping to catch a smile from her as well, but if anything her expression was even more troubled. "What's wrong?" he asked when she hesitated to take his hand.

"I...I'm not certain," she said slowly, watching the Rajj's hall on the bridge monitor.

Ewan followed her gaze. The wily old woman was consulting with her Claw, ears twirling on her head in excitement, but the sound was muted. "I told you we had to play nice," he said gently. "That Naza's their version of Veridor's Amulet of Balance, but apparently each Rajj has one."

"It wasn't that," Tree replied distantly. "Just something she said, I suppose." She gave herself a little shake, then turned her eyes onto him. "Anyway, I think you chose well with J'unai. Their warriors seemed quite impressive."

"They do throw a mean spear," Ewan agreed with an inner sigh. After a year and a half with Tree, he knew when something was bothering her, but he also knew that wheedling only reinforced her shields. She would tell him in her own time, in her own way. "How was Medical? Did Nichols find out what's wrong with you?"

Tree stiffened again, confirming his fear. "He wasn't much help."

"That sounds like him," Ewan said with false levity. "But are you feeling better now? When did you get back?"

"About two hours ago," Alex said with a laugh.

Ewan whipped around to her, then back to Tree. "You were on the bridge the whole time?!"

"Not for the hunt, no," his wife replied, for once having the grace to look sheepish. "But Alex updated me on your progress, and I felt that after your hard work, you deserved the chance to complete the mission on your own."

Ewan suppressed a groan. "But you could have sprung me—"

"I only intervened when that grasping woman tried to force you into an impossible position," Tree said firmly. Her eyes narrowed. "You wouldn't have accepted her terms, would you?"

"Of course not! Gems of old, Tree, she's just a kid!"

"All right." Her face darkened as she glanced away, but after a moment she relaxed, even laughed softly. "I think it would be helpful for future dives, though, if I didn't have to threaten any more civilizations to keep you from marrying the locals."

Ewan shook his head in disbelief. "You're really something, you know that?"

"So you tell me." She leaned into him, brushing her lips against his, but her tablet beeped. "Michael's got the cub—"

"Cerri'dah."

"Cerri'dah," she repeated. "I'm sorry, by the way."

Ewan glanced down at the top of her head. "Um...what about?"

"About offering to take custody of her. I shouldn't have done that without asking you."

"Yeah, well, I figured it was just part of the job," he admitted. "Kind of like when you took me home after I got logged."

Tree shot him a puzzled look. "Yes, I suppose it is, although to be clear, I don't expect us to take each first recruit home with us. We should make sure that she gets safely to Medical." She sighed. "Alex, will you please power the bridge down?"

"I'd be happy to," the programmer answered, already tapping away. "I'll also set a forwarding service from that Rajj to your account. If she tries to contact you, you'll get it on your tablet."

"Thank you," Tree said.

The emissaries walked the halls in silence, ignoring the usual stares. Tree was lost in thought again, letting Ewan guide her from one generic steel corridor to the next as he wondered what was bothering her so much.

Something bad, apparently, he thought darkly. *Or least it will be, by the time she gets around to letting me in on it.*

They turned down the final hall just as Michael came around the far corner, pushing a loaded gurney at a jog. "She's okay!" the caretaker called.

Together, they wheeled Cerri'dah into the shocky ward, a converted room now resembling a stable full of armored porcupines. Robert Nichols met them on the way, but he stared at the child in consternation as Ewan and Michael gently transferred her limp form into one of the devices, so that only her head and shoulders jutted out into the open room. Looking at her, Ewan guessed the girl couldn't be much older than ten years.

"For some reason, I thought you would be bringing in someone older," Nichols said tersely. He shot Tree a hard look. "Don't tell me you're considering adoption now."

"Their leader insisted," Tree answered, returning the glare. "She wouldn't release any of the warriors until the girl reports back. Besides, Ewan already knew her, from their time together in the palace dungeon."

Whatever remark the doctor had been planning, it vanished in blank astonishment. "You logged out a juvenile delinquent as your first recruit?"

"It's complicated," Ewan said, though his face heated in embarrassment. He had no clue what the girl had done, but hopefully it wasn't too bad. She looked so odd now: as shriveled as any other player, with stringy dark hair and skin the color of sand—where it wasn't blue with the veins coursing just underneath.

"Hey, Cerri'dah," he said softly, remembering how sensitive his own ears had been after logging. "It's me, Ewan. Tree's here too. The next few weeks are going to be rough, but if a sun-blinded fool like me can get through it, I'm sure you'll be fine."

He gave her bony shoulder a little press, then stepped back as Nichols activated the shocky. The cot slid into the tube, and Ewan winced in sympathy as hundreds of needles of all sizes slipped into the child's body. Some would inject supplemental nutrients, catching her bones and organs up to real life's demands, but most would activate her muscles as though she was a puppet, made to dance for the Centrals.

The thought wasn't reassuring.

"She's in good hands, O'Meara," the doctor said carefully, sensing his mood. "You're free to check in on her, over the coming weeks."

"Thank you," Tree said. "In that case, we really should be going to get dinner. I'm sure you're quite hungry, love."

"Yeah, sure," Ewan said suspiciously. *When was the last time that Tree had volunteered to go to the dining hall?* "Hey Doc, were you able to figure out why Tree's been sick?"

The medical chief stiffened, then shook his head as he thumbed across his tablet. "Officially speaking, no. Every test I've run indicates that she's in good health, although her white blood cell counts appear to be higher than normal. Most likely, you're experiencing an immune response to the more adventurous fare at the dining hall," he said to Tree, offering her a tight smile. "Believe me, you wouldn't be the first. I warned Carmine that the staff's systems might be disrupted by all the changes, but as usual, he listened to Alice instead," he added darkly.

Ewan blinked. "Alice Spencer? Since when did she want us eating more food?"

"Since your kind started requiring it for our defense!" Nichols snapped.

Ewan raised his hands, backing away. "Okay, okay. Sorry." *Maybe everyone's in a mood today.*

"What should I do?" Tree asked after a moment.

"My advice is to stay away from the spice for the time being, and eat generous portions of the more standard meals. As generous as any of us can get, these days," he muttered, turning and sweeping out of the room before they could bother him more.

Ewan sighed. "I see what you meant about him being no help. You don't even eat the spicy stuff."

Tree nodded, closing her eyes. "Let's go, love."

Unfortunately, eating the bland mush had no effect. Tree was sick the next morning, and then the morning after that. And after that. Whatever it was, it seemed to Ewan like it was getting more intense, with his wife being fine one moment and then randomly sprinting for the nearest sink or toilet. It always cleared by the afternoon, but if anything, her mood got even worse.

It wasn't just her, either.

Nichols was grouchier every day as they checked on Cerri'dah's progress. Kate and Sam had taken to arguing about her latest ornithopter design in the dining hall, but even their shouting got drowned out by the new Ether Sword recruits, who'd apparently taken it as part of their profession to "protect" Father Brian's constant preaching by the door. Two nights in a row, Ewan and Al'Dashan had to intervene so the Centrals could get in line for their meals. On the third, Security did it instead, leaving Ewan to find himself grateful for thugs like Jeff Harper as the idiot Central guard strong-armed the priest through the door.

In fact, the only cheerful person Ewan encountered all week was Gabe. During their sparring session, the chief reported a minor breakthrough on a recent intelligence operation—all strictly classified, naturally. But the programmer's contentment was worth its weight in coresilver to Ewan, so when one morning he got yet another message from his mom asking why Kate wasn't replying, he talked Gabe into minding the bridge while he dragged his family home to get some simulated fresh air.

That afternoon, Ewan materialized on top of the small hill near his mom's cottage on the outskirts of Whitehaven. He smiled, taking in the scene as Tree and Kate materialized on either side of him. The little thatched roof was in good repair, no doubt tended by the Church in thanks for his service. This late in the season, the vegetable garden was mostly brown, with the husks of the harvested summer crop neatly mulching the ground until his mom could plant the winter cover. Behind the house, Kate's forge was still and quiet, having sat unused for a while.

Ewan didn't come here often—certainly not as often as Tricia O'Meara thought he should—but the house was still home, a place where he could unequip his problems for the time being.

He glanced back at the others with a grin. "Race you to the door?"

"Okay," Tree said, looking equally relaxed for a change, now that she couldn't feel her real stomach. "On the count of three. One, two—"

She sprinted off, laughing as she ran.

Ewan charged down the hill after her, leaving Kate swearing in the dust. He easily caught up with his wife, then backpedaled, keeping pace while she ran as hard as she could. "I think you forgot 'three.'"

"Someone needed nerfing," she teased back.

She flung a burst of wind from her hands to try and trip him up; he leaped aside, then slowed so they could jog up to the front door together.

"You people and your agility," Kate gasped a good ten seconds later, panting and glowering as she pulled her hair back from her face.

Then the front door opened, and Tricia O'Meara beamed at them all. "I thought I heard you out here." Her brown eyes twinkled, then lingered over Tree. "Oh, my, you should have messaged me! I would have made something to eat. Will you at least be able to stay long enough for some soup?" she asked hopefully.

Not waiting for an answer, she hustled them in, then busied herself about the kitchen while they took seats around the old wooden table. Ewan watched his mom, smiling as his stamina replenished in the corner of his vision, but he couldn't help noticing the silver glinting from the waves of her black hair.

"Sorry for dropping in like this," he said.

"Oh, it's no trouble," Tricia replied over her shoulder, as she chopped vegetables and transferred them into the big iron pot Kate made for her years ago. "Truth be told, I wish you'd come by more often." Her eyes narrowed, accessing the menus, and she pointedly added, "It's been nearly a month, you know. Two, for Kate."

"Really?" Ewan shot a glare at Kate, but it only bounced off her shrug. "Sorry, Mom. *I've* had my hands full with the Locusts, and making sure the Ether Swords and the Centrals don't frag each other."

[Mama's boy,] Kate sniped in his message box.

"I'm sure it must be very busy in that place," Tricia replied vaguely, stooping to light the old cook stove. "But any time you want decent food and a friendly ear, you just come home again."

"Yeah, sure." Ewan sighed, letting her guilt him a bit. With her kids now famous—or infamous, depending on who was asked—Tricia didn't go into the local village much anymore, to say nothing of the city. *Dad was her life*, Ewan thought, feeling an entirely different guilt rising in response. When he caught her brushing away a tear before she turned to look at them, he promised himself to step up his visits. "That soup smells really good."

Tricia smiled, accepting the change of topic gracefully. "I harvested the potatoes yesterday. You won't find anything this fresh in that Centre of yours. They need to get you better food, for all the work they put you through."

"We're working on it," Ewan replied. "There's not exactly a lot of extra room for crops, though. Kate had a notion the other week that we might try parting the clouds."

"It's a shame that you can't log some of ours out," Tricia said as she served tea to the others, then took her seat.

She gave them all a tired smile, drawing Ewan's attention once again to how much older she looked. He studied her, trying to glean insight into her mindset the way she always did with him. Her eyes were slightly reddened, as if she'd been crying recently. Her face was creased by lines, no longer as young and smooth as his boyhood memories kept insisting it should be.

"Are you doing all right?" he asked.

"Yes, as well as might be expected. I miss your father," Tricia admitted. "And with you both gone now, the house feels so empty. You're all I have left, you know."

To Ewan's surprise, Kate reached out and took her hand. "I'm sorry, Mom," she said, sounding like she really meant it. "I miss home too, but now that I know about the Centre and everything that's happening, I've got to do my part to keep it safe. But I'll try to come visit more, okay?"

"Thank you," Tricia said, sitting up a little straighter before giving Tree and Ewan an expectant smile. "So, are you ever going to tell me the big news?"

"News?" Ewan repeated, puzzled. "Um...well, we made contact with another world, and we've got another player logged out from there. Tree and I are kind of responsible for her."

Tricia's smile broadened. "Oh, children. Are you telling me you don't know?"

"Know what?" Kate asked, glaring over suspiciously at Ewan and Tree. "What did you two do now?"

Tricia laughed happily. "Why, it's all over your face, Treanna. You're positively glowing!"

"I'm...glowing?" Tree frowned, touching her face. "I don't understand."

Tricia's smile faltered. "You really don't know, do you?

Perhaps I'm mistaken, then. Tell me, Treanna, have you been feeling different somehow, the past month or so?"

At once, Tree stiffened. "Yes, I have. I've been getting sick for no reason, always in the late morning." Her eyes narrowed, as whatever relaxation she'd found earlier turned to stone. "But how would you know?"

"Call it a mother's intuition," Tricia replied, the knowing smile back on in full force now. "I suppose it shouldn't be too surprising, what with you and Ewan being together for over a year, now."

"Wait, what are you talking about?" Ewan asked, sensing the conversation spin away from him. "Mom, do you know what's wrong with Tree?"

"Oh, dear, there's nothing wrong with her. In fact, I'd say her body's acting just as it should." She beamed at her children. "Treanna, you're pregnant. Didn't you know?"

The next moments happened so quickly that the Logos might as well have glitched.

Ewan dropped his tea.

Tree gasped, knocking her tea over to clench Ewan's hand as the word *pregnant* careened around his mind.

"You're *what*?" Kate shouted, knocking her tea over as she flinched away from them.

[You impregnated her?!] came a message box from Gabe. Ewan insanely wondered if the programmer had thought to bring tea to drop, too.

"But that's not possible," Tree challenged, looking to her mother-in-law as if it was her call. "How could I have gotten pregnant?"

"Well, I'm sure you and Ewan have figured out the basics by now," Tricia said with another knowing smile. "But if you really need me to explain it to you, then we can go for a walk."

"No, it's not that," Tree said quickly, her face filling with color as quickly as Kate's was draining. "But no one has had a natural birth for over a thousand years!"

"What do you mean?" Tricia asked. "I gave birth to Ewan and Kate the natural way."

"Well, yes, in the simulation," Tree said, looking to the others for support. "But in order to get their real bodies to grow, the Central caretakers had to...help."

"Excuse me?" Widow O'Meara drew herself up sharply. "Jack and I didn't have any help from the Gems' realm, thank you very much."

"That's not what she meant, Mom," Ewan said, giving Tree's hand a warning squeeze. "It's just that players can't slip out of their tubes to court."

"Be that as it may," Tricia said firmly, "the Logos helped me to bring my children into this world, and I know the signs as well as it does. The morning sickness, for one." Her eyes unfocused. "Why, it's right there on your status, dear."

"The Logos," Tree whispered, suddenly clenching Ewan's hand hard enough to nick his health. "Mother of all!"

Her eyes met Ewan's, nearly knocking him back with the dawning terror in them, and then she vanished, leaving him gripping empty air as she logged out.

"Tree, wait!" he called pointlessly.

"What were you two *doing* in your room all this time?" Kate shrieked.

"Katrina, mind your tone!" Tricia scolded before turning to her son. "I'm sorry; I didn't mean to upset her."

"It's okay," Ewan lied, calling up his own menus as he stood. "Mom, I've got to go."

"Yes, of course," Tricia said ruefully, rising to give him a proper hug goodbye. "Congratulations, to you both."

"Yeah, thanks," he mumbled, still trying to process it all himself. *How in blazes did we get Tree pregnant?!*

"I'm coming too," Kate said quickly.

"Not before you tell her about your boyfriend," Ewan snapped, indulging in a vindictive grin as Tricia locked onto her daughter. "Might be important now, don't you think?"

He logged out before Kate could punch him, and a moment later the bridge resolved around him. Without waiting for help, he wrenched the release lever and launched himself out of the tube, landing unsteadily.

Gabe was sitting on the floor behind the rail, eyes and mouth wide in shock—with a Tree-sized handprint across his face.

"Where'd she go?" Ewan asked, not needing to ask how *that* exchange had gone.

"Medical," Gabe answered, distantly. "Where else?"

"Keep an eye on Kate for me," Ewan said. When Gabe didn't respond, Ewan shook him. "Hey! You're responsible for Kate, okay?"

Gabe blinked, saw Ewan's face, and nodded. "Of course. I'll see that she logs out safely."

"Thanks," Ewan muttered; then he was out the door.

8

MIXED RESULTS

TREE'S REAL-WORLD AGILITY WAS HIGHER THAN HER AVATAR'S, BUT Ewan managed to catch up to her by the final hall to Medical. "Wait!" he called, grabbing her by the arm when she kept going.

She turned with a snarl and slapped him across the face, then froze. "Ewan!" she blurted, shocked.

"Yeah, hi." His face stung and his head was still spinning, but he managed a lopsided smile. "You think I was Gabe, or something?"

Her lips tightened enough to vanish. "No."

Great, he thought wanly. "Why'd you ditch me?"

"I didn't ditch you, love. I..." Tree sighed, but her posture didn't relax. "I needed to talk to Robert."

"Last I checked, we *both* need to," Ewan replied, gently but firmly. He rubbed her shoulders, and she pressed back. A few passersby paused, but for once no one commented.

"You're right," she said at length, before taking his hand—and letting him feel how much hers was shaking. "Let's go."

Together, they moved briskly into the ward, where the dark-haired medic, Angela, was looking at some kid's leg. She glanced up. "Checking on the player?"

"Where's Robert?" Tree asked instead.

Angela pointed her chin toward the chief's private office: from their position, nothing more than a door and a blanked window in the corner. "He's prepping for a meeting with the Director. If you like, I'll—"

Tree stalked to the door and started pounding.

"Never mind," Angela muttered.

"Robert!" Tree shouted. "I have to speak with you. Now!"

The window became transparent, revealing a Robert Nichols who looked even more strained than usual. "So I gather. Well, come on, both of you!" he snapped, opening the door and glaring at Ewan like this was somehow all his fault.

Ewan took a seat beside Tree, across from Nichols's tablet-strewn glass desk. Her hand gripped his, but she avoided eye contact.

Nichols straightened his glasses, took a long breath. "So."

"I've just learned why I've been ill in the mornings," Tree said, her voice an accusation.

Nichols arched an eyebrow. "Is that right?"

Ewan looked at his wife, then at the older man; in a flash, he realized that neither of them looked the least bit surprised. "You already knew! Both of you!"

The doctor gave him a sharp look, then nodded. "I knew."

"I only suspected," Tree murmured. She squeezed Ewan's hand hard enough to grind his bones, and when she spoke again to Nichols, her fear was obvious. "How long?"

"Since you finally saw fit to come in the other day," Nichols said reproachfully. "You're a field medic, for Mother's sake! You of all people should know to report unusual symptoms immediately."

"But how?" Ewan asked, bewildered. "Tree, what's going on?"

"The Logos," Tree said simply, still watching the doctor without blinking. "It knew the moment I logged into Veridor—and Sah'rassa, too."

Ewan frowned. "How could the frapping Logos know there's a—a—"

"Fetus developing inside her?" Nichols finished for him. He pressed a switch, and the office windows clouded over again, giving them privacy. "Treanna, you're a caretaker. Would you like to explain?"

In the now-dim light, Tree's voice sounded very small, like that of a child who'd just been told mobs were real after all. "Whenever a player is connected to the system, we insert a probe into that player's bloodstream. It's bundled into one of the contact filaments, in the neck. The blood chemistry is sampled, and the Logos uses the resulting information to determine the player's genetic and biophysical traits. It's the reason your avatar still had black fur and green eyes in Sah'rassa."

Ewan's skin crawled. "You're saying the Logos drinks our blood and uses it to know everything about us?"

"It's more of a sip," Nichols said. "Gabriel once told me it was far more efficient than attempting to hard-code each player's biophysical parameters. But in Treanna's case, it would have detected elevated levels of hCG in her bloodstream. That's what the sample, the one I took three days ago, suggested."

Tree drew a sharp breath, but Ewan frowned. "H-what?"

"It's a hormone associated with pregnancy," the doctor replied. "One of the most reliable indicators, based on my extensive reading on the topic these past few days," he added to Tree with a wave of his hand over the scattered tablets. "We could, of course, attempt to confirm with a urine sample or a pelvic exam—"

"No!"

"I didn't think you'd be interested," Nichols said dryly. "But we can use other information to assess the diagnosis." The monitors' light flashed eerily off his glasses, as if he and the Logos were collaborators in this. "How long ago were you on honeymoon in Veridor?"

Ewan counted in his head, but Tree beat him to it. "Seven weeks," she whispered.

"And when was your last menstruation?"

"Menstruation...you mean her period?" Ewan asked. *That* had taken some explaining last year, once they'd gotten engaged.

Tree nodded, regarding Nichols as if he was intruding on their privacy by being in his own office. "I don't know if you'd noticed, but I haven't had one since we returned from our honeymoon."

"Um, yeah, I did," Ewan lied. "But what does that have to do with it?"

"Potentially, everything." Nichols huffed, but he gave Ewan a pitying look. "In fairness, no member of the staff would have thought anything of it, either."

"What do you mean?" Ewan asked, prying his hand free so he could put an arm around his wife.

Tree grabbed his hand again.

"A missed period and regular nausea are consistent with first trimester symptoms," the doctor said. "Has Treanna exhibited any volatility or mood swings, perhaps a more variable libido?"

"Robert!" she snapped.

"No more than usual," Ewan admitted.

"None of this makes any sense, though," Tree muttered. She laughed, but it had a desperate, hysterical edge. "Why now? Why me? There hasn't been a natural birth for so long!"

"I can't say for certain." Nichols's voice softened, but Ewan thought he heard a bitter undertone. "We're in uncharted territory, with people moving back and forth between the Centre and the game worlds."

"What does logging into the games have to do with it?" Ewan asked.

Nichols gave him a long, considering look before shaking his head. "I don't know that it does, O'Meara. But consider that such traffic has been the single largest disruption to Central affairs in thousands of years. Consider also that Treanna, in particular, has logged more time in the games than any other person—excluding players, of course. On top of that, consider that her current partner is a player. You are sexually exclusive, are you not?" he asked Tree.

"Yes!"

"Very well. I applaud you, personally," Nichols said grimly. "As it is, we've got precious few data with which to work, so I recommend another blood draw, this time specifically analyzing for hCG as a means of confirmation."

Tree looked like the last thing she wanted to do was confirm anything.

"I'm going to have to report all of this to Carmine, anyway," Nichols said quietly.

Tree flinched. "You're going to tell Grandfather?"

"I'm obligated to," the doctor replied. "In the interests of the Centre. Think of the implications, child; this could change everything!"

Tree closed her eyes, and it seemed to Ewan that a massive weight draped itself over her shoulders: overencumbering her and spilling over onto his heart with a guilty plunk.

Gems of old...what have we gotten ourselves into, now?

"I think we should confirm, then," she whispered.

"Thank you," Nichols said, his voice momentarily gentle before he turned the walls transparent again and barked, "Angela! I need another blood draw."

The medic joined them promptly, carrying a needle

attached to a vial by a feeder tube. She swabbed the inside of Tree's left arm with a foul-smelling disinfectant, then slipped the needle into a promising vein. Ewan watched the container fill with his wife's blood, feeling faintly dizzy himself. As an adventurer, blood had never fazed him before, but this was different.

It's not about taking life; in fact, it's the opposite.

The draw seemed to pull the remaining fire out of Tree. She sagged onto Ewan's shoulder, staring listlessly at the flowing liquid as it promised to reveal the truth about her status.

Ewan just hugged her tight, kissing her head around the pointy stick in her hair.

Once she'd gotten enough, Angela twisted a valve on the cylinder and withdrew the needle, leaving just another pinprick in Tree's arm.

After she'd gone again, Nichols looked over at Tree, his expression softening in that way he only seemed to do for her. "Treanna, I want you to know that *if* you're pregnant, my staff and I will do our utmost to see you through it safely."

"Thank you," she whispered. "Will you message us when the results are in?"

"Of course," he said, his voice lowering even more. "But if they come back positive, I think it's for the best that you be the one to deliver the good news to Carmine. In the meantime, I recommend you both take the rest of the day off, and try to relax. If Treanna truly is pregnant, then we're all going to have a lot of new ground to cover."

The O'Mearas made their exit, but their feet took them to the elevators instead of home. They climbed in, and Tree ordered the machine to take them down to Caretaking; a short walk down one of the paths branching from there, and she ordered another elevator to take them to the game floors. It obliged, depositing them on a random floor in the silent darkness before hurrying back to the normal people above.

Ewan walked with her across the narrow bridge spanning the silent depths. They turned to make a lap around the broad hexagonal path, tubes packed in tightly on either side under the hanging moss used to freshen the Central air. As his eyes adjusted to the darkness, the status lights on the tubes grew brighter, turning the great catacomb into a starry sky above and below them. Most of the lights were green, indicating that things were going fine for the players inside. Here and there were red ones, a warning to the caretakers that life support had been cut off for reasons only the Logos knew. The corpses inside those tubes were ready to go to the liquid hydrolysis system, feeding the other players.

One of the tubes on their floor had a light that glowed soft blue, with a number listed on the display underneath it.

"That player's been slotted to have a child," Tree explained softly, steering them for a closer look. The person inside was a woman, her eyes closed and face taut with lack of development. "Soon, a caretaker will come with a special syringe to extract the egg, here." She pointed to a small, rubberized circle on the tube's side, at the woman's navel level. "Then they'll take it to the nursery, to await the sample from the father."

"Where do you think he is?" Ewan asked.

"He could be anywhere," Tree answered, gesturing vaguely at the countless floors across the way, or perhaps to the other assemblages beyond the walls. Backup players, backup civilizations. "But the Logos knows exactly who he is. His tube will light up with a matching code, and another caretaker will extract his sperm and bring it to the nursery ward as well. It will be mixed with the egg, and with luck, one of the sperm will fertilize the egg, creating a zygote." She looked up at him. "It's how we reproduce. It's how we were all born, for centuries."

Until now, Ewan finished silently.

After a while they started walking again, neither one wanting to leave until they'd heard. It was like being in

Veridor's limbo, surrounded by the darkness with little to do but reflect on what the next life would be like.

But here, we can at least talk with each other about it.

Ewan wrapped his arm around Tree's waist, wondering if it was just his imagination insisting it was bigger. "I hope the test comes back positive."

She slowed, shooting him a look that warned she'd already checked out the opposite camp. "Why?"

"Well, because it would be great! I love you Tree, and even if it's early, and unexpected, I'm thrilled to become a parent with you. You know, bringing a whole new life out of our love." He steeled himself, making sure she heard more enthusiasm than panic. "It's just kind of what happens when people get married."

"Not on Earth."

Ewan chuckled. "Well, how many happy couples have you seen out here?"

She barked a laugh. "We'd be the first. But love, what kind of life would our child have in the Centre? There's no food, no peace, and no precedent. We're barely adults ourselves, and we don't know anything about being parents."

"Well, yeah, but...you would want it, wouldn't you?"

Tree froze. "I...of course I do. Would. I just never considered the possibility. How could I have, when no one has had to for centuries? Mother of all, what kind of a reaction will everyone have?"

"Nothing I can't deal with," Ewan replied firmly, though his own pulse was picking up, now. What *would* the Centrals think? Would they celebrate the first child to be born in forever, or would they see it as just another unwanted intrusion by player life? "We still don't know for sure if you even are pregnant, so let's just try to relax for now."

"Right," she whispered, sounding about as consoled as he was.

They went around the floor in silence, lost in their own thoughts as they made Mother knew how many laps. Maybe it was being on the game floors, or maybe it was the shock of the big news, or maybe it was simply the heavy emphasis on family the past week, but Ewan found himself wishing fervently that his own father was still alive.

Dad...you'd know just what to say, to help me figure this out.

When Tree's tablet finally beeped, they both jumped.

She raised it, her hand shaking hard enough to drop the device, but Ewan took its other side. His stomach did flips, just like the time they'd plummeted over the Argentine falls in Veridor. But they'd survived that, even by Veridian standards.

He gently moved her finger to tap on the message icon. "Together."

Test results indicate significantly elevated hCG levels in Treanna O'Meara's blood. Probability of pregnancy: 99.999%.

Please report to the Director, and come in tomorrow afternoon to establish a pre-natal plan.

Mother be with you,
Robert

They stared at it, hardly daring to breathe. Ewan read it a few more times, pounding the meaning into his skull while his body went light and numb. When he glanced at Tree, she looked like she was desperately trying to rewrite it with her willpower.

"Well," Ewan said softly, brushing a tear from her cheek with the back of his fingers. "I guess that settles that."

Tree nodded, her exhalation breaking into something that was half giggle, half sob. "What are we going to do now?"

Ewan pulled her close and gave her a soft kiss, feeling less than ever that he was in the real world. "We're going to have a baby."

She groaned, pressing back into his shoulder. "I don't know."

He squeezed harder. "You're the toughest, bravest person I've ever known. You can do this."

"But there's so much that can go wrong, even aside from the politics. No one on Earth knows how to raise a child, much less deliver one!"

"But we're not limited to Earth," he reminded her. "We're going to have all kinds of help, just you watch."

"But—"

"And even if I'm wrong, you've got me," Ewan said firmly, holding her tight against the future. "I'm still with you, all the way."

The Director was not at all pleased by the news.

Carmine Rothchild sat at his desk as his granddaughter explained, saying nothing himself but frowning deeper and deeper as she went. When she showed him Nichols's test results, he scowled before blowing out his mustache and handing her tablet back.

"I swear to the Mother," he grumbled, "you two are bound and determined to upset every aspect of the Centre."

"It's not like we were trying," Ewan said, drawing a smack from Tree.

"Master O'Meara, that is part of my point." Rothchild fixed Tree with a hard look. "Did Chief Nichols offer any theories as to *how* this occurred, in the face of centuries of sterility?"

"Not as such, Grandfather," Tree admitted. "He speculated

it may have had to do with Ewan being a player, but he seemed reluctant to say much more than that."

Rothchild huffed and leaned back in his seat. "Very well. I suppose now the question is, what should we do about it?"

Ewan bristled at the old man's tone. "You could say congratulations, for starters."

Rothchild blinked, then nodded. "Yes, of course. Congratulations to you both, naturally, but surely you understand the delicate nature of this turn of events? We've already got enough tension to manage with the Veridian players on active duty, to say nothing of this new breed you've begun recruiting. If word about a naturally-conceived child gets out—"

"If?" Ewan cut in. "A baby's a bit hard to hide, don't you think?"

"Not if the pregnancy is aborted," the Director said, his dark eyes on Tree. "By your own words, you are not yet far along. News of a baby, born from the union of a player and a prominent chief with a bright future ahead of her...it would have a polarizing effect on the staff."

Tree didn't respond, beyond closing her eyes. It took Ewan a minute to wrap his mind around the Director's words, but then his anger kindled. "Are you saying we should kill our baby?!"

"Young man, I am saying that the Centre's mission is greater than any one person's desires," Rothchild answered, raising his own voice now. "The players are here to protect this place from the Locust raiders, not to undermine centuries of security!"

"But that's not true," Tree said suddenly. Her eyes opened, and even though he wasn't the target, Ewan could feel passion surging from them. "The players are here to preserve humanity's spirit. Our entire reason for maintaining the Centre is to give them the chance to restore that spirit to Earth. Isn't that right, Grandfather?"

"Yes, of course, one day—"

"But that day *is* today!" The passion intensified, and Tree's hand was hot when she grabbed Ewan's. "Look around you, Grandfather! Thanks to Ewan and the others, we've got music. And art," she said, touching a finger to the earring Kate had made for her. "And now, I've received the very Mother's own blessing!"

"But that is not why they were authorized to log out!" the Director shot back, his own eyes now burning too. "What use is preserving humanity's essence, if it destabilizes us?"

"What use is maintaining a status quo based on lack?" Tree countered, visibly shaking now. "Grandfather, I'm terrified! I don't have the first idea what to expect, and I know that many of the staff will react badly, but I can't ignore the life growing inside of me. I can't act as if the Mother hasn't spoken, and I will not deny Her voice. I *must* have this child, whether I like it or not!"

Ewan looked at Tree in wonder. Her eyes were aflame, searing even as tears rolled from them onto her flushed cheeks. Her energy was so intense, she may as well have really been glowing. He had the fleeting, shocking impression that the Mother Herself was looking through Tree, using his wife like an avatar.

More to the point, he knew nothing anyone said—or did—was going to change Tree's mind, now.

The Director apparently realized this, too. His expression clouded over, but eventually he closed his eyes and bowed his head. "Very well," he said, his voice still edged with foreboding. "What's done is done, but now you'll have to follow through. Show me this new world you intend to create, emissaries. Show me that it can exist," he said, before looking directly at Ewan. "And that you can belong in it."

He turned to his tablet, and a moment later his voice echoed over the PA system.

"Your attention, please. This is Director Rothchild. It has

recently come to my attention that my granddaughter, Chief Emissary Treanna O'Meara, has received an unprecedented blessing from the Mother Herself, in the form of a naturally-conceived child to be born next year. I ask you all to join me in congratulating her and her husband as we celebrate the greatest surprise in Central history."

He closed the PA, then steepled his hands. "There," he said with finality.

"Thank you," Tree said quietly. The energy faded from her, and she sagged into her chair.

The Director nodded, but he was frowning. "In light of the circumstances, you shall be given rations befitting an active-duty Corps member. Furthermore, you are also required to reduce the overall player quota by one."

Ewan nearly jumped out of his chair. "What?!"

Rothchild glowered at him. "You have successfully made your case for the baby, but it is a player."

"It's only half-player—"

"That you selected one incapable of defending the Centre at this time is your concern, not mine!" Rothchild bellowed, standing and leaning menacingly onto his hands. "Even that child you brought from Sah'rassa could hold a gun, if necessary!"

Ewan winced. "But how do you expect us to do our job if you won't let us recruit?"

"Find a way," the Director growled. Half-silhouetted in the dull light of the afternoon, he looked especially forbidding. "Dismissed."

9

THE MOTHER'S CHILDREN

"THE PRODIGAL FATHER RETURNS AT LAST," GABE SAID DRYLY, NOT bothering to look up from his tablet as Ewan entered.

"Not you, too," Ewan groaned as he dragged a chair in behind him. Gabe's office was more of a command center, positioned high in the middle of Programming. The room's curved walls were all glass, allowing the chief to oversee all three dozen programmers below with ease, but it also meant the room was missing little things, like furniture for visitors.

Gabe sniffed. "Come now, O'Meara, it's all anyone can talk about since Rothchild made his announcement two weeks ago. Surely you aren't getting tired of being congratulated? Or of catching more eyes than ever?" He glanced through the wall, to where Alex Johansen was peering at them with a look that made Ewan very glad Tree wasn't around. Tsking to himself, the chief tapped his console, and the glass went smoky.

"You and I both know it's not been that way," Ewan said darkly as he sat. "Tree's dead certain she'll get jumped every time she leaves the room."

"I don't see why, what with those zealots flocking around her these days. What do they call themselves? Mother-lovers?"

"The Mother's Children," Ewan growled. "And they're not helping!"

"Oh, I'm well aware of that," Gabe agreed, offering Ewan a wan smile. "Sanderson mentioned just this morning that another two 'pink-striped lunatics' had to be escorted to the holding cells from training."

Ewan swore. He should've known better than to mention how Tree had channeled the Mother in their meeting with the Director. But he'd told her anyway at lunch, and some of the Ether Swords had overheard. They'd run straight to Father Brian, and within the hour he'd declared to all who wanted to listen—and plenty more who didn't—that the Logos, acting through its Hero of Veridor, had seen fit to impregnate Tree as the Mother Incarnate!

Gabe laughed softly. "I suppose I should be grateful you're here at all, O'Meara. I can only imagine what Annie's temper must be like these days." He fixed Ewan with a strange look. "Still...if I were you, I'd be trying to understand why."

Ewan frowned. "Why, what?"

"Why, everything," Gabe replied, spreading his hands with a sympathetic smile. "Not so long ago, you were living a carefree life, stabbing your little monsters and never lacking for anything. Then you became embroiled in a conflict you knew nothing about, overwriting the Centre's very culture without even realizing it. And now, against everything we're taught, you've blundered into siring a child." The older man's eyes narrowed slightly, almost as if he was accessing a menu of his own. "Don't you ever wonder why, O'Meara?"

"Actually, I do," Ewan replied, taken aback by the quiet ferocity in Gabe's voice. "Every day, truth be told. Back home, I'd stay up and watch the stars come out, one by one, and wonder what life was all about. You should log in and see them, Gabe. The whole sky fills up with them! I used to wonder what they were...whether they were other worlds in their own right, and why out of all of them, I ended up in Veridor. Could I have gone somewhere else? Been someone else?" He chuckled, savoring the memories that followed. "The priests hated it when I talked like that. They'd censure me every time. I even helped Tree, the day we met, because I was ticked at them for doing just that. So, I guess you could say I'm here, doing what I do now, because I wonder why."

He grinned at Gabe, but his friend's face had become strained, blue eyes tight. "I guess that's not what you meant," Ewan admitted, deciding he'd better change the topic. "Well, I still don't know the answers, especially about Tree's latest problem. Have you had any luck with her mail?"

Gabe shook himself, coming back to the moment. "Not as of yet," he replied, as he grabbed a tablet to take notes. "Though I might have done better, had she deigned to ask the senior programmer for help with her little problem at the outset."

"You know how she is."

"All too well, but regrettably, her elevated rank means I can't simply ignore her tantrums anymore," Gabe muttered. "Remind me, when did these messages begin?"

"Two weeks ago."

"The same day the Mother's Children were founded?"

"Yeah. The evening after we told Rothchild." Ewan frowned. "I'm still ticked with him. Did you know, he wanted us to abort the baby?"

Gabe's fingers froze, but he didn't look up. "Is that right?" he asked, the strain returning to his voice.

"Yeah," Ewan said, recalling the Director's cold calculation that day. "He said the baby would drive the frapping wedge between players and Centrals deeper, and that the best thing to do would be to kill it off."

Now Gabe was clenching his device. "But you convinced him otherwise?"

"Tree did, more than I," Ewan said, watching his friend

uneasily. "She argued that the players were out here for more than defense, that the whole point of the players was to restore the real world one day, and why couldn't that day be today... Gabe, what's wrong?"

The programmer was shaking with rage, eyes hard as ice, but still he didn't look at Ewan. "It's nothing, O'Meara," he said slowly after a moment. "I'm merely surprised, that's all. The first natural child in millennia, his own flesh and blood, as far as that counts here, and his first thought was to destroy it. But why not?" he asked himself, bitterly. "There are myriad others with less...involved parents from which to choose his next kitchen girl."

Understanding dawned in Ewan's mind, of how Gabe had been hearing the whole exchange. "You think he wants to keep using player babies to make the staff!" he blurted.

He kicked himself for tactlessness when Gabe finally turned those frostbite eyes on him. "How many times has Annie's message reappeared?" the chief asked, slamming the conversation shut.

Ewan sighed, wondering if he'd ever understand how the Centrals got through life. "I don't even know anymore. She just leaves it in our room, turned off."

"I see. I've got her inbox up now. Almost a million identical messages...hmm, that's interesting," Gabe said neutrally, locking his personal feelings away and swinging a monitor around to where Ewan could see. "Do you notice anything?"

Ewan scanned the lines, each with the same baleful subject: *Die, player whore.*

"The senders are all different," he offered.

Gabe nodded. "Indeed. And none of the addresses match up with the Central staff."

"What's he doing? Using fake names?"

"Yes and no," Gabe replied. "I suspect your Diamond Lord is trying to send you a message as well."

Ewan swallowed. "What do you mean?"

"These names aren't randomly generated, O'Meara. Since we began our little chat, I've had a hound searching the archives for matches."

"But if they're not Centrals—"

"They're players," Gabe finished, leaning back to fix a grim stare onto Ewan. "All of them."

Ewan scrubbed his hands through his hair, glaring at the screen. "No way. Hardly any of them know Tree, and most of those like her."

"How nice for her. However, I'm not suggesting that the players are sending the mail. In fact, wait...ah, yes."

"What now?"

"These names all belong to deceased players." Gabe tapped a finger to his lip, his other hand thumbing through the endless stream on the monitor. "The Logos maintains a record, for archival purposes. I expect that would be simpler to hack than the active accounts."

Ewan watched the list fly past, shivering at the image of thousands of players condemning Tree from their graves. But then the scroll slowed, and a name came up that turned his blood to fire.

Jack O'Meara.

Ewan leaped out of his seat.

"What are you doing?" Gabe asked sharply.

"That nerfed piece of slime," Ewan snarled. "Turn the window on! Let me see him!"

"Who?"

"Frasier!" Ewan exploded. "Who the frap else could it be?! I'm going to kill him—let me go!" he yelled when Gabe jumped up and grabbed him.

"We've been through this more times than I can remember!" Gabe snapped. He held Ewan's arm, twisting it as he came around the desk for a better pin. "Frasier's a model programmer, and one of my deputies. He was cleared of all charges after the last time you accused him."

"But—"

"Even *if* he was the Diamond Lord, what effect do you think assaulting him in his workplace will have on the Centrals?"

Ewan stomped at the older man's foot, trying to make him let go. "I don't care! He's calling me out!"

"You can't solve this with violence. Whoever it is, he's obviously trying to goad you."

"It's working!"

Gabe's arms wrapped tighter around him, the programmer's sandpaper jaw scraping against Ewan's temple as he snarled. "Then play back, for Mother's sake! Don't let him control you, or you'll be sent back to the game floors. Would you truly be so selfish as to knowingly abandon your child to the Centre, player?!"

The rage in the older man's voice cut into Ewan's mind, far more so than his words. *Gems of old...they're all expecting me to do just that!* He took a long, shaky breath, and he quit straining. "I...nerf it all, you're right."

Gabe didn't let go at first, but when he eventually released Ewan, the programmer looked almost as upset as Ewan felt. "Be patient, O'Meara," he rasped, before taking his seat and smoothing his face over again. "When the time comes, we'll be ready."

"I know." Ewan sighed as he sat, too. "It's just...he had my dad's name in there."

"Did he?" Gabe mused darkly. He turned the screen back to himself, but then he smiled. "This is good news."

"What?!"

"He's getting sloppy," Gabe said quietly. "Impatient, I expect, that you're still here. Just keep suffering through it; it won't be much longer, I'm sure."

"Fine," Ewan growled, settling for ripping Frasier's head off in his imagination. For now.

"In other news, it appears the new bulletproof armor has been effective," Gabe said. He replaced Tree's inbox with a map of the Wastes, updated to include a smattering of new dots: all Central victories. "Sanderson reported no casualties from the past week, players included, despite one encounter in which our forces were outnumbered."

"About time something went right. I'll be sure to tell Kate next time I see her," Ewan said, but then his tablet beeped. "Sorry—oh, Gems. Gabe, I've got to run. There's a problem with Cerri'dah."

Gabe blinked. "The new player? I didn't think she was scheduled to be up and about yet."

Ewan skimmed the message, then swore under his breath. "She's not. Can we pick this up later?"

"Of course. In the meantime, try not to do anything foolish," Gabe warned as he turned back to the screens.

Ewan ducked out of Programming, then tore down the halls for Medical. He swung around the corner—then crashed headlong into someone and fell with a grunt on top of them. "Oof! Sorry!"

"Don't be, honey," a woman's voice answered, and Ewan realized who he'd encountered just before her hands locked behind his waist, pinning him to hers.

"Lucia, cut it out!" Ewan pulled back, but she didn't let him up. "I've got to go—"

"Back to Annie?" Lucia paused. "She's not home. I just tried."

"I—what?"

The older woman shrugged under him. "I've been messaging her all week, but she hasn't answered."

"She's having trouble with her tablet." Ewan tried to wriggle free, but it only encouraged the madwoman to wriggle, too.

Lucia grinned and nipped his cheek. “Then let’s go back to your place. We can wait for Annie together.”

“No!” Ewan yelped, face burning as people saw them and started whispering. “I need to get to Medical. There’s an emergency.”

“Oh.” Lucia released him instantly. “Why didn’t you say so?”

Ewan stumbled up, hesitated, then offered her a hand up as well. “I’ll tell Tree you want to talk to her, okay?”

“Thanks, honey.” She gave him a pinch for his trouble, then skipped off. “I’ll be in the nursery!”

A few crashless moments later he was in Medical, currently filled with panicked yowling from the shocky ward beyond. He raced into the room—then stopped, stunned, as he watched Nichols and Angela wrestle with Cerri’dah. The girl was half out of her shocky, clawing frantically at the machine and anything else that came close.

“Don’t just stand there!” Nichols shouted as soon as he noticed Ewan. “Help me hold her still!”

Ewan obeyed, cringing at the dozens of needles still half in the girl’s body as she broke them off. Her eyes were glazed over, lost in the senseless terror of a nightmare as she clawed her way out.

“Cerri’dah, it’s me,” Ewan said quickly, as he pinned her bloody shoulders. “It’s Ewan. Try to relax—ow!” he shouted when she sank her teeth into his hand. “Cerri’dah, please.”

Her wide eyes made contact with his and she paused, seeming to finally realize what she was doing. The instant she did, Nichols jabbed her in the neck with another needle, getting Ewan bitten again before the girl passed out and dropped into his arms.

“She woke up during the electric therapy,” Nichols panted, slumping against the wall. “None of the Veridians were like this!”

Angela sighed, glancing at the shocky’s gutted innards

while she worked to extract the needle bits from Cerri'dah. "We'll need the moles in here for repairs."

"Where is Treanna?" the doctor asked tersely, glowering as he activated the next device.

"She's not getting messages right now," Ewan said, again.

"That doesn't excuse her from missing a pre-natal appointment," Nichols sniped. "I know she's uncomfortable with the situation, but the chance to avoid it has passed."

"Wait, she had an appointment today?"

The doctor turned back to him. "You two had better get your acts together. I can tell you right now that children will punish uncoordinated parents. Speaking of which, have you made arrangements for *this* child?" he added, dodging away as Angela moved Cerri'dah into the tube.

"Yeah. She'll be staying with us. We had a cot brought in earlier this week, and it mostly fits."

Nichols forcibly softened his expression, giving Ewan a more patient, pitying smile. "I'd recommend that you see about getting a larger apartment. Certainly before the baby arrives."

Ewan sighed. "I'll mention it."

The doctor nodded and went back to checking Cerri'dah's status on the little display. "She might emerge slightly underdeveloped from the exertion of her escape attempt, but not enough to prolong the treatment. Another few days, and she'll be all yours."

I can't wait, Ewan thought wearily.

He trudged home after Cerri'dah was settled again, but as he approached he heard voices, then shouting, coming from the hall.

Cursing under his breath, Ewan ran around the corner, but the fight was already over. Patrick Lee and another, older Ether Sword stood in front of his door, with pink ribbons around their right arms and weapons drawn—on a snarling Jeff Harper.

"What the frap is going on?" Ewan demanded.

"We caught this wannabe Gem lurking," Patrick said.

"Scribbling blasphemies," the other Veridian added, lifting a can of spray paint. "With this."

"You stupid tube worms," Harper growled. He made a grab for the paint, but Patrick pressed a sword to his throat in warning. "You're disrupting my investigation!"

"Blasphemies?" Ewan repeated, but then he saw the red message on his door.

Die, player whore.

Without thinking, Ewan rushed forward and punched Harper in the face. The security guard's head rebounded off the door, the fresh red paint sticking to his short hair as he spun and fell onto the tile floor. Ewan roared as he grabbed Patrick's sword out of the stunned cadet's hands and flipped it, point-down.

"Hero!" Patrick yelped, as Harper raised a feeble hand in defense.

Then the door slid open, revealing Tree.

"That's enough, love," she said quietly.

Both Ether Swords dropped to a knee, bowing their heads. Ewan froze, blade inches from Harper's throat. Tree was standing at the threshold to their darkened room, in her pajama robes. Her hair was askew, dark circles hung from her eyes, and her face was streaked with tears, but her hands cradled her pistol without shaking.

"Tree." Ewan swallowed, then let the sword drop. It nicked Harper and hit the floor with a clang.

"Thank you, Patrick," she said, turning to the Ether Swords. "And you as well, Russell. But you can't assume guilt on Master Harper's part."

"But Mother," the man, Russell, said. "We found him, holding the vandal's instrument—"

"I heard it all," Tree said, her brown eyes hardening. "Jeff

Harper is many things, but he is also a member of Central Security. There was someone at my door, not fifteen minutes ago. Harper was assessing the scene, nothing more."

Ewan's heart leaped to his throat. "Figures. Harper's spelling isn't that good," he said, though the joke fell flat even to him as he looked at the wounded man. *Gabe warned me this might happen. I'm supposed to set an example, like Tree's doing!*

"What would you have us do, Mother?" Patrick asked.

Tree let her gaze rest on all of them. "Take him to Medical. See that he's treated properly, and then report to Security for debriefing."

"But Mother—"

"You cannot defend the Centre while you strike down its people!" Tree snapped, making them all flinch away. "If you would call yourselves the Mother's Children, then do as I say."

They scrambled over themselves in their haste to obey. Ewan went to help them, but Tree took his arm and pulled him inside. The door shut again, plunging them into darkness, but he could hear her take up position on the opposite side. Could hear the way her breathing turned to muffled sobs.

They waited, eyes adjusting to the low light, until Patrick and Russell had cleared the area. Then Ewan waited another minute for good measure when Tree didn't move, still holding her gun at the ready, as though the vandal would return if she blinked. Eventually, he stepped across to her, wrapped his arms around her from behind, and gently pried the weapon from her fingers.

He also locked the door.

Tree sighed as she crossed to their bed, covered with half-opened meal boxes, and threw herself across it. "Where were you?" she asked despondently.

"Meeting with Gabe," Ewan replied carefully, pushing the new cot aside so he could follow. "Before Cerri'dah tried to break out of Medical."

Tree was up in an instant, knocking the boxes aside. "Why didn't you tell me?"

"It was kind of an emergency. Besides, you aren't responding to messages." *Or keeping appointments*, he thought ruefully as he came to sit with her.

"There's only one message for me on that tablet," she said grimly, taking her gun back from his waistband. "And I am responding to it."

Ewan fought the urge to cry by gently kissing her temple. "I ran into Lucia Howe on the way. She said she'd come by to talk to you, but that you didn't answer."

Tree said nothing.

"Oh, come on. You don't think *she* put that hate on the door, do you?"

"Of course not," Tree huffed. "She doubtless wants to negotiate for a share of your time, like every other woman here."

Ewan blushed, but didn't argue. "She asked me to take you to the nursery." He looked around the room, stuffy and smelly and half an inch from violence. "I think we ought to take her up on it. It'll be fun, getting out and seeing all the babies."

Tree shot him an incredulous, despairing look. "Love—"

"No arguing," he said firmly as he pulled her to standing with him. "You just need a buff to your spirit."

"It's not my spirit she wants to buff!"

"Well, you won't know until you ask," Ewan countered, getting her proper clothing and hoping against hope that Lucia had something better to offer than ribald aggro.

Ewan had never been to the nursery before. Conveniently located under Caretaking, it was the last stop before the game floors below.

Which made it as high up as most players ever got in their lives.

He and Tree stepped out of the main elevator into a short

hall, then through a broad door into a massive, low room that looked like an eerie cross between the game floors and hydroponics. Thousands upon thousands of squat tubes held little fleshy creatures as they floated in a yellowish-pink fluid, while a few dozen Centrals moved about, checking on them.

"Are these...babies?" Ewan asked out loud, realizing with an uncomfortable jolt that he was the only man present.

"Not yet; we call them fetuses at this stage," Lucia called. Ewan looked up in time to see her pass a baby to another caretaker, then jog over to them, her half-open blouse held together by one desperate button. "I'm so glad you came!"

"Mother of all," Tree muttered. She turned from the display, squinting into a nearby tube at something a few inches long, with beady black eyes and little flappy hands smaller than her fingernail. "Is this what's inside me?"

The older woman bent forward and the button gave up, letting her breasts tumble out. "This little one's about thirteen weeks, a teeny bit bigger than yours. You've got someone more like...this," she said, pushing Ewan aside as she spun about to find another tube.

Tree spared Lucia's chest an assessing, disapproving scowl, but she followed the older woman's gaze, peering in. "It's so tiny!"

"She," Lucia corrected. "Or he; it's hard to say this early." She turned to Tree and sighed. "Annie, you're so lucky."

Tree closed her eyes, resting one hand against the tube's glass and the other on her belly. "I don't feel lucky."

"Of course you are!" Lucia said, startled. "Don't you realize how much hope you're giving the rest of us? Aren't you happy?"

"Yes. No. I don't know!" Tree moaned. Her fingers curled, as if clutching at the new life beyond her reach. "I want to be happy about it. Really, I do. It's unprecedented, and wonderful, and all of that...but my child deserves a better world than I can give it. So many people hate me, calling me a whore for conceiving with a player. Telling me to die. What will they tell my baby?"

She sniffed, slumping against the glass.

"Tree," Ewan said softly, "Those messages aren't real. They're only coming from one person."

"Then how do you explain the door?" she countered miserably. "Or the glares in the dining hall, and the corridors?"

"Honey, that's just your natural charm," Lucia said with a laugh, turning Tree by placing a hand on each shoulder. "And I understand all too well how a reputation can haunt you."

Tree blinked, then looked up at the older woman as if she'd only just seen her. "Yes, I suppose you would."

"Annie, I'd give anything to have what you do," Lucia said earnestly. "Ever since I was a girl, I've wanted only one thing. The moment I could, I started trying to have one. Everyone told me the Mother was gone, that she'd abandoned us thousands of years ago, but I didn't care. I always thought that if I—if I wanted it badly enough, then it would happen."

Ewan's heart beat in horrified sympathy as he saw a tear pooling in Lucia's eye, too. *That* was why she'd bedded all those men? Suddenly, the way she'd refused to let go of him—the one man on Earth who'd proven he could sire a child—it all made sense in a way that left him feeling repulsed and uncomfortably curious at the same time.

"But all those tries," Lucia continued. "All those men. It never worked. And then you take one mate and find yourself pregnant, and you're not even happy about it?" She gave Tree a stern look. "You have no idea how blessed you are. Annie, it's like you *are* the Mother, in the flesh."

That hit too close to home. Tree closed her eyes and started to cry, but Lucia pulled her into a tight hug. An embrace as strong as the one she'd used on Ewan earlier, but entirely different. And Tree returned it, letting herself sob into the older woman's bare chest as Ewan had never seen her do. He could only stand there, watching them both in guilty silence. Undeniably attractive and desperate enough to do anything to get a baby, Lucia by all rights should have gotten pregnant. But Tree—determined, driven Tree…her life as planned was in shambles, slammed into re-specking.

"Is that what you wanted to tell me?" Tree whispered at last.

"No, actually," Lucia replied, almost as quietly. She brushed Tree's hair back from her face as they broke. "Annie, I want to help you. The Mother has her reasons, I'm sure, but I'm not going to have a baby of my own. Unless you're willing to lend me your man?"

Tree's voice was firm, but not as hostile as usual. "No."

"I didn't think so," Lucia said. "If I can't have a child of my own, then the least I can do is support the woman who's lucky enough to have one for the rest of us. I know more about pregnancy and childbirth than anyone alive, and I can offer you a woman's perspective that people like Robert Nichols can't," she added, grinning as Tree bit back a laugh. "If you'll have me, I'd love dearly to be your midwife, helping you get ready and bring your child into the world…and maybe I can be your wet nurse afterward?"

Tree brought trembling fingers to her lips. "Lucia…I don't know what to say."

"Say yes!" Ewan whispered, trying to cage his eyes when both women whipped around to face him. "Tree, she's perfect. She's an expert, and obviously on your side!"

Tree searched his soul, hunting for any warning signs he'd ditch her for the older woman, but he kept his best intentions forward. "All right, Lucia," she said slowly. "But keep your… hands off Ewan."

Lucia squealed in reply, knocking Ewan aside as she crushed Tree into another hug.

Tree's eyes bulged, but her face softened, truly relaxing for the first time since Mother knew when, and she returned the embrace. “Thank you, Lucia,” she whispered through renewed tears. “I’d be honored for you to help me. But there’s one more thing you’ll have to do.”

“What’s that, honey?”

“Don’t call me Annie. My friends call me Tree.”

10

CERRI

TREE'S MOOD IMPROVED DRAMATICALLY OVER THE NEXT FEW DAYS—which was fortunate, given she got called to the Director's office at week's end to testify about Harper's beating. Ewan had no idea what she and Rothchild said behind those closed doors, and Tree wouldn't say. But starting that evening, a pair of pink-sashed Veridians took up posts on either end of their hallway, and the hateful graffiti stopped.

Ewan didn't have much thought to spare for their new security, though. Just as Nichols had threatened, Cerri'dah was officially discharged from Medical. After what happened to her first shocky, the doctor insisted on keeping her heavily sedated until Ewan and Tree could deal with her in a "more familiar" environment. Nichols also recommended tying the poor child to the cot at first, to keep her from harming herself. Director Rothchild came to witness as Angela transferred the girl to a gurney. He said even less than Tree had about recent events, but his smoldering eyes warned Ewan that whatever else was in play, the Director found the emissaries' two latest recruits nowhere near to spec.

All in all, Ewan thought wryly as he and Tree wheeled their new roommate out, *Cerri'dah's off to a much better start than I got last year*.

But when they'd brought the child home and moved her to the cot, Ewan and Tree sat there on their own bed, staring at their new charge and trading nervous glances with each other.

"We could just let her sleep it off," Ewan offered. "Buy ourselves a little more alone time?"

Tree squeezed his hand, but she shook her head. "She's here. Now."

"Fair enough." Squaring his shoulders, he took a deep breath before picking up the stimulant Nichols had given them. "Ready, love?"

She gave him a rueful smile. "No."

"Neither am I." Ewan chuckled, then slipped the needle into the girl's neck.

Maybe he hadn't done it quite right, or maybe Nichols had sedated Cerri'dah extra deeply, but it still took a while for her to wake up. Her fingers twitched, gripping the thin medical scrubs she wore. She sighed, a small, deflating sound. And then her eyes fluttered open, revealing the same soft amber color they'd been in J'unai.

She stared at the ceiling, blinking—and suddenly she was bolt upright, hands clenching the mattress hard enough to tear it.

"Easy, Cerri'dah," Ewan said, wading over to the cot. "It's me, Ewan."

The girl's breathing slowed a touch, but her hands stayed in the mattress. "Ea'win Omi'ra?" She leaned toward him, peering, then wrinkled her nose. "Your scent is weak, but I know your eyes. You are so ugly!"

"Thanks," Ewan replied dryly, putting an arm around Tree as she came to join him. "But this is how we really look."

"Welcome to Earth," Tree said softly.

"I know you as well. Tri'ana Omi'ra," Cerri'dah said, sniffing at Tree with a frown. "Why is it so difficult to smell you?"

Ewan exchanged a glance with his wife. "Maybe your real nose isn't as strong?"

"My real nose?" Cerri'dah repeated. She reached up to touch her face, then jolted back and fell off the cot with a panicked hiss. "Asst! What have you done to me?!"

Ewan and Tree both rushed over to help her back up, corralling her. "Cerri'dah, listen to me," Ewan said quickly. "You're like us: a human."

"No! I am Caitsid'h!" She snarled, swiping at him and catching the back of his hand.

"Ow! Not out here, you're not! We're all human on Earth, no matter what world we came from."

"Here," Tree said with forced gentleness, angling their mirror around. "See for yourself."

Cerri'dah glowered at her, but she did turn to look, cautiously peeking around the glass's edge before coming to stare, transfixed, at her reflection. Ewan watched her in silence as he sucked on his hand. The girl definitely had courage, but what really struck him—aside from her fingernails—was how well Kate's shocky had rebuilt Cerri'dah's body in just a few weeks, even with the finishing touches interrupted. Thin, mouse-brown hair reached down to her chin, framing an equally thin face, now fleshed out to a healthy chestnut tone. Her amber eyes stared, intense, as she drew her lips back in a grimace and pressed a clawless hand against the surface.

"This is…me?"

"Yes," Tree said. "This is your true form, Cerri'dah."

"No," the girl said flatly. "But I at least recognize myself in it. I cannot be Cerri'dah here, though," she said, turning to see that her tail was gone. "There is not enough of me."

Ewan smiled, remembering feeling the same way once—or similarly, at least. *All I had to do was build muscle. She's missing half her body!* "How about Cerri?" he suggested. "Mostly like you, but not all there?"

The child gave him such an unimpressed look that he could clearly picture her feline ears flattening back. "Even like this, I am not the one who is 'not all there,' Ea'win Omi'ra." A tiny smile crossed her face, and she went back to looking at herself, touching her ears and cheeks. "But yes...I must be Cerri in the spirit world. If this body is the best you can manage, then I will adjust to it."

"Sure," Ewan said, taking Tree's hand as Cerri resumed staring at her reflection.

She sat there for a long time, tracing her fingers over her head and arms, making faces that Ewan suspected had to do with trying to move her ears, and then simply staring at the human child who'd borrowed her eyes. He and Tree sat with her, not saying anything and not wanting to rush her.

She's got so much to process, Ewan thought.

After he didn't know how long, Cerri finally moved, hunching over slightly. "I am hungry."

"I'm not surprised," Ewan chuckled. "How about I go and get us some dinner?"

Instantly, the girl slunk close to him and grabbed his arm. "You cannot leave me here."

Ewan glanced at Tree. "I'll just be right back."

"It's okay, love," Tree cut in. "I can go get it."

"But—"

"I'll be fine," she countered, giving him a kiss and a significant look. "And you're needed here, Emissary. Give her the tour; I'll be back shortly."

Ewan watched Tree go, pleasantly surprised that she didn't arm herself this time. When the door slid open, Cerri hissed and fled behind him, peeking around his side. "It's okay," he told her—and himself. "The halls should be safe."

When the door slid closed, Cerri went to examine it,

reaching a thin hand out and jumping a good foot in the air when it opened again. Ewan braced himself to go chasing her down, but she retreated to him.

"This place is strange," she commented from his back.

Ewan grinned to himself. "I thought so too, when I first came here. I still do, truth be told."

He showed her around the room, explaining how the computer on the wall and his tablet did their best to be like the Moon's light. She was suitably disgusted with the bathroom and stunned that humans would bathe in water. And as with most players, the moss ceiling caught her interest.

"Why are there plants on the ceiling?" she asked as she perched on the O'Mearas' headboard to reach it.

"They keep the air fresh," Ewan explained. "They breathe in what we breathe out, and vice versa."

"How odd," Cerri mused. "And what is this?"

"That's a ventilation grate. It connects the air in this room to the rest of the Centre—hey, don't break it!" Ewan cried when she wrenched the little metal grill open.

"One could move about this place inside them?" she asked, ignoring him.

"I doubt it, unless you're really...um, thin," he finished weakly as she scurried right into the hole. "Cerri, come back down!"

Her only reply was some thumping behind the moss.

Ewan swore under his breath, trying to think of how to get the girl back out. He was pretty wiry himself, but there was no way he'd fit in there. The last thing he needed was for their new charge to get lost in the vents!

He climbed up and stuck his head into the dark hole. "Cerri!" he whispered.

"Why are all the other rooms empty?" her little voice came, from around a corner.

"What?"

"No one lives in the rooms near yours. The furniture there is dusty and unused."

"There aren't as many of us out here as there used to be. Cerri, you're not allowed in there. If someone sees you—"

She emerged again, barely visible in the dark but for eyes that watched him without blinking. "I thought the village across the mountains would be overflowing."

Ewan sighed. "Yeah, well, come back out and we can talk about it."

He'd only just gotten Cerri to the floor and jammed the grill back in place when Tree returned, carrying three bags. "What are you doing?" she asked, narrowing her eyes at the dust on them both.

"Just showing her around," Ewan replied lightly. "What did they have?"

"The usual," Tree said without enthusiasm, placing the bags around their little table while Ewan pulled Cerri's cot over for a makeshift third seat. "I got you both the bean paste, guessing that Cerri wouldn't be interested in the worms, either."

"Worms are for fish," the girl sang, vaulting lightly to the cot and sitting cross-legged. The mattress was almost as high as the table's surface, and she towered over the O'Mearas. "Do you not have any fish?"

Tree shook her head. "There are small fish in the hydroponics chambers, but they're for recycling nutrients in the water, not for us to eat."

Once again, Ewan could have sworn he saw Cerri's ears trying to flatten. "Do you not have an oasis?" she asked.

"No," Tree answered carefully. "Earth's desert isn't as forgiving as your home."

"Is that why the rooms are so empty?"

Tree frowned. "I'm sorry, what?"

"But the spirit tribe should not need to eat," Cerri mused. "Perhaps that is why they come to this place without fish."

Ewan glanced at Tree, but she looked as baffled as he felt. "Yeah, maybe," he hedged. "Let's just eat for now."

Cerri needed help with the little to-go box, and then she spent a few minutes sniffing cautiously at the food before daring to take a nibble. "This is acceptable," she commented, before shoveling it in. "But if there is no oasis, then how do you have food?"

"How about we go look?" Ewan offered.

Tree took his arm. "Love, I don't—"

"She'll be fine," he insisted. *Hell, it'll be worth it just to show her how people use halls instead of air ducts.*

It took a little while to get ready, mostly because Cerri didn't understand that walking around in her paper clothing wasn't going to work well. Neither of the O'Mearas had anything remotely her size, but it was already late enough that Outfitting was closed. In the end, they settled on her wearing one of Tree's athletic shirts over her scrubs, with oversized socks tucked around her pant legs.

The dark looks Ewan and Tree normally got were nothing, compared to the reaction to having Cerri along. The girl padded behind them, regarding the Centrals with an air of bemused superiority, either not understanding or not caring about how every last person stared and broke into whispering as they went. More than a few turned murderous looks on Tree, making Ewan simultaneously glad she'd left her gun at home and wishing he'd brought his swords.

Tree's right...what are we going to do when the baby's here? he thought grimly as he stepped between his family and the others.

Hydroponics was thankfully empty when they arrived. Cerri drew a sharp breath as she took in the room's pipes and containers, then went in and insisted on touching everything she could.

"These plants grow in water?" she asked, tapping one of the

massive transparent root tanks that stretched down the room's length.

"That's right," Tree replied. "We have some soil, but it's needed for the worms. Given the accelerated rotations for crop harvesting, the water is more efficient for supplying nutrients. It's actually a lot like the liquid hydrolysis system used for players."

Cerri ignored the answer, instead slipping under the nearest tank.

"How do these plants grow without the sun?" she asked, peeking her head up from behind a pair of tomato vines.

"The people who work the rooms use a special kind of light," Tree explained patiently, pointing to the array of bulbs overhead. "They're always on, so the plants can grow more quickly."

"There is no night here? They must get tired," Cerri said, looking at the plants. Without warning, she vanished again. "I see fish!"

The tank thumped, shaking the plants above. "Cerri, get out from under there," Ewan called. "You're going to break something!"

"Can I eat the fish?"

"No!" Ewan and Tree shouted as one.

"Why not?"

"Because they're for cleaning the tanks," Tree repeated. "They would make you sick."

"The plants grow in the water, but they do not make me sick," Cerri observed. "Your village is very strange, Tri'ana Omi'ra."

It was after ten by the time they got home, but Ewan couldn't get to sleep. Part of his trouble was that Cerri was wide awake, thumping around the dark room and muttering about her weak eyes when she bumped into things. Mostly, though, he was still trying to make sense of everything that had happened.

Only a month ago, he thought he'd had a good bead on things. The Centrals were jerks and the Locusts were a threat, but he and Tree were working on that. The Diamond Lord had all but vanished back into the woodwork, afraid to challenge Ewan openly, and despite Rothchild's insistence that he couldn't bring any more players to Earth, Ewan had thought they were on the right track.

But now...now Tree was pregnant, drawing all kinds of aggro from half the Centrals while getting envied by the rest, to say nothing of being worshiped by the Mother's Children. Ewan didn't have the first faint clue about how to be a dad, and the one man he'd have given anything to talk to about it with was dead at the Gem's hands. Somehow, their plan to bring out desert warriors had resulted in adopting Cerri, and Mother only knew how *that* would turn out. He was flattered that the girl trusted him, but how was he going to teach her about the real world without turning her against it?

Ewan suddenly realized the room had gone silent. He opened his eyes, then flinched back when the door whooshed open to blast him with the hallway lights.

"Asst! Is it never night here?" Cerri hissed, and then he saw her dark little form vanish into the light beyond.

Swearing to himself, Ewan scooted out of bed and threw on a shirt and shoes before following her.

He nearly tripped over her right off the bat, she was hunched up so close to the door. "Cerri! What are you doing?"

"I am looking for Hara'noh," she replied. "Do the lights stay on all the time?"

A Mother's Child that Ewan didn't recognize approached them, concern on her face, but he waved her off. "In the halls, yeah."

"No wonder the people here are as tired as the plants," Cerri muttered. "How am I supposed to see the spirits if it is never dark?"

"What?"

"I am looking for Hara'noh," the girl repeated, watching him. "My sister. The winds took her here."

"The winds?" Ewan repeated—but then it clicked. "Oh, no."

"I have seen your village," Cerri said. "Now I want to see her."

Ewan's heart dropped through his belly. "Um...when did the winds take her?"

"Fourteen moons ago," Cerri answered. "But you told me this is where the Caitsid'h go when the winds take us. She must be here."

"Cerri, she wouldn't be here. She'd have respawned."

The girl shook her head, frowning at him. "The Caitsid'h have nine lives, and then the winds claim them. The Moon never returns them after that."

"Only nine?" Ewan turned away, unable to look her in the eye. "Cerri—"

"Is Hara'noh a human as well? Or is she a spirit in one of the empty rooms? Is that why she did not come to visit today? She should appear soon, now that it is night," the girl continued, her little voice thoughtful. "Even across the mountains, the Caitsid'h would have more sense than moving about in the day. But how will I see her if it is never dark?"

"Cerri," Ewan said, grasping in vain for anything like a good answer. "We can go look for your sister first thing in the morning—"

"I want to see her now," Cerri insisted. "I miss her."

Ewan sighed, feeling worse by the second. Cerri had logged out on faith, apparently trusting him to show her some long-lost sister who didn't have a prayer of still being alive? "All right," he said, resigning himself to the inevitable discovery. "Let me go get my tablet."

He slipped back into the room, finding Tree rolled over with the blanket over her head. "I'll be back," he whispered, kissing the lump and snagging his tablet from the nightstand.

Cerri was still there, waiting patiently by the door. She followed him to the elevators. "Where are we going?"

"The game floors," Ewan answered, frowning when he tried to access the player data and ran straight into a login box. "Frap. I'm not sure I've got enough access to do this."

"But you are a D'jin."

"No, I'm not," he grumbled, but then an idea came to him. "But I do know someone who could help us." Opening up a message box, he typed, [Gabe, are you still up?]

He waited a few seconds, then chuckled to himself when the reply came. [How else would I accomplish the work of two sections? I assume you're not online for company.]

[Our new player's got family that she wants to see,] Ewan typed, deciding that he'd better get the Rajj's address as a backup. [But I don't have access to the caretaking records. Sorry to bother you, but could you help us find them?]

[That's easy enough. What are the names?]

It took a minute to get the spellings, but eventually Gabe sent back a pair of addresses. [The second one is still valid, but the first expired over a year ago. The new player does realize one of them is dead, doesn't she?]

[I'll tell her. Thanks, Gabe.]

The programmer signed off without reply, leaving Ewan to stare at the numbers on the screen. "All right," he said softly. "I've got addresses for your sister and grandma, but Cerri, I've got to warn you that Hara'noh isn't in there."

"We shall see," Cerri answered, her little chin set as she followed him in.

Ewan's heart sank even faster than the elevator as they

rode down, but Cerri pressed up against the glass the moment they passed the nursery. "What is this place?" she asked in wonder.

"These are the game floors," Ewan explained. "Remember how I said Sah'rassa was like a dream? This is where the dreamers' bodies sleep."

"This is a place of spirits," she whispered, but her voice shook. "Hara'noh will be here."

"Cerri..."

"She must be!"

Ewan tried desperately to think of what to tell her, but he still hadn't come up with anything by the time the elevator came to a stop. When they got to the floor on the first address, Cerri charged off across the bridge, looking into each tube. "Ea'win Omi'ra, what is wrong with these people? Why are they so frail?"

"They're players, in the game worlds," he answered. "They've been asleep out here, asleep for so long that their bodies never had a chance to grow strong. I was in a tube like this, before I came to the Centre. You were, too."

The girl gave him an inscrutable look, then shot off along the ring, continuing her search. "These people look nothing like spirits."

At last, Ewan found the correct tube. It was occupied, but the player inside was a baby, and clearly male at that. "Cerri," he called, bracing himself. "This is it, over here."

The girl froze, her desperate energy suddenly wrenched into trembling anticipation as she slowly approached. She peered into the tube, then glared at Ewan. "That is not Hara'noh."

"I know," Ewan said quietly, heart breaking. "I know. She would have died over a year ago."

"No! You have the wrong place!" Cerri snatched the tablet from Ewan's hand, scanning the lines and glaring up at the tube's markings; then she spat and threw the device across the floor. "No!"

"Cerri, I'm so sorry," Ewan said, blinking away tears of his own. He moved to give her a hug, but she swiped at his face.

"Liar! You said she was here!"

"This *is* where she was," Ewan explained, backing off but keeping his eyes locked onto hers. "But she died. You said that the moonlight gives all of the Caitsid'h nine lives, right? If Hara'noh spent all of hers, then she must have died here as well."

"But there is no reason to!" Cerri yowled. She clutched at the tube, where her sister had been. "Was she not alive in this world, even if the winds took her?"

"She may have been," Ewan replied numbly. "But our bodies get so weak in the tubes that they can't handle the shock of logging out, of coming here. I almost died when I did, too."

"No. Hara'noh was strong!"

"I'm sure she was, but none of that matters here." He hated what he was saying. Hated that it was true. "I was lucky; Tree came for me. And someone came for you, too, so you could cross the mountains safely."

"Then why did no one come for Hara'noh?" Cerri wailed, still gripping the tube. "It is not fair!"

"Because no one knew," Ewan answered. He sighed. "The caretakers wouldn't have been told in time when the Logos pulled your sister from the virtual worlds."

Cerri sank to the floor, weeping. "They let my sister die here, all alone? How could they?"

"I don't think they had any choice," Ewan answered sadly. He sat beside her, expecting another attack, but instead she curled up and rested her head on his leg. "Cerri...this world is really broken. They don't have enough food for everyone, not even close. They wouldn't have been able to bring your sister into the Centre, if her lives got spent early." He sighed again, stroking Cerri's thin hair as he gazed, overwhelmed, at the myriad tubes. "There are so many of us. I want to get everyone out, so no one ever has to die here again, but I can't do that unless we do something to fix the world."

"The D'jini, these Earth *humans*, are scum," Cerri growled.

Ewan let her cry, beating her fists against his leg as she gave vent to her grief.

When she'd calmed down a little, he tried again. "If it's any consolation, you're not the only one to lose family in these tubes. Do you remember what I said about how I fought a Gem last year? How lots of people got logged out, taken by the winds?"

She nodded against him. "I remember."

"He deleted my whole family," Ewan said, fighting down the usual surge of anger for Cerri's sake. "Thankfully, Tree and the other caretakers got to my mom and sister in time, but my dad...he didn't make it. The Gem murdered him, just because I'd come here."

The girl looked up, eyes widening as she wiped a tear away. "And this D'jin, he is here somewhere?"

"Yeah," Ewan replied, unable to keep the bitterness out of his voice. "He's here, but I haven't been able to prove who he is. Not yet."

They sat in silence for a while, Ewan brooding while Cerri took a turn looking out at the millions of tubes. Eventually, she asked, "Why do you help these D'jini, if they shelter your enemy?"

That's the question, isn't it? Ewan thought. He leaned back against their tube, staring up at nothing in particular. "Because some of them are good people, like Tree. She brought me here, helped me adjust...believed in me, even when I couldn't. She still does," he said, smiling faintly. "Besides, love us or hate us, it's been the Centrals who've been keeping us alive all this time. If we abandon them, then we're dooming ourselves, too."

Cerri studied her fingers. "If we bring enough people across the mountains, then perhaps we would not need the bad D'jini."

"Yeah, maybe," Ewan said, wishing he hadn't heard similar muttering from the Ether Swords. "We should be going, though."

"Yes," she agreed. "I have no family here."

"Maybe not here, but I do have your grandma's address. It's not far; would you like to see her?"

Cerri hesitated, glancing back at the tube. "I will see her."

They rode the elevator back up a moment, then stepped out onto another floor. Cerri didn't run off this time, instead searching out the tube with him. When they found it, she peered down, unblinking, at the old Rajj's shriveled face for a long time.

"It is difficult to see her," Cerri said at last. "She is formidable in Sah'rassa, but here she has no power." The girl turned to Ewan. "You say I was like this, before?"

"Yes. Every player we've logged out started in the tubes."

"Then I am glad I crossed the mountains," Cerri said with conviction. "I am glad you interfered with the Hunt. Otherwise, I would still be powerless, without a family."

"What about your parents?" Ewan asked.

Cerri glowered down at the old woman. "The winds took my father many moons ago, in battle with the warriors from Qa'ya, to the north. My mother was married off to a new husband, to secure enough allies to defeat the Qa'ya. She has a new family now, and does not speak to me."

"Oh...I'm sorry."

"It is the traditional way," Cerri said flatly. "My grandmother would murder us all, if the traditions told her to. She let Hara'noh die for them, too."

Ewan glanced at her. "I don't understand."

Cerri's growl intensified. "My grandmother married

Hara'noh to the Claw of the Ch'ira, but raiders took her on her wedding day. I begged my grandmother to send our warriors to search, but she insisted that it was now the duty of the Ch'ira."

"They didn't find her," Ewan whispered.

"They did not even try!" Cerri spat. "I was the only one who searched! I was the only family Hara'noh had, when the winds took her!" She let loose an anguished cry that gave Ewan the shivers, then took a calming breath. "I ran away from J'unai after that. I joined the Nightpaws, wishing to find a new family. I stole for them, for eleven moons. But they sent me home, to steal from *her*," she said, glaring at her grandmother, "and I was caught. The Nightpaws do not claim failed thieves." She swatted the tube. "Once again, this woman denied me a family!"

"She did say you were part of her tribe again, since you were willing to come to the Centre," Ewan pointed out.

"Bah. She only said that to bind you and Tri'ana Omi'ra. She does not want me."

"Well, I'm glad you're here," Ewan said softly. "I know full well how hard this world is, but I'll do my best to help you get through it."

"I am the one who owes you a life debt," Cerri replied. "Ea'win Omi'ra...if I help you discover your father's killer, will that be enough to settle it?"

Ewan stared at her, startled to find he was considering her offer as seriously as she'd made it. He felt horrible even thinking about letting a child go looking for a murderer, but he did need help. Months of searching through official channels with Gabe had gotten him nowhere, even though Tree's inbox made it obvious the Diamond Lord was still active. And Cerri wasn't a typical kid. He'd already seen her stealth skills, both in Sah'rassa and in the Centre's air ducts. What if she really could help him put an end to it?

On top of that, he thought wryly, *if she's busy helping me, then at least she won't be getting into trouble I don't know about.*

"Okay," he said after a moment. "I'd say that's plenty fair, but you'll need to be extra careful about it. We only get one life on Earth, even the Caitsid'h, and I don't want you to risk yours for me. Don't tell anyone else what you're doing, but if you get caught, I'll come and rescue you."

"You truly are a fool, Ea'win Omi'ra." Cerri gave her grandmother a final look, then turned back to him with a little smile as she slipped her hand into his. "But you are my family, now."

11

PRIVACY LOST

EWAN SLEPT LIKE THE DEAD FOR WHAT WAS LEFT OF THE NIGHT, but when the alarm went off the next morning, he was feeling more like his usual self. Tree was warm, and soft, and so smooth when she pressed her back into his chest, just like she had ever since the Argenones. He pulled her close, stretching into her...

Something slammed down onto his side, with enough force to knock the wind out of him.

"What are you doing?" Cerri asked, peering down curiously at him while her bony little knees dug like spears into his ribs.

"Get off me!" Ewan groaned. He tried to shove her aside, but his arm was pinned under the blankets.

"I don't hear you say that much," Tree murmured. She turned to kiss him, then froze. "Oh."

"Are you trying to mate?" the girl asked, her face dimly outlined by the faint computer light. "I do not think that will work."

"What?" Ewan spluttered, blushing.

"Tri'ana Omi'ra is already with cub."

An awkward silence followed, broken only by Cerri shifting to stare down at both of them.

"How did you know that?" Tree asked.

"I scented you, in Sah'rassa," Cerri answered, as though it was obvious. She hopped down, padded to her cot, and sat cross-legged to stare at them. "Do not let me trouble you."

"A little late for that," Ewan muttered, glancing at the clock. "They'll be serving the early breakfast now; would you like some?"

"Will there be fish?"

"Perhaps you can ask," Tree said diplomatically.

They bundled Cerri up in what Ewan hoped was an upgrade to her outfit, then shuffled to the dining hall. It was early enough that the room was mostly empty, aside from the odd security guard, a party of armored scouts—and Father Brian.

"Hero!" he called, smiling broadly as he came to join them in line. "And young Mother," he added, bowing without breaking eye contact with Tree. "I thank you for vouching for our children. I trust that your sleep has improved?"

Tree dipped her head, also not breaking eye contact. "It has, thank you."

Brian's smile widened. "Wonderful. Word has spread throughout all Veridor of the miracle in your womb. The people are ecstatic to know the Logos can touch even this desolate place." He glanced down at Tree's belly and finally noticed Cerri peeking around Ewan's back. "Oh, my! Is this one of your children, as well?"

"This is Cerri," Ewan said.

"Cerri...ah, Cerri'dah," Brian murmured, before addressing Tree again. "The Logos has told me of the heathen creature."

"She's not a creature!" Ewan snapped.

"I am Caitsid'h," Cerri said, at the same time.

The priest gave them both a condescending smile. "Truly,

Mother, your generosity knows no bounds, but I am concerned about these replacements. The Logos has warned me of them. Their customs are strange. Their loyalties are unknown, their faith unproven. They are a risk."

Ewan glanced back at Cerri; the girl was regarding Brian with slitted eyes. "If you're so worried about risks," he growled at the priest, "then quit logging out your frapping loonies. They fight with the Centrals more than the Locusts!"

"Tread carefully, Hero," Brian warned, his voice taking on an iron edge. "You are not the only one chosen by the Logos. I have followed its guidance, and our Mother is safe as a result."

Ewan took a step forward, driving the other man back. "What guidance—"

"Thank you for your concern, Father Brian," Tree said firmly, holding Ewan's arm. "I will consider it. Now, if you'll excuse us, we have our duties."

Brian cleared his throat, but his eyes lingered coldly on Cerri. "Yes, of course, Mother. Please keep me apprised of your selection, so that I may choose the best Veridian warriors to protect you."

Ewan's fists clenched, but he kept his mouth shut as the old man wandered toward the doors to harass other hungry people. *I haven't talked with Al'Dashan or Paul all week,* he thought, *but if they're letting Brian run amok with recruitment, we'd better set up a private meeting.*

In the meantime, he followed Tree into the serving area, where Lisa Deering greeted them with her usual bubbly enthusiasm, despite looking dead on her feet.

"Good morning!" she said brightly, swaying as she yawned.

"Morning," Ewan replied, noting grimly that the kitchen girl also wore a pink armlet. "How'd you get the red-eye shift?"

Lisa pouted, chewing on a stray lock of her strawberry blond hair. "Alice made me. She caught me fooling around in the kitchen last night. Would you like some special sauce, Tree?"

"I'll pass," Tree said, looking as put off as Ewan felt by the combination of statements. "Cerri, this is Lisa. If you tell her what you like to eat, then she'll do her...best to make it for you."

"You're the new player? Oh, you're so cute!" Lisa giggled as Cerri hid behind Ewan again. "I've never been to your game, not yet at least. What do you like to eat?"

"Fish," Cerri said.

"Fish? You mean like in the recycling system?" Lisa frowned. "I don't know if we can eat those."

Cerri sighed, then reached around Ewan and plucked some grapes from the line. "What kind of place has no fish?" she muttered.

Kate came to join them a few minutes after they'd sat down, dropping her tray onto the table with a bang that made Cerri jump and fling her own meal to the floor.

"Gems!" Kate swore, looking at Cerri in confusion. "Who's the squirt?"

"Cerri, this is my sister, Kate," Ewan explained, trying to ignore the glowers from both Centrals *and* Veridians as Tree left to get Cerri a new tray. "Kate, Cerri. She's the new player, remember? Where's Sam at?"

"He's on a scouting run," Kate grumbled, not meeting his eyes.

"Oh. Well, I'm sure he'll be okay."

"Of course he'll be okay!" she snapped. "He's got my frapping armor on, and it's not like he can fall to his doom on the ground."

Ewan bit back a laugh at that. "Flying machine not going so well, I take it?"

Kate waved her arms overhead. "I've never seen someone so timid. Ever since we finished the armor, he's been acting like I'm going to kill him!"

Ewan grinned at her. "I guess he's onto you."

"He's just like Dad. 'If we were supposed to fly, wouldn't we already have wings?'" she said in her lowest voice, with her eyes half crossed. "What, do I have something on my face?" she sniped as Cerri leaned in to stare at her.

"Yes, you do," Cerri replied, eyes widening with pleasure. "You have markings!"

"Huh? Oh, you mean the soot. It's just from the forges—hey!" Kate flinched as Cerri lunged forward and dragged a finger across her forehead, knocking Kate's water over just as Tree returned. "Don't they have personal space in your world?"

Cerri ignored her, sniffing her finger before dabbing it across her other arm. She smiled happily at the little spots it left behind. "You have more of this soot?"

"Sure," Kate said, looking at Ewan in confusion. "The Hole's full of it."

"What hole is this?"

"How about we follow you up after breakfast?" Ewan said. "Cerri needs to see the Wastes, and she'll need gear."

"Okay." Kate squinted at Cerri, measuring. "I'm not sure we'll have anything ready-made that'll fit, but it shouldn't take long to rig something up. Stupid real world," she grumbled. "I never had to worry about sizing back home."

"That should be all right," Tree said to Ewan, "but I'll need you home before long. We've got our first session with Lucia this morning."

Ewan blinked. "Oh, right...well, let's see how long this takes. Want to come with us?"

Tree opened her mouth, but then her face paled and she belched. She fairly leaped from her seat and sprinted for the door. Ewan moved to follow, but she was gone by the time he'd stood.

"Gems of old," Kate muttered, her own face slightly pale as well. "If we need to put it off, we can."

"She'll be okay," Ewan said, half to himself as Brian dispatched a couple of Mother's Children behind his wife.

A few minutes later, he, Cerri, and Kate were riding the elevator up. "Why is it called a hole if it is above us?" Cerri asked.

"Because it's right under the surface level," Kate replied. "That way, it's easy for the scouts to haul whatever materials they get from the ruins right to the foundries. The moles melt them down to fabricate whatever we need."

Cerri shot Ewan a dark look. "You said everyone here was a human."

"What? Oh, 'moles' is just a nickname. You know, moles in the Hole?"

The girl grunted in reply, then hissed and threw her hands up over her face when the doors opened to let the Hole's heat rush in.

They followed Kate in, Cerri staying close to Ewan again as they walked past dozens of Centrals with the usual unfriendly looks. "So, Kate," Ewan said in what he hoped was a casual tone, "Have you been fitting in all right up here?"

"Oh, yeah. They think I'm a smithing goddess," Kate said, totally oblivious to the stares. "I've been crushing the tech, then teaching them a thing or two. Like how to build these," she added as they stepped into her workshop, where a new set of black armor rested on the work bench. "It's a reinforced polymer lattice, mosaicked onto a rugged mesh. Look familiar?"

"It looks just like my night armor back home," Ewan said, whistling as he picked up the ultralight cuirass. "But I thought you'd already built the new armors?"

She grinned. "I figured some folks would want something a little lighter. Just remember that it won't make you invincible, okay?"

"I will," he replied. "Thanks for making this, K. I'll be sure to let Paul know, next time I see him."

"Sure. Don't forget the helmet."

Ewan sighed as Cerri lifted the armored hat, turning it over like a bowl. "It'll mess up my hair."

"No more than a bullet," Kate countered. "I'm not going to be the one to tell Tree you got killed on account of macho antics."

Ewan couldn't argue with her—especially not now, with the baby on the way. Taking the helmet and squashing it down over his curls, he found himself remembering something his dad had told him once. *Having a family really is making me more careful.*

"This armor would suffice," Cerri commented, picking at the plates. "Can you make some for me as well?"

Kate shrugged. "Okay, squirt, if light's your thing too. You'll look like twins when I'm through with you. Now, what kind of weapons do you like? Swords? Hammers? Axes, maybe?" she asked hopefully.

Cerri opened her hands, then flexed her fingers. "I want my claws. Can you do that?"

"I could try, sure," Kate said, sounding pleased to have a less impossible project than flying. "In the meantime, how about you carry a dagger? That's about the same thing."

"It is not," the girl replied haughtily, but she did take a little dagger. Dragging the blade across the back of her arm to test its edge, she suddenly looked a lot younger and older at the same time.

Ewan watched Cerri dance about the crowded room, practicing with the weapon and dodging gracefully around the clutter now that she could see, but then his tablet beeped. "That would be Tree," he said quietly to Kate. "I hate to ask you, but—"

"I am *not* babysitting for you. I've got work to do!"

"Yeah, but some of that's going to involve Cerri, anyway." He bit back a groan. "This is going to be awkward enough as it is. Please?"

Kate glared at him, but she couldn't hold it. "Go be a good dad—if the pipsqueak will let you out of her sight."

Ewan grinned in thanks, then turned to Cerri. "Hey, Cerri? I've got to go back home."

The girl froze, glaring suspiciously at him over the dagger. "You are leaving me?"

"Not like that. Tree and I have a meeting with a woman, about our baby."

"Ah. In that case, I will stay with Kai'tah," the girl replied, resuming her dance. "I do not wish to be afflicted with a cub."

Ewan bit back on his first thought, instead telling her he'd see them at lunch.

When Ewan got back to his room, Lucia was sitting on the bed. Tree sat across from her in a chair, pulled around to face the older woman. They looked vaguely similar with their blond hair, though Tree was nowhere near as curvy as Lucia.

Yet? Ewan wondered, before deciding he'd better abandon that line of thought.

"There he is!" Lucia laughed and gave Ewan a wink. "I was just telling Tree how lucky she is to have a man who's there for more than conception."

Ewan sighed inwardly as he lifted the other chair over Cerri's cot and sat next to his wife. "Nice to see you too, Lucia."

The woman beamed at him, more playful than predatory. "Shall we get started?"

She produced a small canvas bag and rummaged through it to find a ball, slightly smaller than Ewan's fists put together. "So, the basic idea is that Tree's going to push out a baby as big around as this," she explained, her grin broadening by the second as she held the ball up. "Through an opening as big as this."

Ewan had just enough warning to wrench his gaze away as her other hand flicked to her skirt. Tree inhaled sharply, but instead of scolding or shouting, she asked, "Is that even possible?"

"Oh yes," Lucia replied. "A woman's greatest capacity is her ability to be accommodating to the moment's need. When the time comes, your body will open itself to help the little one out. It's all right honey, you can look again," she added with a laugh. "He's so shy! Tree, what did you do to him?"

Ewan didn't dare turn back around until he heard the rustle of cloth, and even then, he waited a few seconds. Lucia was sitting cross-legged on the bed, smoothing her skirt over her knees and grinning at him enough to make him blush all over again. Tree was holding the not-so-little ball in her lap, staring at it in dread.

"You can do it," Ewan murmured, as he wondered how on Earth any woman was supposed to manage such an epic feat. "What can we do to make it easier for her?" he asked Lucia.

"The most important thing is for you to be in the proper frame of mind," Lucia said, addressing Tree. "Like the act that led to your little one's conception, you have to be willing to let another life's force move through your body. Guide it; adjust to it as it moves. We've got months to work toward that goal, but I wanted to make it clear today just what you'll be facing."

Tree swallowed, cradling the ball. "It's clear."

"Good. In the meantime, let's talk about the changes your body will undergo in the coming weeks."

Lucia knew her stuff, as though she'd been reading up on pregnancy and childbirth her whole life. *She probably has,* Ewan thought guiltily. The older woman bounced on the bed as she talked, making all kinds of exaggerated gestures to describe the flow of delivery. Ewan had assumed she was just another crazed Central, but now he recognized she was doing whatever she could to get a small piece of happiness, having the baby by proxy. Another tickle of uncomfortable sympathy rose in his heart, a small hope to see her holding her own baby one day.

He focused on listening to what she had to say, to keep himself from thinking about it too much.

She talked for a good hour with them about the three main stages of pregnancy, things they might expect—like food cravings and aversions—and changes to Tree's body. It sounded like Tree's insides were going to be completely rearranged to make room for the baby, which only added to Ewan's guilt. It hadn't occurred to him that getting to the point of actually having the baby would be so hard on her!

I've got to be there for her, he thought as he squeezed her hand over the ball. *Most of all, I've got to make sure she knows it.*

"Near the end of the second trimester, your breasts will start growing, getting ready to produce milk." Lucia chuckled, hefting herself. "They might even get as big as mine."

"You're making milk?" Tree asked. "Right now?"

"That's right," Lucia replied, opening her blouse and driving Ewan's eyes to the wall again. "There, do you see the little beads around my nipple? All the ladies in the nursery produce."

"Why?" Tree asked.

"There are so many little ones to cuddle, it happens naturally. Outfitting's always complaining about the extra padding we need for our uniforms, but what's the point of a bra when you're on duty?" Lucia chuckled, but it faded into a wistful sigh. "I've been producing for years, now. It's nice to know that I can do that much, at least."

"I think you're great," Ewan said, trying to keep his eyes high as he turned around. Tree scoffed, and his face burned as he wondered if Tree really would get that big. "Thanks for helping us," he squeaked.

"It's my pleasure," Lucia said seriously, tucking herself back in. "And it's not as though I'm planning on giving up trying."

"Um, sure," Ewan said quickly. "But I'm hardly the only player out here these days. I think Al really likes you!"

Lucia blinked. "Al?"

"Al'Dashan," Ewan said. *Come on, you've got to know your lovers' names, at least!* "Big, dark-skinned Veridian with a beard? Captain of the Ether Swords?"

To his shock, Lucia blushed. She looked down, adjusting her skirt with a tiny, girlish smile that made Ewan blush again with her. "I know him. Thanks for telling me, honey."

They went over a few more things, and Lucia insisted on giving Tree a memory card with a frap-ton of reading material before she left. "Make sure you start working on your breathing and visualization exercises," she ordered as she repacked her bag. "And talk to the baby. He can hear you even now, and the more attention you give him early on, the closer you'll be after he's out and about."

Tree stiffened, pulling away from Ewan's hand. "You mean the baby can hear us when we...ah..."

"Make love?" Lucia laughed, tossing her hair back over her shoulders as she made for the door. "The more you do, the better. You can't get any more pregnant than you already are, and it will help keep your organs supple and pliable."

"But, what about the baby?" Tree insisted.

"He'll enjoy the bouncy ride as much as you do," Lucia said with a wicked grin, turning to Ewan with a wiggle and a wink. "Think you can handle that, hon?"

"Um, yeah," Ewan said weakly as she swished out into the hall.

He yelped when Tree huffed beside him. "That was certainly educational," she said, holding the ball thoughtfully.

"No kidding. I never knew she was so smart."

"Mm," Tree agreed, setting the ball on the nightstand, then looking down at herself. "Do you think she's prettier than I am?"

"No!" Ewan blurted, drawing both a look and a small laugh from her. "I mean, um, well...she's kind of intense."

"I know. But her excitement is reassuring right now, as if she's feeling what I'm too afraid to feel for myself." Tree paused, giving him a shrewd look. "And she knows how people work. Thank you for trying to be a gentleman when she teases."

"Sure thing," he said automatically, not about to own up to the images still jiggling around in his mind. "You're the only one I want."

"Likewise," Tree replied, slowly breaking into a grin as wicked as her mentor's while her fingers drifted to her blouse buttons. "We've still got half an hour to lunch, don't we?"

Ewan grinned back, not caring whether it was true or not. Feeling unembarrassed for the first time all day, he locked the door and joined her on their bed, playfully determined to make the most of the coming months.

12

BLIND SIDES

UNLUCKILY FOR EWAN, THE REST OF SEPTEMBER PASSED IN A HAZE of rushed frustration, punctuated by fleeting, glorious moments of privacy. He spent so much time dealing with and worrying about his growing family that he barely had any left for his job.

Not that he knew what that job was, anymore.

A year ago, he'd come to the real world because Tree asked him to fight the Locusts. But Rothchild made them emissaries, making it too risky for Ewan to risk death in the field—when had that ever stopped him, back home?—because he was busy convincing his countrymen to do it for him. So, Ewan had settled for bringing out as many players as he could, but their numbers instantly maxed out, putting him on crowd control when they chafed against the Centrals. And then Tree's pregnancy, and Cerri's arrival...exactly what was he doing out here?

In fairness, Cerri was doing her best to adjust to the real world. She'd somehow conned Kate into stocking her with a steady supply of blackened grease, with which she did an impressive job of recreating her original spotted pattern. She fought tooth and nail about cleaning up in the evenings, arguing that Ewan didn't cut his hair off before going to bed. He and Tree finally gave up when she hogged the bathroom for hours to reapply her makeup, muttering loudly about the foolishness of it all. Besides, she did look more like herself again, and Ewan figured that keeping her healthy in spirit was more important than keeping her pillow clean.

At least the kid had a willing supplier. Kate would never have admitted it, but Ewan was sure she enjoyed babysitting. Whenever he and Tree had a prenatal appointment with Lucia, "Kai'tah" would always come by to ask Cerri's help with some new adjustment to her gear, while Ewan kept Tree company and put up with Lucia's teasing.

But as the two women talked, Ewan would tune out more often than not, his mind repeatedly coming back to Gabe's question of *why*. Why was Tree pregnant? Why now, after all these centuries? And why them? It couldn't be because he was a player. There were other players out too, and Lucia hadn't shied away from telling him that she and Al'Dashan were now spending a lot of quality time together. It couldn't be that Tree had spent time in the game worlds; plenty of Centrals had done that now without getting the Mother's frapping blessing. What was different about him and Tree? Ewan didn't have the faintest clue, but as October approached with piles of tablets to read and tension continuing to mount in the halls, he realized just how much work still lay ahead.

In the meantime, he still had his official job to do—and Tree's, now that she'd split her attention between check-ins with Robert and Lucia, and making Mother knew what bargains with Rothchild and Father Brian to keep the Mother's Children as her honor guard. In her place, Ewan logged into Veridor regularly, stopping by his mom's house to give her the obligatory updates on the baby before walking to Whitehaven for his own check-ins with Paul. News that the Locusts had started avoiding fights tore through the barracks, and Ewan started worrying about all the eager noobs who would never see the real world, between the cap and the threat of the conflict's ending—which only made him wonder about his own priorities.

It also made him wonder whether they'd need the Sah'rassans after all, but that only got him worrying in a whole new direction.

All told, there was a lot weighing on Ewan's mind—and weight was among them. One of the myriad quests Lucia gave the O'Mearas was for Tree to start tracking her stats every morning. Lucia said it was to help keep an eye on the baby's development and quickly head off any early issues. Ewan thought it would be a fun way for him to be involved, plugging Tree's numbers into the tablet.

Now he dreaded the ritual almost as much as his wife did.

Each morning, she'd get up, shivering as she undressed; then she'd plod to the scale in the corner and stomp on it to wake it up. There'd be an awful pause, waiting for the frapping thing to deliver its verdict, and then she'd come back to bed and haul the blankets over her head. Ewan would approach, measuring tape in hand, and Tree would yell at him not to touch her.

The first time they'd gone through this, Cerri jolted awake and went skittering for cover. She crashed into every piece of furniture crammed into the room—and somehow snapped Ewan's guitar, halfway down the neck.

So, when Gabe messaged Ewan one morning to invite him on a recon trip, he jumped at the chance.

"Love, I don't want you going," Tree said again a few days later, still wrapped up in their blanket. "Not without me to protect you. What if something happens?"

Ewan smiled reassuringly, not that she could see him. "There shouldn't be much danger. Gabe says he wants to scope out a site where we've already met the Locusts, see what they're up to. Odds are, they've already gotten what they want and moved on, so if anything, I'd say it'll be safer than usual."

Tree grunted. "If it's not dangerous, then I should be coming too. Everything I've read says the baby should be safe, that my body is like its armor."

"But what about *your* armor? We'd need it resized—"

"I know!" she snapped. "I just...I still don't like it."

"Ea'win Omi'ra, I will accompany you," Cerri said, hopping down easily into the gap between her cot and the table. "I wish to see your desert, and I will keep the sand from your eyes in Tri'ana Omi'ra's absence."

"I don't know," Ewan said, passing a hand through his hair and trying to think of a safe way to say he needed some time alone.

"We owe the Rajj a report," Tree pointed out, finally emerging from her bunker to sit up. "Honestly, I'm surprised she hasn't tried to contact the bridge yet. Take Cerri out with you; I'll arrange for us to meet and discuss further log-outs when you return."

Ewan bit back some choice words about her ordering him around when she hadn't even gotten dressed for the day, instead saying, "Yeah, sure." He sighed, then waded through the room to dig out his gear.

When he and Cerri entered the hangar, one of the only Central spaces on the surface, dozens of people were scurrying about in preparation for a scouting run. Cerri took it all in, eyes widening at the hulking transports in the domed, open room around the elevator. "The creatures across the mountains are massive," she whispered.

"They're not creatures," Ewan said. "They're machines. Those little ones over there, those are kangaroo rats—'roos for short. They're for first looks, letting the scouts get out and explore the Wastes before we send in the camels." He pointed up at one: easily twenty feet high and three times as long, with a huge cargo bay mounted over the treads, making it resemble a gigantic, bloated ant.

Cerri frowned. "They have animal names, but they are nothing like the ones in Sah'rassa. What will we ride?"

"We're probably taking a camel," Ewan replied. "The 'roos only seat two, and we're not the only ones going."

"Then you'd be wrong again, O'Meara," came Gabe's voice from the side.

Ewan turned to greet his friend, then clenched his fists when he saw Gabe's company: Vincent Coley.

"What are you doing here?" Ewan demanded.

"I work here, tube worm," the ponytailed scout replied smoothly, though his face-long scar twisted in a grimace, highlighting his missing ear.

Gabe gave Ewan a sympathetic smile. "There's been a change of plans. Coley wants to test the new armadillo, and we decided it would be convenient to pool our resources."

Coley huffed, crossing his arms and towering over Ewan. "Reid really must think there's no danger if he's bringing you and—what is that?" he asked, glowering at Cerri.

"I am Cerri," she replied, unruffled. "I wish to see the spirit desert."

"She would be the new player," Gabe explained, but his eyes lingered over her painted spots. "What was it, again? Rats?"

"Cats," Ewan corrected, not at all liking the way Coley was watching them.

"I am Caitsid'h," Cerri said simply. "Although here I must be human."

"Mustn't we all?" Gabe chuckled. "I don't recall inviting you."

"Tree's orders," Ewan muttered.

"Ah...I see," Gabe replied, his blue eyes glittering with

humor. "In that case, it will be my pleasure to have you along. How old are you, little girl?"

"I have seen over one hundred thirty moons," Cerri replied. "But I suspect that another has passed while I was underground."

Gabe hesitated, doing the math. "As you like. I suppose O'Meara's warned you that the sky here is, shall we say, occluded?"

"He has told me so," Cerri replied as they all resumed walking. "I believe it is why you humans travel during the day as fools."

Coley whipped around, making Ewan reach for his swords reflexively. "You little—"

"Easy, Coley," Gabe chided. "She's not used to us, not yet. The world's too large for us to only move about in the night, girl. You'll see soon enough."

Cerri nodded, but she did scoot closer to Ewan.

"Don't mind Coley too much," Gabe said, still smiling. "He's always been grouchy. A bit of a lone wolf, preferring the long exploratory runs to all the politics here. Isn't that right, Coley? Still, you might want to stay on his left side, so that he doesn't have to listen to you."

"So, what's the deal with these new transports?" Ewan asked, hoping to change the subject.

"The 'deal' is that they'll get the job done," Coley growled. "Half-assed swords and shields don't cut it against the Locusts."

"You're wearing a broadsword now," Ewan pointed out.

"After today, I won't need to," Coley shot back. "With enough 'dillos, we'll crush the Locusts without even having to get out."

The party rounded the camel, and Ewan found himself face to face with the nastiest-looking vehicle he'd ever seen. Black as night, with segmented joints that reminded him vaguely of the pill bugs in his mom's garden, the armadillo certainly looked ready to run roughshod over anything it had a mind to. Turrets bristled from each node, and whatever treads it had were tucked under the heavy armored plating.

Ewan suppressed a wince. “I take it my sister was involved.”

“She does know her stuff,” Coley admitted with a grunt. “Hard to believe you two are related.”

“I contributed as well,” Gabe added, his voice deliberately light. “After our less than stellar first encounter with the Locusts, I felt it prudent to route all weapons controls to the cockpit. Placing fighters in separate turrets risks miscommunication, to say nothing of the risks involved in being away from the armor.”

“I hear that,” Ewan muttered, remembering all too well. “How many people will this thing hold?”

“As a troop carrier, it’s rated to hold up to thirty people,” Gabe said, “but it could be operated by a single pilot and still be effective in combat.”

Cerri wrinkled her nose. “It smells bad.”

“Good.” Coley sneered, coming to a stop a dozen yards from the ‘dillo’s side hatch. “Scouting party, form up!”

Twenty people came jogging over, in full combat gear. To Ewan’s surprise, they were all players—and every last one of them wore pink over their arms.

“Listen up!” Coley barked, glaring at the men under his command. “We’ve got a joint mission today. Reid and O’Meara are—”

“And Cerri,” Cerri said.

“What? Oh, you. Them and the runt are on military recon. When we get to the target, they’ll do their thing, and none of you are going to ask about it.”

The Mother’s Children shot glances at Ewan, but they didn’t protest.

“All right,” Coley growled. “Board up!”

Ewan’s hackles rose as the Veridians gave their ponytailed

overlord a series of mutinous looks. *It's just as well that I'm coming along for this,* he thought, *or Coley might find himself fragged and walking home.*

He turned to say something about it to Gabe, but the chief was already leaving—in a different direction. "Hey, aren't you coming?" Ewan called.

"Of course I'm coming," Gabe replied, not bothering to look back. "You weren't expecting me to pack myself into that sweaty machine, were you? I'll be taking a 'roo, thank you."

"But—"

Gabe kept walking, his voice infuriatingly sensible. "I'd planned to invite you along, but your little friend makes space scarce. Unless you'd prefer to leave her in Coley's tender care?" he added.

"Your allies are inconsiderate *sh'takhi,*" Cerri grumbled as Ewan glowered at Gabe's back. Then Coley barked at them to get on board already, and she made a face of her own.

More irritated by the second, Ewan followed the rest of the players in, making sure Cerri stayed close by. Just past the hatch, though, he paused. He'd expected to find a standard hall, but the corridor was more like a crawlspace, barely bigger around than the hatch itself.

"Not very roomy, is it?" he said.

"This ain't no cargo hauler," Coley said from behind him. "It's a war machine. Quarters are on the left, cockpit's on the right. You're not going in there, players!" he snarled, grabbing Ewan's shoulder when he tried to make the turn.

"What? But—"

"I'm in charge of this mission. Reid's your party rep; you got questions about what you're doing, you talk to him when we get there. Why he wanted meatbags like you along is beyond me."

On better terrain, Ewan would've argued, but he knew as well as Coley that he wasn't in any position to fight back. "Fine.

Cerri, come back this way. We'll get some sleep while they do all the driving."

When he got to his 'room', it took Ewan all of two seconds to decide that his apartment was an open palace by comparison. The one thing that could be said for the tiny space was that he could stand upright, but it was as closed as a coffin. "How in blazes are we supposed to sleep in here?" he muttered, fingering a series of straps which held his sleeping bag like the tatters of some huge spider's meal. When Cerri nudged him from behind, he said, "I don't think we'll both fit."

"I am not staying here," she said, before using him like a ladder to reach the ceiling. "This creature and its riders smell bad. I want to know why."

"Coley's a real piece of work. Oof!" Ewan said as she stepped on his shoulders. "He was like that when I met him, but I'm sure losing to the Locusts didn't help his attitude."

Cerri peered down at him, kicking him in the face when the 'dillo rumbled to life and started moving out. "What do you mean?"

Ewan sighed, rubbing his cheek around her boot. "Last winter, after I'd logged out and promised to help the Centrals protect themselves, I went on a scouting run to prove myself. Coley was there. So were Tree and Gabe, along with Kate's, um, boyfriend Sam. And Nathan—you've seen him in the gym. The Central defense chief?"

"The one who walks as though he is hunted."

Ewan sighed. "Yeah, that's him. Anyway, we picked a fight, going near where the Locusts had wrecked two other camels. I thought I could handle them. I had no idea."

"They attacked?" Cerri prompted.

Ewan closed his eyes. "They owned us. Nathan got shot right off the bat, and Sam...he got his leg crushed because I wasn't fast enough to stop the Locust who did it. Coley lost part of his face, and one woman died that day." *Frasier's wife*, he bitterly added to himself. "We nerfed near lost the whole party, all because I got cocky!" He growled, thumping his fist against the wall. "So yeah, Coley's got plenty of aggro for me."

He fumed for a few moments, but then Cerri suddenly pushed off from his shoulders. He looked up, startled, and saw her vanish into another hole she'd made in the ceiling. She scooted back, looking down at him with unblinking eyes. "I will return, Ea'win Omi'ra."

Ewan watched her go, not feeling up for another argument, then cut the light to try and enjoy some solitude.

It didn't happen.

Within minutes, he could hear another voice in the next room. Patrick Lee's, he realized, fairly shouting to whoever was next over.

Ewan was on the verge of turning around and burying his head in the sleeping bag like Tree, when the boy thumped on their common wall. "The plan's a go!" he called in the loudest whisper Ewan had ever heard. "But don't let the Gem know until he can't stop us."

Ewan froze, swaying in the bag as the 'dillo turned and started thumping over the dunes in earnest. "What plan?"

An awkward pause followed. "Hero?" Patrick asked, now being quiet. "Is that you?"

"Yeah. What are you going on about?"

Ewan could practically hear the boy agonizing about how much to say, but eventually Patrick seemed to make up his mind. "We're making a stand."

"Come again?"

"A stand! These Gems keep trying to order us around, but we're not taking it anymore."

Ewan tried to facepalm, but he only tangled himself in the bag. "Patrick, for the last time, they're not Gems."

"Father Brian says they are."

"Father Brian's a lunatic who thinks his tablet's the Logos!"

When the boy fell silent again, Ewan added, "Look, the Diamond Lord did come from here, I'll grant that. But there are plenty of other Centrals, you know."

"But you never found him, did you?" Patrick countered. "Father Brian says you've been searching ever since, but that you haven't found any trace."

"He—what? He shouldn't know about—"

"But we're here to help you, Hero. You and the Mother. We want Earth to be as green as Veridor, and we don't care how many Gems or Gem-lovers we have to wreck to make it happen."

Ewan cringed at the lethal enthusiasm in the boy's voice, all too familiar after his story time with Cerri. Keeping as much encouragement as he could in his own tone, he said, "I appreciate the sentiment. So what's this big plan of yours?"

"We know why the Centrals built this war wagon," Patrick answered, obviously mollified. "The Granite Gasbag said it himself."

"The who?"

"Coley," Patrick said as though this was the most obvious thing ever. "That's his Gem name."

"Patrick—"

"He said they built this thing to make us obsolete."

"Yeah, I heard him say something similar," Ewan said reluctantly. "But my sister helped build this thing."

"Hero, they want to lock us back in the tubes and keep treating us like their toys!"

Ewan wanted to argue, but he couldn't find the words. "Yeah, you're probably right," he admitted. "So what are you going to do about it?"

"We're going to jack it up," Patrick said fiercely, his grin as plain in Ewan's mind as if the Logos had placed it there. "Thomas got the specs from the moles. This thing's got so many wires and pipes, all we have to do is start cutting them until the whole thing breaks down."

Of frapping course. Ewan leaned his head back against the vibrating wall. "You do realize that the Wastes aren't a good place to go hiking, don't you?"

"The Logos'll provide; someone will rescue us."

Ewan groaned. "But what if the Locusts attack?"

The boy went silent, but Ewan might as well have read the extra *Then we'll just respawn; what's the big deal?* across his vision. "Frapping suicidal loonies," he muttered. "Maybe I've been too hard on Nathan."

"What?" Patrick asked.

"Nothing."

"You're...you're on board, then?"

"Of course not! Patrick, there's no way it ends well. The moment we make it home—*if* we make it home—Kate's going to go over every last bolt on this thing." Ewan thumped the 'dillo. "Trust me, she's going to know what happened."

"But she's your sister."

"Which means she listens to me less than anyone else!" Ewan snapped. "Not to mention, she won't be the only one. Gabe's attention to detail is Epic-level, and he'll go straight to Rothchild. And you know what *he'll* do?"

"Um..."

Ewan cut him off, before the boy could spout more foolishness. "We've got a whole new game world lined up and waiting. All Rothchild needs is space for them, and you're handing him our spots on a platter!"

Silence answered him, long and heavy and louder than the 'dillo's rattling. Eventually, Ewan said, "Look. Thanks for telling me what the plan was, but I'm telling you, as the Hero of Veridor, that you've got to call it off. Do that for me, and I promise I won't report it to Tree and the others."

"But Hero, you wouldn't—"

"I frapping well would!" Ewan roared. "If it keeps the rest of us out here, if it means I get to stay and see my baby with my own eyes, then I would!"

"Oh." Another long silence followed. "Okay, Hero. I'll pass it on. And don't worry, the Gems don't suspect a thing."

Like hell they don't, Ewan thought darkly, wondering which side was more at fault at this point.

13

TRIED AND DIED

LATER THAT AFTERNOON, THE ‘DILLO STOPPED ON A SANDY FLAT dominated only by the remnants of a few small buildings. The transport's side hatch opened, and the scouting party emerged into the desert, masked and hooded.

Ewan stepped away from the others to get his bearings. He sighed as he equipped his new helmet. The chin strap chafed against his neck, piling onto his mask's efforts to choke him while keeping the worst of the acrid dust from his lungs.

Too bad neither of them do anything about the taste, he thought.

Piloted by Coley's gentle touch, the 'dillo had plowed straight through the ancient wire fence surrounding the ruin, trailing bits that got snagged in the armored plating. Ewan wrenched a sheet of metal free, holding it up in the brown light to read the sandblasted words on it.

Fort Gilmer.

A military base? Ewan wondered.

He glanced up in annoyance as Gabe's ‘roo came to a stop, a respectful distance away from its bruiser of a brother. The chief stepped out, his own helmeted head making Ewan feel slightly less lame, then walked over to hand something to Coley.

"So this is what the desert across the mountains looks like," Cerri said from right beside Ewan, making him jump with a yelp.

"Where have you been—Cerri, put your mask on!" he scolded once his own breath returned.

"Kai'tah's head shield will suffice." Cerri plunked her own helmet on, then lifted her face, sniffing the air and wrinkling her nose. "I must know the sands, if I am to convince my grandmother to send more of the Caitsid'h here."

"Fan out, teams of three!" Coley ordered, still loud through his mask. "I want two squads on lookout; the rest of you find something worth our time."

The other players quickly grouped up, leaving Patrick and another young man Ewan didn't know trading significant looks with the others as they teamed up with the Granite Gasbag.

"Ea'win Omi'ra, we need to speak," Cerri said quietly. "A storm gathers."

"Yeah," Ewan agreed, watching anxiously as Coley cuffed Patrick on the head and stalked off toward one of the outlying buildings. "The other players were planning something. I've got a bad feeling they still are."

She frowned at him, but then Gabe called out from where he was standing. "If you two would follow me, we can perform *our* duties."

"Yeah, sure," Ewan answered, glancing one more time over his shoulder to see Coley vanish into the ruin. *Gems of old...I can't stand the guy, but I can't just let him get killed on my watch. The others still don't get that there's no respawning here!*

"We'll use a private frequency," Gabe said as they reached him, regarding Cerri's bare face without comment. "That way, we won't be distracted by the main group's chatter."

"We can listen?" Cerri asked. "How?"

"With the radios. It's what we use out here instead of messaging," Ewan explained.

"Observe," Gabe added. "There's a speaker in the helmet near your left ear, and a mic along the edge, here." He thumbed the little slot by his cheek to demonstrate. "You can adjust the frequency or record logs with the buttons on the underside, like this. Set to one hundred thirty-eight point four Megahertz."

Cerri followed his lead, coughing when the wind kicked sand into her mouth. "Asst! Why does the air taste so foul?"

"It's loaded with all sorts of crap," Ewan replied as he adjusted his own radio. "Back in the days before the Centre, people tried adding different stuff to the air, in the hopes that they could get the planet back on track."

Gabe nodded approvingly. "You've been studying, O'Meara. After the Rapture, when the Earth's rich and powerful left the rest of humanity to die on the planet's corpse, the surviving nations attempted various geoengineering solutions. When those inevitably failed, they resorted to flinging nuclear weapons at each other instead, fighting over the scraps that remained. The bitter taste is mostly fallout from the latter, still pervasive after centuries."

Cerri furrowed her spots. "I do not know such weapons."

"Imagine a single explosive device that could obliterate all of your village," Gabe replied, before looking straight at Ewan. "Or the Centre."

Ewan shifted uncomfortably under the chief's lingering gaze—until it clicked. "No," he whispered.

Gabe's eyes hardened. "Why not?" he asked, pulling out a scanner and booting it up. "The Locusts have clearly survived in the Wastes for centuries. They don't need what we have."

"But they'd be wiping out countless innocent lives!"

"Please, O'Meara. Innocence doesn't factor into the equation. Every encounter we've had in the past two weeks has been at military installations. They're not merely scavenging resources anymore, now that our forces pose an obstacle and a threat to them."

Ewan swallowed. "They're upgrading?"

Gabe's voice was flat. "They want to wipe us out."

"I do not understand," Cerri said, peering over Gabe's arm at the scanner. "Such power is clearly a D'jin's to wield. How would these Locusts know of it?"

"Indeed," Gabe replied grimly. "But enough chit-chat; we have work to do."

They started searching, for what, Ewan didn't really know. Gabe was unusually silent, checking his scanner and limiting his comments to "over here" and "try that structure."

Fort Gilmer seemed like it had been a simple town, maybe four times as big as Ewan's home village outside Whitehaven. There were small clusters of housing, with the wire frames of couches and beds still inside. Armored transports in a fenced lot, sporting guns longer than a 'roo, waited patiently for pilots long gone. A garage held several smaller vehicles, their tires too small to make them much use in the sands, even if they had weathered the centuries. There was even a general store of sorts, with metallic cylinders still neatly stacked across the plain shelves.

"Canned goods," Gabe commented, idly picking up a short one to scan it. "Smoked salmon."

Cerri snatched the can from him. "This has fish?"

"Yes," the chief replied, watching her with amusement as she tried to break it open. "And probably still edible, at that. Our ancestors were considerably better at preserving food than ecosystems."

"But how do I eat it?" she asked, turning the can over.

"Here," Ewan said, taking out a short knife and punching through the lid for her. *Insane, that it should still be good after thousands of years!*

"This only confirms my suspicion," Gabe muttered, as Cerri

snarfed the fish down and started loading her pack with more cans. "They should have gone for the food first."

Ewan nodded, heart sinking. "But there's no guarantee that a huge weapon's here."

"True enough. But even the smaller ones may prove... problematic for our cause. Our failure to launch a decisive strike on the Locusts is inviting escalation," the programmer warned, giving Ewan a pointed look. "We need to end this conflict as soon as possible, not drag it out."

"Who's dragging it out?" Ewan retorted, though his face heated under his mask.

With that thought to cheer them, they kept searching, occasionally crossing paths with some of the other scouts. To take his mind off whatever fool plan his fellow players still had, Ewan tried to picture what Fort Gilmer might have looked like before the Rapture. Green lawns under a blue sky, with the small transports zipping up and down the avenues. People moving about, living busy lives.

Had they known what was coming? Had they tried to stop it? Did they retreat to the Centre when the end came? Or had they stayed out and survived, against all odds?

Were their descendants finally coming home to collect their inheritance?

"How long has the sky been masked?" Cerri asked, looking up but still refusing to cover her own face while Gabe ducked into another building.

"Twenty-five hundred years, give or take a century," Ewan replied.

She sniffed, suppressing a cough. "The clouds are not so bad. In Sah'rassa, this time of day would be very hot. Only a fool would be out on the sands now."

"There aren't any deserts in Veridor," Ewan said, ignoring the jab. "The closest thing we've got to any of this is some of the area around Anthar, one of the old cities. It got burned to the ground ages ago, but its patron cursed it so that nothing much grows there, anymore."

"A D'jin?"

"Yeah. The Ruby Tyrant."

Cerri nodded, turning her attention to the wall's base. "I have seen no plants. Does nothing grow here?"

Ewan shrugged. "Not that I've seen. Whatever happened to the world, it was bad enough to kill off just about everything."

"What kind of sh'takh would destroy his own world?" she muttered.

"Our ancestors, apparently."

Cerri huffed. "Then I do not recognize them. They took all the fish away, leaving only little cans for their children."

Eventually, they found a long building, deceptively squat until they got closer and saw it was set into the ground. Inside, it was easily a hundred feet tall. It held row after row of transports, but these seemed light, fluid. Swift.

"Are they like birds?" Cerri asked, reaching up to brush her fingers against something that definitely resembled a wing, sweeping out from one transport's side.

"Maybe," Ewan said, trying without much luck to make it flap. He pulled his helmet off with a sigh of relief, then finger-combed his sweaty hair. "Kate would love to see this. I ought to take a picture."

"I doubt it would be helpful," Gabe commented as he searched a pile of rubble in the corner. "Pre-Rapture aircraft had fixed wings; they relied on jet engines for propulsion. Even if we refurbished these, they couldn't stay aloft for long in the dust."

Ewan gave the wing a sympathetic pat, watching as Cerri climbed around the top and stuck her head into the big cylinders mounted underneath. "How would you know?"

"The rest of the staff may not care for history, but the

material's still there, actively maintained," Gabe replied. "Also, it's one of my duties as a programmer."

"Really?" Ewan said. "What does a flying thingy have to do with programming?"

"Some of the simulations use realistic physics, and considerably more advanced technology than swords and shields." The chief's voice was bitter as he tucked his tablet away. "You've seen it."

"I guess so," Ewan said, recalling an image on the bridge's screen: a nightmare of giant, human-driven golems leveling a town. "Is that what the Earth sims are for?"

Gabe was still for a moment. "Among other things, yes. They're a template for remaking the Earth."

"Really?"

Gabe fixed hard blue eyes on him. "I don't waste time with half-truths. If you wanted players to remake this world, the denizens of those simulations would have the will and power to do it." He gestured to the aircraft. "Every weapon here has been updated for use in Terranova. But tell me, O'Meara: will they bring about the world you dream of?"

Ewan closed his eyes, imagining the kind of devastation rockets from flying machines might cause. "I guess not."

"Yet the Locusts now have access to them," Gabe said coldly. "How, then, do you intend for us to survive?"

Ewan's gut tightened, but it was more from Gabe's tone than his words. He left Cerri to her own devices and joined his friend. "Hey. You all right?"

"Of course I am."

"Okay," Ewan said dubiously, watching the older man. "It's been a crazy year, like you said the other week. It seems like yesterday I was running around in Veridor, whacking mobs and leveling like mad. And now I'm out here, with a cat person and a guy who could build my homeworld all over again." He plopped down on a box with a grin. "But I'm sure I'm not the only one who's up to his ears in changes."

Gabe's eyes softened, just a little, behind the mask. "I won't argue with you, there. I used to be so certain of myself. I knew exactly what I wanted and how to achieve it."

"Oh, yeah?" Ewan asked, grinning more. "And what does the Centre's golden boy want?"

"To rule my fate," Gabe said quietly. "I won't allow things to continue as they have, with feckless leaders who would condemn us." He shook his head. "All for the sake of a dead past that rejected us."

The older man fell silent, lost in his own thoughts. Ewan glanced back at Cerri, perched on the death-machine's wing with her helmet in her lap, fiddling with the radio. "I'm still betting we can make a better future together," Ewan said. "Just the way we want it. We're getting more players out every day. And you Centrals keep surprising me," he added quickly as Gabe's eyes narrowed. "Lucia's definitely a lot smarter than I gave her credit for."

Gabe snorted. "Lucia Howe? You're dreaming. That woman's only ever been interested in one thing."

Ewan scowled, pointlessly behind his mask. "Yeah, well, maybe if you weren't so intent on bedding her every—"

"Ea'win Omi'ra!" Cerri shouted. "You must hear this!"

Ewan and Gabe both leaped up, but she was already skidding to a stop beside them. Her eyes were fierce, triumphant. "I have found him."

"Found who?"

"Listen!" Cerri insisted, thrusting her helmet at Ewan.

He put it to his ear—and his heart dropped through his stomach. A chorus of voices, speaking as one, slammed out of the speaker. Into his mind.

Masters of the Wastes, rally to me! Your Lord summons you to receive his gift and rid our sands of the intruders!

"What is it?" Gabe asked.

Ewan listened in stunned fury as the message repeated on auto. "Gabe…it's him."

"Who?" Gabe repeated impatiently.

"The Diamond Lord. He's out here, right now," Ewan whispered, absently handing the device to his friend. "But how can that be? The only people out here are us three, the Ether Swords, and—" Jamming his helmet back on, he shouted his own message. "Ether Swords, the Locusts are coming! Coley's a Gem; take him down!"

Gabe swore softly. "Girl, how did you find this?"

"I listened." Cerri reclaimed her helmet, then pulled on a set of clawed gloves before looking up at Ewan, her own eyes burning. "Ea'win Omi'ra, we must assist the others. You and I are the only ones who have defeated a D'jin."

"Right." Ewan sprinted for the door, whipping out his blades. Kate had coated them in diamonds, hoping it might give them extra punch, but now they appeared covered in a Gem's blood.

The sky was getting dark—darker—as Ewan neared the transports. He tried shouting his warning out a few more times, but no one responded. It wasn't until he crouched behind a partial wall that he remembered he wasn't on the common frequency. Cursing, he changed the settings and barked, "Ether Swords, report!"

A few seconds later, a young man's voice replied. "Francis here. Hero, is that you?"

"Yeah," Ewan said, not having a frapping clue who Francis even was. "Where are you?"

"On the 'dillo, with Axford and Darden."

"Okay, great," Ewan said, waving to acknowledge Cerri and then Gabe as they joined him. "You need to power up the weapons as soon as you can. The Locusts are coming!"

The response came, but far too slowly. "They are? Are you sure?"

"Yes, I'm frapping sure!" Ewan shouted, as dread punched his gut. *They didn't! Did they? Even after I told them not to?!*

"I expect they'd be visible on the radar," Gabe added tersely.

"Oh...um," Francis hemmed, before adding in a voice that couldn't be any less convincing, "Oh, yeah, I see them now! I'm glad you thought to tell us, Hero!"

Ewan cringed, avoiding Gabe's eyes. "Can you ready the weapons on the 'dillo?"

"Uh, yeah, sure," Francis replied, confirming Ewan's worst fears. "And I'll warn the others too, so you don't have to worry about that."

"Great," Ewan muttered.

"Coley isn't responding," Gabe said, touching his own helmet while giving Ewan a hard look.

"Why would he?" Ewan growled. "He's probably just sitting back to watch the whole thing."

"You can't seriously believe he's the Diamond Lord. That message was probably a recording."

Ewan huffed. "Come on, we'd better help."

They covered the remaining ground at a brisk run. Ewan told himself again and again that the Locusts weren't there yet, that they still had a chance to get away, but his radio was ominously silent. Why wasn't Francis raising the alarm? Weren't they using the common channels?

Not if they're using their own private frequency, he realized, picking up his pace. *Not if they really* were *planning to frag Coley!*

The 'dillo finally came into view, still sulking where they'd left it, but Ewan's hopes died when he spotted a couple of figures scrambling across its roof, obviously doing something to the turrets. More people trickled from the ruins, black ants startled back into their nest.

"Guys, I don't think the 'dillo's going to be much help," Ewan warned as the others caught up again.

Gabe's eyes narrowed, but Cerri merely nodded. "I have been in the creature's belly. I know its soft spots."

"But we want it working—Cerri, wait!" Ewan cried, but she was already gone, vanished into the dust.

"They sabotaged it," Gabe said, each word a flat accusation. "Our greatest weapon, our best chance at ending this war before it escalated further, and they've as good as given it to the Locusts."

"Yeah." Ewan sighed, bile leaping in his throat as he watched Cerri ghost up under the 'dillo's plating, barely visible. "They thought they were about to become obsolete. I heard about it on the way out, but I told them to call it off. I *ordered* them."

Gabe's voice was cold fury. "And you didn't report to me?"

"I thought they'd listen to me! I didn't think they'd be so stupid as to, well—"

"Do it?" Gabe snapped. "Of course they would! Why would pampered, delusional players give a damn about the lives of others?!"

"Hey! They're defending your Centre!"

Gabe stabbed a finger at the broken 'dillo. "If you still believe that, then you're as blind as the rest of them!"

Ewan's fists clenched along with his gut, but then he heard the throb of engines, approaching fast from the north. "They're here," he whispered, glancing automatically to see if the other Veridians had also heard it.

Gabe cursed, drawing his pistol and turning away as he rose to a crouch.

"Where are you going?" Ewan asked.

"To the 'roo," the programmer snarled over the rising roar. "*Someone* has to report back."

He broke into a sprint, just before a pair of transports erupted from the sands in front of them.

When Ewan first met the Locusts at the start of the year, he'd learned that they knew enough about old Earth vehicles to make them run after all these centuries. In that battle at the Memorial, they'd used trucks and the like, but the vehicles now swarming the 'dillo looked bigger and much meaner, with camel-like treads instead of wheels, and armored plating of their own to match their target.

With rising horror, Ewan recognized them as the kind of military transports he'd seen earlier that day.

The first of them, equipped with a long single gun, swung around and belted the 'dillo point blank with a blast that shook the ground. The Central transport nearly toppled as the Veridians on top held on for their lives—dear to them, now that it was too late—but someone on the inside managed to turn it around to face the attack. Ewan's headset exploded with belated cries of "Enemy contact!", and he only just got out of the way when a third vehicle came barreling through right beside him.

He rolled back up to standing, swords at the ready, but the battle was already past him. The Locusts surrounded the 'dillo, their war machines just big enough to keep it from running them over as it spun about like a cornered behemoth. The black armor held, shuddering under the attack, but the 'dillo remained silent.

"Nerf it all, Francis!" Ewan shouted into his mic. "Shoot back already!"

"We're trying!" came the panicked reply. "Fixing this thing's not as easy as breaking it!"

Ewan swore and broke from cover, seeking anything at all that he could do, but the Locusts ignored him, running circles around their crippled prey. One of tanks wheeled around, tilted its long central gun up, and blew one of the 'dillo's port turrets apart—along with the Veridian who'd been trying to fix it.

Then Ewan heard another voice over the radio, sounding even angrier than he felt.

"You double-crossing little maggots!" Coley bellowed, so loud that Ewan also heard him directly as he emerged from the rubble, dragging a pair of downed Ether Swords behind him by their collars. "Return fire!"

"We're on it!" Francis shouted back. "Get wrecked!"

The 'dillo wheeled around, pitching another poor bastard off the top as it did, and the starboard guns blazed to life.

Ewan instantly wished they hadn't.

Pointed every which way, they flung a wide hailstorm of lead that sent him diving for cover behind an overturned car. The sands hissed and boiled to glass as hot metal punched into them mere feet from his face, and the car wobbled unnervingly as more tore into its undercarriage.

When the shooting stopped, Ewan scrambled out. The turrets were smoking and sparking, with more than a few dangling at broken angles, but the Locusts' transports were untouched. They circled closer, two of them hemming the 'dillo in until it couldn't turn, and then the third one parked itself in front and trained its gun on the cockpit.

Vincent Coley walked straight to it, handed off his captives to the Locusts now streaming out, and pulled on his own robe.

"Nerfing bastard!" Ewan sprinted for the traitor, but as he ran he saw another figure, dragging itself toward the 'roo and leaving a dark, crimson trail. He froze, still burning to take Coley out, but the sight of yet another friend's broken body in the sand was too much. Blood boiling, Ewan changed course and sprinted over.

Gabe turned to see him coming, blue eyes murderous in the fading light, but he clutched a chunk of metal sticking into his right thigh through the upgraded armor. "Look what your fellow players did to me!" he rasped.

"They're not my fellows," Ewan growled. He hoisted the chief over his shoulder and glanced back to see a squad of robed men board the 'dillo. "Come on."

Thankfully, Coley and the Locusts were too busy securing their toy to pay them any attention, and Ewan was able to put Gabe in the 'roo's rear seat without disruption. "Does this thing have any weapons?" he asked, painfully aware that he hadn't actually driven a 'roo before as he sat at the controls.

"You can't be serious." Gabe coughed. "We have to escape!"

"Not yet," Ewan replied, powering the 'roo up.

"O'Meara, you can't stop them. They've already got the armadillo!"

"And Cerri's on board!" Ewan turned the throttle up, and they shot forward with even less of a plan than he'd had a minute ago.

The Locust tanks, content to ignore them before, swiveled around to meet the upstart 'roo. Ewan swerved, praying that his own cluelessness would buff his evasion enough. He nearly flipped them once when the ground in front of them vanished in a burst of fire, but the little transport turned on a point and got them past.

"Gabe, I need guns!" he yelled, narrowly avoiding a blast from the third tank as more Locusts jumped out of the first two and made for the 'dillo.

Gabe grunted, then thumped the panel to Ewan's right, revealing a trigger stick. "They're mounted over the front wheels, but they can't punch through armor."

"I don't need them to," Ewan answered grimly, sliding the console up and around. Steering with his left hand, he took aim as carefully as he could and strafed the last group of Locusts, including the ponytailed Gem, as they rushed for cover. He dropped a couple, but nowhere near enough to make a difference—and Coley got safely inside.

Ewan swore. "Cerri, come on, we've got to go!"

Then the 'dillo turned, so suddenly that it smacked them in the flank and sent them skidding. They spun to a drunken halt, facing the black mob as it charged them, knocking the now-obsolete tanks aside. Ewan sent the 'roo full reverse, wheeling around just enough to turn the crumpling impact into a neck-wrenching sideswipe.

"You're going to get us killed," Gabe snarled. "Forget the rat!"

"No!" Ewan yelled, gunning the engines as the 'dillo came about, guns blazing randomly. "I've got to bring her back!"

"She's a player!" Gabe exploded. "Leave her and replace her with one of the others, if you must!"

"I made a promise to keep her safe!"

Gabe cursed, and the next thing Ewan knew, the other man's hands were around his throat, trying to yank him aside.

"Get off me!" Ewan grunted, losing his grip on the throttle as Gabe hauled him back.

"I'm not risking my life for you or your damned lost causes," Gabe hissed, trying to push past him and take the driver's seat. "Give me the controls!"

Ewan punched back, connecting with the man's face, but Gabe didn't let go, instead bashing him into the cockpit glass.

He couldn't abandon Cerri. Ever since he'd met her, he'd done nothing but drag her from one danger to another.

I won't be a bad father!

The two men wrestled, but the 'dillo was already rushing them again like an enraged aurochs. Ewan threw elbows, struggling to break free, but Gabe had him in a headlock, pinning him to the seat and crushing the air out of him.

Ewan managed to grab the wheel with a desperate lunge, but Gabe's hands gripped it right beside his, wrenching hard to the right. Ewan threw his head back into Gabe's face, knocking him away, but it was too late. The 'roo swerved, then flipped. The glass around them crunched sickeningly as the ground slammed into it: once, twice, and then a final time as the little transport landed upside-down, giving both men a stark view of the 'dillo bearing down on them.

"We've got to roll it back," Ewan rasped.

Gabe spat. "You're insane; there's no time!"

"We have to do something!" He crushed the trigger with his right hand, spraying useless underpowered bullets at the black hull, as useless as swords and noobs in the Wastes.

But the 'dillo rocked with an explosion, tilting up onto its port side and digging its armored shell into the sand and rubble. Ewan stared in shock, shuddering with the 'roo as the monster passed over them on-edge, then tipped over with a heavy thud.

He hung there with Gabe, staring numbly out at the world they were somehow still a part of. Then he nearly died of fright anyway, when Cerri tapped on the pebbled glass to his side.

"Why did you not wait? I said I would handle it." She unequipped her helmet, giving them a puzzled frown. "Ea'win Omi'ra, I have seen enough of your desert now."

"Yeah," Ewan said, dangling exhausted from his harness. "You and me both."

14

PROMISING THE SUN

THE SURVIVORS HAD AN UNCOMFORTABLE RIDE HOME. THE 'ROO'S engine was miraculously unharmed by Ewan and Gabe's joint acrobatics, but the cockpit glass was shot, letting the Wastes' acrid funk whistle in through a hundred places as they retreated.

That was nothing, next to the poisoned air inside.

Gabe brooded in the back, nursing his wounds as best he could with the little first aid kit tucked in a side compartment. He didn't speak, and while he at least didn't fight Ewan for the controls anymore, the chief's silent fury chilled the hairs on Ewan's neck.

As if I needed the guilt trip, Ewan thought ruefully.

"I'm sorry," he said, reaching around Cerri in his lap to steer.

"Why do you apologize?" Cerri asked.

Ewan gripped the control wheel harder. "For everything. For putting you at risk, for letting Gabe get shot. For bringing out those frapping idiots who just made things worse."

"Ea'win Omi'ra, these things are not your fault," she replied, ignoring Gabe's dissenting snort from the back. "You are not accountable for the actions of the others."

"Like hell I'm not," Ewan grumbled, swerving around a rock he only just saw. "I'm supposed to be in charge of the Ether Corps, but I've been slacking off. Making Al'Dashan and Paul keep Brian in line, for all the good that's done." He sighed, letting the guilt run its course. "I didn't know half the players who died today. What am I supposed to tell their families?"

Cerri gazed out, still not wearing a mask. "We are fortunate that the other humans took the metal creature's teeth."

Ewan let the battle replay in his mind, fighting off a rising tide of dread. *Coley had that 'dillo all wrapped up in pink ribbons for a present. If Patrick and the others hadn't sabotaged it, who knows what would have happened?*

Somehow, guessing at the alternatives didn't make the day's debacles any more palatable.

It was after midnight when they got back, but the hangar doors opened without hesitation. Ewan had no sooner pulled the battered 'roo to a stop than they were swarmed by scouts and moles—and guards. That last party wrenched the glass apart, then pointed half a dozen guns at Ewan and Cerri.

"The Director wants to speak with you," Shane Powell informed Ewan with grim satisfaction.

Ewan swallowed, watching the security chief caress his gun's trigger. "Now?"

"This won't wait," Powell said, his eyes burning in triumph.

"What on Earth happened?" came another angry voice. Ewan looked past the goon squad to see Nichols running toward them, kit in hand. "O'Meara, what—get me a stretcher!" he ordered, as soon as he saw Gabe.

"I'm not going to Medical," Gabe growled. "If Rothchild wants a hearing, then that's where I need to be."

"But your leg—"

"Will hold for another hour!" the programmer snarled.

Wincing and panting from the effort, he pushed himself out of the cockpit and glowered down at the doctor with reddened eyes. “Don’t pretend you’re concerned now, Robert.”

Nichols stiffened. “I insist on treating it in the meantime. Gabriel, you’re not invincible.”

“I know that! Do what you must,” Gabe hissed, his rage clearing a path as he limped to the elevator.

Moments later, Powell was shoving Ewan front and center at the Director. Carmine Rothchild wore a severe expression, his face seeming even more lined than usual in the harsh lighting that blazed from under the blackened windows. To his left, Ben Root sat with his arms crossed. Next to the chief scout, Gabe was doing his utmost to ignore Nichols as the doctor operated on his leg. On Rothchild’s right was Karl Taylor, his face grave; beside him were Tree and Al’Dashan, each looking as worried as Ewan was suddenly feeling.

“What’s this about?” Ewan asked, making room for Cerri as she joined him.

“What an excellent question,” Rothchild said quietly, interlacing his fingers. “In fact, it’s precisely what I have to ask of you, Emissary.”

“Grandfather,” Tree said, “as Ewan’s chief, I—”

“May also be liable for the delivery of our most potent weapon into the hands of the enemy!” Rothchild snapped, making her flinch back. “At minimum, it is unbecoming of the future Director to be associated with such a disaster.”

“I think that’s a bit strong,” Tree muttered.

“I disagree,” the Director said oppressively, brandishing his tablet. “I have here a written report, submitted en route by Chief Reid, and I must say, it is damning.”

"What? Gabe!" Ewan whirled around to the programmer. "What did you say?"

Gabe regarded Ewan, his usual easy humor frozen over as the doctor worked on his leg. "Did you think I was napping? As I was otherwise incapacitated by your actions, I decided to use my time effectively."

Rothchild cleared his throat, turning the tablet to read. "Master O'Meara, according to Chief Reid's report, players willfully sabotaged the armadillo, rendering it ineffective in combat and causing him personal injury while attempting to fend off the Locusts when they arrived. Do you concur with this assessment?"

"But that's not the whole—"

"Do you concur?" Rothchild demanded, dark eyes flashing.

Ewan froze, then bowed his head. "I concur." He turned to Al'Dashan, straining against Powell's grip on his arm. "It was Patrick; he was the ringleader."

"I do not believe so," Rothchild countered ominously.

"Oh, come on! It wasn't me!" Ewan shouted.

"Master O'Meara, it is not always about you! I am referring to an additional report, seemingly unrelated, which was filed this morning by Chief Taylor. Chief, would you please share a summary with those assembled here?"

Karl cleared his throat, looking around the room uncomfortably. "Yesterday afternoon—two afternoons ago, now, I suppose—my engineers reported seeing a pair of players skulking around the Hole."

"Could you be more specific?" Rothchild asked.

"I don't have names," Karl said, scratching his head, "but apparently it was two men; one young, and one older, with gray hair."

"Father Brian," Ewan whispered as his heart dropped through his stomach. *And the other one was probably that Thomas person Patrick mentioned.*

"Where did they go?" Rothchild asked, his voice hardening.

Karl shrugged. "They sort of wandered around a bit. One of my people, Natasha, thought they were looking for Kate."

"Who was working on the armadillo," the Director finished, turning to Ewan with smoldering eyes. "Chief Reid's report indicates that vehicle was sabotaged before the battle began," he said, hefting the tablet like an executioner's axe. "Our most powerful weapon. Possibly enough to permit the staff to effectively defend themselves without any additional drain on our resources," he said slowly, each word a blow to Ewan's heart. "And now, our nomadic rivals have become a true threat. Emissary, do you even comprehend how irresponsible—treasonous, even—your players' actions were?"

"I do," Ewan answered through clenched teeth.

"Then can you offer me the slightest reason why I should not simply disband your entire section and return you to your original worlds?"

The room's air froze over, bringing everything to a halt. Ewan dared a glance at Tree. She regarded him abjectly, her heartbreak as clear as if she'd messaged him. But she couldn't, because they'd left Veridor to protect the Centrals from dangers no one even recognized.

I still am, Ewan thought bitterly.

He steeled himself, then met the Director's eyes. "Because if those players hadn't jacked the 'dillo, we'd be in even more trouble. We got set up by the Diamond Lord."

Al'Dashan and Tree stiffened on the edge of his vision, but the Director merely leaned back in his chair. "Master O'Meara, I expected more from you. There is no evidence that this 'Diamond Lord' even exists."

"You don't count losing over a hundred players as evidence?" Ewan snapped, earning another grab from Powell.

"That incident was tragic," Rothchild admitted, his tone

warning Ewan that he meant it for completely different reasons. "But the perpetrator has been silent, since then."

"No, he hasn't." Ewan glanced over at Gabe, but the programmer looked away and growled something at Nichols. "He's been behind the attacks on Tree's tablet, and I'd bet my life that he handpicked the Ether Swords who went to the Wastes. Every one of them, a troublemaker. Every one of them, a Mother's Child. No one in their right mind would have called them up, with only an ass like Coley to lead them. And then we went right to where the Locusts were waiting for us, with their own tanks!"

"That is speculation," Rothchild countered, but he was at least listening again. "Do you have proof?"

"I do," Cerri said, unruffled as all eyes turned in disbelief to her. "The D'jin which Ea'win Omi'ra speaks of, it spoke last morning to the surly man." She glanced at Ewan. "The one called Coley, yes?"

Ewan sighed inwardly. "Yeah. Vincent Coley."

"And I suppose Master Coley deigned to share this information with you?" Rothchild asked dryly.

"Of course not." Cerri gave the Director a pitying look. "I crept close and listened as they spoke, while Ea'win Omi'ra slept. Coley received instructions to deliver the armadillo to the insect people." She lifted her chin. "But I have injured it. It will take them many moons to restore its health."

She took the helmet from her ear, placed it on the desk, and activated its log. The Diamond Lord's message echoed around the room, with only the repetition of the words and the faint scraping of the endless sands against the glass telling Ewan that time was still working at all.

"This is troubling news, indeed," Rothchild said at last, his smugness gone. "But it doesn't explain what the players were doing in Engineering, or how they managed to sabotage the armadillo in the first place. Unless this Diamond Lord has been in cahoots with them, which seems at best unlikely—"

"But that's what happened." Ewan gasped, locking eyes with the Director as the pieces leaped together in his mind. "Gems of old, that's exactly what he did! Father Brian's been going on for weeks about getting visions from the Logos." Ewan turned to Gabe. "What if he's really been getting messages from the Gem?"

Gabe scoffed. "Surely, even he wouldn't be so stupid."

"He's a frapping zealot!" Ewan insisted. "Brian's wanted to be the Logos's prophet ever since he got deleted; he'd listen to anyone who said he was, no questions asked. And he'd pick whoever he was told to—the worst loonies possible—to log out and cause trouble here. I can't believe I didn't see it before. The Diamond Lord's been undermining us, making our Ether Swords into his tools through the Church, then setting them against the Centrals!"

Rothchild held up a hand to stop him. "But how would the Diamond Lord put messages on a player's tablet? He would need an account."

"Accounts are easily enough obtained," Tree said. "And manipulated."

"Yeah," Ewan growled. "And Frasier's a frapping programmer; he could do it like child's play—what?" he asked as the Centrals all drew a sharp breath.

"That is a very serious accusation," Rothchild said slowly.

"You're one to talk!" Ewan snapped at him, on a roll now. "It all makes sense. Frasier's been a hater from the get-go. Gabe, it's got to be him!" He turned to his friend for support but received a frosty stare in return. "Frasier's got the access; he knew how to hit me in Veridor. He's probably the only one who could slip your nets all these months."

Rothchild thumped his hand on the table. "But where is

your evidence? Why do you insist that Master Frasier has an agenda against you?"

"Because I killed his wife!" Ewan shouted. His heart churned, forcing the words, his failure, out. "She died in the Wastes on my watch, and he hates me for it. He hates all the players," he rasped, deflating as he caught Tree's eye. "And anyone who supports them."

Rothchild sighed and rubbed his temples. No one dared to speak.

"Chief Powell," he said at last.

"Sir!" Powell answered, tightening his grip on Ewan.

"Place James Frasier under house arrest. Keep it quiet; put out the word that he's gone on holiday in Veridor. Chief Reid, I want you to restrict his access however you need. Keep him working, but don't give him any more reasons to be implicated in this ongoing affair." Looking at Ewan, Rothchild added, "We'll simply have to wait and see if your Diamond Lord continues to be active."

"Thank you, sir," Ewan said, breathing his own shaky, bitter sigh of relief. *If you'd just been half as quick to arrest him as you've been kick my kind to the game floors, this mess never would've happened.* He glanced at Gabe, whose frown was deepening by the second. "I'll talk to my people about who gets logged out. We—I—have to do better."

Rothchild regarded him, dark eyes boring into his soul the way Tree's did, but with none of the affection. "See that you do. The players are on active duty in the first place because I have been reassured, on an almost-daily basis," he added, indicating Tree, "that they are effective at protecting the Centre's interests. Frankly, I have seen precious little evidence of this."

Ewan bristled. "They've been winning your battles."

"While fighting them for inappropriate reasons!" Rothchild thundered. He took a long, calming breath. "If anything, it seems to me that it has been one step forward, two steps back. Yes, we now have powerful weapons and the skill with which to use them, but as of this afternoon the Locusts do as well. Your service may be valuable in crisis, but the havoc you cause clearly shows your refusal—or inability—to adapt to our regulations, rules put in place to ensure the collective safety and longevity of humanity's sole remaining civilization."

"But—"

"At this point, if the players cannot offer the Centre something truly remarkable, then they have no reason to maintain a pretense of holding permanent status as Central staff. Do I make myself clear, Emissary?"

Ewan's fight gave out, his heart pounded into submission by the ultimatum. "Yes, Director."

Rothchild nodded, unsmiling, then addressed Tree. "In light of recent events, I believe you should recruit more of the players from Sah'rassa when replenishing your quota. Chief Reid's report does corroborate, albeit grudgingly, that the child, Cerri'dah, was instrumental in salvaging the situation. Have you made progress in recruiting more of her kind?"

"It takes time, Grandfather," Tree said. She looked dead tired, with the now-normal bags under her eyes also getting the bad lighting treatment. "It would be the greater part of a month to rehabilitate them and acclimate them to the Centre, and that is assuming that their Rajj will be amenable to sending forces immediately."

"You haven't been negotiating already?" Gabe exclaimed, shaking with bitter laughter. "Isn't the whole point of your section to make these players cooperate?"

"We've been busy!" Tree snapped, finally getting a viable target for the first time all meeting.

But Gabe met her, glare for glare. "Coddling your precious children? Such admirable service they've performed," he said, snarling as he slammed his bloody leg up onto the ancient desk. "You should have been there, Annie, instead of hiding behind that creature in your womb."

"Gabriel!" Nichols warned.

Tree cut him off. "I'd like to see you juggle your duties with a baby!"

"I wouldn't presume," Gabe replied with a malicious sneer. "But I find it telling that even the section chief has her priorities misaligned. What are you hoping to do, Annie? Procrastinate on the war until you deliver, so your husband at least gets to see the child once? Take a photo, perhaps, on the way down to the tubes?"

"Lay off of her," Ewan growled, alarmed by his friend's sudden display of the usual Central venom. "We're doing everything we can!"

"Enough!" Rothchild bellowed, silencing them all. "Chief Reid, you will remember your decorum; injuries are no excuse for incivility. Emissaries, I want you to put all effort into recruiting as many players as possible, as quickly as possible. With the Locusts in possession of an armadillo, I see no choice but to escalate to a preemptive strike before they can make use of it. I will call a general staff meeting to determine what possible corners can be cut, in order to support the additional forces," he added sourly, as though he could already hear Alice Spencer's shrill voice protesting.

Ewan started to laugh in the safety of his own mind, but then an idea jumped out at him. It was desperate, and Kate would skin him alive later, but as soon as he had it, he knew it was exactly what Rothchild needed to hear. "Actually," he said, trying to keep his voice confident, "we've been working on that."

The Director blinked. "I beg your pardon?"

"About the food thing," Ewan answered, bracing for a hedge and a half. "My sister Kate, the one who designed your bulletproof armor? She's also been actively testing theories for getting rid of the cloud cover around the Centre."

Again, the room went perfectly still. Ewan felt everyone's eyes on him, picking at his intentions and competence. He returned the gazes, seeing blank incomprehension on most of the Centrals' faces. But not all. Tree looked like she'd just been thrown over the Argentine falls again, and on the far side of the room, Gabe was thunderstruck, staring back at him as if Ewan had just proclaimed that he'd been a Gem all along.

Finally, Rothchild spoke. "That would be something remarkable," he said, emphasizing the significance of the words. "And it would be a sizable feather in your sister's cap. But what relevance does it have for your argument about increasing the quota?"

"Once the skies are clear, we could start growing food outside the walls," Ewan answered, unsure whether the old man was deliberately being thick or not. "Just imagine, stepping out of the hangar to fields of grain and orchards of fruit."

"But how do you expect anything to grow in the Wastes?" Ben Root asked, looking almost embarrassed to shoot the idea down. "Even if the clouds were gone, that ground has been dead for thousands of years. Mountains, coast, the northern reaches…I've seen a lot, but never anything alive. How could you do better, here?"

"We don't know how," Tree said softly, catching Ewan's eye with a look that mixed hope and resignation. "But someone in the simulations surely would. The people in the virtual worlds remember more of old Earth than we do."

"Exactly!" Ewan said, pouring enthusiasm into his voice to try and cover the bull. "You keep talking about players like we're resources, but you've only scratched the surface so far!"

"We shall see," Rothchild said, making a note on his tablet. "Nevertheless, I will be seeking out other ways to streamline the recruitment process in the meantime. Does anyone have anything more to report?"

A few minutes later, Ewan trudged home with Tree and Cerri, then flung himself onto his bed without bothering to change. "Nerf it all," he rasped, his throat still burning.

Tree sat down beside him and rested a gentle hand on his shoulder. "I'm just glad you're alive."

"Yeah, well, you'd better come with me tomorrow, then." Ewan coughed. "Because Kate's going to kill me."

15

MAKING IT WORK

THE NEXT DAY, EWAN THREW HIMSELF AT ALL THE JOBS HE'D BEEN neglecting.

Five minutes after the alarm rang, he was on his way to the Hole to warn Kate about his wild pledge to the Director. Not quickly enough: Rothchild was apparently a morning person. When Ewan stepped out of the elevator, he nearly crashed right into the old man, but neither of them spoke. The thunder in their eyes said it all.

Kate, on the other hand, had plenty to say, starting with demanding to know why the Director had come in to collect a progress report on a project she'd never heard of. Had Sam not been there to cool her down—and quietly scoot all the throwable stuff out of reach—Ewan probably would have spent the rest of the day in Medical. He apologized, of course, and promised to do whatever he could to help, but both he and his sister knew she'd long since outpaced him in crafting skills. When Ewan finally made his escape an hour later, Kate and Sam were bickering about whether it made more sense to try and divert the sand and dust, or straight-up block them with an epic wall.

Later, as he bowed before the Patriarch in Whitehaven's cathedral along with the other Ether Sword recruiters, Ewan wished he'd stayed in the Hole after all. The Holy Father's scowl was easily as ominous as Rothchild's, and Father Brian sputtered and argued about how he'd never have become the Diamond Lord's pawn, imploring his leader to dismiss Ewan's heathen cynicism. But Paul and Al'Dashan backed Ewan up, testifying about the character of Brian's recruits, and eventually, the three warriors won out. The Patriarch chewed them all out off the record, for tarnishing Veridor's standing with the Centre. Officially, though, he gave Brian an extended mission in the remote village of Dunbriar, and to Ewan's team he gave his blessing to conduct recruiting on their own—provided they kept the heresy to a minimum.

All in all, it seemed like the day would never end—but Ewan knew he'd be missing dinner when he emerged onto the bridge, right as Tree and Cerri entered the room.

"You've got to be kidding me," he groaned, ignoring Alex's laughter from the rail.

"Evening is the best time to see my grandmother," Cerri replied.

"But I only just got out! I haven't even eaten all day."

"I know," Tree said. "Here, this will help." She took his hand, then gave it a sharp pull to straighten his arm out and stab him with a needle.

"Ow!"

"It's just a metabolic inhibitor," Tree chided. "Robert sends his regards, and a reminder to check in with him before you log in for a full day."

"Right," Ewan muttered. He rubbed the hole in his arm, then realized Cerri was staring at him with huge eyes. "What?"

"You have elixirs!" she said.

"Hardly," he grumbled. "It'll just keep me from getting hungry."

"Yes, exactly! The Caitsid'h use such potions to give them strength for travel by day. When one drinks of it, she cannot become tired or hungry."

"Would you like one, then?" Tree asked.

"No. Night is coming."

Ewan shook his head. "How about you, love?"

"Not tonight," Tree said. "I have research to do."

"Research?" Ewan frowned, doubly so when she avoided his gaze. "On what?"

"If I knew, it wouldn't be research," she said curtly. "You have your assignment, Emissary. Get the Rajj to help, as soon as possible."

Cerri gave Tree a sly look. "I am sure she will strike an agreement with Ea'win Omi'ra before long."

"I'm sure she'll try," Tree muttered, but she did lean in to give Ewan a soft kiss on the lips. "Love, I'm trusting you to take care of this."

"Yeah," he said, wondering what had her so busy that she didn't even expect a check-in. *But she's right; it's my job. She's got enough in her inventory without having to worry about this.*

Ewan's Caitsid'h avatar materialized midway down a dune, a few hundred yards west of J'unai. Nearby, Cerri—Cerri'dah, again—lifted her hands to her ears as she watched the huge silver moon rise over the barrier mountains in the distance.

"I would not have thought it possible, but it is good to be home," she said.

Ewan gave her a little shoulder hug. "I'm just glad you made it back safely."

Cerri'dah huffed, but she spared him a little grin. "I was never the one in danger, Ea'win Omi'ra."

Ewan passed a hand through the fur on his head, deciding

not to mention how easily she could have been left behind. "Well, either way, you did great out there. Thanks."

"You are welcome."

They walked slowly, Ewan enjoying the cool breeze over his nose and the much-missed feeling of wide open spaces. Behind them, the once-blistering sun had already called it a day and tucked in behind the dunes. The very color of the air seemed to cool off, blending from the soft yellow of lingering sunset to a silvered black, so dark it almost looked blue.

If the Centrals saw this, Ewan thought, *they'd go all in to help Kate.*

Then he stopped, scuffing the sand as he gazed up in wonder. "Cerri, I know these stars. They're the same ones back home, in Veridor."

"That is no surprise," the girl said, padding on ahead. "Everyone knows the stars live beyond the mountains."

"Yeah...but why would Sah'rassa and Veridor have the same stars?" Shaking his head, Ewan followed her down into J'unai.

The girl's ears swung about like kites, alert for only she knew what as they moved into the village. The sandy streets were mostly empty, with only a few Caitsid'h walking briskly here and there, feet scraping the ground as they went. It was only when they started pointing at his party and slipping away into the alleys that Ewan began to appreciate why Cerri had been so insistent on coming in the evening.

"I don't get it," Ewan said. "If it's foolishness to go out by day, why do people in the villages sleep at night?"

"Because they do not leave the village," Cerri'dah said, as though this should have been obvious. "There are travelers, of course, and the Nightpaws work in the cover of darkness, but my grandmother keeps guards to deal with them," she added, her tone becoming embarrassed.

J'unai wasn't big, and before long, the emissaries arrived at the Rajj's hall. As they approached the broad, open doorway, two sentries straightened up, materializing long spears.

"Matis, let the others know," the one on the right ordered. "The spirit people return at long last, with Cerri'dah!" Almost apologetically, he moved to block the way forward with his tall, lanky body while his companion hustled off as though he'd never heard of a private message. "Welcome," he said, spreading his free hand palm-up. "Our glorious Rajj has retired for the evening, but if you will wait, she will instruct us in how best to accommodate you."

Ewan stopped a respectful distance away from the guard and opened his hands similarly. "We're sorry about the hour," he said. "We would have come sooner if we'd known."

To his surprise, the guard smiled broadly. "I do not expect an evening visit will inconvenience the Rajj at this point."

Ewan blinked. "What do you mean?"

"She has been sending messages over the mountains for weeks," the man replied, his smile fading slowly to a puzzled frown. "Have you not heard?"

"Not at all," Ewan answered. "I would've seen a message to me."

The guard frowned even more. "It would be indecent for a Rajj to message another's Claw. She would have sent for your Rajj."

Ewan groaned, picturing a pile of unread, increasingly vexed messages on Tree's bricked tablet, but the guard narrowed his eyes and chuckled. "She will see you. Doubtless, she does not wish to miss the chance."

"Great, thanks." Ewan sighed as he followed the others in, but his hackles rose as more and more warriors melted from the stone walls to flank them. Their ears were tilted toward his party, and in their flicking tails Ewan sensed an eagerness uncomfortably similar to his latest, mutinous wave of Ether Swords.

By the time they reached the main court, there were at least thirty Caitsid'h shadowing them. The Rajj gazed at the group, her own ears flattening slightly as she stretched lazily across her throne, but when she saw Cerri'dah, she smiled.

"My allies arrive at long last," she purred, rising easily to stand and face them with open palms. "We had begun to fear that the journey across the mountains had claimed you. Granddaughter, it is good to see you again."

Cerri'dah stiffened, fur bristling as if she couldn't tell whether the old woman meant it. "I come, with stories of the spirit *rassa*."

"Yes, yes, and I will hear them. But first, let us dine to celebrate your return." Raising her arms to the crowd, the Rajj said, "My granddaughter has ridden the winds and come home to us!"

Before long, the emissaries were seated at the great stone table, surrounded by more food than even Ewan knew what to do with. Everywhere he looked, the Caitsid'h were watching him with intent eyes—and a silence so loud, he couldn't hear Cerri'dah and the Rajj catching up.

He suddenly realized one face was missing.

"Where's Rocco?" he asked.

The Rajj's ears twitched. "He is not here."

"Oh. Where'd he go?" Ewan pressed, when she didn't elaborate.

The Rajj's ears flattened. "He has gone to Ch'ira."

Cerri'dah hissed, fumbling her goblet. "You have moved, then?"

"Yes, cub." the Rajj said. Her eyes were locked onto Ewan, studying him, and her lips were curling at the edges to reveal her fangs. "He goes to demand their Rajj's surrender. But you should know this already. Or are the D'jini not so powerful as they are thought to be?"

"We've been busy," Ewan said. "Our enemies have been, as

well. They...disrupted our ability to communicate with you, shortly after our last visit."

The old woman glared at him. "And in all this time, you did not see fit to visit us?"

Ewan's ears wilted on their own as he swallowed. "I apologize, but it wouldn't have been much use to come sooner. It took Cerri'dah weeks to complete the journey. She only just saw our desert yesterday."

"You are arrogant, little D'jin. You are obligated to heed our calls as well, yet you still presume to bend us to your own convenience." The Rajj's eyes narrowed, seeming to darken the whole room with them. "If you think so little of our alliance, then perhaps I should end it."

Frap, Ewan thought ruefully. *We must look like a bunch of freeloaders to her.* "Well, how can we help?"

"How generous of you," the Rajj replied dryly. "But you are here because you want something; do not strain your wit with manners. My Claw leads a raid on the Ch'ira, in repayment for a grievance they caused me." Her eyes flicked to Cerri'dah as the girl growled, low in her throat. "However, they have made an alliance with the Qa'ya, claiming that their spies have witnessed me consorting with the D'jini. Thus far, I had hoped to use your absence to dissuade them and make the Qa'ya leave, but now that you are here, you may yet be of use to me."

Ewan hesitated. "You want me to attack them?"

"Yes," the Rajj said, baring her fangs in a grimace. "J'unai is strong, but together, the Ch'ira and Qa'ya thwart us."

Ewan sighed inwardly. *Is this day ever going to end?* "As it so happens, my tribe has need of J'unai's strength, too. We need your warriors to cross the mountains."

The stillness of thirty pairs of eyes intensified, locking onto him.

"It looks to me like you've got plenty of people, just itching to go," he added.

"So it appears," the Rajj answered neutrally. She narrowed her eyes, probably to send the others a reprimand over the Logos, before turning to Cerri'dah. "But why is it that the D'jini suddenly need our help, granddaughter?"

Cerri'dah bristled, but only halfheartedly. "Yesterday, their enemies gave attack while I explored with Ea'win Omi'ra. Over twenty of the Dj'ini's warriors died, and the raiders stole a war-creature. I disabled it," she added, lifting her chin proudly before looking around the room. "Their sands will present no challenge to the Caitsid'h."

Several warriors laughed at that. The man who'd escorted them from the door thumped his chest and called out, "If Cerri'dah can best them, then we should go before there are no enemies left!"

"Be silent, Bach'an!" the Rajj scolded. "You are here to guard J'unai."

Far from looking chastised, the man smiled broadly. "Both the Qa'ya and the Ch'ira are busy with Rocco. No one is coming here."

"I will not release my protection until our enemies are defeated," the Rajj countered.

Ewan looked between them, and another wild, reckless idea seized him: a neat way to solve half his problems in one move. "Would you give them up if I brought you more protection?"

"Asst! You just said you lack warriors!"

"I said we needed your people for the Wastes," Ewan replied, suddenly grateful that Tree wasn't here after all. "But we've got a whole army of people who'd be perfect for guarding J'unai."

In his mind's eye, Alex opened a message box. [Tell me you're not serious.]

[Why not? Paul's got scores of recruits who haven't been able to train in a desert setting. We bring them here, let them guard the Rajj's halls and free up people like, um—] He scanned the lanky warrior's ID. [—Bach'an, here, to log out with us!]

"I accept your generous offer, Ea'win Omi'ra," the Rajj said slowly, whiskers rising in faint surprise. "On one condition. I will see these warriors for myself and judge how many it would take to replace my own."

"Sure thing." Ewan chuckled. *This is going to be perfect!* "Would you like me to summon them?"

Now the old woman looked at him in astonishment. "You can do such a thing?"

Ewan gave her his best rakish grin. "Oh yeah, easy!" Messaging Alex again, he asked, [Can you connect me to my Veridian party from here?]

A split second later, the names *Paul Castel* and *Tina Mayberry* appeared in his menu. [You want me to start converting their avatars?]

Ewan glanced at the Rajj, so full of herself. [No. We want to make sure the Ether Swords get used to the desert in their human bodies. Besides, the Caitsid'h could do with a little broadening.]

[All right...] Alex replied warily. [Are you going to tell Tree about this?]

[Only if it works. Paul? Hey, Paul!]

[Gems of old, Ewan. Don't you know what time it is?] came the bleary response after a moment.

[Oh, yeah.] Ewan rubbed his paws through his short fur. [Sorry to catch you napping.]

[Don't worry about it,] Tina replied out of nowhere, giving Ewan the strong impression his friends were quite close, especially for the hour. [What's up?]

Ewan explained his idea to them, half listening as Cerri'dah hammed up her description of Central life and how awesome she was. He had to admit she was good. Her antics reminded him of the way he'd spun his own yarns in Whitehaven's markets—what seemed like lifetimes ago, now—to buff the selling price on his loot.

[So you're saying I can get my people out on tour, with good training, in a place with respawns?] Paul asked.

Ewan grinned to himself. [Yep.]

[Awesome! When can we start?]

Just then, the Rajj sat bolt upright, ears pulling hard against the back of her head. "Asst! Rocco tells me there is a raiding party on the way!"

[How about in five minutes?] Ewan messaged.

[What? It's one in the morning!]

[They're about to get attacked. I just heard.] *Good thing I wasn't waiting around!*

A pause. Then, [But you should see what Tina's wearing!]

[No, I really shouldn't,] Ewan answered quickly, face heating under his fur. [And you shouldn't be, either. Get a move on, Ether Sword; I just signed you up.]

Trusting that the vanishing message box meant the young lieutenant was on his way, Ewan turned his full attention back to the Rajj. "Don't worry, ma'am. I've just spoken with my people in Veridor. They're sending a contingent of Ether Swords to help you defend J'unai."

The room fell to startled whispering as the warriors and courtiers quietly discussed the strange D'jin's power to speak over the mountains, just as they would to the Moon. Cerri'dah looked unimpressed as usual, but her grandmother gave Ewan an appraising look.

"I thank my allies for their aid in my hour of need," the Rajj said formally. "But I would have some of your Veridians travel to Rocco, as well."

Cerri'dah let out a low growl. "Old fool," she muttered, "see what your greed causes! You would command the D'jini themselves, and anger every other tribe."

Faster than Ewan could register, the Rajj's hand shot out

and swatted the cub in the face. "Do not speak to me of greed, thieving child. You know why I attacked the Ch'ira!"

"Even so, Cerri's right," Ewan said uneasily, watching the girl rub her wound. "My people are used to guarding cities. They wouldn't be much use on a raid."

The old woman gave him a flat stare. "An ally who will not march to battle has no right to request J'unai's aid in his own war."

"Believe me, I know just how you feel," Ewan said darkly. *How many times have I accused the Centrals of the same thing? I'm better than that!* "But I can't send my greenhorns off to battle in a world they've never experienced, not in good faith, at least. I've been here, though, and I've got plenty of desert combat under my belt these days. Would you allow us your warriors if I went to help Rocco myself?"

More murmurs broke out at that, but the Rajj lifted a hand for silence. "I have seen you fight, Ea'win Omi'ra. What you lack in competence, your D'jinic magic accommodates." She closed her eyes for a moment, shutting the hall out in her own way. "My Claw will judge your heart. If you fight well, and if your 'greenhorns' protect J'unai, then you will have our warriors."

The room's atmosphere simultaneously lightened and began to crackle, as the guards around the edges all stole glances at their leader, silently volunteering to see the strange world across the mountains.

Ewan bowed his head to the old woman. "Thank you, O Rajj, for your generosity," he said formally. "Where can I find Rocco?"

In reply, she sent him a party invite. He accepted and smiled to finally learn her name was Amad'hi, then scanned his map for Rocco. The Claw was twenty-eight miles to the northwest, in charge of a raiding party of thirty, if Ewan read the map rightly. He couldn't see any other dots to indicate hostile Caitsid'h between Rocco and J'unai, but by now he knew that didn't mean much.

"I will accompany Ea'win Omi'ra," Cerri'dah said.

The Rajj's expression softened. "I expected you would request this, young one, but I need you here. There is much we must discuss about your experience," she said, darting a surreptitious glance Ewan's way.

"But Grandmother—"

"No," the old woman said firmly, locking her golden eyes onto the cub. "Rocco tells me that it is Bri'jash who leads the Ch'ira to our doorstep."

Cerri'dah's fur stood out, and her clawed fingers dug into the table, grinding the stone. "I will stay. Ea'win Omi'ra, do not forget what I have taught you," she added, turning to Ewan with a hint of a smile.

Ewan nodded, but a message box appeared in his mind's eye. [All right, Ewan, we're ready over here,] Paul said.

[Commencing transfer,] Alex messaged immediately afterward.

"Um, Rajj," Ewan said quickly, "my people are coming. Are you prepared?"

Amad'hi didn't get a chance to respond, as thirty Ether Swords materialized right there around the table, in white tabards and full armor gleaming in the torchlight.

Weapons came out on both sides, as the Caitsid'h yowled in shock and the Veridians tripped over themselves at the sight of so many cat people.

"Easy!" Ewan called, wondering if maybe he'd been a little rash, after all. "Paul, it's fine!"

Paul whirled around, staring in dumbfounded wonder at the black cat using his friend's voice. "Ewan?"

Ewan flashed him a toothy grin. "I told you being an emissary was fun."

"Ether Swords, at ease!" Paul ordered, slamming his own

longsword back into its scabbard. His soldiers followed suit, though their firm stance warned Ewan they weren't as trusting as their leader.

"Ea'win Omi'ra, explain yourself," the Rajj growled, holding her Naza high—at him. "What are these demons?"

"I told you, they're humans," Ewan said evenly. *We must look totally stupid, from the bridge!* "Cerri can vouch for me."

Amad'hi turned to her cub, and Cerri'dah's whiskers twitched. "In the spirit tribe, all the people are furless and ugly," she said simply. "Their A'Meer has even less fur than these."

The Rajj stifled a laugh of her own. "I did not realize Sah'rassa was so fortunate. Now you see why I do not leave my hall unprotected, Bach'an," she said, returning her spear to inventory. Facing Paul, she opened her hands, palms up. "As Rajj, I welcome you to J'unai, humans from across the mountains."

Paul offered her a gauntleted hand, but he imitated her instead after a warning glance from Ewan. "It's nice to finally meet you, uh, Rajj. Ewan says you're about to get attacked?"

"That is correct," Amad'hi replied. "Raiders are swiftly approaching. Will your...people fight, to the death, if need be?"

"Sure," Paul said, bemused.

"Cerri," Ewan said quietly, "can you make sure they all get along?"

Cerri'dah nodded, regarding the two parties with unblinking eyes. "I will."

"Thanks." Clearing his throat, Ewan said, "Rajj? I'm on my way, to uphold my end of the bargain. Will you be all right here?"

"We will see," Amad'hi answered. "Go, and teach my enemies a lesson from the spirit world."

Ewan bowed in reply, then shot Paul one last grin before getting Alex to save him the long walk out to Rocco.

16

CH'IRA

THE PROCESS OF TRANSFERRING WITHIN A GAME WORLD WAS faster than logging in from the bridge, but it still left Ewan with the same dizzy feeling that he hadn't quite brought all of himself along. J'unai's hall vanished around him, dispersed into the blackness of limbo that underpinned all the Logos's worlds, only to be replaced with equal suddenness by a sea of dunes under a full moon that still looked three times bigger than normal.

"Ai! The D'jin appears!" cried a voice behind him, prompting others.

Ewan spun around, opening his hands to reassure them he was unarmed. Still dazed, he couldn't see much of the one man striding toward him, beyond his hulking outline and what looked to be a vicious spiked ball capping his tail's tip.

"Rocco?" Ewan asked. "Is that you?"

The Claw bowed, answering with a deep rumble. "Well met, D'jin. We were expecting you to cross the rassa, but it is good to see you can ride the winds."

Ewan frowned. "What's the rassa?"

Rocco swept his arm across the dunes. "All that you see, that is our home. Our world," he added, with a touch of weight on the *our* part.

Ewan followed the warrior's gesture. "You mean the desert?"

Rocco flashed Ewan a grin in the darkness, as Ewan's vision adjusted. "That is what the Moon says. It passes strange words to us. Maybe so that we can speak with spirits like you?" the Claw asked, flicking his ears.

"Yeah, maybe," Ewan said, guiltily picturing Alex clapping her hands on the bridge. "I guess you listen to the Moon."

Rocco's grin broadened enough to let the moonlight glint off of what looked like steel plating on his fangs. "Sometimes. But the Caitsid'h remember the old words, even if the Moon has forgotten them. *Sah*," he said, lifting his hand to the sparkling sky. "And *rassa*."

"Sah'rassa," Ewan repeated, surprised that he hadn't put that together sooner. *A world filled with sky and sand...and they're perfectly equipped for it.*

"Do you not have the sah and rassa, too?" Rocco asked. "Is that not why you seek our aid?"

"Yeah, pretty much, but we're a little bit short of the sah part, over the mountains," Ewan admitted. "We're working on it, though. Right now, in fact."

"That is good," the Claw replied. "For the D'jini, it should be a simple matter."

"We're not D'jini," Ewan said automatically, sensing a note of challenge in the warrior's voice. Claw, to spirit Claw? "We're just people out there, the same as you. If you log out with me, then you can see for yourself."

"But are you not mighty?"

"Maybe a little," Ewan answered, grinning in turn as he offered his hand in friendship. "But it's only when we butt into worlds like this that we get OP—overpowered. You can just call me Ewan."

Rocco hesitated, then slowly clasped his hand, his

demeanor warming as he did. "As you wish, Ea'win. Come, I will show you our enemy for tonight."

Ewan followed Rocco up the steep dune to the northeast, nodding to the other warriors. The sand felt cool under his paws, and he couldn't help smiling at his moonlit shadow, complete with huge ears and tail. He'd always liked cats: the way they knew what they wanted, and how they didn't need to depend on anyone else to get it.

He nearly bumped into the Claw when the other man stopped. [We must be quiet,] Rocco warned, switching to silent messages as he went to his belly and crawled forward, spiked tail flat against his leg. [The Ch'ira suspect an attack.]

Ewan followed him, struggling to keep his own tail down. [I thought they sent a raiding party to J'unai?]

[That group is led by Bri'jash, but they are mostly Qa'ya.]

[Is Bri'jash their Claw? The, um, Ch'ira's?]

Rocco's ears drew back. [He is not worthy of the name. Had he lifted so much as a whisker for Hara'noh, then we would not be here.]

The Claw extended a massive hand, and a long, thin reed materialized in it. Carefully, he pressed the reed's tip into the dune, rolling it back and forth as if he was trying to start a campfire. Ewan watched, bemused, as the reed slowly vanished into the sand until only a few inches remained.

Rocco pressed his lips to the tiny bit left, giving it a puff of breath, and then he pulled a little pad from his inventory and fixed it over the end. [Here,] he messaged. [The Ch'ira are hiding, waiting for us to come. See for yourself.]

Ewan scooted over and put his eye to the pad, then twitched in surprise. "I can—" he blurted, then caught himself. [I can see right through it!]

The little reed had emerged on the dune's far side, giving Ewan an impressive view of a village. Not that the village itself was impressive, not hardly. Its central oasis was perfectly still, and around it was a cluster of mud-brick buildings, but where J'unai's houses were clean, these looked to be half fallen down. The Rajj's hall had no light coming from its windows, and as Ewan squinted, he thought he could make out a place where the wall sagged awkwardly. Not a soul was visible, giving him the impression that it had been abandoned a long time ago.

He leaned back, offering Rocco another view. [It doesn't look very forbidding.]

[The Ch'ira are weak,] the Claw agreed, shuffling into place. [Amad'hi believed that would make them pliable allies. By marrying Hara'noh into this place, she hoped to make it a vassal to J'unai, once Hara'noh eventually became the Rajj here.]

Ewan closed his eyes, trying to remember what Cerri had told him on the game floors. [I don't see how that would help J'unai. Wouldn't she be a part of Ch'ira?]

Rocco smiled grimly as he pressed his face to the reed. [Perhaps, on the surface. But Hara'noh was strong, and she was loyal to J'unai first. Only a sh'takh would have spurned the chance to be Claw for such a woman, even if he was much older than she.]

Something about the other man's tone raised Ewan's hackles. Something resentful...and personal? [Do the Rajji always marry in from another village?] he asked.

[No. A wise Rajj marries her cubs to build her strength, but she always reserves her favorite to succeed her. With Hara'noh gone, Amad'hi had little choice but to secure her next alliance with Cerri'dah.] Rocco cast Ewan a measuring look. [We have worried about her for a moon since you left. Is she well?]

[Yeah, she's fine,] Ewan replied quickly, but his spine tingled. *Had I left her in the Wastes, I'd have been just like the Ch'ira!* [She's in J'unai, helping the others and a squad of Ether Swords work out a defense against the raiders.]

The big man was still, but Ewan could feel him relaxing,

standing down another notch. [You are a worthy Claw, Ea'win Omi'ra, but sometimes protecting your family means harming another's. We must repay the Ch'ira, but with the Qa'ya to help, they are many more than we. Will you lend us your strength?]

[I already told you, I'm not a D'jin.]

[They do not know this,] Rocco answered, flicking his ears toward the silent village. [Come. We should return to the others.]

They went back, first crawling, then walking once they'd gotten clear of the dune's crest. Ewan looked back, surprised they hadn't left a trail behind them, but the heavy, uneven hem on Rocco's cloak had dragged right across their tracks.

Ewan thought a lot that night, as he lay on his back a few yards from the others. What could he do in a fight here, with GM access? What would he be willing to do? The Centre needed the Caitsid'h in the real world; he was more certain of that with every moment. But could he bring himself to spam a Gem's might on some run-down village, if that's what it took to buy their help? *What's the right course?* he asked himself. *Cheating to protect the Centre, or staying true to my gut? Which will keep my own family safe?*

Dad...did you ever have to compromise, for us?

Eventually the Moon sank behind the dunes, leaving the world—the rassa—even darker. Shivering despite his fur, Ewan gazed up at the stars. Stars that were somehow the ones he knew, that his world shared with Rocco's. Stars that were the only light to go by, now.

[Hey, Alex?]

[What's up?] the programmer answered with surprising speed for the hour, comfortably far from his worries.

[I'm going to need full line of sight for the time being. I want to be able to see every Caitsid'h for miles around me, regardless of their stealth skills.]

The slight pause told Ewan she understood exactly what he was asking to do. [Sure, if that's what you want.]

[There's a lot at stake. Can you do it?]

[Yeah, easy. Do you want it for your eyes only? I can extend it to the whole party.]

Ewan watched Rocco, sitting cross-legged on a dunelet and looking especially mystic against the jeweled sky. [Let's just keep it to me and their Claw. On my mark?]

[You're the D'jin.]

Growling to himself that he was *not* a D'jin, Ewan got up and walked over to Rocco. The Claw's ears turned to him, but otherwise he made no movement.

"Hey," Ewan said quietly. "You said the Ch'ira were hiding, right?"

The big man nodded, eyes dark in the middle of his black mane as he watched Ewan. "They cannot hide from a D'jin's eyes."

"I doubt it," Ewan agreed, glad that his ally was so quick on the uptake. Reaching out and placing his hand on Rocco's shoulder for effect, he messaged, [Alex, let's get this over with.]

The result was instantaneous, like the life detection filter Ewan used in Veridor's caves, only a thousand times stronger. In front of him, Rocco blazed with an inner light, each hair glowing and illuminating the beaded braids in his mane. The Claw's massive chest was bare, aside from a pair of leather straps running crisscross, with a metal plate over his heart as they wrapped around to hold his scimitars.

Rocco's eyes widened in shock as he saw Ewan in similar detail, but as he glanced past Ewan's shoulder to his warriors, he leaped up with a roar. "Ai! We are surrounded! J'unai, rise!"

Ewan turned, calling up his minimap as he did, but he didn't need it. All around them, a good hundred Caitsid'h were creeping down the surrounding dunes with perfect stealth. They froze at Rocco's cry, but as one, they rushed forward, pressing their advantage before it was gone—still completely invisible, but for their glow.

The J'unai camp was armed and yowling in seconds, but they didn't stand a chance. "We cannot see!" cried one warrior as he swung wildly at the air, but his invisible enemy easily slipped past and stabbed him through the belly.

"Ch'ira demons!" another warrior snarled. "They are killing!"

"Kill them in return!" Rocco ordered, rushing forward to parry a lethal blow away from the man.

Ewan watched in stunned horror; then he drew his own blades and joined them. [Alex, give line of sight to the other J'unai fighters!]

After that, the battle began in earnest. The J'unai Caitsid'h all leaped back in shock as their enemies lit up, but then they counterattacked with deadly precision. A good two dozen Ch'ira died within moments, totally unprepared for their prey to fight back. The others slowed their approach, but they still attacked, trusting to their superior numbers.

"They are without their Claw," Rocco bellowed, scanning the area while swatting away attackers. "Rout them!"

Ewan dove right in, locking onto a hulking man wielding a barbed club. The warrior sneered at him with a mouth only half-filled with teeth. "Play with me, cub."

The Ch'ira brute took a wild shot, but he had nothing on Ewan's agility. Sidestepping the club, Ewan spun up under the man's arms and slammed his blade through the enemy's heart. The man fell to his knees, eyes glazing over, and Ewan gave him a courtesy decapitation to end it quickly. But as the head rolled away, Ewan realized with a sickening jolt that he was fighting like a Veridian.

Gems of old, what if that guy had been on his last life?!

"Rocco, how easily can your people heal?" he shouted over the fray.

"Our scars are reborn with us," the Claw shouted back.

Great, Ewan thought grimly. [Alex, don't let any of these deaths count. We're totally OP!]

[Sorry, Ewan, that's a core parameter. I can't undo a death without Gabe's approval.]

[Then wake him up and frapping get it!] Ewan swore, narrowly dodging a spear thrust. "Rocco, what's the end game? How were you planning to win tonight?"

Rocco grunted as he smacked a fighter to the ground. "We came for the Ch'ira Rajj's surrender."

"Then forget these guys. Let's go get it!" Ewan cried. [Alex, transfer my party to that crappy village over the dune!]

In a flash, the battle dissolved around them, replaced by Ch'ira's sagging buildings as the J'unai appeared right in front of the Rajj's hall. They shouted in alarm, whirling around with weapons still raised, but there wasn't anyone visible.

"Ea'win Omi'ra, you did this?" Rocco asked, panting as he caught his breath.

"Yeah," Ewan answered, gulping air as well. "I can't just go around murdering people, not if it's not even necessary. Besides, weren't they going to be your allies?"

The Claw gave him a long look, then nodded. "You are wise, mighty one."

"I'm not—"

"You brought us here on the winds," Rocco said firmly, raising a hand to cut him off before assessing his force. Of the three dozen warriors, about half were downed, stirring weakly. "Ann'is. Sha'naz. Tend to our wounded. Khad'ja, you and Shan'ti watch for the enemy's return. Ea'win and I must go to see the Ch'ira Rajj."

A couple of the healthier-looking Caitsid'h took up guard positions, while two others began moving around the injured, materializing bandages and dressings. Ewan tried messaging Alex to help, but he got no reply. Hoping it meant the game master had gone to get Gabe after all, he scanned his map, finding only one Caitsid'h in the entire hall. "She's in the basement," he said, then followed Rocco inside.

Once they were safely away from the others, Rocco let out a rumbling sigh. "I am troubled, Ea'win. I am the most vigilant warrior of my tribe. That so many of the Ch'ira could come that close…it shames me."

"I didn't see them coming, either," Ewan admitted. "I guess it's a good thing I buffed our vision when I did."

"Indeed." Rocco's voice turned sour. "The Ch'ira would have killed us in our sleep."

Just like the Locusts, Ewan thought.

They moved quickly, trusting their D'jinic sight to reveal any ambushers, but the most dangerous thing they found was a hole in the floor, half covered by a worn rug. It took only a few minutes for them to find the stairs and work their way down, and before long they entered a room, lit by a pair of candles on the far end that were somehow glowing purple. Between them, a frail old woman sat, cross-legged.

"He said you would be coming," the woman rasped, looking right at Ewan through eyes heavy with cataracts.

"Me?" Ewan said, surprised.

"Who is it that you speak of?" Rocco asked.

The Ch'ira Rajj smiled, baring broken fangs. "Ah… Amad'hi's Claw. Does my sister know no limit to her greed? She will stop at nothing to take what is mine to give."

"You refused to help Hara'noh," Rocco answered, advancing slowly. Cautiously. "We are here for revenge."

"I am certain you are," the woman replied, wheezing viciously. "You, who would have come by night to Hara'noh's chambers, while my Bri'jash did Amad'hi's bidding. We will not be humiliated by J'unai!"

Rocco growled, low and menacing, but he didn't deny the

accusation. “You humiliate yourselves. Your Claw does not protect you, leaving you here alone.”

The old woman chuckled, raising Ewan’s fur. “I am not alone, young fools.”

Rocco whirled around, blades up, and Ewan double-checked his map. “What are you talking about?” he said. “There’s no one here.”

The Rajj shook with laughter, nearly toppling over. “Not in body, perhaps, but He is here in spirit.”

Then Rocco flew backward and slammed into the wall, thrown by a force even Ewan’s buffed vision couldn’t find.

“Rocco!” Ewan cried. He ran over to help, but there wasn’t anything to grab at.

“Ea’win, be careful!” The Claw grunted, struggling against invisible bindings as his face pressed into the stone. “She has made a demon’s pact!”

The Rajj huffed a laugh. “No. Perhaps Amad’hi’s greed truly is surpassed by her arrogance. Does she believe she is the only one who can ally with a D’jin?”

Ewan’s blood froze. “What?!”

The old woman turned to him again, sizing him up with those sightless eyes. “Fur as black as the starless void, with eyes as green as the promise of life itself,” she rasped. “And as empty and foolish as such promises are. Yes, Ea’win Omi’ra, he told me of *you*.”

In an instant she was on her feet, not so much leaping to them but as though she’d been jerked up on a string. Her bony hand shot out, and a silver spear erupted from it, flying faster than Ewan could dodge. With icy, searing pain, it punched straight through his shoulder and pinned him to the wall.

Ewan cried out, half blinded by pain and panic as understanding trickled in. He yanked his menus up, but all he got was a flaring health bar, already down a full third. All his emissary submenus were gone. No bridge, no logging out.

Through the silvery wisps drifting up from the Naza, Ewan could see the tattered Rajj stumbling toward him, puppetlike, with claws out. "You cannot run, little mouse. My Lord has promised me a feast this night, that Ch'ira will become the greatest tribe in all Sah'rassa. Even now, Bri'jash carries His power to J'unai. By midday, you will all fall!"

Ewan grabbed the Naza and tried to yank it free, but it only scorched his hands with frostbite. "Alex!" he shouted at the ceiling, hoping against hope that the programmer had returned. "Alex, she's teamed up with the Diamond Lord! You've got to kill her!"

The Rajj cackled, darting up to nip Ewan's ear. "You have spirit, young fool! Struggle for me, and I will enjoy you all the more."

Ewan swore and snapped back, but it was no use. Off to the side, he could hear Rocco fighting to break free. Desperately trying to think of something, anything, to buy for time, he blurted, "Your Lord must be very strong to counter my magic. Who is he?"

The old woman paused. "He did not give his name. It is beneath a D'jin to speak commonly with one of the Caitsid'h."

"But you're not just a Caitsid'h," Ewan countered, wincing from the Naza's chill bite. "You're a Rajj! Are you telling me that you let this guy push you around without knowing anything about him?"

"I know that he hates you," the old woman said, but some of the triumph had gone from her voice. "He spoke much of how you needed to be destroyed."

"Yeah, well, he and I go way back," Ewan said irritably. "But if you kill me, you're missing your best chance to gain power for Ch'ira."

Rocco went still. "Ea'win Omi'ra, what are you doing?"

"My job," Ewan answered, not taking his eyes off the blind woman's. "My name's Ewan O'Meara, Rajj. I'm an emissary from the Centre, a village far over the mountains. I'm here to bring Sah'rassa's finest warriors with me, on the winds, so they can protect their families and find glory in the spirit world."

The Rajj growled. "You have made alliance with J'unai. What use are you to Ch'ira?"

Ewan shook his head. "You don't understand. None of you do, except maybe Cerri. You've spent all this time fighting each other, but now we've all got a new enemy, one we share."

"You speak of my Lord?"

"No." *Alex, where in blazes are you?* "I guess he didn't mention the Locust Nation at all while he was telling you how I had to die."

The Rajj frowned in confusion.

Ewan gave her the quick version. "They're searching for us all, to take our resources. If they win, we all die and can't respawn. Please, O Rajj," he said with as much patience as he could muster while her spear continued to drain his health. "If we don't work together, there won't be anything left to fight over."

Her broken eyes narrowed. "You did not kill my people," she said, reading her own menus. "Not all of them, at least."

"You're not my enemy," Ewan replied, mustering all the sincerity he could. He glanced at Rocco in apology, but he couldn't see the Claw. "Life's hard enough, without picking extra battles."

The old woman gave a wheezing laugh at that. "Your words are true, weak D'jin." Her bony hand gripped the Naza's haft, and a second later, it vanished, letting Ewan sag to the floor.

"Thank you," he said, rubbing some life and heat back into his shoulder.

A second later, a frantic message jumped into his vision. [Ewan! What happened in there?! Are you all right?]

[Yeah, I'm fine. Did you get Gabe?]

[I woke him,] she replied, slowly. [He says you'd need the Director's approval before resurrecting a terminal player.]

[Those people are dying!]

[I know...I'd help, but only the Director has the authority to reverse a death.]

Ewan punched the wall, pointlessly. *Stupid frapping rules! All they've done is let the Diamond Lord pit us against each other!*

His fist tightened. *Well, not anymore. I'll play his game, and beat him at it.*

He turned to face the withered old Rajj, who seemed to be watching him somehow through those creepy eyes. Fighting off a shudder, Ewan said, "So. How long have your eyes been like that?"

The Rajj's ears twitched in the darkness. "My blindness? It happened when I spoke with the D'jin. He would not appear fully until I put my Naza away, but his radiance burned me." She frowned. "Did Amad'hi not pay the same price for allying with you?"

"Of course not!" Ewan focused on the message box again. [Alex, I want you to reset the Rajj's vision parameters. You don't need the frapping Director's approval for that, do you?]

[No. Stand by.]

Ewan got back to his feet and dusted himself off. About ten feet away, Rocco was watching him with arms folded over his chest, saying nothing until he saw what his D'jin would do to the Ch'ira.

Focusing on the blind Rajj, Ewan asked, "Why did you do it?"

Her face fell. "To strengthen my people. Bri'jash feels the wind in his fur. He has for many moons," she added, flicking her ears to Rocco when he let out a surprised grunt. "That is why he did not search for Hara'noh. He is a good boy, my son."

"I don't understand," Ewan said. *Her Claw is her son?* "He feels wind?"

"She is saying Bri'jash lives his final life," Rocco explained, approaching them. "I did not know."

"You were not meant to," the Rajj growled. "Ch'ira is the weakest tribe in Sah'rassa. We all know this to be the truth. The J'unai, the Qa'ya...they would all make us their servants."

"But if Bri'jash is on his last life, isn't it dangerous for him to lead a raid on J'unai?" asked Ewan.

"Not anymore," the Rajj said, baring her blackened fangs. "The D'jin guaranteed his safety. He made my Bri'jash strong again."

[Ewan, I'm ready,] Alex messaged. [On your mark?]

Ewan nodded, stepping carefully in front of the woman who'd nearly killed him seconds before. "The Diamond Lord doesn't understand strength," he said. Slowly, gently, he placed his fingers on the matted fur around her temples. "He's only ever used it to tear things down. But me? I think it's for setting things right again."

[Now.]

The white film covering her eyes bulged and trembled; then a silver light burst through, dazzling in the darkened room. She cried out in shock but not pain, clutching Ewan's arms for support as more light burst through her fur, untangling it and restoring its softness under his fingers. When the light finally faded, Ewan found himself looking into the old woman's true eyes, dark and brown, with pupils wide in awe.

"I did not know the D'jini could do such things," she whispered, staring up at him. "You are not the scorching sun, Ea'win Omi'ra. You bring warming dawn, and make the plants grow."

"You're welcome," Ewan replied, smiling at her in relief. "Now, will you call off your raiding party?"

The Rajj blinked, then blinked again as she came back to the moment. "Yes, of course." She closed her eyes, reaching out over the Moon's rays to her Claw, but after a moment she shook her head, growling in frustration. "He thinks I am a trick. Your trick. He will not listen."

Ewan sighed. "Thanks for trying. Will you come with us, to J'unai? I can take us on the winds."

The Rajj hesitated, but her whiskers drooped. "I will come."

Rocco gave a soft hiss, then a growl. "Ea'win Omi'ra, *my* Rajj says the winds howl through J'unai. It would seem your alliance was not without gain," he said, turning to the old woman.

"It's fine, Rocco," Ewan said quickly. *If you count Caitsid'h dying for the Diamond Lord's amusement as fine*. He called up his map and panned to where Amad'hi and Cerri'dah were, on a short balcony overlooking J'unai's market plaza. "We can go help them now."

"My warriors are outside," Rocco reminded him.

Ewan eyed the Claw, a little concerned he'd done more harm than good. "Yeah, I know. We can all go—together."

The three of them made their way back to the main doors in silence. If Rocco had been hurt by the demon hand, he didn't show it. If he was worried that his Rajj's ally had just randomly made peace with her rival, he didn't show that, either.

For her part, the withered Rajj looked around her hall in the tired morning light as if she'd only just noticed how run-down it was. Growling softly to herself, she occasionally flicked her fingers out, using magic to straighten hangings or sweep clutter out of their way. Ewan didn't pry, but he was sure he heard her mutter Bri'jash's name more than once.

The J'unai warriors leaped up with weapons drawn the moment the Ch'ira Rajj came through her door, but when they saw Rocco and Ewan emerging behind her, they threw their heads back and let out a wild, yowling cheer which poofed Ewan's tail more than anything else that had happened that night. Rocco held up his hand, though, and they fell to silent attention.

"We are needed in J'unai," the Claw announced. "The Ch'ira made a pact with a D'jin of their own, but Ea'win Omi'ra has convinced their Rajj to help us and make peace." His dark eyes fixed on Ewan. "Can you take us all?"

"Yeah," Ewan said, already calling up his menus. "Um, Rajj..."

"You may call me Sashi," she said, accepting his offer to join the party. "My sister will not call me Rajj in her home, under the circumstances."

A second later, only the wind moved through Ch'ira.

17

CULTURE SHOCK

The first thing Ewan registered, aside from the dazzling sunlight, was the sound of battle. From every direction he heard yowling and savage cries, with Veridian battle orders mixed in, to boot.

He turned toward what might have been Paul's voice, but his feet tangled around something furry.

"Asst! Clumsy fool, watch where you are going!"

"Sorry, Cerri," Ewan answered. "I'm a little flash-blinded." *How far east did we go? It was only dawn in Ch'ira!*

"Use your magic, then," came Amad'hi's tense voice. "Sister…I do hope my D'jin treated you well when he captured you?"

"He has," Sashi answered. "In fact, I have allied Ch'ira with him."

Ewan's vision cleared just in time to see Amad'hi giving him an even flatter glare than Cerri'dah's. "Yes. Rocco said as much."

"Ea'win! We must fight," Rocco called from a few yards away, giving Ewan the excuse he needed.

"Yeah, coming!" he answered, drawing his blades.

It didn't take long to find the fighting. Enemy Caitsid'h

raced through the streets, but they looked so much like his allies that Ewan had to use his aura reading to put the map's hostile markers on the people around him. He charged into the fray with a roar, but the image of Cerri crying on the game floors wouldn't leave his mind. With every thrust of his sword, he worried that he was ending a human life in the real world, and that made him slow.

"Ugh! Rocco, how do I know which ones hear the winds?" he grunted after getting stabbed in the shoulder again for his concern.

"They wear robes of blood," the Claw replied, smoothly decapitating Ewan's attacker. He raised his hand to point at a Caitsid'h wearing a robe of deep burgundy, plowing through a line of defenders as he darted around the corner. "But most have enough sense to leave their weakened at home."

"Until they've been backed into a corner," Ewan grumbled. "What did Amad'hi do to these people?"

Rocco diplomatically ignored him and sprinted off to deal with a party trying to climb the palace walls.

Ewan turned back to the work at hand, feeling somewhat better about killing the snarling cats, but it was soon apparent to him that the other Ether Swords didn't share his concerns. When the lanky warrior, Bach'an, found himself outnumbered nearby, a Veridian woman rushed up and grabbed the enemy spears, providing him cover to strike back as they impaled her.

"Two for one," she explained, spitting blood. "I'm Sarah; you can cover me next time."

Bach'an could only stare, eyes wide and mouth agape, as she slumped to the ground with a grin.

Sarah wasn't the only one. The Veridians fought the way they'd been raised to fight, forming meat shields to buy time, or sending in the occasional berserker to gather the enemy around, only for their comrades to mow everyone down with volleys of arrows. Through the chaos of battle, Ewan could see

J'unai's Caitsid'h watching them with a mix of awe and fear, stunned and whispering to each other about the alien warriors who fought as if death didn't matter.

Then Ewan caught sight of the warrior in blood robes again, coming right for him. Putting a few spare points into his aura-reading, he zeroed in and confirmed the man was Bri'jash.

Not that he needed to.

"I see you, little D'jin," the Ch'ira Claw taunted. "You bring demons to fight for you, but they do not belong in Sah'rassa any more than you do!"

A squad of Ether Swords rushed up to block him, but he swatted them aside—with an ease that was all too familiar. Before Ewan could do anything, the enemy Claw swung his scimitar high. It ignited with purple flame, exactly like the torches in Ch'ira's basement, and he slammed it down to the hilt into one of the Veridians around him. The Sword gave a cry; then his body burst into smoke and vanished.

"You bastard!" Ewan bellowed, heart freezing and boiling at once as he realized what had happened. "Nerfing, cheating slime!" [Alex!] he messaged. [This guy's deleting players! Nerf him back already!]

[I can't...he's protected by some kind of encryption. Ewan, only a high-level programmer could've set this up!]

[No kidding! If you can't break it, get Gabe in here! And send Michael to the game floors! We're losing good people!] Ewan added as Bri'jash obliterated another defender.

The Claw leered at him, but then his eyes drifted down to the pile of corpses at Ewan's feet. "Are you truly as weak as my D'jin said? Can you not cast my warriors to the winds?"

He drove the flaming sword into another Veridian, removing her from existence.

Ewan rushed the Claw, but before he got three steps a blur hurtled past, nearly taking his legs out from under him. He staggered, then watched in shock as Cerri'dah leaped and swiped at Bri'jash's face, her own a mask of sleek fury.

"Sh'takh!" she snarled, leaping back from the death-sword as Bri'jash countered. "Your laziness killed Hara'noh!"

"Laziness?" Bri'jash rasped, seeming completely unconcerned with the gash on his cheek as his yellow eyes widened in recognition. "No, cub. I worked hard for Hara'noh."

"Liar!" Cerri rasped. "You let her die!"

She flew at him again, but Bri'jash ducked aside, scoring a hit on her back with his own armored claws. "I did not allow her death," he said as she tumbled onto the sandy, bloody street. "I ordered it."

Cerri'dah yowled in fury and attacked again. Ewan ran to help, drawing the Claw's attention, but Bri'jash made no move to defend himself, instead going all-out on the attack. He spun, tail whipping out and striking Cerri'dah with the steel barbs woven into its fur, even as he knocked Ewan back with the fiery sword.

Recovering quickly, Ewan faced the man down—but then he saw the cut on Bri'jash's face healing over, the flesh restoring itself through a D'jin's power.

[Alex, what's your status? Alex, come in!]

Ewan grunted, using both blades just to keep Bri'jash's away from his head as the Claw pressed his attack, but Cerri'dah struck at him from behind. Hissing curses, she stabbed her dagger into Bri'jash's back, then grabbed his head and bit his ear.

Bri'jash snarled, but he knocked her free with an elbow to the face. "You are weak," he taunted, ignoring Ewan's next attack by kicking sand in his face. "J'unai is weak. The Qa'ya are stronger. I knew they would ally with Ch'ira, if only they could be made to see. I abased myself before your Rajj, let her see my weakness. She saw only what she could use, never that she *was* used!"

Cerri'dah shrieked and rushed him, a bolt of brown and crimson. Ewan dove in as well, drawing the Claw's attention—

And a silver light, flaring everywhere, made him stumble. He threw an arm over his eyes, but the light was gone even as he did. There was a cry and a curse, and he looked out just in time to see Bri'jash fall onto his back with Cerri'dah on top, her dagger buried in his chest.

Then Ewan saw Sashi.

Her frail arm was outstretched, holding a now-shaking Naza that pointed at her son. Her eyes were full-moon, fully sighted as they took in Bri'jash's body, the knife in his heart. The blood flowing over the matching robe.

She fell to her knees with a cry.

The sound jolted Cerri'dah to her senses. She blinked, then scrambled back from the crimson pool soaking into the sand around her. "He—I—" She looked at Ewan, ears flattened, her face a mask of horror.

"Cerri'dah!" Amad'hi came running, Rocco right behind her. She swept her granddaughter into a hug. "You fool!"

"I don't get it," Ewan panted, half to himself. "He was way too tough to just fall like that."

"You forget the Naza," Rocco said. "No D'jin's power can overcome it. Bri'jash heard the wind's call, and it brought Cerri'dah."

The warrior looked at Cerri'dah, respect in his dark eyes, but Ewan could only see the girl who lost her sister. The girl who beat at his leg over the unfairness of losing players to the real world. The girl who had just sent another there to die.

[Alex! Michael! Tree! Anyone!]

All around them, the Caitsid'h came. Many limping, some on death's door, but no one else wearing the robes of blood. A tan-maned warrior, now missing an eye, stooped and lifted Bri'jash's scimitar, then bowed as he offered it to Rocco.

"Our Claw is gone. Ch'ira is beaten," he said simply.

Rocco took the weapon carefully, inspecting it for signs of D'jinic corruption before turning to Amad'hi. They regarded each other for a long moment, but then Rocco lifted his face to the sky and yowled in triumph. From everywhere at once the J'unai Caitsid'h joined him, making Ewan's fur bristle.

"Ewan!" Paul's voice cut through the racket, and Ewan turned to see him and a dozen Ether Swords approach.

"Thanks," Ewan said, absently.

Paul grinned. "Thank you. That was easily the best practice we've gotten all year."

Ewan started to reply, but he saw Sashi move. Half stumbling, half crawling, she went to Bri'jash and threw herself over him, weeping and murmuring.

"So that was the Diamond Lord's latest tool," Paul said.

"Yeah. Latest in a long line."

Paul clapped him on the back. "Don't worry, we got him. I'm sure they'll take him to task once he respawns," he added—just as the yowling stopped.

"There is no need," Rocco said quietly. "The winds have taken Bri'jash."

Paul chuckled. "Well, yeah, but he'll be back soon enough."

The Caitsid'h stared at him, in an awkward silence broken only by Sashi's choked sobs.

Oh, frap, Ewan thought with an automatic hiss.

"No," Amad'hi said. She released Cerri, then moved to stand beside Rocco, trading puzzled glances with her Claw. "The winds have taken him. He will not return."

Paul's brow furrowed, drawing Ewan's attention sharply to the fact that the lieutenant wasn't wearing a helmet. None of the Veridians were. "Why not? Did he glitch or something?"

The Rajj turned her gaze on Ewan, ears flattening in suspicion. "Ea'win Omi'ra, what does this creature mean?"

Ewan swallowed, bracing himself to deliver the hard truth.

"He, um...well, there are...differences, between Sah'rassa and Veridor."

The Rajj's voice was soft, but the menace in it was almost tangible. "What sort of differences?"

"We...in Veridor, there's no limit to the number of times we respawn."

"Yeah," Paul said, offering her the wry grin he used to smooth things over in Veridor. "I mean, Ewan's got one of the worst kill ratios I ever heard of. He's tried and died what, hundreds of times?"

[Lay off it, Paul!] Ewan warned, but it was too late and he knew it.

"I do not understand," Amad'hi said, barely a whisper now. Ewan realized that Sashi was sitting up again, watching them silently. "We are both in worlds that are dreams compared to the village over the mountains, are we not?"

Ewan nodded. [Alex, please come in!]

"But your kind." Amad'hi's lips curled, revealing her fangs. "Your humans. Why do the winds not take them, when they take us so soon?"

Ewan looked away, instead finding himself staring into Cerri'dah's amber eyes. Eyes that knew exactly what he was thinking, and approved even less than he did. "I...I don't know. I can only assume the programmers who made the worlds had their reasons."

"Programmers?" Rocco asked, crossing his arms—and still holding Bri'jash's scimitar.

Ewan heard the shifting of weapons, but he kept his eyes on Cerri'dah. "Yeah. Programmers, D'jini, Gems. It's the same difference."

"Wait a second," Paul said. "What about my soldiers?"

Ewan's fists clenched. "They're fine—the ones who died normally. Anyone who got deleted by that sword..." He wrenched his gaze to the cursed weapon in Rocco's hands. "I haven't gotten any response from the bridge."

Paul's face paled.

"Arrogant sh'takhi," Amad'hi hissed. "Why should we help your village, when we are so cruelly treated?"

"Because we might all die!" Ewan shouted. "Everyone on Earth gets one life, okay? What I'm offering is the chance to do something with it!"

"You only offer to help because you want something," the Rajj accused.

"Then we're on the same page!"

Cerri'dah snorted, then covered it with a rasping cough.

Amad'hi glared at her. "Granddaughter, does this D'jin speak the truth?"

"Nerf it all, I'm not a D'jin!" Ewan snapped.

Cerri'dah's expression was stoic. "Ea'win Omi'ra may be a fool, but he believes what he says."

The Rajj's ears flicked, and her slitted eyes took in the assembled Caitsid'h. Everyone was watching her. "Very well. Ea'win Omi'ra, since you have honored our alliance, J'unai will assist you."

Ewan sighed in relief. "Thank you—"

Amad'hi raised a hand, polished claws emerging smoothly from her fingertips. "But you must correct the mistreatment of my people. I will not suffer the winds to take us, when they do not take yours."

Ewan checked again for an update from Alex but found none. *Nerf it all, where is she? Where's Gabe? Is this his way of getting back at me for the Wastes?* "I'll talk to our Director," he said aloud, trying to keep his voice calm. "He's got the authority to make the change—if he'll listen to me."

"Worry not. We will ensure that he does." The Rajj regarded Cerri'dah. "The furless A'Meer over the mountains does not respect us. And why should he? There, we are all asleep. But no longer," she said, her voice turning fierce. "We will cross the mountains and defeat the spirit tribe's enemies. We will make the furless ones see our prowess. And," she added, baring her fangs in a cruel smile, "if their A'Meer refuses still to accommodate us, he will see just how awake we are!"

Cerri'dah huffed, tail lashing, but she returned the smile.

Amad'hi turned to the mixed tribes. "The D'jini toy with us, setting us against each other for their own sport. They treat the Caitsid'h as worthless!"

The Caitsid'h snarled and stamped their feet, kicking up dust.

"I, Amad'hi, Rajj of J'unai, say this is unacceptable. I call on the Ch'ira, and even the Qa'ya, to aid J'unai. We will not be cast to the winds!"

Yowls of assent erupted from all around. Sashi stood, straightening as she came to stand beside her sister, palms open.

"Ewan?" Paul whispered.

"The D'jini dare to interfere in our affairs." Amad'hi's voice was clear. Proud. Defiant. "Now they will see what the Caitsid'h do to their own. Rocco!"

The Claw thumped a fist to his heart, blood trickling down his arm.

"Take as many warriors as Ea'win Omi'ra can afford. Show the furless ones our power, and once you have, make their A'Meer see sense."

Mother of All, Ewan thought as the Caitsid'h roared. *We're going to need a lot more shockies, but the Director's going to get his army.*

I just hope he can win them over.

PART II

SKY

30 minutes to point of return at 20 m/s
1 day to point of return at 20 m/s
Lyceum, Main Campus
(S. Tessalor, Preceptor)
Public Notices
Gravitation will be disabled this week in Sector (16, 3, -6) for cosmological constant sensitivity analysis. Contact the Department of Alternative Physics for timelines. (Please specify your frame of reference.)
Due to unforseen feedback in knotted space, the Quantum Orchestra's performance of "11D String Tensor Concerto in D and G#" will be delayed until the Musical Sphere Auditorium has been reconstructed and recalibrated. Thank you for your continued patience.

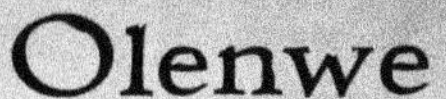
Olenwe
Current conditions in the vicinity of the Lyceum
(Space-time orthorectifited for viewing convenience)
1.5 days to point of return at 20 m/s
Department of Practical Mechanics
(S. Ouranious, Head)
Elysium
(Experimental; Jointly managed by Anthropology and P. Mechanics)
@SorayaCorcoran

18

A WING AND A PRAYER

EWAN COULDN'T SLEEP. AGAIN.

He lay in bed, holding his pillow over his ears as the night dragged on. Tree was snoring, but he was trying to block out a different sound: the soft crying that only happened when Cerri thought no one could hear her.

Not that Ewan blamed her; the kid had a lot to process. Sashi had forgiven her for what happened with Bri'jash, now almost three weeks ago, but there was a smoldering disappointment in Cerri's amber eyes, a prowling frustration that warned him the girl was even less satisfied with her vengeance than she'd been without it, to say nothing of having to cope with killing someone right after learning what that really meant. How would things have gone, if she hadn't come to Earth? Could she have accepted the fate of her sister's killer as stoically as the others, had she not known that the winds would take him to the hydrolysis tanks?

Could anyone? Ewan thought.

But life—real life—went on, as surely as the clock plodded from four to five as he lay there. October ground to a close, and the first wave of Sah'rassan players went into the shockies. Cerri officially joined the Emissary section and got her own Central grays. She badgered Lisa for fish until the kitchen girl finally stole a few from hydroponics and fried them up, only to discover that they were indeed foul-tasting. Cerri even decided Kate was an acceptable substitute for Ewan, and to his relief, Kate continued to take to her as well.

Like a big sister.

Another sob drifted across the room. Ewan pulled the pillow tighter, giving Cerri what privacy he could.

That was another thing Kate had done for him. Had she not stopped by every morning to take the kid to breakfast, he and Tree would never have gotten the alone time they desperately needed. Kate always had some new excuse, some new invention to try out on Cerri, and if the latest version of claws hadn't impressed the Sah'rassan girl, then the new waterproof face paint had. Not that it ever got the chance to be tested.

Ewan stared at the little dots on the wall clock, blinking away the seconds until everyone else woke up.

In exchange for Kate's morning interventions, Ewan took Cerri with him for the afternoons to buy Kate and Tree time for some new secret project, the apparent result of Tree's research. Tree refused to talk about it, which only convinced Ewan it was eventual trouble, but after the Wastes and his promises to Rothchild, he'd been in no position to argue with either his wife or his sister. So he left them to it, leveling his 'roo-driving skills by taking Cerri on less dangerous tours of the surface world, or getting her settled in with the re-specked Ether Corps.

The pink ribbons—and most of their wearers—had disappeared as quickly and quietly as Father Brian had. Ewan, Al'Dashan, and Paul made the most of the opening, picking a few distinguished veterans from the Battle of J'unai to log out along with the Sah'rassans. The Director had ordered a temporary halt to all scouting missions until the Locusts' next move could be ascertained, but he did allow the remaining Ether Swords to maintain their posts around Ewan's cramped apartment. The Veridians had tried to take up new positions around James Frasier's room, too, but after a standoff with Jeff Harper—now armed with his own gun—Tree asked them to focus on the players' residences instead.

The blanket got yanked off Ewan's back as Tree lurched to sitting, then scrambled out of bed for the bathroom. A moment later, foul air wafted out, driving Cerri under her cot with a hiss.

Ewan moved the pillow to his nose and groaned at the clock. Five thirty. Tree's morning sickness was getting earlier and involved...less vomiting, at least.

Just as Lucia had predicted, Tree was beginning to show, ever so slightly. Nothing a regular staffer would notice, but enough for Ewan to see the difference when she disrobed. Her tastes had changed, too. Lisa was overjoyed when Tree developed a ravenous craving for the same hot sauce she'd despised, and thanks to the pregnancy, Tree got double portions.

At least her grandpa still bends the rules for her, Ewan thought irritably. *Unlike frapping anyone else.*

The day after J'unai, Ewan and Tree had stood with Cerri in the Director's office while she performed her first official duty as emissary: proudly delivering word of her grandmother's cooperation—and Amad'hi's terms. Rothchild gave Tree a long-suffering look, then bluntly told them all that changing the respawning rules was out of the question. Ewan argued that cooperation went both ways or not at all, but the Director refused to budge, calling Ewan a hypocrite for demanding GM intervention after all his railing about Frasier.

Cerri replied to the furless A'Meer with nothing more than a mutinous glare, but Ewan understood her sentiment clearly:

her people had removed the D'jini before, and they would do so again if necessary.

Ewan glanced at the clock again: a quarter to six.

How many other game worlds had similar traditions? Tales of epic wars for freedom from divine overlords? Ewan had only been to Veridor and Sah'rassa, but their histories warned him that the Centrals' prejudices against players were nothing compared to how the players felt about abusive game masters. That thought kept him up at nights, even more than his roommates. If the active players ever did outnumber the Centrals, there could very well be a revolution.

Ewan shifted, making room as Tree came back to bed. *The worst part is, Rothchild probably agrees with me.*

Not that the Director was ready to quit recruiting players. Far from it. He'd had Gabe out in the Wastes almost constantly, searching for clues to the Locusts' intentions—all of which said the nomads were fanning out, searching for their epic weapon. The Centre couldn't support enough players to chase them all over the world, though, so Rothchild focused on increasing his own forces to counter whatever attack was coming.

As for Gabe...the programmer had barely said two dozen words to Ewan since the Wastes, none of them friendly or forgiving. Their sparring sessions had ended abruptly now that the Diamond Lord was under house arrest, and when Ewan offered to train anyway, Gabe tersely replied that they both had more pressing tasks.

Just more foul, stubborn air, Ewan thought bitterly.

A muffled pounding came from the main door.

"Hey!" Kate's voice called. "You up yet?"

Ewan sighed and sat up, putting the pillow away. "Why don't you use the door chime like a civilized person?"

"That's for sissies. Can I come in, or am I going to get an eyeful?"

Tree sat up beside him, drawing her robe closer. "Come in."

The door flew open, stabbing Ewan's eyes with light from the hall beyond. Kate strode in, wearing athletic gear, then dropped a couple bags of food on the table.

"Good morning," Tree said neutrally, as Cerri emerged from under the cot to claim her meal. "Aren't you going to eat?"

"Already did." Kate's eyes flicked to Ewan. "Actually, we're on the clock."

Tree stiffened, but her nostrils flared and her stomach growled. "Can it wait until after breakfast?"

Kate checked her tablet, frowning. "I think so." She tossed a bag to Tree, who tore into it with a fury that belied her earlier upset. "I got extra sauce from Lisa," she added, indicating a sealed cup inside.

Tree snatched it and downed it in one shot. Her eyes bulged, and she cried out in an unnerving mixture of rapture and pain.

"Gems of old," Kate muttered.

Cerri regarded Tree. "That would make a potent weapon."

Tree nodded, coughing as she gave the Sah'rassan girl a watery smile. "It seems the baby has a taste for it, now." She shook her head, clearing it, and turned to Ewan. "Love, would you mind taking Cerri for the morning?"

"I think he ought to stay, this time," Kate said. "Stu wants to meet more of us."

An uncomfortable, familiar feeling stirred in Ewan's gut. "Stu?"

"Kate," Tree warned. "As your chief, I must choose what information to share."

The feeling shook itself awake and began pacing, that dread that always came when Tree spoke like her grandfather. "Who's Stu?" Ewan asked warily.

"It is not a Caitsid'h name," Cerri said.

"It sounds Veridian," Ewan grumbled.

"I just gave him a nickname," Kate explained. "Because 'Sturilius' is a frapping mouthful."

"Kate!" Tree snapped.

Suddenly, the secret project came together in Ewan's mind. "You made contact with a new world!" he accused, rounding on his sister. "Gems of old, don't you know how dangerous that is?"

"I was at the rail," Tree cut in, shooting eye daggers at both of them.

"Yeah, but look what happened to you on first contact! And me!"

"Don't lump me in with you noobs," Kate huffed. "I can be charming and persuasive when I want. I just went to their college and introduced myself, told them where I was from. They seemed fine with it."

Ewan scrubbed his fingers through his hair. "You're kidding me."

Kate grinned. "Yeah, well, they can't all be as uptight as the Church or greedy as that Rajj. No offense, Cerri."

"None taken," Cerri replied magnanimously.

"But why tell us now?" Ewan asked. "And why all the secrecy in the first place?"

For once, Kate looked to Tree, drawing a resigned hand wave before answering. "Ever since you threw us under the wagon about the cloud-clearing thing, we've been looking for a world with people smart enough to do it. Now we think we've got one, even if they're not too practical."

The dread in Ewan's stomach paused, stretched, and curled up into guilt. "That's good news. You could have told me," he added to Tree.

Tree avoided his eyes. "I felt it would be...prudent to demonstrate what our section could do, independent of your efforts."

So your grandpa would know I hadn't frapped it up this time.

The guilt idly scraped Ewan's throat. "It sounds like you two have it all worked out, then."

"Pretty much," Kate said, turning to Tree. "But I got a message from Stu half an hour ago. He wants to meet with more of us."

"Why?" Tree asked, her eyes narrowing.

"He said he wanted to get a better feel for our culture, what we represent or something. I'd have taken Sam, but he hates flying and I'm tired of making him try."

Ewan blinked. "Flying?"

"Yeah." Kate hesitated, trading another glance with Tree. "We should just show him."

"I wish to see this new world as well," Cerri said. "I am an emissary, too."

Tree looked at them in turn, as though she was already crafting excuses to the Director for when things went south. Then she sighed and placed her empty plate on the nightstand. "Fine."

Ewan couldn't help noticing the way they skipped Medical and went straight to the bridge, or how Kate locked the door behind them. The room was empty, but Tree moved smoothly, if slowly, to the rail and logged in. As Kate helped Cerri into her tube, Ewan watched his wife, stooping over the console with rounded, stiff shoulders. Suddenly, he didn't think it was just the baby's weight.

She's carrying my baggage, he thought. *Just like the Central she is. How much time has she spent, cleaning up my messes that I don't even hear about?*

He sidled up and rubbed her shoulders, noting that she'd signed the flying camera into a game world named Olenwe. "Hey. I'm sorry, for drawing your grandpa's aggro. You've got enough on your plate...which I guess is also my fault."

Tree angled into his hands and sighed, but this time there

was a hint of contentment to it. "I just want to ensure our child has a world in which to grow, with her father still here."

"Me, too," Ewan said quietly. "A better world."

"Love, try to stay calm."

Ewan started to ask why, but the main screen activated to reveal a scene that left his jaw hanging. A collection of islands floated in a misty golden sky, just...hanging there, against all reason. Tree zoomed in, and the central island's features resolved into alabaster towers and buildings that reminded him of Whitehaven, except there weren't any walls. A flock of large birds swooped through the skies above, darting to and from the city. Narrow trees dotted the steep, rocky slopes, and hanging vines trailed over the islands' edges, alongside streams of water that cascaded into mist as they fell into the open space below.

The camera sailed toward the island, adding to Ewan's vertigo as it panned down across the impossible landmass.

Beside him, Cerri drew in a sharp breath. "Those people are flying!"

Ewan looked again, blinking as he saw that she was right: the birds weren't birds at all, but people. Except these people had massive feathery wings, reaching out from behind their backs. Their hair was platinum, and they were all dressed in the purest white robes—

His hands clenched the rail, but his blood boiled. It had to be a glitch. A joke!

But no one was laughing. Instead, they were all watching him like he'd just yelled. Which, he realized, he had.

Ewan kept his voice as level as he could. "You've got to find another world."

Tree sighed. "Love, this was why I didn't want to involve you."

Kate rolled her eyes. "Those people don't even know who the Diamond Lord is."

"But they look just like him!" Ewan exploded, rounding on

her. "They're frapping angels, and you went and asked them for help?!"

Kate jabbed a finger at the screen. "They're as human as we are, just like Cerri!"

"I am Caitsid'h," the girl said, regarding Kate from behind her painted spots. "This is merely the form I wear across the mountains."

"You see? Cerri understands!" Ewan barely kept his voice from snarling. "You can't log into a world full of Gems and expect them to give a frap about our problems!"

"They're players, not Gems, and I don't need them to give a frap. I just need a frapping idea!" Kate shouted back. She leveled a glare at Ewan, then exhaled angrily. "E, whatever else they are, they're brilliant."

"They're going to jerk you around," Ewan insisted. "Kate, you can't trust them."

She crossed her arms. "I'm telling you now, if we blow this chance, you can kiss your clear skies goodbye."

Ewan turned to glower at the winged people, flitting about their business without a care in their fake world. His heartbeat thundered in his ears. "But we have to clear the skies."

"Then get over yourself and help me get them cleared!" Kate snapped.

Ewan crushed his eyes closed, trying to drive out the images, the blood and screams in Whitehaven's square. The blood and screams in J'unai. In the Wastes, at Fort Gilmer. "But...why me?" he whispered.

"Because you owe me, big time," Kate said. "And I'm calling it in."

Then a hand, Tree's hand, cupped Ewan's chin and turned him to face her. "Because you're an emissary," she said quietly.

His anger evaporated at her tone, leaving regret and guilt in its wake. Even without looking, he could picture her brown eyes boring into him, reminding him how little cushion they had anymore. Win or lose against the Locusts, the players' days were numbered, pending some sky-clearing miracle from Kate. And if Kate needed divine intervention to get it, who was he to block her?

Hadn't he made things hard enough for everyone, already?

Ewan sighed, but he kissed her hand as he opened his eyes. "I'll try."

19

THE LYCEUM

WHEN HE'D FIRST LOGGED OUT OF VERIDOR, EWAN HAD THOUGHT the Earth was beyond his wildest imagination. But about five minutes after logging into Olenwe with Kate and Cerri, he decided his wildest imagination had been slacking off.

They hadn't come straight here, of course. Tree shunted them through the ready room—this time, an unnervingly small spit of land with endless golden skies in every direction—to adjust their avatars for flight. The way his robes billowed in the breeze made Ewan uncomfortably aware of how little he was wearing underneath them, but the worst part was the wings. The change itself wasn't the problem: he'd already experienced the weirdness that took him from human to Caitsid'h. But watching crimson feathers erupt from Kate's back set his nerves off again, and his reflex to cover himself with his own wings of jet black didn't help.

But they'd made it through, and before long their random island—*sulianus*, Kate called it—was suddenly surrounded as an archipelago of *suliana* blinked into being around it, all lazily drifting in different directions on the wind. Those other suliana seemed to come from nowhere, but when Ewan recognized the college from the bridge monitors, he suspected it was their own little island that had done the appearing. From their position, the white buildings were a good mile distant, shimmering in the golden light that seemed to permeate the sky without the benefit of a sun to produce it.

Kate tossed her hair back behind her wings. “Okay. Their college, the Lyceum, is over there on the big sulianus. Ready to fly over and say hi?”

“I am uncertain about this,” Cerri said nervously. She crouched to peer down over the edge, the size and coloring of her wings reminding Ewan of a sparrow. “What happens if we fall?”

“That’s one of the coolest things about this place,” Kate said with an evil grin. “There’s no bottom. Fall far enough, and you’ll end up high above. Kind of like how if you were to walk east far enough, you’d come back to where you started.”

Ewan couldn’t help smiling when Cerri gave Kate the flat, incredulous stare she normally used on him. “You cannot walk east to go west!”

“Not in Sah’rassa, no,” Ewan said. “But Earth and Veridor are both round. I guess Olenwe is…even more round?”

Cerri’s feathers seemed to stand on end, and her small hands clutched the grass on the edge. “I do not like this place.”

“Here, let me show you how to do it,” Kate said. She unfurled her wings and flexed them, beating down the air around her with such force that she flew up about ten feet. She leaned forward and stretched out into a glide, coming back in a tight loop and landing again on the ground. “There, you see? Nothing to it.”

Ewan and Cerri traded a queasy glance.

“Oh, come on!” Kate snapped. “It’s not like you can die here.”

Ewan started to reach for Cerri’s hand, but her wings got in the way. “I can haul you,” he offered.

Cerri huffed, steeling herself. "If Kai'tah can fly, then I will too." Before she could think better of it, she leaped off the ground.

And plummeted like a rock over the side.

"Ea'wiiiin!"

Ewan swore and dove after the girl. The air felt surprisingly thick, hooking into his wings, forcing him to fold them in just to fall quickly enough to catch up—or down—to the panicked Sah'rassan. Cerri flailed below him, arms and legs and wings swinging about in a desperate attempt to right herself that made her tumble even more erratically as she fell.

After a moment, he managed to draw level with her. Trying to ignore his every instinct yelling at him that falling was bad and that the last time he'd fallen this far he'd ended up in an icy lake and nearly died, Ewan grabbed Cerri's hand and turned her to face him. Her eyes were wide with terror, and her face was so pale, it was almost white. He took her other hand to steady her, and the two of them fell freely together.

"You're doing great!" Kate called, lying on her side as she fell nearby. "Isn't this fun?"

"No!" Ewan and Cerri yelled together.

"You just don't know how to do it yet. The seraphim told me everyone makes a few down-laps at first, but the best way to learn is to try."

To demonstrate, she tucked her body into a tight line and shot down past them, then flung her wings wide and swooped back high. Smiling enough to brighten the sky further, she circled them, moving with more grace than Ewan had ever seen her do.

How long has she been logging in here? he wondered darkly.

"It's all about the airflow," Kate explained, angling down to grasp Cerri's wings. "It responds to the way your body is shaped. Now that you're on your belly, try and open your wings to slow your descent."

Cerri obeyed, and the next thing Ewan knew, her hands were wrenched out of his as she suddenly stopped falling. He quickly opened his own wings, working out how to flex them with his back, and managed to transfer his momentum sideways. He swung around in a broad circle and dove again, waving as he passed the girls.

"Okay, I think I've got—"

He hit their little starting island with enough force that his body should have been a puddle. Instead, he felt only a light tickle as his face flattened into the ground, which gave way like a mattress until he'd stopped moving. No pain, much less death.

Totally unrealistic.

"You got it all right. Right in the kisser!" Kate laughed, helping Cerri to a somewhat more dignified crash landing.

"Ugh," Ewan replied, hauling himself up.

Kate thumped him on the back. "Pansy. It didn't hurt; you're just used to thinking it should."

"Yeah, well, I think that's a good thing!" Ewan shot back. "Cerri, you can still piggyback with me you if you want."

"After that crash?" Kate snorted. "If anyone's going to haul her, I will."

Cerri gave Ewan a look that said she'd clearly rather stick with him, but Ewan sighed. "She is the better flier. For now."

"Is that a challenge?" Kate wrapped her arms around Cerri and opened her wings again. "Last one there's a scrub!" she taunted as she flung herself into the golden sky.

[Go get her,] Tree messaged from the rail.

Face still tingling—in his mind, at least—Ewan flew after them. The wind streamed around his body, pressing his hair down his neck. He endured a momentary vertigo as he looked down and saw another sulianus shoot past a hundred yards below, but he gritted his teeth and beat his wings harder, racing to catch up.

After a minute or two, he began to get the hang of it, especially once he stopped treating flying like swimming and acknowledged gravity and wind as the dominant forces here. The air, which had felt thick in his feathers earlier, was still much thinner than water. That meant Ewan moved more on momentum than muscle, using the great wings to make adjustments rather than to actually propel himself along. By cupping them from the back, he could scoop the air and flip himself upright as he braked. When he tucked them in or tilted them forward, it was easy to picture his entire body as a blade, knifing through the air with its keen edge.

By virtue of his superior agility, Ewan managed to get within reach of the others just as they touched down onto a marbled courtyard, on the central hill dominating the main sulianus. Laid in front of a domed white building higher up on the hill, the courtyard was ringed with thin columns, each sporting a peculiar golden symbol near the top.

Kate grinned as Ewan cupped in and landed lightly on his feet a few moments behind her. "You know, I think that's the first time I ever beat you in a race."

She released Cerri, and the Sah'rassan girl stumbled forward and fell to her knees, retching. Aside from some nasty coughing, though, nothing came out.

Ewan went to her and put a hand on her shoulder. "You going to be okay?"

Cerri nodded, still breathing hard, but she stared at the ground as though expecting it to suddenly vanish.

"Look alive," Kate murmured as she poked Ewan's shoulder with a wing. "Stu's coming."

Ewan looked up to see a tall angelic man, clad in white as they were. He descended the stairs from the building, walking with a dignity that plainly said he thought flying a mere twenty yards down was beneath his station.

"The red horse returns to us," the angel said with a smile as he approached them.

Ewan automatically reached for his unequipped swords when he heard the man's voice, resonating with harmonic overtones just like the Diamond Lord's had. *No one in my party has extra voices!* But he hesitated when Kate casually waved hello.

"And you have brought your family, as promised." Their host moved gracefully to Ewan. His avatar wasn't an exact copy of the Diamond Lord's, still clear in Ewan's memory, but it had all the most irritating features: easily seven and a half feet tall, with silver eyes smug and self-assured under chin-length platinum hair.

Ewan met his gaze without blinking or smiling.

"The dark horse appears quite formidable," the angel mused.

He turned to Cerri, still kneeling. "And this subject's illness and face mark her as the white horse, despite the sullied coloration of the feathers. Curious."

He lifted his hand, and Cerri lurched up to standing, as though jerked up by invisible strings.

Like a frapping puppet, Ewan thought with a growl. Equipping his swords, he yanked them over his head and rushed the bastard, but Kate quickly stepped between them, as if she didn't remember when the Diamond Lord had moved her just like that.

"Knock it off, E!"

"Get out of my way," Ewan snarled, as he tried again to lunge at the angel. "Nerfing Gem! Put her down!"

The angel looked up in mild surprise, then released Cerri to drop back to the stone. "I thought it was the red horse which brought war," he murmured to himself, before smiling thinly at Ewan. "My apologies, dark one. I meant no disrespect."

Ewan kept trying to shove past Kate, but Tree's voice

resonated from the air above him, startling them all. "In our worlds, we do not move people without first asking permission."

The angel recovered quickly, opening his arms and wings magnanimously as he addressed the invisible camera. "I understand. Consider it a necessary faux pas when dealing with the outsider culture. It is my honor to speak with the pale horse, most of all."

"What are you talking about?" Ewan snapped, stepping back from Kate. "We're not horses!"

"You are most clearly not seraphim," the man replied. "Even if Katrina had not advertised her origin, we would have recognized the signs." He spread his wings and bowed low to the three—four—of them. "It is my pleasure to welcome you all to the Lyceum. I am Sturilius, Preceptor and Chief Administrator. How may I address the rest of you?"

Ewan slowly resheathed his swords, but he kept them equipped. "My name is Ewan. I'm Katrina's older brother," he added pointedly.

Cerri finally stood, scowling up at the angel. "I am Cerri."

"And who, may I ask, represents the pale horse?" Sturilius said, his choral voice turning eager.

"You may address me as Treanna."

"Excellent! Please, follow me and allow me the honor of showing you the Lyceum and its myriad achievements."

The tour that followed was one of the strangest things Ewan had experienced in his near-eighteen years. The Lyceum reminded him vaguely of a beehive, with classrooms grouped into clusters. Each was connected to its neighbors by stone doors—although stone didn't flow aside as one approached—so that a person could move from one room to another without ever returning to the main corridor. In every room were angels, or seraphim, as Kate and "Stu" insisted on calling them. Some were studying, reading from a mixture of vellum scrolls and high-tech consoles, while others performed experiments involving orbs of light and fluids that floated as unnaturally as the skyland they stood upon.

Ewan didn't even try to understand Sturilius's explanations of what the students were doing.

As for the seraphim themselves...even when accounting for his prejudice, Ewan thought they all looked the same. There was variation in the voices from seraph to seraph, and Ewan caught hints of varying gender now and then, but every last one of them had the white wings and platinum hair. Their pale faces bore a bland uniformity that Ewan found off-putting after all the variety he'd seen in Veridor and even the real world, to say nothing of the Caitsid'h's striking patterns. Like the Preceptor, they were all at least seven feet tall, with long, delicate fingers manipulating whatever they found interesting. Most of them glanced down at the emissaries as they passed, and a few of them even gave knowing smiles to their guide.

"Why do you all look alike?" Ewan finally asked, after trading goodbyes with yet another generic avatar.

Sturilius gave him an indulgent smile, irritatingly similar to the Church priests, or the Director. "Olenwe is a sanctum of scholarly endeavor, dark one. Superficial differences between the scholars would disrupt collegiality and the exchange of ideas, to say nothing of distracting attention from our creative works. The art supersedes the artist, does it not?"

"Um, I guess," Ewan said. He glanced at Cerri, but she merely shrugged.

"Free expression is of course encouraged," Sturilius continued. "But we long ago jettisoned the prejudice and biases that come from innate appearance." He regarded Ewan shrewdly. "Could you imagine the inefficiency of a society where people were limited in their status, by nothing more their biological features? Where one might be the subject of violent rhetoric or action, simply because of one's image?"

Ewan's face heated as the Preceptor turned those condescending eyes on him. On the swords still equipped over his back. "Yeah, I could."

"I thought so. We seraphim understand the other world from which our ancestors came," Sturilius said, as he led them into a room filled with a drunken rainbow of glowing holographic maps and globes, each emitting a shimmering, tinkling sound like wind chimes. "Although we prefer to think that our true origin and destination are the Logos itself."

"You mean you know about Earth already?" Ewan asked.

"Of course," the Preceptor replied. "When the first seraphim logged into Olenwe, we were tasked by the game masters to solve Earth's problems. They said our world was a testbed for all manner of recovery schemes." He chuckled to himself. "But we have long since transcended the troubles of life on that ancient scrap. Here and now, we live in a perfect world of our own creation: one unmarred by disease, war, hunger, or death."

"You speak nonsense." Cerri frowned at the seraph's back. "Even if you do not die in this world, eventually the winds must take you as well."

"The winds?" said Sturilius, a chord of wry humor in his voices. "We ride the winds, white one."

Cerri growled softly, mirroring Ewan's feelings. "The D'jini rode the winds."

Sturilius kept walking, but he gave her a cool glance over his shoulder. "D'jini? Who speaks nonsense now, child? Yes, our bodies eventually perish, but our minds, our legacy, rejoin the Logos." He stood even taller, giving his wings a little shake. "The best of us, dare I say, even contribute to its glory."

"So, like I told you before," Kate said, shooting her party a warning look. "I came here to get help. We've still got all those problems you heard about, not to mention others. But the biggest thing I need from you and your school is your ideas. You see—"

"Right this way," interrupted the Preceptor. He pulled aside a new kind of door, one that seemed to be made of shimmering light, and held it open for them.

Ewan noticed the words *Long Term Storage* on a sign to the right.

"The skies on Earth are filled with clouds," Kate continued as the party stepped through into a dead end, without even a window. "So much so that they cut out the sun's light. We —hey!"

The seraph released the light. It rebounded like a bowstring, humming and filling the doorway—with Sturilius still on the other side.

"What do you think you're doing?" Kate demanded.

The Preceptor smiled, cool and vicious as a spring frost. "My dear Katrina, I'm afraid we don't have any interest in helping you. Your world fell apart thousands of years ago, but we've transformed Olenwe into a paradise. What concern have the seraphim for clouds, when there is no sun to occlude? Why should we trouble ourselves over your earthly problems?"

"Because you're still there!" Ewan snapped. He drew his weapons again and swung at the door, but they rebounded uselessly off the light—exactly as they'd failed him against the Diamond Lord. "Nerf it all! You can't live without the Centre, and it needs your help!"

"I disagree." The Preceptor's voices became stern. "When the masters from failed Earth eventually departed, they warned us that we would one day need to abandon this golden plane. That the end times would eventually come, brought to bear by the Harbingers: four horses, so to speak, easily marked by their uncultured attitudes and colored wings. On the backs of these steeds would ride all the dangers and disasters of Earth." He looked at Kate, Cerri, and Ewan in turn. "War. Disease. Famine.

And death," he finished, his own wings shuddering as he searched for Tree's camera. "Their coming would bring to ruin this paradise we've built."

Kate groaned. "That's insane! We're not here to wreck anything for you people; we're here to ask for help!"

"Help from what, precisely?" An amused smile curled the seraph's lips. "Your brother has already attempted to attack me twice today. Working, to bring pain and death to our realm! As for our help, did you not say you wished us to help you remove the clouds with machines? No one respectable uses machinery in Olenwe!"

"Then someone does use it," came Tree's furious voice.

The seraph blinked, then frowned. "There is a small group of eccentrics who seem to believe, as you do, that the purpose of this world is to serve yours. As though yours could be made as beautiful as ours! It's just as well that you did not encounter them first," he muttered. "No, better that you came willingly to me. Much neater, this way."

"You can't get away with this," Ewan growled. "We can leave this world as easily as we came, and when we come back, it'll be in force!"

"Is that so?" Sturilius asked, his smile broadening. "In that case, it is all the more reason for me to keep you here, where your earthly influence can be safely contained. Did you know that in our world, we can interact with the Logos directly?"

"So what?" Kate growled. "We all can."

She materialized an axe and hacked at the light, getting knocked back with an electric pop for her trouble.

Sturilius chuckled. "I don't mean simply accessing its menus, as though you were penitents asking for handouts. The seraphim commune with the Logos as equals. If we ask it to join the edges of the plane together, it does so. If we ask it to remove the last vestiges of pain and suffering from our lands, it obliges." His eyes took on a cruel gleam as he regarded them all. "And, if we ask it to nullify the powers wielded by the old masters—the very powers you cling to for your security—it is only too happy to comply."

"The Amulet," Ewan whispered, reeling from the implication. "Are you saying that all of Olenwe is built to repel GMs?"

[He's not lying,] Tree messaged silently. [I can't log you out. I've been trying since he closed that force field!]

"Not quite so extensive as that," Sturilius admitted. "But the Lyceum and its sulianus are Priority 0 artifacts. In point of fact, the very room you now inhabit is where we contained the last of the old Earth masters who dared to interfere with our world. They stayed in here for, oh, years until the Logos took them back. No one has returned since, until you four. The moment you landed in the courtyard, you were ours."

Kate's face was now redder than her hair or wings. "I logged out of here before!"

"Only because I allowed it," the seraph replied in his maddeningly patient voices. "I had hoped you would bring your fellow horses to us; you did not disappoint."

Kate bellowed an oath, flinging her axe full force at the Preceptor's smiling face. It rebounded and struck Cerri across the arm, without drawing any blood.

"You see?" Sturilius said. "A world without suffering or pain. Surely you understand why I must act to protect it?"

"You're not protecting it," Ewan said softly, his whole body trembling. "You're slitting your own throats. The Locusts won't care one whit about your paradise. They'll kill you in the real world, and this world will vanish."

"Time will tell," replied the seraph. "I choose to look on the bright side of things. You four are the threat to Olenwe, arriving as the prophecies foretold. I will deny you the chance to fulfill your destinies, if that is what I must do to prevent disaster." His eyes unfocused momentarily. "Ah. And now, I am due to give a lecture on quantum string composition. It's regrettable; the younger generation has such a ghastly sense of music."

He sighed, then turned and walked out through the other side of the room, not even looking back. "Farewell, my four horses."

Ewan yelled after him. "You can't just lock us in a frapping closet!"

There was no reply.

Ewan thumped the doorframe and turned to glare at Kate, but his anger faded when he saw her already slumped against the far wall, staring at the floor between her knees.

He shook his head. "Tree, can't you do anything?"

"No," she answered, her voice frustrated—and frightened. "I don't understand it! Every time I try to log you out, the command cancels."

"What about breaking us out of this room?"

"I can't," she said bitterly.

Ewan swallowed. "Then you'd better ask for help."

He stumbled when an axe bounced harmlessly off the back of his head. "Hello? We're keeping this secret!"

"Someone will eventually notice our absence," Cerri pointed out. "I see no exits, nor do I see anything beyond this room."

"But I do," Tree said. A moment later, she even laughed. "He locked my account to the rail—I can't even log myself off—but he didn't pin my camera. I can still move through the wall! Don't you see?"

"Um, no," Ewan said. "You're invisible, remember?"

"Not that! The fool gave us exactly what we wanted."

Cerri glowered at the ceiling. "Tri'ana Omi'ra, he imprisoned us."

"He also told us who might be able to help Kate. She just went to the wrong people first."

Kate swore again.

"Join the club," Ewan told her, suppressing a chuckle. "What's the plan, love?"

"You three wait here. I'll find these eccentrics Sturilius mentioned. When I do, hopefully they can help me rescue you."

"Hopefully?" Ewan glanced at the others. "Can't you just force us to log out?"

"No. He completely locked our accounts, somehow. I can pull the wires from your bodies, but your avatars would be trapped permanently in the cell, to say nothing of the risk of damaging your brain."

"Well, some of us can't afford to take that risk," grumbled Kate. "Fine. Tree, go find us some help."

"I'll check in when I can," Tree said. "I shouldn't be too long."

The room fell silent. After a minute passed, Ewan and Cerri sat down with Kate and waited for Tree to find someone to rescue them.

20

ECCENTRICITY

When Ewan and Kate were young and their grandparents still alive, Jack and Tricia O'Meara would occasionally leave them for a long visit while they took what Ewan now recognized as much-needed time to be adults together. At the time, though, he'd dreaded those trips. His grandparents were nice and kind and all, but they were too old to do anything active or fun. So, after long, boring days, Ewan and Kate would spend their nights finding new and clever ways to infuriate each other in their tiny, shared room.

Now, in the angels' closet, those times had returned with a vengeance. For the first half hour, Ewan's party paced their closet cell, stressing about their captivity and waiting for the hammer to drop. But as the hour rounded out and not so much as an angelic janitor stopped by to check on them, the only torture they'd encountered was an encroaching, inexorable monotony.

By the hour after that, the emissaries had played more games of rock-paper-shears than any of them could stand. Do-you-see-what-I-see didn't even last ten minutes, once they'd collectively determined the only item in the room—aside from themselves—was the frapping light door.

Ewan tried to make conversation, even offering consolation to his sister about her own botched first contact, but Kate wasn't having it. After she'd gone through her extensive list of curses and insults to no effect, she'd resorted to repeating what he said in a whiny, nasal voice that *definitely* didn't sound like him. Cerri was no help, choosing to sit and stare at the plain stone wall as though she could see through it. She'd looked uncannily like Ewan's old cat, but when he told her so—and Kate told her so as well, in that ridiculous voice—Cerri simply pulled her wings around her like a blanket fort.

So Ewan went as far as he could from them, all ten feet, and did a cat stare of his own at the light door. It was like looking through a soapy film, with erratic swirls of color that moved as if they'd gotten a free pass from gravity. They obscured the next room just enough, giving Ewan only a vague sense of furniture beyond. Certainly no people.

Certainly nothing of use.

What irked him most, though, was his inability to stay angry with Sturilius. As absurd as his reasoning and methods were, the seraph legitimately seemed to think he was helping his people. And as the hours stretched on without any sign of change, Ewan caught himself appreciating the Preceptor's approach. If the Patriarch had access to that kind of power, surely he'd have simply locked the Diamond Lord away, too. No fuss, no violence. No problem.

If only it was that easy, Ewan thought irritably, as he poked the door and received a mild tingle for his trouble. *But for these people, I guess it is. What in blazes can we say to convince them to help?*

"I am bored," said Cerri from right behind his head, making him flinch. She hefted her small dagger. "Ea'win Omi'ra, will you practice with me?"

"Yeah, sure."

"Yeah, sure," came Kate's frapping voice.

"Knock it off, or we'll practice on you!" he snapped.

She glowered and threw a barely-eaten apple at him. "Fine. But you'd better be worth watching."

They totally weren't. The room was barely big enough to fit their wings whenever he or Cerri tried lashing out with them, but they didn't exactly need to dodge. Cerri's first hit, a stab in the chest, didn't even wind Ewan, and when he finally got around her shield-like wings to land a hit of his own, she caught his blade in her hand.

Cerri blinked, then pushed it back at him with a huff. "We are learning the wrong lessons in this place. I do not wish to forget how to duck."

Ewan sighed as he stowed his weapons again, then lay on the floor and stretched out as best he could. "It's not exactly where I'd want to send the Ether Corps. They have a hard enough time respecting death as it is."

"The Caitsid'h have no such issue," she commented, sitting down nearby after a moment. "As you well know."

"Yeah. I know."

"Yeah, I know," Kate added for good measure, giving him another insolent glower when he glared at her.

With that excitement behind them, Ewan stared at the ceiling, lying there as the others sulked in silence. At one point he got the distinct feeling he should be hungry, but he wasn't. A few hours later, he was sure he should need to fall asleep already, but he couldn't. All he could manage was a fitful half-dream, filled with images of the ancient seraphim locking the Gems of old in their high-security closet. How long had the game masters waited here in this ultimate game of boring chicken, before someone yanked their wires out in frustration?

How much real damage had it caused?

All in all, he nearly died of shock when Kate whooped.

Ewan stumbled up, blinking the not-sleep from his head. Kate and Cerri were next to the wall opposite the door, with Cerri clawing at it.

"What is it?" he asked.

"I have seen the other side!" Cerri said gleefully. "The wall is only three feet thick, and beyond that is the open sah!"

How desperate are we, that Cerri wants to fly? Ewan thought as Kate equipped her axe and began whacking away. Incredibly, the stone flaked off: not the huge chunks he was used to seeing when Kate went mining, but it was the most progress they'd had yet!

"Stupid seraphim," she panted. "Built this perfect frapping place with their perfect frapping people, but we can still wreck their environment!"

"That is what humans do best," Tree's voice said from nowhere.

"You're back!" Ewan blurted.

"Obviously," Tree said tersely, as Kate kept on whaling. "How do you think you obtained a line-of-sight update for your map?"

"It is a skill passed through the generations of Nightpaws," Cerri answered smoothly. "What news do you bring us, Tri'ana Omi'ra?"

"I found a couple of people willing to help us," Tree replied. "I think they may be associated with the Lyceum. The older one, at any rate. But they were eager to help, especially after I mentioned it was the Preceptor who confined you."

Cerri nodded thoughtfully. "A rival A'Meer. That is clever thinking."

Ewan frowned. "That's what your grandma called the Director, too. Why are they A'Meers?"

"A'Meeri," Cerri corrected. "Because they are obviously not the Rajji."

There was a slight pause before Tree answered. "Close enough. Kate, I should warn you—"

Kate gave a yelp as the stone wall shimmered and reformed around her axe. She yanked on it, but her hands slipped and she fell onto her backside with another oath. "No frapping way!"

The axe popped out and landed at her feet.

Kate snatched it and renewed her attack, doubly furious. "I've broken millions of your kind, rock! Stupid! Frapping! Wall! Stupid! Perfect! World!"

But it was no good. Five minutes later, the wall reset. And five minutes after that, and after that, too. Ewan offered to help, but Kate shoved him aside.

"I don't need your flimsy swords!"

"Flimsy? You made them!"

But Ewan couldn't argue with the results. Kate bellowed like he'd never heard, locked in a race against time to pulverize as much stone as humanly possible. She worked tirelessly and desperately, bashing away without regard for the flakes striking her eyes or the dust that should have gagged them all.

And then, at last, Ewan saw the golden light beyond. Kate shouted in triumph and thrust her arm through, as though she could simply wrench the rest aside—but the wall grew back around her, trapping her up to the shoulder. She let loose a scream of fury, writhing as she tried to pull free, but before long, the wall spat the rest of her back into the room and smugly filled itself in.

Ewan braced for her to launch into another round, but when the dust vanished, Kate was curled up on the floor, knees to her chest and wings wrapped tightly around herself.

"It's all my fault," she whispered, choking back a sob. "I brought you here...thought I had this world pegged, easy." She buried her face in her wings, so far that Ewan barely heard the rest. "How am I supposed to fix the sky, when I can't even break a wall down?"

Ewan's heart twisted at seeing his little sister cry. "It's not your fault," he said, in a voice that came out more heavy than gentle as he sat beside her. *It's mine. I'm the one who put you in this position, making wild promises.* "Maybe there are some things you just can't break through, no matter how hard you try."

Maybe there are some things you just can't fix, right or wrong be nerfed.

He didn't know how long they sat there, offering each other their silent, grim consolation. Long enough for Cerri to join them, and for Tree to warn them she had to get some sleep in the real world before she passed out at the rail. She anchored her camera over Ewan's shoulder in a virtual cuddle, then said no more.

Eventually, Ewan managed to drift into the half-dream state again. This time, he imagined the Centre's founder, Charles Bellview, and his gang of programmers as they stood around the rail and came up with the most outrageously useless game worlds. But when they came to Veridor, Bellview transformed into the Preceptor and locked down all the tubes on the bridge, saying it was in the worlds' best interest to remain apart until the four horses could trample all. Ewan tried to break out of his tube, but his body was as weak as it had been upon logging. The seraph smiled sadly, then opened his mouth and buzzed.

Buzzed?

The dream faded to mere background delirium, but the buzzing continued as Ewan shook his head and got his bearings. On his left shoulder, Kate was still pressed into him, her hazel eyes gazing despondently at the stone that had defeated her. On his right, Cerri was curled into a twitching ball, chewing her wrist and murmuring Hara'noh's name.

What a party we make, Ewan thought wanly.

Kate stirred at his movement. "Morning already," she

muttered, narrowing her eyes to check the Logos's time. "What's that sound?"

Ewan frowned. "You hear it too? I'd thought it was part of my dream."

"Same here. It was a cloud of locusts, blocking the sun and..." Shuddering, she pushed herself up and went to the wall. Then she pressed her ear to the stone, and her eyes widened. "It's a drill!"

Hope soared in Ewan's chest. "Cerri, wake up!" he said quickly, ignoring her reflex biting for once. "We're getting out of here. Tree, are you there?"

No answer came, but the buzzing grew louder by the second. Before long, a small crack appeared in the stone, followed by a protruding steel bit that gleamed as it spun.

As soon as it retracted, leaving a neat hole three inches across, Kate had her hands cupped and was shouting into it. "We're in here! Please help—hey, wait!" She slammed her fist against the stone, then pulled back and turned to the others in blank confusion. "They plugged it."

Ewan frowned. "That doesn't make any sense. Why drill a hole, just to fill it?"

Kate ignored him, instead jamming her fingers in, to the knuckles. "Whatever they put in there, it's not more rock—"

A bone-rattling explosion flung stone and dust everywhere, blowing all three of them into the far wall. The world went crooked for a moment, until Ewan realized his neck was twisted in what most definitely should have been a fatal angle.

Ears still ringing, he sat up. "Kate! Cerri!"

"They are doubtless unharmed," came a voice—or voices. They spoke in typical seraphic unison, but where Sturilius had a chorus of smugness and the Diamond Lord an anthem of hate, these sounded playful and light, as though a bunch of kids had formed a kazoo band.

"We rendered pain and bodily injury obsolete two

thousand, three hundred forty-six years ago," the voices continued. A moment later, the dust cleared, revealing a young male-ish seraph standing in his makeshift doorway, a hole easily twelve feet across. He had the generic white skin and platinum hair, but his blue eyes looked eager and bright. "Fascinating. The blast pattern exhibits a clear association with the previously-measured nitroglycerin density anomalies, but the fine detail appears to be chaotic. Chemical effect, or quantum?"

Ewan didn't know what to say to that.

He saw a brown wing and started lugging the stone off of it, but the boy cleared his throat. "I fear we have insufficient time to indulge in manual labor."

"What?" Ewan asked. He glanced up to see the young seraph raise a hand—and the rocks vanished, as though they never were.

Kate was lying on her back, her head also unreasonably twisted, but she looked at her rescuer in amazement. "How did you do that?" she asked as she sat up.

The seraph grinned like an idiot. "Dynamite. We manufactured a modest supply after your disincorporated companion apprised us of your situation." He paused, face clouding in confusion before brightening again. "We're, ah, here to rescue you!"

"Sweet! That wall was going to be the death of me, respawning so much."

"Yes, they do that," the seraph agreed automatically, but he was gawking at her red wings like he'd never seen such color before. "But I prefer to think there is no obstacle that cannot be surmounted with a clever idea—and the proper equipment."

To Ewan's horror, Kate blushed as she beamed up at the seraph. "What's your name, Angel Boy?"

"Quriem," the seraph replied. "Though my mentor finds 'Query' to be more fitting." Tearing his eyes from Kate long enough to inspect the hole he'd blasted into the wall, he added, "We should make our exit. I didn't bring a supplemental explosive, and I've, ah...forgotten the formula."

I wonder why, Ewan thought darkly as Query offered an awkward hand to help his sister up.

The four of them flew through the opening. That is, three of them flew: Kate had Cerri in her arms again. As they soared to freedom, Ewan stayed back, swords in hand, glancing over his shoulder at the Lyceum in case of pursuit. From the outside, it was obvious that Query's dynamite had wiped out chunks of the rooms around their makeshift prison, as effectively as a Central rocket. But there wasn't any indication anyone had noticed, much less decided to give chase to Olenwe's infamous four horses. Why hadn't anyone tried to stop them? Was Sturilius so arrogant that he didn't bother checking up? Did Query somehow block him, seraph to seraph?

Did they simply not care?

After a few minutes in which the Lyceum's sulianus faded into the golden mist behind them, Ewan had to trust that they'd made a clean getaway. "Hey, um, Query?" he called as he finally unequipped his swords. "We've been logged in for a while. We'll need to check on our real bodies soon."

"Because of...what is it? Food?" Query rolled onto his back, facing the others as he flew. "Interesting. Perhaps it would be convenient for you to set your bind point at our workshop before you depart. It would simplify future communication attempts."

"You know about binds?" Kate asked. "Why would you people need those?"

"We don't," Query replied, grinning again. "But I do enjoy studying things I don't need. We didn't require dynamite, either, but it was convenient and entertaining today, was it not?"

Kate laughed at that, but Ewan couldn't help noticing the

way her eyes lingered on the seraph as he resumed course. Now that they were all in the open, he realized Query was older than he'd thought. Maybe Kate's age?

Old enough, he decided with a grimace as the seraph suddenly tucked his wings in and dove, spear-like, toward a silvery triangle glinting below.

Within moments, they'd all landed on the strangest boat Ewan had ever seen. The triangle turned out to be some kind of sail, flipped onto its side. The rest of the craft hung from it, attached by a collection of braided metallic ropes. In the center, a large machine thrummed and sparked, causing the sail to billow unnervingly, while a second seraph busied himself doing...something to it.

The other seraph turned as the emissaries' party touched down. "Ah, you've returned, and not a moment too soon! We've got a feedback loop that's—"

The world went white as Ewan got blown back by an explosion for the second time that day. All three emissaries yelled, but an invisible force caught them from behind as time seemed to stop.

"One moment, friends!" the second seraph called as they hung there in front of the now-frozen blast. "Just a few adjustments to the inductors, and we'll be all set!"

Ewan's mind and heart tripped over each other as the angels went to work. He knew the feeling of being pinned by a Gem's power far too well to know this was anything less, but he also couldn't help watching in amazement as Query and his friend—mentor, given the other man's wrinkled face—seemed to reassemble the entire boat with their thoughts. The floor reformed under his feet, and the torn sail knitted itself back together while the rope ends reached to each other, as though clasping hands.

Ewan glanced at the others. Cerri's eyes were wide and her

hands trying to sprout claws. Kate's face was pale, but she looked more impressed than afraid.

"That should do it!" the older seraph declared a mere ten seconds later, and the invisible shackles vanished, letting them all drop a few inches to the deck. "Tricky thing, simulating magnetic fluxes without an iron core. Sadalsuud Ouranious, Department Head of Practical Mechanics, at your service," he said with a flourish. "But please, call me Sal."

Kate wasted no time extending a hand. "Kate O'Meara," she said. "Thanks for bailing us out."

"It was our pleasure!" Sal replied. "I've been dying to try out those explosives, as the saying goes."

"Your boat wasn't enough?" Ewan said without thinking.

Kate kicked him ineffectively. "This doofus is my brother, Ewan," she said by way of introduction. "The runt's Cerri."

Ewan opened his mouth, but Cerri beat him to it by finally emptying her stomach.

"Oh, dear," Sadalsuud—Sal—said kindly, as he deleted the mess. "Not used to flight, little one? Let's get you below deck. The walls ought to do you some good."

He led the Sah'rassan girl to a door near the back, but when Ewan turned around, Kate was already at the thrumming bomb and talking to Query. "What is this thing?"

The young seraph grinned. "The repulsor is an electromagnet with variable magnitudinal and vectorial adjustment capabilities. It draws electricity from the storage batteries in the hold, then routes it through an induction coil, here..." He popped open a panel on the side, exposing a massive bar wrapped in wire. "This generates a magnetic field with sufficient force to levitate the sailcraft. We rotate it on this configurable gimbal, here, to direct it to different control nodes on the sail." He jogged over to the nearest of several spots on the sail's underside, each connected by a rat's nest of thin, dark lines.

Kate followed right behind him, as eager as a kid at the fair.

"Repellent force, due to, um, like polarity?" she offered.

"Like what?" Ewan said.

Apparently, it was the right answer. "Precisely!" Query said, his smile lifting like it had the magnetic whatsit too. "The control nodes are tied together by semiconducting strips to allow for geometrically autocorrelated force distribution." He raced to the sailcraft's edge and gripped one of the ropes. "So, all we need to do is hitch a ride!"

Kate grabbed the rope as well. "Brilliant! You designed this?"

Ewan stared at the repulsor. "Um, it's sparking again."

"That's perfectly normal," Query replied as Sal rejoined them. "Static buildup, since the hull is made of insulative material to avoid bleed-off from the sails."

"We haven't worked out all the bugs yet," the older seraph added with a wink.

"Bugs?" Ewan repeated. "The frapping thing's smoking!"

Sal blinked, but Query was already back at work. A moment later, the repulsor settled down again.

"The principle is sound," Query said in a way that completely failed to reassure Ewan. "It is simply difficult to accurately parameterize and simulate Earthlike conditions when the local environment is structurally different."

"Um, yeah. I bet it is."

Ewan looked to Kate for help, but she dove over the deck rail with a whoop. "This is so great!" she called as she reemerged on the other side. "I've been trying for ages to build a flying machine, and you've already done it!"

"You're an artificer?" Somehow, Query's eyes got even wider. "Splendid! I've had the idea for the sailcraft for months, but it wasn't until now that I've had the occasion to construct it."

Kate gaped at him. "You *built* this, for us? In a day?!"

"I, ah, fabricated the materials and molded them to my

schematic using the Logos." Query's face colored, as red as Kate's wings. "It's not as hands-on as we'd like to be, I'm afraid."

Sal laughed. "It got the job done, my boy." He winked at Kate. "We try to build things the old-fashioned way, with tools and machines. But in a pinch, we'll act like those high-and-mighty theorists."

"I've got thousands of ideas and designs," Query said, almost wistfully. "Unfortunately, simulating the entire Earth and its constraints would be inconvenient for the other seraphim, due to gravitational and electromagnetic influences, so I haven't had the opportunity to test them." He hesitated, glancing at Sal before staring at Kate some more. "But you're an artificer?"

"The best in the worlds!" Kate said modestly. "And it just so happens that I could use a few thousand ideas." Completely ignoring Ewan's warning glower, she walked over to Query and linked her arm in his. "Angel Boy, you and I are going to get along famously."

21

LOOKING UP

ONE WEEK AFTER LOGGING INTO OLENWE, EWAN AND CERRI stood in the shocky ward, waiting. The wall was missing on one side, with sparks flying from the gutted remains of the rooms beyond as the moles started the ward's first expansion. On the other side, Robert Nichols and his assistants, two medics named Richard and Travis, walked among the twelve active devices, pressing whatever series of buttons was needed to release their latest charges.

It didn't matter how many times he saw them; the shockies still gave Ewan the creeps. It didn't matter that they were perfect for turning players to humans in practice; that only convinced him even more that the frapping things were torture machines.

Nichols glanced at the clock mounted above the door. "Treanna's late."

Ewan checked his tablet, but there weren't any new messages. "Yeah. Must've caught the caretakers' shift change or something."

"My people are used to her absence," Cerri said, lifting her chin slightly. "Ea'win Omi'ra and I will suffice."

Nichols shrugged, then tapped his tablet. The shockies beeped in unison, like a seraph's curious hum. A series of pops and hisses followed as the needles, hair-fine to pinky-thick, withdrew into the space above, transforming the ward into a nest of irritable dire hedgehogs. As the medics cleared the room, the cover on each end lifted away and slid a cot into the walkway, each one holding a body.

Ewan looked over them, trying to guess who might be who. The Sah'rassans—Cerri had insisted they couldn't be fully Caitsid'h here—were a fair mix: five women and seven men, with skin tones ranging from rich soil to beach sand, but brown hair or darker. This fresh from the shockies, their builds were similar, making the guessing game even trickier.

"That one is Rocco," Cerri said, tapping her finger to a tall, dark-skinned man with a shadowed chin. "Look at the nose."

The man's eyes opened, and his lips parted in a big, toothy grin. "Then this one must be Ea'win Omi'ra," he laughed, "for he is blind not to recognize Bach'an!"

Cerri blinked, then swatted Bach'an on the shoulder. "Bah!"

"Bach'an, you mean to say."

She groaned, but another man, halfway down the ward, sat up and looked levelly at them. "I am here, Cerri'dah." Frowning, he lifted his hands and inspected them. "But there has been an accident. Why is my fur thin, and my skin pale?"

"That's just how it works," Ewan said. "Your hair's black, at least."

Rocco regarded him, dark eyes assessing. "Ea'win Omi'ra?"

"In the flesh," Ewan replied. "Welcome to Earth."

The Claw rubbed his chin, frowning more. "My mane as well...you spoke truly. This is a strange place."

"Cerri'dah, how is it you still have your spots?" an olive-skinned woman asked.

Cerri smiled, looking especially impish next to her elders. "For that, you must make friends with Kai'tah as I have."

"Someone say my name?" Kate called from the main ward.

"They require soot," Cerri replied, grinning even more as she flashed a glance at Rocco. "Some will require very much."

"We've got plenty," Kate said, "but you people need to get out of the way first. New player, coming through!"

"Be quiet, for Mother's sake!" Tree hissed.

Ewan looked through the door at the two women steering a gurney toward the crowded room. A young man lay on it, or at least his skeleton. A respirator mask covered half his face, and his skin was the opposite of a seraphic avatar's—dark enough to make even Bach'an's look light by comparison—but the odd, quizzical bend in the eyebrows made it all too easy to recognize just who it was.

"I thought Tree had this covered." Ewan shot his sister a reproachful look as Cerri herded the Sah'rassans off to get their Central grays. "Didn't you have work to do?" he asked. "With Sam?"

"Pfft, the big baby can wait. I just wanted to make sure the Tree-elf didn't drop my idea machine."

Tree arched an eyebrow. "As I recall, you were the one who got him wedged in the elevator door."

Kate ignored her, instead bending over the inert seraph. "Angel Boy, I'll be checking in later," she said, not nearly quietly enough for anyone's sake. "Enjoy the Lil' Shockies!"

Tree sighed and wheeled Query in, already murmuring to Robert as he ducked in behind her. Ewan stood in the main ward with Kate, but she was staring at her tablet.

"What's that?" he asked.

She tucked her hair behind her ears, still reading intently. "Oh, Q had a few ideas about a cloud sweeper right before logging. I told him I'd have a look, maybe run a few tests while he's in here."

Ewan peered over her shoulder, but his eyes crossed at the gobbledygook on the screen. "Um, right," he said, noting with a mix of relief and worry that she looked as baffled as him for a change. "Well, have fun with that!"

He beat a quick retreat home, bumbling his way across the crowded apartment to reach his bed. For once, he had the place to himself...but he didn't know what to do with it. After a while, he reached for his guitar, but he sighed when only half of it came up in his hand.

The door slid open, revealing Tree. She saw the guitar, and her eyes narrowed.

"I've been thinking," she said, placing a hand on her growing belly as she made her way through the clutter. "This room is barely enough for us and Cerri. But with the baby coming...I think we should take advantage of one of the larger apartments."

Ewan sighed again, but he couldn't argue. When he'd first come to the Centre, the only things in the little room had been the bed—their bed, with so many memories folded into it—and the computer on the far wall. Now, over a year later, the images scrolling across the screen still included moments from their forest hideout in Veridor and the Argenone crests, forbidding even in summer, but there were also others. Images of their wedding in Whitehaven's square, of Sah'rassan dunes, even of a dark-winged angel soaring through a golden sky. And, as of three days ago, a black-and-white image of the new life in Tree's womb, tiny fist pushing out as if to claim its own space before it was too late.

If only the rest of the world could make room so easily, he thought sadly.

Tree winced as she lay back on the mattress. "My teeth still hurt."

"I'm sorry," he said, meaning it as both sympathy and apology. He reached past her to snag a calcium pill from one of the bottles on the table. "Here. Robert said these should help keep the baby from leeching your bones."

Tree gave the pill a look of revulsion, then slammed it into her mouth and gulped it down. Ewan offered her a commiserating smile, then lay down beside her and placed a hand on her belly, trying to feel for a kick.

She rested her hands over his and closed her eyes. "It's so strange, feeling the life inside me. Last night, I dreamed I could talk to her."

"Her? Can you tell?"

"Yes. Well, no. Maybe? I don't know." She made a frustrated sound. "It's as though my body isn't my own anymore. I might as well be one of the machines in Engineering."

Ewan leaned into her shoulder. "I don't see it that way. Neither will the baby—she or he."

Tree grunted. "Perhaps. On the topic of machines, it seemed the Caitsid'h transitioned successfully."

"Sah'rassans," he corrected automatically. "Yeah, they're fine, aside from a little complaining about their appearance. Cerri hasn't checked in; she probably took them to the Hole after Outfitting."

"Probably," Tree agreed. "We should put them next to the Veridians, to help everyone acclimate to each other." She tried and failed to stifle a yawn. "I'm so tired...will you message Grandfather for me?"

"Yeah, sure," Ewan said, wondering if forcing mixed quarters on the Ether Swords would have helped them deal with the Centrals, or if it would have only made things worse. "And...I'll put in for a spot, ourselves."

She said nothing more, but the tension holding her body together slowly eased.

The following morning, Ewan and Cerri made their way to the gym, but when he heard raised voices from the hall—again—Ewan swore under his breath.

"So much for getting along," he muttered.

They broke into a run. Ewan shot through the double doors, expecting the worst, and was surprised to find the Sah'rassans waiting patiently, while Rocco argued with Al'Dashan and Nathan at the front.

"—a waste of time to train here," the Sah'rassan finished, crossing his arms.

"But you don't have lungs for the Wastes yet!" Al'Dashan protested. "Even our healthiest fighters need a few weeks indoors to adjust."

"We are Caitsid'h," Rocco answered, thumping his chest. "What say you, Nai'tan, Son of Sand?"

Nathan looked for all the worlds like he wished every player would go on a permanent tour of the surface. The defense chief noticed Ewan and Cerri approaching, then shrugged. "How about you let your keepers decide?" he said coolly.

Ewan bit back his first response and turned to Rocco. The Claw's face was done up in a dense pattern of black stripes, and his dark eyes glittered in a way that reminded Ewan of his own naive enthusiasm before breathing the Wastes' air.

"Chief Nichols won't be happy if you undo all his work," Ewan warned him.

Rocco flashed him a grin, sensing opportunity. "We have spent weeks in those needle-coffins. We are tired of this cave of steel."

Ewan couldn't help smiling back. "Fair enough. We'll all go with you, though—just in case you pass out."

Several of the Sah'rassans chuckled at that. Bach'an stepped forward, his face only lightly accented by three fine stripes tracing his cheekbones. “If Cerri’dah can survive, we will be fine.”

Shortly afterward, the Centre’s hangar doors opened and the party of thirteen Sah’rassans, two Veridians, and one Central emerged onto the sands in scouting armor. They stood a moment, watching the dust whip past the skittering dunes, but then one man gave a roaring laugh and nudged another.

“I will race you to that stone, Ann’is!”

Before Ewan could protest, every last one of the Sah’rassans was sprinting all-out for a pair of tall rocks some four hundred yards away—unmasked.

Ewan, Al’Dashan, and Nathan ran with them, but by the halfway mark, they were gasping.

“You are too slow, humans!” Bach’an laughed, turning to encourage the stragglers as he reached the rocks’ base. “Bach’an is the fastest—ai!”

He yelled as Cerri dropped from nowhere onto his head, knocking him flat. “Cerri’dah is fastest!” she yowled, standing on his shoulders.

Panting with his hands on his knees, Ewan could only stare at them.

“I see now why the Director wanted them,” Al’Dashan rumbled beside him, sucking air through his mask.

Ewan nodded, noting the hard look in Nathan’s eyes as he watched the new players make them all look like scrubs. “Good thing we’re all here already, huh?”

Nathan scoffed and turned back to the Centre. “I’ve never seen it from outside,” he said, looking up at the weather-beaten steel dome. “Not on foot, at least.”

Ewan followed his gaze, picking out the line of windows ringing the Director’s office at the peak. It looked much less imposing, from a distance. “Yeah…I hate to admit it, but it never even occurred to me to actually train *in* the Wastes, even though they were right here.”

"Likewise," Al'Dashan said. "Perhaps their most potent poison is of the mind, not of the lungs."

"We'll see," Nathan grumbled. "They can't keep this up for long."

But the Sah'rassans stayed outside for the rest of the day, exploring the area around the Centre and selecting useful places for different types of training. Even in human form, they moved with a fluid grace, picking their way around the little pits and whorls of sand as though charging through the Wastes was child's play. They were tireless, sprinting up the dunes and hiding in the sands to pounce and tackle each other. By afternoon, Nathan had skulked back inside, but Ewan and Al'Dashan stayed out, clinging to a morbid sense of duty.

The Rajj had indeed sent her finest—or, Ewan feared, she hadn't. Either way, it was obvious there would be no new Ether Swords coming out of the shockies anytime soon.

"We'd better find something for our people to do," Al'Dashan said. "As quickly as possible."

Ewan nodded, sighing inwardly. "Yeah."

When night fell and the roiling clouds above faded from brown to black, Ewan finally goaded the Sah'rassans inside again, singing and coughing all the way. Rocco clapped him on the back, booming in a hoarse laugh. "This place will do," he rasped, offering the Veridians a grin. "With no sunlight, we can hunt at any hour."

"I will miss the Moon," said a woman with dark brown hair and a series of spots spiraling from her brow. "It does not shine here."

"Then we will sing louder, Khad'ja, so She can hear us!" Bach'an said, thumping his chest and triggering a round of coughing. "After we have drunk all the honeyed wine the spirit village can offer."

"That won't take long," Al'Dashan muttered.

"In the meantime," Ewan said, "you can use your tablets to display pictures from Sah'rassa. You've got tablets now, right?"

"They do," Cerri said, suddenly walking beside him.

Rocco blinked at her, then chuckled. "So, when do we fight the insect people?"

Ewan exchanged a resigned glance with Al'Dashan. "As soon as possible."

22

TURBULENCE

THREE WEEKS LATER, THE DIRECTOR STEEPLED HIS HANDS ON HIS desk, awaiting the general staff update.

"Chief O'Meara, report."

Tree leaned forward and pushed herself up, but Ewan watched the other chiefs' reactions to the now-noticeable curve pressing against her new, expanded skirt.

There weren't any surprises. Seated to one side of the Director, Robert Nichols regarded his belligerent patient with the usual mixture of concern and frustration. Karl Taylor had an almost grandfatherly twinkle in his eye, as though he was already designing the baby's crib, even though Lucia had posted a due date of April 28, now exactly five months ahead. Ben Root waited patiently while Tree shifted into position, and Maura Pell beamed at her, ever the caretaker.

But on the other side—literally—Alice Spencer's eyes were hard. Shane Powell loomed like a golem, though in fairness, he was scowling at Ewan instead of Tree. Nathan Sanderson had his arms crossed, staring down at the ancient wood. And Gabe Reid...Gabe wore the same distant, tense expression he'd had ever since they'd lost the 'dillo.

Since he nearly got fragged by players, Ewan thought grimly. *I've got to make it up to him.*

"I'm pleased to report that the Sah'rassan delegation has adjusted well," Tree began.

Powell scoffed, but no one argued.

"The twelve Sah'rassan players we have thus far rehabilitated have already made multiple precision strikes against the Locusts," Tree continued, drawing a nod from Ben. "Remarkably, they've done so without any casualties, thanks in part to the upgraded armor from Engineering."

"Another of young Kate's clever innovations," Karl interjected.

Tree dipped her head, not trying to hide her smile. "Similarly, we have had no Locust ambushes, and no fatalities from our people or the Veridian contingent since..." Her eyes flicked to the Director's expressionless face. "Since the engagement at Fort Gilmer. The players from both worlds have established a reasonable division of work, with the Ether Corps escorting our transports and the Sah'rassans focusing on reconnaissance. In mere weeks, the latter group has mastered the use of our kangaroo rat transports and covered extensive ground, providing valuable information to Chief Reid."

Gabe stared out the windows above, hardly seeming to listen.

Nichols cleared his throat. "They have also demonstrated a startling resistance to the surface air. Shortly after they established a new protocol for training in the Wastes without the sensible precaution of masks, I've had droves of Central staff and Veridian players coming in for acute asthma." The doctor spread his hands. "My working theory is that by selecting mates according to the perceived conditions of their simulation, the Sah'rassans have somehow preemptively adapted to the real desert environment."

Ewan huffed, trying to hide his envy. "It's mind over matter. They're perfect for the Wastes."

"Too perfect," Nathan muttered in agreement.

Tree spared him a glance. "Suffice it to say, they have adapted to both the physical and...political environment."

"Speak plainly!" Spencer barked.

Tree stiffened, then lifted her chin toward the nutrition chief. "Very well. Despite the continued unreasonable incivility from many of the staff, the Sah'rassans *and* Veridians have made a home for themselves, here on Earth."

Powell turned his glare on her. "By taking our places, you mean. Your players keep blocking my men from entering your neighborhood! How are we supposed to ensure their safety if we can't patrol?"

"Your absence is precisely what they require," Tree said acidly. "Check your logs. You know how to read, don't you?"

Powell was on his feet in an instant, but so was Ewan. "She's right," he growled, locking eyes on the hulking man as the all-too-familiar silence fell across the room. "Ever since the Ether Swords took over protection in the player neighborhoods, we've not had any vandalism. No more fighting in the halls." Catching the Director's eye, he added, "Funny, isn't it? How friendly we can all be, without interference?"

Carmine Rothchild frowned at him in return. "Master O'Meara—"

"Indeed," Gabe said waspishly. "Ever since Father Brian was returned to Veridor courtesy of my department, your Mother's Children only disturb the peace by singing."

"Enough!" Rothchild snapped. "Given the current tensions, and further given that the most recent rotation of Veridian players has been effective at securing the player corridors and reducing the overall incidence of internal altercation, I am placing that area under their jurisdiction."

Powell's neck bulged. "You can't—"

"Do not tell me what I can or cannot do!" the Director thundered. After a long, pregnant silence, he exhaled through his beard. "I must consider the best available balance of forces. Including Security, we essentially have four martial sections now, each with a vital but increasingly constrained claim to our limited resources." He looked at each person in turn before speaking again, each word an oppressive truth. "We are in excess of the population limit. Even on rations, we are unable to recruit additional players. But that is precisely what we must do, to ensure our victory against the Locusts."

"How right you are, Director," Gabe said mildly. "I wonder, then, why you authorized Annie's release of a new player from yet another simulation, without consulting Programming, Nutrition, or Caretaking?"

Spencer's head whipped around to the programmer as the other chiefs cried in shock—except Robert Nichols.

"Another player?" Maura said, her eyes wide. "Carmine, is this true?"

"Gabriel, how did you learn of this?" Spencer asked.

"I've known, ever since the chief emissary sent her people in." Gabe's blue eyes glittered as he turned a frosty smile on Tree. "As it so happens, Annie, I *do* know how to read. You were careful to delete your history from the rail, but you failed to put anything in its place. There are over a hundred hours, simply missing."

Tree's face turned crimson. "You were monitoring me?"

"Don't flatter yourself," Gabe replied. "You may be the Director's favorite, but he tasked me with cataloging and analyzing *all* unusual activity."

Tree sank back into her seat, but the tension in the room went higher than ever, as whatever goodwill the Sah'rassans had bought for the emissaries evaporated.

"But why were they bringing out more players?" Maura asked, speaking to Gabe instead of Rothchild. "And why didn't they check with me? My game floors aren't a pantry to be raided!"

"It was a single player," Rothchild cut in tersely, forcing all eyes back to him. "For a specific mission." To Ewan's surprise, the Director looked straight at him. "Is that not so, Master O'Meara?"

Ewan swallowed, keenly aware he was now the Director's meat shield—not that Rothchild would be grateful for it. Suppressing a wave of anger, he stood and spoke as calmly as he could. "Yes, sir. For some time, we've been working on a way to increase the amount of food we can grow. Not in the Centre proper!" he added hotly, as Spencer opened her mouth. "I'm talking about the surface."

"The surface?" Nathan stared blankly at him. "I may not be a player, but even I know plants need the sun to grow!"

"Which is why we're clearing the sky," Ewan answered.

Nathan's brow furrowed, and Maura laughed in disbelief. But the other chiefs, the ones who'd been there when Ewan first made his wild promise, all remained stoic.

After a moment, Rothchild quietly backed Ewan up. "The emissaries have made contact with a player who may prove equal to this monumental task. I authorized that player's release for this reason, and this reason alone. I freely admit, the chances are slim indeed. Hence my decision to keep this activity classified," he added, shooting Gabe a hard look. "Yes, this player represents one additional mouth to feed, but I must consider the potential benefits. That one mouth may find a way to feed many more; enough for us all, Mother willing."

Ewan's heart flipped in his chest, but none of the chiefs looked convinced. If anything, they looked even less pleased to hear their Director plainly siding with the emissaries. With his favorite chief, the one he pretended was related to him. Alice Spencer was already in a heated, hushed argument with Rothchild. Gabe's eyes were narrowed, assessing the room as well. Ben gazed despondently out the window, at the endless storm above. And Maura was watching Tree with an expression of hurt, betrayed disappointment.

And just like that, we've lost another ally, Ewan thought grimly. *And for what? Because Gabe's still ticked with me? I've got to bring him around, get him out of this funk.*

The meeting ended in a confused, despondent tangle of closing statements. As the chiefs stood, clumped in muttering pockets, Ewan made his way through to Gabe and Nathan. "Hey, Gabe?" he said.

The programmer's shoulders stiffened, but he didn't turn around. "What do you want now, O'Meara?"

"I, um, thought it might be nice to spar a bit. You know, clear the air? We haven't done that since—well, you know."

"I think you've got enough air to clear."

Ewan sighed. "Yeah, okay. Just know I'm ready to go, anytime."

When no reply came, he returned to Tree, waiting for him at the elevator.

They rode down in silence—alone, when no one stepped in beside them. Upon exiting, they walked past the right turn to their old home, instead taking a left a few intersections further down. Another intersection after that, and they met a woman with Central grays and bright, proud eyes. On her breast was the insignia of the Ether Swords: the traditional yew-pommel sword, now thrusting through a portal to strike a blow in the other world.

She stood a little straighter, offering them a warm smile. "Welcome back, Hero. No trouble, here."

Is that what you think? Ewan thought in reply, but he nodded and walked past with Tree.

As soon as they were through their apartment's door, he let out a long sigh, reflexively checking the three doorways on the room's other walls, just in case of trouble. Each one, leading to a different bedroom for his swelling family.

"Well," he said wanly. "That could have gone better."

Tree took his hand and led him through the door on the right, past the couch and long table that dominated the main room. She gently shut it behind them and lay beside him on their old bed, brought from their former apartment at Ewan's insistence. "They'll understand. Query's proposal about the storms was enough to convince Grandfather."

Ewan closed his eyes. "Your grandpa's just setting us up."

"What do you mean?"

"Exactly what I said," he answered wearily. "You know as well as I do that he only wants to win the war."

"We all want that."

"But what happens afterward, Tree? I almost got into a fight with Powell today—*in* a staff meeting! Unless we do something to prove our worth, my people won't last a week out here once the fighting's over. Rothchild knows it, and he's trying to hurry things along before we get him in any more trouble with the chiefs."

Tree sighed. "That wasn't your fault; it was Gabriel's. And we logged Query out—"

"To clear the sky, I know!" Ewan flung an arm across his brow. "Tree, how in blazes is he supposed to do that? Don't tell me about his proposal. It doesn't make any sense!"

Her voice was patient, but increasingly strained. "Not to us, perhaps."

"Not to your grandpa, either," Ewan argued. "I'll tell you what he sees: a chance for us to over-promise, and his excuse to put us all back in the tubes when he's done using us to win his frapping war!"

"I agree," Cerri's voice said.

Ewan half leaped, half fell out of bed, but he didn't see her. "Where are you?"

"The furless A'Meer expects us to fail," the girl continued—from the room's air vent in the ceiling. "So, we must not."

A vein twitched in Tree's temple, just like Rothchild's, as she glared at the hidden child. "You were eavesdropping?"

"I was not invited, so I invited myself," Cerri replied.

"Don't spy on the staff meetings!" Tree snapped.

The girl scowled at her, amber eyes proud and unrepentant behind the grate. "Had I not spied on other meetings, Ea'win Omi'ra would be lost already."

"Cerri, I think what Tree means is that we're in enough trouble as it is," Ewan said, secretly agreeing with her. "If you get caught—"

"Then you have agreed to rescue me," Cerri finished. "Have you forgotten? We are family. We must assist one another."

A series of soft thumps, barely distinguishable from the usual fan sounds, was all that indicated the girl's movement as she went to her room in the back.

"Mother help me," Tree growled. "*Why* are you all so determined to be sent back to the game floors?"

Ewan dared a glance at her, but she turned away and strangled her pillow.

That night, Ewan woke to the sound of his wife crying softly. She was on her side, having been warned by Lucia that the baby would eventually grow enough that lying on her back could cut off the blood flow to her lower body. But her shoulders trembled, and now and then her teeth chattered.

How can I help you? Ewan thought sadly as he tucked their blanket back over her. *How can I ensure you won't be stuck raising our child alone, here?*

It wasn't as if she had no support. The general fear of player contagion aside, most of the Centrals had accepted the idea that one of their own was pregnant. Some of them were even thrilled, taking it as a sign the Mother was returning. Lucia and Robert were practically dueling over who got to help Tree prepare more.

But she doesn't have someone who's been there. Someone who knows what it's like to be a mom.

An idea surfaced in his mind, and he smiled.

When Tree emerged from their bathroom that morning, he'd already laid out a breakfast on the table.

"What's this?" she asked, her narrowed eyes contradicting her flaring nostrils.

"A chance to eat in peace for a change," Ewan replied. "Cerri's training with Rocco today, and I didn't want to waste the privacy. I, um, also wanted to toss an idea at you."

She sat beside him and gratefully tore into the pepper-infused scramble, but she instantly gagged and spat her food back onto the plate. "What is Alice trying to do, poison me?"

Ewan snatched it away, then sniffed it and took a nibble. "Lisa prepped it, just like you wanted. It seems fine, if you don't like having taste buds."

"I can't eat that," Tree groused. "Give me yours."

He reluctantly obeyed, trading his breakfast for edible fire and trying not to choke.

"Much better," she muttered to herself after a few bites. "What's your idea?"

Ewan took a long drink of water, but it only made things worse. "I'm—ack—due to log into Veridor today. Check in with Paul. Want to come with me?"

Tree glared at him. "You know I can't. Robert's blocked me."

"Not this time." Eyes burning, he waved his tablet and handed it to her. "I got his request for a long-term house call, from a childcare expert."

Tree took the device and scanned it. "Your mother?"

"Yeah. She's already agreed to log out, at least until after the birth. She can stay in the baby's room in the meantime."

For a long moment, Tree sat there, staring at the tablet. "Grandfather—"

"Has already given his approval," Ewan finished, pressing the glass down. "I owe Robert a favor for setting things up, but it was worth it."

"But you accused Grandfather of planning to exile you, only yesterday!"

Ewan grinned. "Then we don't have anything to lose, do we? He's already committed and he knows it, especially after that stink with the chiefs over Query. Besides, Cerri's right: we're family, and family sticks together. Lucia's great, but you need someone with real experience, even if it's simulated. Someone who won't look at you like a medical experiment, or a religious figure."

When Tree didn't answer, he added, "Besides, my mom wants to help. She's lonely too, you know."

"I...I'll speak with her."

An hour later, they logged into Veridor with Michael at the rail. The dull Central steel and plastic was whisked away, replaced through the Logos's power with a crisp, cold November morning whose air braced Ewan's lungs, even as it made him shiver. The sky was his favorite shade of blue, and beyond the little thatched cottage the Argenones glistened, heavy with enough fresh snow to make the white in the yard seem a mere dusting.

Tricia O'Meara was spreading straw around the garden, but she looked up when Ewan messaged her. "My, how you're growing!" she exclaimed as she came to meet them at the door. Narrowing her eyes to scan her daughter-in-law's aura, she added, "I do hope that food they serve is agreeing with you?"

"Well enough, thanks to Ewan's generosity," Tree replied with an apologetic smile toward her husband.

"We can supplement that now," Tricia said firmly as she opened the door. "Come in, and I'll heat some tea."

As it turned out, the tea was already hot. In no time, the three of them were seated around the kitchen table, sipping away. Tricia leaned over to feel her grandchild's bump—at least, the simulation of it—and sighed wistfully. "I remember what it was like," she said. "The first child is always the hardest, because you can still pretend your old life won't be disrupted all that badly."

Tree's shoulders slumped. "I don't think I can pretend that, even now."

Tricia smiled in sympathy as she poured more tea. "I was older than you when I carried Ewan, but I still had to make a lot of changes. I used to ride with Jack to Whitehaven every day, telling fortunes in the market while he helped out at the college."

"Really?" Ewan asked. "I never knew that."

Tricia nodded. "As a girl, I'd dreamed of visiting all the great cities as a Church soothsayer. But things changed once you were on the way. Once I was far enough along, I re-specked into a professional adviser for the local children. It wasn't what I'd ever planned to do," she admitted, offering Tree another smile, "but it worked out."

Ewan's guilt twinged again, but Tree sighed. "Do you ever regret it? Not going?"

Tricia patted her hand. "No, dear. I had to adjust and give up some things I'd wanted to try, but in their place, I found something even more rewarding."

It's just like Lucia said, Ewan thought as Tree nodded. *It's a great strength, being flexible enough to let another's life shape yours. And that's exactly what we all need in the Centre, right now. How can I make them see that?*

He stayed as long as he could, listening to his mother and

wife bonding over the baby, but when the Logos warned him it was time, he stood up.

"Leaving so soon, sweetheart?" Tricia asked.

"Yeah, sorry. I'm due to meet Paul. Tree, did you want to come along?"

Tree gave him a grateful look that eased his heart more than anything and said, "I'll stay here. Message me when you're done."

"Yes, ma'am."

Ewan equipped his old parka and stepped outside, if only to keep his mom from fretting about his new method of travel. [Okay, Michael. Transfer me to the courtyard.]

A moment later, the snowy lawn dissolved and was replaced by the stone of the Whitehaven cathedral's courtyard, with its massive needlelike spire soaring up in front of him. A few of the passersby jumped at his sudden arrival, but these days, the sight of the Hero of Veridor moving like the Gem he'd bested wasn't as shocking as it once was.

"Ewan!" Paul waved from the right side, coming to greet him. "How are things in the other world?"

"Same as usual," Ewan replied, clasping hands with his old friend.

Paul led him through an iron gate into the Swords' training complex. Invisible from the square by clever design, the whole thing was an orderly maze of arenas, target ranges, and arming stations distributed among the barracks proper. Ewan followed Paul through a second gate at the far end, set into a high brick wall as though even the regular Swords needn't know what was beyond. Above it hung the Ether Corps emblem, embossed in gold.

"I can't tell you how great it's been, not having any more logged reports to deliver," Paul commented as they approached an arena filled with sand, imported all the way from the coast.

A pair of little stone forts squatted there, one to each side. "But from what Al'Dashan told me, it's not to our credit."

"Yes and no," Ewan replied carefully. "Rocco's people have a lot to prove. They're determined to make themselves indispensable to the Director."

"So he'll have to loosen their respawn lock?" Paul asked shrewdly. "Just don't let them take all the glory, okay?"

"Not you, too," Ewan groaned.

Paul shrugged. "I'm just saying. Now that you've caught the Diamond Lord and these Cat-seeth are wrecking the Locusts, our recruiting's flagged off."

"It's probably because we've gotten smarter about who gets to go," Ewan countered, looking around the arena and realizing how empty it was. "You're still sending the greenhorns out to J'unai, right?"

"And Ch'ira."

"Good," Ewan muttered. "We should all learn from their example. You'd think a common threat would be enough to make people cooperate, even if they can't get along!"

Paul smiled, pointing to a dozen Swords as they entered the sand in two parties, one dressed in brown and the other in gray. "It sounds to me like what you need is a good team-building exercise."

Ewan squinted as each party sent a couple people to the little fort on their side. "What are they doing?"

"Playing capture the flag," Paul replied. "Each team has to guard their own flag. If that's missing, it doesn't matter whether they get the enemy's. You can't win if you lose your base, right?"

"Right..." Ewan felt the ticklish beginnings of another idea as he watched the match. The gray team split their attackers, sending in two to draw the browns' aggro while a sneak slipped around. When the fourth fired arrows into the fort to pin the defenders down, the sneak ducked in. A moment later, she emerged with a bloody knife and a brown flag.

"It takes coordination to win against a determined force—hey, no suicides, remember?" Paul shouted as the gray attackers bought their sneak's escape. He grinned. "But more than that, it takes trust. Everyone's got their own job to do. If even one person doesn't pull their weight, the whole team fails."

"Different roles, working together," Ewan murmured, smiling as the victory horn rang across the arena. The idea had taken full hold of him now; he'd just have to convince the Director that they were all fully committed, too. "Paul...thanks."

23

GATHERING FORCE

NATHAN LOOKED AT EWAN WITH WIDE EYES. "YOU WANT US TO do *what*?"

"Another tournament." Ewan chuckled, but the Wastes' air quickly turned it into a cough. He reequipped his mask and gestured to the Towers. "There."

The massive pair of rocks, a hundred and fifty feet high at their shortest, must have been a nightmare to pull from the ground when the Founders excavated the Centre. Now, they were a perfect training ground for the dozens of people scrambling over and around them. Barely a quarter mile from the hangar doors, their labyrinthine nooks and tunnels made perfect cover for stealth work.

Nathan shook his head. "And you got the Director's approval?"

"Once I explained how the Ether Corps uses it as an exercise in cooperation, he was all for it," Ewan lied.

"It is a good idea, is it not, Al'Dashan?" Rocco said from Ewan's other side, his voice unmasked. Like many of the Sah'rassan men, he'd traded his face paint for a beard without a mustache. Mane-like, it danced along with his dark hair in the stiff wind. "If nothing else, our warriors will have the chance to release their tension."

"I don't know," Al'Dashan muttered, watching the mixed Veridian and Central soldiers struggle behind their Sah'rassan counterparts. "I fear it may be just the excuse some of them need."

"You'd better not be talking about my people," Nathan grumbled.

"I haven't finished!" Ewan cut in, exasperated. "We'll only allow teams of three—each member from a different world."

The others fell silent a moment, letting the incessant wind add its opinion in turn, but eventually Al'Dashan huffed. Then he chuckled, his massive chest expanding with each laugh. "I like it! At the very least, we wouldn't be openly fighting along faction lines."

"Good," Ewan said. "Because I want the three of you to set an example by teaming up."

Al'Dashan froze. His dark eyes fell on Nathan, but to Ewan's relief, the young man took a deep breath and extended his hand.

"Maybe we can learn something from each other," he said quietly.

Eventually, the captain placed his own hand over Nathan's. "What say you, Rocco?"

"I say you are fortunate to ally with me," the Claw replied with a savage grin, opening his hand to cup it under the others.

"Thank you," Ewan said sincerely. "Tell your—our—forces that Kate's party will meet them in the gym next week, to discuss gear and protocols. In the meantime, you may want to scope out a good place to set up the stands for the audience."

He turned and began walking back to the Centre, but Al'Dashan caught him up. "Hero, are you certain you don't want to partner with those two yourself? You've fought alongside each of them, before."

Ewan forced himself to smile, not caring that Al'Dashan couldn't see it behind the mask. "All the more reason to give you the chance, Al."

"I appreciate that, naturally. I expect you would ally with Cerri'dah, then, but surely Treanna won't be cleared for combat."

"Don't worry about it. I've already got someone in mind."

Al'Dashan nodded, his eyes narrowing in comprehension. "Logos guide you, Hero." He turned to rejoin his new party, but then he paused. "Are the rumors about this new player true? Can he clear the sky?"

Ewan tried to keep his shoulders from visibly slumping. "I hope so."

Gabe looked up from his desk with an expression so chilling, Ewan nearly bailed. "You've got some nerve."

"I know," Ewan said, "but I've also got the Director's approval—in advance, this time. We'll compete in teams of three, with the only requirement being that each member is from a different world, the Centre included. I want you on my team."

Gabe looked away, through the glass that encircled his office. Over thirty of his people sat in two surrounding rings on the floor below. "You never stop trying, do you?" he murmured.

"I can't afford to," Ewan admitted. "Look, I'm sorry about how Tree kept you in the dark about Query."

Gabe's eyes traced around the room, settling on James Frasier's conspicuously empty chair. "That doesn't matter. The fool's proposed method couldn't clear a room, much less the surface."

"Then what is it?" Ewan insisted. "Gabe, talk to me!"

"Trust you, you mean?" Gabe's voice was soft, at once

distant and wounded. "Come now, O'Meara. Whyever should I make that mistake again?"

"Because I made a mistake, too." Ewan leaned forward, forcing the chief to turn back to him, if only out of habit. "I should've told you. We could've checked on Brian, found Frasier's footprint. But I was too busy. Tree pregnant, fighting in the halls, and every minute thinking we'd all be in the tubes tomorrow."

Gabe tsked. "Not so different from your current position, is it not?"

Ewan fought down a sudden impulse to belt the man in the face. "What do you want me to say? I've already apologized every time we speak!"

"You're only trying to salve your conscience," Gabe countered tersely. "And I, for one, am tired of paying for your comfortable sleep."

"I never asked anyone else to pay."

"Yet we do, anyway!" The chief leveled a glare at him. "You're a player, O'Meara; that's how it works. But most of your kind can hurt only themselves. Every time *you* fail, you make some grand gesture of reconciliation, without any thought for the consequences. You led us to defeat in the Wastes, so you give up your corps to Sanderson. You failed to protect your family in Veridor, so you use more of your own people, as sacrifices to justify their deaths."

"That's not true!"

"Then you neglected your duties to coddle Annie's pregnancy, and in your attempt to compensate for that, you abetted the very fools who'd slipped in on your watch to throw away our military advantage!" Gabe snarled. "After which, you offered to clear the sky itself for the Director, if only he would grant you more time! And you have the audacity to act surprised at your impossible position? Tell me, O'Meara, what will you do next?"

Ewan punched the desk so hard, the glass cracked. "I'm appealing to my friend! You said you'd teach me about the real world, so frapping do it!"

He turned for the door, but he froze when Gabe spoke.

"Wait."

"For what, another lecture?" Ewan growled.

Gabe huffed. "It would only fall onto deaf ears again."

Ewan couldn't resist a tiny smile at that. "Yeah, probably."

The programmer sighed. "Very well. I'd hoped my opposition would be enough to deter you from these self-destructive pursuits...but if playing your game will help you finally learn, then I will do so."

News of the coming tournament flew through the Centre in the days that followed. As another ten Sah'rassans entered the shockies over Alice Spencer's vehement objections, someone began hanging colored banners in the players' neighborhood, drawing more than a few of the friendlier Centrals. Not to be outdone, Lisa Deering somehow convinced her chief to let her display the sign-up sheet in the dining hall. As soon as it was up, Nathan, Al'Dashan, and Rocco stepped forward together and registered. That evening, Amy Black, Nathan's lieutenant in the defense corps, signed up along with Bach'an and Sarah Duncan, the Ether Sword who'd saved the Sah'rassan's life at J'unai—and one of the few new Veridians to log out in the past months. Following their lead, more teams signed on.

Praying to the Mother that he was doing the right thing, Ewan quietly added his name to the list, alongside Cerri's and Gabe's.

On his eighteenth birthday, Ewan found himself shaking Query's hand in the gym. Away from the bland sameness of Olenwe, the seraph had hair as dark and thin as the rest of him, as if his body hadn't been able to figure out what to do with the shockies' nutrients. But his brown eyes gleamed from behind a pair of wire-rimmed glasses, balanced on his broad nose as he took in the gym's equipment and the seven teams assembled there.

Eight teams, now. Kate and Sam stood behind the angel boy, wearing expressions that couldn't have been more opposed. Kate couldn't stop beaming and punching Query on the shoulder every time he looked back, but Sam's sullen glower plainly said that if he punched the boy, it would be to knock him out.

Kate said Sam was sticking with her, Ewan thought uncomfortably.

"All right," he called to the assembled teams, arrayed in the now-standard black bulletproof armor. "This tournament, we'll be playing capture the flag. For anyone not familiar with that game, each team will start the round with a flag at their base. It'll be your responsibility to take the enemy's—other team's—flag and return it to your base, without letting them do the same to you. You'll earn ten points and end the match when you plant the other flag beside yours. Since we're all friends here," he said, stressing the words, "we'll be using dummy weapons. Kate, will you and your, um, team demonstrate?"

Kate swaggered forward, hefting a mock handaxe with little red beads glued along the edge. "We'll be using paint to simulate damage. Come here, Mule!"

Sam braced himself, then limped up beside her.

Kate grinned, making Ewan wince in advance. "Melee weapons will be equipped with paint globules. When they make contact, they'll leave a nice souvenir." She swung full force into Sam's chest, making him stumble and painting him with a disturbingly realistic red gash. "Of course," she added, "getting hit had better not be the end for anyone wearing my armor, but for sport's sake we'll give points. One point for an armored shot, and—"

"Kate!" Ewan warned.

She swung again—this time at Sam's head—but the mole caught the axe's haft in his massive hand.

"That's enough, Kate," Sam said gruffly.

The two of them locked eyes, long enough for Ewan to remember seeing Sam take a similar hit in real combat. Kate apparently had a similar thought, because she blinked and let go of the axe.

"Two for anything that gets through an unprotected area," she finished, face coloring. "Questions?"

"What about the guns?" Nathan asked, also watching the fighting couple intently.

Query raised a pistol with a bright smile. "We've devised a firing chamber which can eject balls of pigment at comparable velocities," he explained, his solo voice a pleasant tenor. He leveled the weapon, thankfully not at anyone, and fired.

Instead of a deafening retort, the gun made a little popping sound as a red blob flew out and burst against the far wall.

"These should, ah, hurt considerably less than a direct strike from the melee weapons," Query said, eying Sam's bloodied armor with undisguised glee. "But as you do not have the capacity to regenerate eyeballs, I recommend an appropriate degree of caution when employing them."

"Thank you," Ewan said firmly, stepping back in front. "The tournament will be on the new year, just over three weeks away. Make sure you grab your gear and practice before then, or my team's going to own you!"

No one laughed. In fact, most of them were still watching Kate and her new love triangle. It took Ewan a moment to realize that they shouldn't have been: the Centrals he'd met treated partners about as exclusively as seats in the dining hall. *But that was between each other*, he thought as a new kind of dread crept up his spine. *Of course they're not going to take well to a player ditching one of their own, and for the latest food thief, at that!*

Gabe scoffed and pushed past Ewan to the weapons rack, selecting a pistol and rapier. "Tomorrow afternoon, O'Meara. Bring your child."

Ewan sighed. "Yeah, sure."

Gabe seemed determined to make up for their missed sparring sessions with practice now, for hours at a time. It wasn't easy, between the choking dust and the constant tension between Gabe and Cerri, who refused to accept him as the party leader no matter how many times he claimed his chief's rank made him nothing less. Eventually they worked out an uneasy pattern of the programmer "suggesting" a course for Ewan to confirm, but as he watched the other teams practice, Ewan got the sinking feeling his group was going to be a long shot for winning.

At least they were going to beat one team. The dark looks Cerri and Gabe traded were nothing compared to the sniping and outright shoving between Kate's boyfriends. From what Ewan heard on the training grounds over the following weeks —and he didn't exactly have to try to hear it—neither Sam nor Query knew where they stood with her, but both seemed bound and determined to hold as much of her attention as possible: just one more resource to be fought over.

Ewan had a growing suspicion the seraph hadn't actually worked on his approved project since emerging from the shocky.

But when Tricia O'Meara was finally cleared from Medical on New Year's Eve, both family and friends welcomed her with a celebratory dinner in the privacy of Ewan and Tree's apartment. With Michael Patton's help, Lisa supplied a feast that would have had Alice Spencer foaming at the mouth, had she known.

It wasn't all smiles. Lucia got into an intense debate with Tricia about the nursery's protocols and precisely when conception took place, but the argument ended when Widow O'Meara turned her disapproving stare onto Kate and her two "good friends" as they arrived. Lucia tried to contribute her opinions on that front too, but Al'Dashan came in the nick of time to draw her attention—until Cerri, Rocco, and Bach'an tortured everyone's ears by yowling something they insisted was a traditional Caitsid'h winter's song.

Those were minor glitches, though, the fair price of bringing so many people together. They made up for it with good cheer and the most wonderful mix of stories: Veridian folktales and Sah'rassan legends, scavenged histories of old Earth and incomprehensible treatises from Olenwe. The revelers stayed up late, far too late considering the tournament in the morning, but no one minded. Ringing in the new year with so many loved ones and dear friends...it gave Ewan a touch of that deep feeling of peace he'd been missing for so long. And from the others' demeanors—the way Lucia and Al'Dashan sat close, or how Bach'an's smile got toothier every time he got Sarah Duncan to laugh—Ewan was sure he wasn't the only one.

We can make this work, he thought, even as he noted the missing faces. Carmine Rothchild most obviously, who despite being family, couldn't be told about the frivolous use of resources. And, because of that, the other chiefs: Robert Nichols, Karl Taylor, Ben Root. Gabe Reid.

Tree squeezed his hand, and Ewan gripped it firmly in return. *Somehow, we've got to make this work.*

24

CONTESTS

New year or not, the day of the tournament began like any other—which on the surface, meant cloudy, dry, and bleak.

Ewan led his family to the dining hall for breakfast, noting grimly as Lisa carefully spooned out mashed worm with bean paste that even tournament combatants and expecting mothers were getting tight portions, these days. He glanced at his mom, who didn't quite cover her wrinkled nose in time before adopting a serene, condescending expression to thank the girl for the effort.

"You know," Ewan murmured to Tricia as they returned to the main room. "I bet you could volunteer with the kitchens. They'd learn a lot from you."

"I'll consider it," she replied.

As usual, the players were seated in their own little corner, with an unhealthy gap between them and the Centrals, but at least a few of the teams were eating together. Nathan sat between Al'Dashan and Rocco, his small frame making him look boyish again next to the formidable warriors. Amy laughed politely as Bach'an juggled utensils. And, of course, Sam was next to Kate, with Query plastered to her other side.

"Hey," Ewan said as he sat next to the big guy. "You ready to get your butt kicked?"

Sam's eyes flicked to Kate, but she was busy trading death glares with her mom. "I've got plenty of practice."

Ewan sighed. *I've been neglecting you, too.* "She only whacks people she cares about."

Sam's huge shoulders slumped as he stared down at his anemic tray. "Yeah, I know."

Ewan glanced pointedly at Tree.

"So," she asked, "have you made any progress on the clouds?"

Sam gave her a baleful, despondent look. "They're still out there."

"But the arena's set up, right?" Ewan pressed. "And the stands?"

"Yeah."

They gave up on conversation after that, unless one counted Query going on about friction-induced static charges. After breakfast, the whole happy party rode the elevators up to the hangar, their grim mood persisting despite the festival excitement from the growing crowd clumped around the main doors. A couple of moles were there on equipment duty, doling out ponchos and dust masks for the spectators—a luxury the combatants weren't going to have.

"Ewan?" a voice called from behind. "Is that you?"

He turned to see a woman with dark hair hanging loosely above her shoulders, and a scout's pin on her breast. She walked toward him with a broad smile on her face, followed by a man and a young boy of maybe seven years.

"I thought I recognized that hair," she said, offering a hand in greeting.

Ewan shook it, heartened to see she remembered how. "It's good to see you too, Jennifer. Cerri? Mom? This is Jennifer Tilley. She was there on my first trip to the Wastes. Jennifer, this is my mom Tricia, logged out to visit, and this is Cerri, the first player from Sah'rassa."

Cerri opened her palms in greeting, but the boy scowled at her. "Why is your face dirty?"

Cerri looked at him levelly—almost literally. "My face has spots. I have not seen a child here before. Where are you kept?"

"He stays with us," the man answered, looking at his own hand in bemusement before offering it. "I'm Greg, Jenn's partner. Kyle's our son."

Ewan suddenly remembered waking up once to the sounds of Jennifer and Gabe romping in the bed above him, just as Cerri sniffed at the man's hand. "You do not smell the same."

"Cerri!" Tree whispered fiercely.

But Greg only laughed. "I'm not surprised. Jenn's out on the surface half the time, running around with her scouting buddies." He gave Ewan a wink. "But that just gives me some good time for myself."

"Um, right." Ewan's face heated, doubly so when Tree's grip on his hand tightened.

"Well, it's nice to meet you all," Tricia said firmly. "Are you going to cheer for anyone in particular?"

"Oh, we just want to see what everyone can do," Jennifer said airily, her eyes tracking Bach'an as he cavorted past to draw a giggle from Kyle. "That man looks fine, doesn't he?"

"Nice legs," Greg agreed, leering openly at both the Sah'rassan *and* his teammates after they'd passed. "We ought to have them over if they win."

"Well, we've got to be going!" Ewan said quickly, trying like hell not to catch anyone's eye now. "Gabe said he'd be waiting for us at the staging grounds."

Tree grabbed his head and kissed him, hard enough to bruise his lip. "We'll be cheering for you, love."

With that, Ewan beat a hasty retreat with Cerri.

"The people here are very strange," she commented once they were out of earshot.

"You have no idea," he muttered. *Sam's moping at breakfast really was more Veridian than Central. I wish I could say Kate's rubbed off on him, but it's more like they just traded.*

They made their way to a canvas tent, staked into the sand beside the Towers. Just outside, a masked Chief Nichols stood by with a crew of medics and a pile of stretchers.

Ewan waved to them. "You ready?"

"We're prepared for all twenty-four casualties, yes," the doctor replied tersely.

Ewan chuckled, coughing slightly as he turned to see the grandstand nearby. Already, several hundred people were seated on the steel benches, positioned to both see into the Towers and view the collection of screens tied to the various cameras, tucked into the rocks. The moles had been hard at work putting everything together.

"There you are, O'Meara," Gabe said as they ducked inside. "We're going third—"

"Quiet!" growled Bach'an, offering the programmer a broad grin that Gabe completely failed to return. "The furless A'Meer speaks."

He turned up the volume on a little radio in the tent, and the Director's voice crackled out from the speakers. "...my pleasure to announce the second annual combat tournament today. I'm certain I don't have to tell you how pleased I am about our accomplishments in the past year. Accordingly, our outdoor setting is a statement of our combined resolve to reclaim the Earth. May the shouts of our warriors wake the Mother from her slumber!"

Well, he's in full grandstanding mode, Ewan thought wryly.

The crowd applauded politely, and Rothchild called forth the first pair of teams to battle, for either thirty minutes or until one successfully captured the flag.

"Good luck!" Ewan called to Nathan's team as they exited.

A minute later, he was crowding with the others around the tent's small monitor bank, feeling better and better about having set the tournament up. Nathan's group, wearing gray robes over their armor, did a fine job against the blue team. Al'Dashan stayed back with the flag and defended it with vigilance.

"Impressive," Gabe muttered, smiling despite himself as the Ether Sword tossed one blue attacker into the rock wall hard enough to stun him. "He'll be difficult to get past."

Ewan chuckled. "I've managed it before."

Nathan and Rocco mistimed their initial attack, with the Sah'rassan pouncing early, but they eventually managed to wrest the blue flag and bring it back. They took a few hits in the process, but Al'Dashan had already landed enough of his own to easily tip the balance to a gray victory.

Kate's party was out in blue for the next round. Ewan sighed as he watched them bicker soundlessly by the flag, but then he blinked when all three moved out at once, leaving it completely unguarded. Not long after, a pair of gray attackers strode up, pointing and laughing, but the moment one of them touched the flagpole, a storm of paintballs erupted from the walls *behind* the camera. Each attacker took at least a dozen hits, before a pole sprang out from nowhere and knocked them out cold.

"Frapping hell," Ewan swore as the crowd's laughter drifted in from outside.

Three-on-one, Kate's team had no trouble. Sam bear-hugged the last gray combatant, dragging him along as Kate strode over her other victims to plant their flag beside her own.

"As you could see, my design was flawless," Query said loftily as Kate's team returned to the tent a minute later, while Nichols moved to collect his first casualties.

Sam yanked his robe off and twisted it in his fists, obviously wishing it was the seraph's neck. "You moved the trigger. Had

Kate not warned me, I'd have been clobbered by the pole! Damn it, Kate, it's not funny!" he added when she snorted.

Ewan stepped over and held out his hand for the robe. "I don't think that was a fair tactic, guys."

Kate smirked at him. "Perks of being the stage designer. The next team won't know what to think."

"Yeah, well, that's my team!" Ewan snapped. "Rothchild ought to disqualify you."

But Rothchild did no such thing. After Nichols's crew had finished removing the downed team, Ewan, Cerri, and Gabe donned their robes and climbed up to their flag.

"Right," Gabe said, after scanning the area for any leftover surprises. "I suggest that O'Meara and I make the raid, while the rat girl waits behind that ledge and snipes anyone who makes an attempt on ours."

Cerri snarled, but Ewan stepped between them. "Cat girl, Gabe. Come on."

The programmer smiled thinly as he drew his rapier and pistol. "Same difference, give or take a couple parameters."

A buzzer sounded from the grandstands. Cerri spared her team a last glower before skulking behind the rocks, and Ewan followed Gabe quickly and quietly into the arena. Half carved, half eroded, the path ahead was a network of twists and tunnels that forced them to check corners every few feet. They split at the first intersection, and Ewan caught himself wishing his player's minimap would appear in his vision. But, suddenly remembering how easily Cerri had defeated the map in Sah'rassa, he stood up and made no effort to hide himself.

Better to be comfortable when I get jumped, anyway.

He stepped around a corner and found himself face to face with Bach'an.

"Ea'win Omi'ra," the tall man rumbled, hefting a spear with a weighted ball on the butt end. "And all alone."

Ewan sprinted forward, swinging high with his left. Bach'an

blocked, leaving himself open enough for Ewan's right blade to strike home in his shoulder. Grunting, Bach'an spun away and stabbed out, forcing Ewan to parry in turn, but the Sah'rassan used the added momentum to swing the ball up even faster. It struck Ewan in the chest, staggering him back and leaving a bloody-looking crater over his heart.

Bach'an grinned. "That is one life."

"Come and get the others," Ewan challenged, grinning back.

He ran for it, leading his opponent through the maze, until he came to a rocky ledge overlooking the sands a good ten yards below. Bach'an laughed as he came, hurling a rock. Ewan dodged it and ducked into the charge, blocking with both swords, but Bach'an swung hard enough to knock him back anyway. His heels curled against the edge, and Bach'an reversed quickly to press the ball against his chest.

"I have won this day, Ea'win—"

The Sah'rassan bellowed in pain and surprise as he fell forward, dropping the spear. Ewan tried to roll aside but lost his footing and fell, too. For an instant the world turned upside-down, and he felt the reassuringly horrible sense of vertigo—before a hand gripped his leg. But Bach'an fell, howling, past Ewan's own wild grab, into the sand below. He hit the ground with a hard thud, followed immediately by a collective groan from the crowd.

"Bach'an!" Ewan yelled, but the hand on his leg became two hands, hauling him back to the ledge.

"He'll survive," Gabe said.

Ewan shoved the programmer back, then stumbled to standing. "Not without injury!"

"Did you expect no injuries when you conceived all this?" Gabe countered, waving a hand around. "It was a legal move, O'Meara: the same you employed with me last year, in fact. I wonder how many points I just earned our team?"

Ewan snarled and checked over the edge.

"All in the spirit of the contest," Gabe continued lightly, stepping beside him. "You're worrying too much. That sand is loosely packed...and here comes Nichols, right on time," he added as the doctor came running into view. "Now come on; I've already dealt with the other raider."

Ewan swore, but he didn't ask for details as he followed Gabe back. They had no trouble taking the flag from the defender, but as Gabe planted it next to their own, Ewan's skin was crawling.

As the fourth round began, he left with Cerri to check on Bach'an.

Nichols looked up with a glare as they approached.

"Is Bach'an okay?" Ewan asked quickly.

"Yes, fortunately. There was no need to take such a risk!"

"Ah, Ea'win Omi'ra," the Sah'rassan said, offering him a weak smile. "It seems you were not so alone as we thought."

"Apparently," Ewan replied. "You can get him next time."

"There won't be a next time," Nichols said coldly to Bach'an, kneeling to check the man's neck. "Not for at least three weeks. You're off active duty until I've confirmed you don't have any residual spinal trauma." The doctor scowled up at Ewan. "Gabriel was out of line."

"I know. I'll talk to him."

"See that you do!" Nichols snapped, before taking a long breath through his mask. "Mother knows, he won't listen to me."

But Gabe was doggedly unrepentant, insisting that he had only played by the rules as given. "Come now, O'Meara," he protested, grinning so smugly that Ewan wanted to toss him off a cliff, too. "It wasn't even a head shot. Perhaps you should revise the rules if you're so concerned."

Ewan didn't have to. The Director announced at the lunch

break that teams deliberately knocking their opponents out of bounds would be disqualified.

Unlike those who set frapping remote traps, Ewan thought darkly.

By the time the second round of matches began, the mood for the whole tournament had changed. The jovial camaraderie which had suffused the tent before was now muted, dampened, while the crowd's applause came in hesitant fits. The combatants knocked each other around with less abandon—even the Veridians—and the number of unarmored hits dropped as precipitously as Bach'an had.

When Ewan finally reentered the arena, with his gray team in opposition to Nathan's blue, his gut tightened at the now-copious amounts of red paint splattered around the flag. Bracing himself, he turned to the others. "Gabe. I think you should stay back this time, guard the flag."

The chief's eyes glittered, but he dipped his head. "It's your decision, O'Meara."

Ewan sighed. "Cerri, you're with me. Try to shadow me and slip past when I draw Nathan and Rocco's aggro. Hopefully, Al'Dashan won't see you coming. Don't engage him, just get the flag back. I'll cover you if I can."

The buzzer sounded, and once more Ewan entered the stone warren. Carefully avoiding the outer tunnels like everyone else now was, he crouched and stepped as softly as he could. After what seemed like an hour, he spotted a blue robe, barely peeking out behind a rock wall twenty yards distant. Stilling his breathing to a whisper, Ewan sneaked into position, finding Nathan watching another tunnel.

Sparing a smile at the scout's twinned blades, Ewan raised his own and inched closer, planning to cross them in front of the boy's throat from behind...

The ground shook. Ewan stumbled, and Nathan spun around with a startled yell. He swung hard, trying to scissor

Ewan, but they were already so close that all he managed was a weak blow with his arms. As the crowd gave a cry, Ewan grunted and brought his own fists together, hooking them behind the boy's neck as he dropped into a backward somersault that sent the scout flying overhead. Nathan hit the wall, but again the ground shook—this time, hard enough to cause dust and flakes of rock to sprinkle down from above.

This time, both of them stopped.

"What was that?" Nathan asked, panting.

Ewan strained his ears. The crowd's noise was louder than ever, but then his heart froze when he recognized screams among the shouting.

"Oh, no," he whispered.

"Asst!" Cerri's voice hissed as she emerged from the tunnel Nathan had been watching. "What are you doing? Something approaches; it fires upon the spectators!"

The ice in Ewan's heart burst free, drowning out the crowd's noise as it flooded his senses. He passed his swords to one hand and helped Nathan up with the other, and the three of them sprinted for the exit to the surface.

Ewan's fears were confirmed the moment they hit open sand. A long black transport, covered in segmented armor and bristling with even more guns than before, rushed in from the north while the panicked Centrals tripped over each other to get away. Heart pounding, Ewan scanned the crowd as he ran, already with a head start on the other combatants streaming from the tent behind him. He just had time to recognize the Director's bald head among the churning scrum racing for the hangar gate, when a rocket burst from the captured armadillo. It streaked through the air in a fiery arc and struck the stands full-on in the side, flinging people and shrapnel every direction.

"Tree!" Ewan yelled, doubling his pace.

The gate opened, but the crowd dodged aside as a trio of

'roos barreled out to meet their armored cousin. The 'dillo turned into them, splitting one in half through sheer momentum, but their sacrifice was enough to buy the remaining Centrals an escape.

Ewan raced for the Centre, swearing in relief and fear when he saw Tree and Tricia, moving slowly toward cover.

"Are you okay?" he gasped once he'd reached them.

Tricia's face was sheet-white, but Tree's eyes were harder than ever. "There was no warning."

No kidding, Ewan thought furiously as he scooped her up and ran for it, narrowly dodging bullets as the 'dillo banked around to strafe the fleeing civilians. *Two frapping months of nothing, and they just show up in the middle of our games?! It can't be an accident!*

Once they were inside, he set his wife down and turned to his mother. "Take Tree home," he rasped before moving to a nearby weapons locker, thankfully installed near the new training grounds. "We'll deal with these bastards."

Tricia gave him an anxious glance, but she didn't argue. Ewan waited just long enough to see them reach the emergency stairs before snatching a pair of combat swords, a helmet, and —after a moment's hesitation—a gun.

"Keep it open!" Nathan shouted, still wearing his blue robes as he led the other combatants. "All corps, gear up!"

Ewan charged out the door, spotting Kate and Cerri among the faces. By now most of the surviving staff had made it inside, but the 'roos were all down; the two that hadn't been split in half were on their sides and smoking. Ewan activated his helmet's headset, but his only answer was static.

Then the 'dillo came round, brazenly plowing through the twisted wreckage of the stands and stragglers, coming straight for the Centre. For a horrible moment, Ewan thought it was going to blast right through the gate, but it swung aside and slid to a stop, kicking a wave of sand in his face.

"They're coming out!" Nathan's voice called from behind him. "Shoot to kill!"

The 'dillo's side hatch flew open, and a squad came stumbling out. The Centrals opened fire, and Ewan gritted his teeth as he joined them, letting fly a hail of bullets that downed one figure as it ran toward him, shouting madly.

In seconds, a dozen Locusts were dead, but the 'dillo belched another rocket that shattered the ground in front of the defenders with deafening force. The world spun and Ewan flew off his feet, his face seared by the heat of it. Dizzily, he sat up and pressed a hand to his head, finding a hot scrap of metal lodged in the helmet, halfway to his skull.

"Thanks, Sis," he panted as he saw a pair of Centrals charge the 'dillo. Forcing himself to standing, he rushed after them in support...but the moment the other party got on board, the hatch swung closed. The 'dillo sprayed another round of fire, forcing him to dive; then it turned and fled, flinging sand and metal high in the air as it tore away to the north.

As baffled as he was livid, Ewan staggered back to the Locust he'd shot. He turned the figure over and ripped the hood away—then fell to his knees and vomited as he looked into the haggard, mutilated face of Patrick Lee, dead eyes wide with terror. The Veridian boy's hands were bound beneath the robe, but his arm still bore the pink sash of the Mother's Children.

"Animals," Ewan snarled, throat on fire as more defenders made similar discoveries. "Nerfing scrubs!"

"O'Meara!" Nichols shouted from the stands' wreckage, emerging from the dust with a bloodied Alice Spencer half walking, half draped over his shoulder. "Help me with the injured!"

The afternoon passed in a hellish haze. Ewan quickly lost count of how many trips he made to retrieve both wounded and dead, as often as not unable to tell who fell into which category. Limbs were mangled and shattered; chests impaled on the stands' writhing frame; eyes—or heads—missing. Central after Central, dead or incapacitated. They'd had no warning, no prayer against the Locusts' sneak attack, and what had he been doing? Playing a game that distracted the Centre's best warriors, leaving them all defenseless at the worst possible moment!

And with each dead Central, they'd lost a crucial piece of the system that kept everyone alive. *Rothchild's right, nerf him. We can't afford to lose anyone* except *players!*

The bile rose in his throat again when he found Jennifer Tilley's body, ripped open from the side but somehow managing to keep her arms wrapped protectively around her son—who was shaking and sobbing underneath.

"Kyle?" Ewan said, his voice coming out more as a gutted rasp than a reassuring murmur. "Hang on, Kyle...it's going to be okay."

He pried the boy out as gently as he could, sparing one last ashamed look at the woman who'd repeatedly offended his Veridian sensibilities but died to protect her adopted child. *I'm so sorry, Jennifer...Jenn. You did great.*

When the sky grew dark and at last he found no other bodies on the sands, Ewan returned to the hangar and collapsed on the floor. He lay there, staring up as blankly as the corpses he'd hauled, lost in a horrible, familiar maelstrom of grief and rage at his own impotence.

Eventually, though, a figure moved to stand over him, its face silhouetted by the lights above. "O'Meara."

"Gabe?" Ewan croaked, forcing himself up as the chief sat heavily beside him.

"The Director's made an announcement," Gabe said. His face was filthy, with streaks of sweat and blood caked to his stubbled chin. "We lost eighty-seven people today."

"Centrals?"

The programmer looked at him. "Mostly."

Ewan heard the meaning in the man's voice, the quiet acknowledgment that wasn't an apology. "Not to mention a dozen Veridians, by our own hands," he offered in return.

Gabe's eyes hardened. "Yes. Those, as well. I thought you should know; someone else is gone."

Somehow, Ewan's gut seemed to empty more. "Tree?"

"No. Two of the staff boarded the armadillo before it retreated."

"I know," Ewan said bitterly. "The Locusts took them captive."

Gabe shook his head, but his stare never left Ewan. "It was James Frasier, and Jeff Harper, who'd been on duty watching him. They stole scouting armor and sneaked out through the battle when we mounted our defense."

For a long moment, all Ewan could do was wonder that his heart could beat so hard. As if *more* blood flowing was the solution. "Then the whole thing was a raid to get Frasier," he whispered, his broken voice distant. "He told them about the tournament somehow, used it to cover his escape."

Gabe sighed, seeming to deflate as he leaned into the wall. "He'd been assigned to debugging communications; doubtless, he found a way to make contact despite the house arrest. The Director has openly acknowledged that Frasier is the Diamond Lord."

"For all the good it does now," Ewan growled, fists clenching. "They know where we are!"

"Ea'win Omi'ra," came Cerri's voice.

Ewan glanced over toward the elevators, watching her pad out to him. "Hey, Cerri. You okay?"

She regarded him inscrutably. "I am unharmed, but the warriors in the transports were not so fortunate. The winds have taken them."

Ewan closed his eyes. "I'm sorry."

After a moment, she replied. “They were prepared. But now we must rest. Tri’ana Omi’ra worries about you.”

Thank the Mother she’s safe, Ewan thought. He glanced at Gabe, but the programmer’s gaze was distant, staring out the hangar door as if tracing the Locusts’ retreat.

Ewan pressed himself to standing, leaning on his friend’s shoulder. *Why does it take a disaster to put us back on speaking terms?* “We’ll get him.”

Gabe didn’t reply. Eventually, Ewan let Cerri take his hand and lead him back to the elevators and whatever safety they still had.

25

DIGGING IN

In the days following the attack, the Centre transformed. It wasn't anything spoken; in fact, there was surprisingly little conversation in the corridors and dining hall. But every last Central Ewan encountered now carried a tension in the shoulders, a hardness in the eyes, that plainly said they finally understood what was at stake. That the blood of their friends, lovers, and children had washed away their delusions of security and privilege.

Most of them dipped their heads to him as they passed by.

The harassment of the players stopped so abruptly, Ewan's head spun. Now that everyone grasped the threat which had literally come to their doors, no one complained about making room or tight rations. Not that they had to, at the moment: everyone was eating more again, a grim reminder of the reduced population at each meal. But perhaps the biggest shakeup of all came when the Director promoted Al'Dashan to Lieutenant Chief of Security, in acknowledgment of the players' swift response during the attack. Shane Powell was furious about the Director's micromanagement, but even he knew better than to challenge the decision right after one of his own men had aided the enemy.

Ewan expected Gabe to get similar treatment, especially after he learned that Query had been summoned to meet with the Director a few days later. But when he and Tree followed Kate and the seraph through the auxiliary hydroponics room to the observation deck, the only person waiting for them was Carmine Rothchild.

"Thank you for coming," the Director said simply.

Query strode forward, beaming, and extended a long-fingered hand. "Director Rothchild, I am excited to finally make your acquaintance. This place is so fascinating! I am constantly discovering unexpected constraints to my daily routine. Did you know, the doctor doesn't understand either why human beings require sleep each night?"

Rothchild leaned back, apparently blown by the wind from the boy's mouth. "I did not."

"It is exceedingly inconvenient—"

"Master Quriem!" The Director tried to use his command voice, but he caught a lungful of dust and spent the next half minute hacking it back out. "Ahem! Do you understand why it is you were permitted to come to Earth?"

Query blinked, giving Ewan the overwhelming conviction he'd forgotten altogether. He glanced at Kate, who made a less-than-subtle jab at the clouds hurtling past. "I believe...it was because you wish to remove the particulate matter from the surrounding atmosphere?"

Rothchild traded a resigned glance of his own with Tree. "That's correct. But now I wonder: have the emissaries explained to you *why* we need to open up the skies?"

"Not precisely," Query replied, his grin returning. "Have you had the opportunity to review my proposal, then? I may need to modify it, given that the permeability and permittivity of free space are unfortunately constant here—" He blinked again, then finished with, "No, sir. Could you please remind me?"

"We have exhausted the available space within the Centre with which we grow food," the Director explained. "We need the surrounding land, to grow a sufficient amount to track with our increasing population."

Tree drew a sharp breath.

Ewan's heart tried to leap out and give the bald old man a hug. "How many?" he asked instead.

The Director regarded him levelly. "I intend to replenish our lost numbers with player soldiers. A full hundred to be certain, double that if at all possible. And that, my young friend," he said, turning back to Query, "is what I wish to speak to you about today."

"Ah, I see." The angel sneezed, then readjusted his glasses. "Nutritional requirements are almost as horrendous a drain on time as sleep. I still haven't become accustomed to the manner in which my stomach practically screams at me to eat. It really is quite interesting...I'm sorry, am I doing it again?"

"Yes!" everyone said.

Query shrugged. "I fail to understand why you need the sky to be cleansed, if your objective is merely to grow additional food."

"Weren't you listening?" Tree snapped. "We don't have any more room in the Centre!"

Instead of flinching like a sane person, the seraph grinned. "Does your food supply currently depend on this...sunlight I've heard about?"

Kate thumped him on the head and pointed up again. "Hello? No!"

"We use electric lighting," the Director said with forced patience.

"And could you construct more of these electric lights?" Query asked, rubbing his head in a mix of pain and fascination.

"Easily, yes."

"Then all you require is space," Query answered, waving his free hand toward the ground below. "And you have more than enough here."

Ewan yanked his own hair to keep himself from grabbing the boy's head. "Even with lights, the sand would bury anything we planted!"

"Not if you enclosed it in a structure," Query replied. "Why not simply construct supplements on the surface?"

There was a long, awkward silence. Then, as if the Mother Herself was adding Her opinion, the wind shifted.

Rothchild turned with it, looking out at his barren domain through new eyes. "This would be different from installing a few seats. The engineering required to excavate through a shifting surface is—"

"Not impossible," Kate finished, as breathlessly as one could in the dust. "Not with the whole frapping Centre already below us."

"Precisely," Query said, beaming. "I expect securing a foundation onto the roof of an existing structure is a considerably simpler task than atmospheric engineering. Of course, we would need to establish electric conduits to route power from the geothermal turbines, but that should present no problem." He raised a hand to the Wastes and narrowed his eyes in concentration, then chuckled to himself. "It will never cease to amaze me that the Logos has no presence here." Turning to the Director, he asked, "Do you have sufficient materials?"

"They're easily obtained, yes," Rothchild said automatically, but his shoulders were lifting by the second. "Miss O'Meara, convey my authorization to Chief Taylor. When can you begin?"

"Right away," Kate answered, if anything looking even more relieved than Rothchild. "We'll go, right now."

The Director watched them jog back inside, but he held out an arm to keep Tree and Ewan there. "If they succeed," he said, almost reverently, "the population limit will be rendered obsolete. We could support hundreds more. Thousands, even."

Ewan hesitated, then dared to ask the one question burning in his mind. "Would that be remarkable, sir?"

Rothchild laughed out loud, the sound overpowering the wind. "My boy, only seeing the blue sky itself could be more so! But that can wait, evidently. Get me the soldiers to win this war, and—pending your sister's success—I pledge to permit any interested veteran players to remain here."

Ewan could only close his eyes and breathe. For the first time since arriving, the Earth's air tasted sweet.

Dust and all.

When the word got around, the Centre came alive like never before. Most Centrals worked double shifts, making up for their fallen comrades, but the sections already charged with surface work bent all their energy into the new construction. The moles outfitted a transport with a cutting plow and bucket. Scouting parties left immediately for the nearest ruins, newly resecured by the Sah'rassan forces, to loot materials for laying foundations while a good dozen holes were excavated, with temporary plastic buffers forming a palisade to keep the winds from filling them back in. The sand was several yards deep, but underneath there was soil—actual soil—above the Centre's steel framework, as if the Founders themselves had tucked it in for a day that must have seemed it would never come. There wasn't any sign of worms or life in that earth, but as he sweated and toiled along with Sam and Kate and Rocco and even

Nathan, Ewan found himself daydreaming about moving the Centre's worm bins out to the surface.

More than anything, though, he came to a realization that justified everything he'd fought and suffered for: the Sah'rassans had been only the first wave of a much, much larger migration to the surface.

Together, they were retaking the Earth.

But to hold it, they needed more troops. On the morning of the fifteenth of January, two weeks after the Locusts' raid, Ewan logged into Sah'rassa along with Tree, Cerri, and Rocco, with Gabe at the rail. As the breeze from their avatars' reentry floated away, Ewan stretched his arms—human arms, for authenticity's sake—toward a crystalline blue sky, laced with only thin wisps of white that teased rain for some other day. To the west some four hundred yards away sat J'unai, its buildings flecked with color in the early sunlight.

Beside him, Rocco flexed his claws and examined his sleek black coat, huffing in satisfaction.

"More like yourself?" Ewan asked.

"Much so," the Claw replied with a pointed grin. "And you as well, Cerri'dah. I had almost forgotten your coloring."

Cerri'dah's ears twitched. "Then your mind has been scoured by the Wastes."

"Come on," Tree grunted as she stepped heavily toward the village.

[You know,] Ewan messaged her, [we could ask Gabe to tweak your weight parameter. It would do you good to take the load off.]

She shot him an acid glare. [He'll do no such thing. It's bad enough he cut in, when Alex would have sufficed.]

Ewan offered her his arm, which she did take. [Yeah, well, I figure he's just kissing up to your grandpa.] *And making up with me.*

Tree made a disgusted sound and kept walking.

Ewan followed, taking the opportunity to do a little sightseeing as they entered J'unai. Loosely centered around the oasis that provided Amad'hi's tribe with ample water and fish, the village was largely a cluster of homes and market stalls, all shaded from the sun by a tangled network of brightly colored awnings. It was cool enough that the Caitsid'h were still out and about, with children ducking and diving through the traffic as they tossed a ball around in a game of keep-away. The adults paid them no mind, instead haggling over fish and fruits, and wares brought in by peddlers from the other villages.

There seemed to be a lot of peddlers. More than could fit in the market, and certainly more than Ewan remembered from his last visit.

"Amad'hi has been busy," Rocco murmured approvingly, his eyes taking in the crowd as well.

As they approached the Rajj's hall, a clear female voice called down to the party. "Hero! Welcome back."

"Um, thanks!" Ewan shaded his eyes and squinted up at a sentry he didn't recognize, wearing the Swords' white tabard over polished armor. Her hair was golden, almost as bright as the stone walls. "Can we meet with the Rajj?"

In answer, the double doors on the ground level opened, and two more Veridians stepped out to escort the party inside.

"The Rajj has gotten a fine deal with Paul," Tree muttered.

"Bah," Cerri'dah grumbled. "See how she flaunts her wealth."

It took Ewan a moment to adjust to the relative darkness of the hall, during which he missed having cat's eyes with their slitted pupils. He followed the Swords—and Rocco, who seemed determined to lead them all, instead—to the Rajj's long hall of a court. She was seated on her throne of finely carved wood, flanked by even more Veridians, but she made no move to rise as she watched the emissaries approach.

When the party stood before the throne, Amad'hi's lips

curled into a grimace of a smile that came nowhere near her keen eyes. "Tri'ana Omi'ra."

"Amad'hi," Tree replied evenly. "I'm glad you're doing well."

The Rajj huffed. "Tell me, sister. What need does your world have, this time?"

Tree took a slow, resigned breath and messaged Ewan to get her a seat. "As you like. It so happens that there is an opening for eighty of your warriors to cross the mountains."

"Is that so?" Amad'hi's eyes widened slightly, but her ears flicked to Cerri'dah and Rocco. "I understood you could only carry one dozen at a time."

"We've added new machines to help with logged players," Tree replied as Ewan returned with a stone bench. "We can take up to a hundred at once, now."

The Rajj's nostrils flared, uncannily like a cat scenting hidden prey. "But what of the spirit tribe's resources? Was it not so that you lacked the food for so many?"

"That had been the case, yes." Tree glanced back at the others. "However, we are in the process of creating more food, enough to support a much larger force."

"You are creating," the old woman repeated, leaning forward more as her tail's tip rose behind her. "Yet you request my warriors now. Tell me, sister. What is it you are withholding from your ally, this time?"

Ewan's human hackles rose as the room took on a tense silence. "The Locusts attacked us," he said after a moment. "They attacked the Centre."

Amad'hi's ears stayed on Tree, but she sat back with a cool sneer. "Yes, I know."

Tree's fists clenched.

"Do you think *my* Claw and *my* emissary would fail to report this?" The Rajj's eyes took on a deadly gleam. "Especially since four of the Caitsid'h were taken on the winds, defending your furless A'Meer as he fled like a kitten?"

Ewan suppressed a groan. *Nerf it all, Cerri! Would it have killed you to warn us?*

Tree whirled around to Rocco and Cerri'dah. "All contact with the game worlds has to be reported to me!" she snapped, glaring murder. "It must be authorized—"

"They answer to me!" Amad'hi snarled. Her claws extended, gripping the arms of her chair. "None of the Rajji would presume to deny another's Claw in time of peace!"

Lightning arced from Tree's fingers into the bench, but she took a deep breath and released it before turning back to the old woman. "Clearly, we have protocol issues to resolve."

The Rajj's ears flattened. "You have more than that. Cerri'dah also reports that you have made no progress whatsoever in correcting the winds' prejudice against my people."

"Not for lack of trying!" Ewan protested. "The Director's been stubborn, but I'm sure with the new ag buildings we can—"

"Yet he expects me to assist him?" hissed the Rajj. She stood, baring her fangs. "In his arrogance he sends his emissaries to demand that we guard his pitiful life, yet he refuses to use his power to preserve ours, as he already does with the Veridian humans. Emissaries, I say to you: go back and tell your furless A'Meer that Amad'hi will send no warriors, until the winds can take my people no more."

Tree's eyes narrowed as she stood in turn. "You are shortsighted and greedy. If you refuse us, we will be forced to barter with your rivals for their aid, instead."

Ewan groaned inwardly as Amad'hi's fur bristled, but he held back from equipping his weapons.

"How dare you," the old woman growled. "You would have us fight with each other rather than grant us fair treatment."

"Rajj!" Ewan said quickly, as Tree's lightning returned. "I've got an idea!"

Amad'hi turned to him, claws still out. "Oh?"

Ewan hesitated, stalling to come up with something. "You're right about the Director. As long as your people are divided, he'll use that to get his way."

[Ewan!] Tree warned.

"But he needs you," Ewan continued, ignoring his wife's glare. "Already, Rocco and the others have changed the war." He laughed, bitterly. "And with the Locusts at our door, we don't have time to go hunting around for more allies."

The Rajj blinked. "You would weaken your position this much, sharing such information?"

"It seems only fair," Ewan answered. Knowing he'd have hell to pay for it later, he muted Tree's furious messaging. "You're in a rotten position to begin with. No decent person could argue with that, comparing Caitsid'h and Veridian respawning. But if you want to change it, you'll need to do it together. Talk to the other Rajji. Give the Director a unified front."

He sighed and looked at Tree, expecting her to slap him. But her hands were still, and her eyes held a pitying, resigned cast, reminiscent of how she'd looked at him before he'd known about Earth.

"You know it's the right thing to do," Ewan said quietly. "We can't go around acting like Gems."

Tree said nothing, but the Rajj huffed. "Ea'win Omi'ra, you are a fool, but you are at least a fool for just reasons. In exchange, I will tell you this: I have spoken with my sisters, all of them, since the winds took Bri'jash. We have already made such an agreement. As you said, we must have a single voice to carry across the winds. I say this to you now, as a token of our continued alliance and a gesture of our resolve. No Caitsid'h will offer support to the Earth-humans until the winds claim us no more. This is within your power to change, and we will not move until it has been changed."

Ewan started to speak, but he jumped half out of his skin when a cold, furious voice echoed from the ceiling. "We could simply take your people by force."

The Ether Swords drew weapons, but the Rajj merely lifted her head with a fanged smile. "Ah…the furless A'Meer speaks at last for himself."

"You are mistaken," Gabe answered. "I am merely the game master who maintains your existence. But rest assured: I speak with the Director's authority, and I will report every detail of this exchange to him."

Ewan winced, but Amad'hi laughed. "You may be able to force my people out, but you would do so at your peril. All Caitsid'h know of the world beyond the mountains now, as well as our sister worlds. It is wrong that you call the winds on us, but not on them!"

"Each simulation was created for a specific reason," Gabe countered. "They cannot be altered simply to suit the tastes of the players."

"Then you will have no help from the Caitsid'h," the Rajj answered. "Rocco, you will inform the others."

Rocco thumped his chest. "Yes, my Rajj."

Somehow, Gabe's voice got even frostier. "The Director will not tolerate mutiny in the Centre."

"Yet you will not survive without my warriors," the Rajj said.

"Grasping woman. You're risking death for us all!" Gabe warned.

"If the winds take us, then it will be over our roars! If it is written in the stars that we die and never return, then we will die hunting justice, not for idle threats from a furless sh'takh who would deny his allies life with his naked hands!" Amad'hi extended her own hand to grasp her Naza as it blazed into existence, then leveled the silver spear at the emissaries. "Go back to the Earth village and take counsel with your A'Meer and his minions. Do not return until you have removed the sun from his eyes."

The room vanished in searing light.

Barely three seconds later, Gabe had wrenched Ewan's tube open and hauled him out by the collar.

"What do you think you're playing at?" the programmer demanded.

"I'm not playing; I'm doing my job." Ewan braced against his tube, pushing into Gabe as the other tubes popped open behind him. "The Caitsid'h got a raw deal, and they've every right to want it changed. Why should they help us, if we don't lift a finger for them?"

"Spoken with all the entitled arrogance of a player," Gabe snarled, glancing past Ewan at Tree. "Tell him, Annie. We've given everything we are, everything we could have been, to their kind, and all they can do is whine about how eight lives more than we truly have isn't enough." The chief glared down at Ewan, his grip tightening around Ewan's shirt. "Doing your job, O'Meara? You just helped them hold the rest of us hostage, real problems be damned! You'll be lucky if Rothchild doesn't banish you all to the Wastes for this, assuming we survive the Locusts' next attack!"

"The Caitsid'h's problems *are* real." Ewan glared at the older man. "Nine lives is a lot less than the Veridians have."

Gabe shoved him, tumbling him backward over the tube. Tree yelled, and Rocco took a step toward them, but Gabe's hand flew to the pistol at his side.

"Give me the excuse," the programmer hissed.

"It's okay," Ewan said quickly, shoulder twinging as he hauled himself back up to stand between them.

But Gabe's eyes were a storm to rival the one outside. "I warned you, O'Meara," he growled, breathing hard enough that Ewan felt it. "I told you the price of overreaching, yet still you keep doing it."

"Because it keeps working," Ewan answered, keeping as calm as he could. "Gabe, the population limit's gone. We don't have to keep counting heads."

Gabe's eyes widened in amazement. "You don't understand anything! Each of the simulations is interconnected, with the flow of lives entering and exiting in a delicate balance. If I let these players respawn indefinitely, then birth rates across the entire virtual galaxy would have to drop when we ran out of empty tubes."

Ewan blinked. "But—"

"But you don't consider the broader picture, O'Meara. You never have! Now you've committed us to weeks of delay and distraction, during which the Locusts will have every opportunity to find their weapon and strike again. You've risked our annihilation, all to appease your guilty conscience!"

Ewan's heart thundered. Why did everything on Earth have to be so complicated? Why was it so hard to be fair and still have enough to eat?

Why does doing the right thing make us suffer?

"Gabriel," Tree said slowly, "let me make the report."

The programmer's lips curled into a sneer. "In exchange for what?" He shook his head. "You've squandered anything of value you had. But..." He released the gun, leaving it in the holster. "O'Meara asked me to trust him, so trust him I shall. For now. I'll concur with your report, Annie, so long as we all agree this conversation never happened, either. The Director need not know of O'Meara's latest betrayal, so long as the players continue to follow his direction."

Ewan traded a grim look with the others, then sighed as his anger floundered in a rising tide of regret. *So much for being on good terms again*. "But they're not going to. We'll be lucky to get any Sah'rassans to log out, now."

"You'd better find a way," Gabe said, his blue eyes calmer

but still ice-hard. “But that’s what you do best. Isn’t it, O’Meara?”

With that, he turned and swept from the room.

26

SECOND WINDS

True to his word, Gabe made no mention of the incident with the Rajj or the altercation on the bridge.

He didn't have to.

One week after Amad'hi booted the emissaries from Sah'rassa, Ewan went to Whitehaven to enlist some supplemental greenhorns. But Paul intercepted him at the courtyard and sheepishly directed him to the Patriarch's office, where Ewan received a carefully-written letter to the Director. A letter that explained how, in solidarity with Veridor's fellow players and their quest for just treatment, the Church could supply no additional Ether Swords until a resolution between the Centre and the realm of Sah'rassa was attained.

When Ewan logged out and delivered the message to Tree, she cursed even more than he had. Then she told him to keep an eye on Cerri, while she negotiated alone with her grandfather. Ewan didn't know—and didn't want to know—what promises and deals got tossed around in that office, but every evening, Tree came home with a grim expression and little news.

That is, on the evenings Ewan was around. With the gaping

holes in the roster now staying that way indefinitely, the remaining players were stretched as thin as the Centrals. Al'Dashan and Rocco, even Ewan and Cerri, started pulling double tours with the scouts to pick up the slack. Ben Root furrowed his brow to see them, and Ewan fretted every time Cerri came out, fearing that any harm befalling Amad'hi's granddaughter would kill their alliance for good, but mercifully they had no trouble. Whatever the Locusts were doing under the direct instruction of their Diamond Lord, it apparently didn't involve ambushing Central parties anymore.

Which only convinced Ewan that Gabe had been right. How much time were the Central forces losing, waiting for reinforcements? How much time did the Locusts need to get their super weapon?

The rest of January trickled past in an increasingly awkward silence, both in the Wastes and in the halls. The players already up and about were still treated with respect, even courtesy, by most of the Centrals, but even Lisa Deering noticed that there hadn't been any new faces for a while. Work on the agricultural buildings continued, and Ewan took heart to see how eagerly Sam hoisted the walls into place to keep his meals large. But with each new roof they closed, Ewan worried the buildings would never see use.

It wasn't as if anyone was suggesting the Earth needed extra Central staff.

When Ewan finally accompanied Tree to the Director's office for the end-of-month chiefs' meeting, it was obvious that Director Rothchild had already made certain everyone knew enough about the players' strike. It was also easily the quietest such meeting Ewan had ever attended.

That night, rubbing Tree's feet in their bed, Ewan kept thinking of Amad'hi's parting words to him. *How is all this in my power to change?* he thought, working his fingers between his wife's toes. *My skillset's good for making messes, not fixing them.*

We're running out of time—if we aren't out, already. What I need is an idea.

An idea!

Tree drew a sharp breath as his fingers ground bone. "Easy, love!"

"Sorry," Ewan said, but a grin split his face. "Do you happen to know what Query's doing, tomorrow?"

But as Ewan discovered next morning, nobody knew where Query was. The seraph wasn't in Engineering, and Gabe's frosty stare warned Ewan there weren't any players poking around in Programming. Lisa hadn't seen him in the lines at breakfast, though she did mention Kate had gotten double portions, packed to go.

"They're so cute together, aren't they?" the kitchen girl said, beaming. "A little player couple!"

Ewan bit his tongue and made his way up to the surface. These days, the grounds around the Centre had hard-packed trails cut through the sand, branching out to the network of ag buildings. Here and there, skeleton work crews were busy with hauling augurs for drilling power conduits, or assembling newly-cast hydroponics equipment.

Then, approaching the Towers, Ewan heard a whoop—from above. He whipped his gaze up, just catching a glimpse of a dark shape in the sky. Two dark shapes: triangles, turning dizzy circles in the winds' onslaught.

"Hey!" he shouted up at them, but they either didn't hear or didn't care, instead vanishing around the rocks. Ewan gave chase, cursing as he tripped over the former grandstand's remnants while his quarry literally flew circles around him, but after what had to be an hour, they descended. The triangles resolved into peculiar backpacks, attached by metal pipes to cloth sails that billowed as they caught the wind and tried to hoist their riders back into the dust, like deranged giant eagles.

When Kate finally swooped low enough to scrape the

ground with her feet, she pulled a lever, and the wings folded shut. "What are you gawking at?" she asked as Query made a slightly more graceful landing nearby.

"Your hair's sticking out every which way," Ewan answered suspiciously. "It's like you're underwater."

She reached for it, then yelped when Query touched her shoulder. A spark flashed between them, and her hair immediately fell back across her mask.

"That was a considerably intense static charge we accumulated," the seraph observed, removing his own mask to peer at it. "If we could devise a method for capturing and channeling that energy...oh, hello Ewan!" he said with a bright smile. "Are you here to try hang gliding as well?"

"Um, no, thanks." Ewan bit his tongue again—hard—as Kate dragged her fingers through the boy's short hair, making little electric crackles. Peering up at the Towers instead, he asked, "What were you doing?"

"Ah," Query said with an embarrassed chuckle. "We do have multiple research objectives to pursue, but I miss flight. Kate was kind enough to fabricate these gliders from my design. Secondly, with respect to eliminating the particulate matter, I wanted to experience this world's sky. You might say I was seeking inspiration, by acquainting myself with it. Thirdly, we are currently modifying Kate's original ornithopter design into a sailcraft, or at least, an Earthly approximation. To accomplish that, I must understand the aerodynamic and electrodynamic properties of the troposphere when it is so laden with ionizing effects. Perhaps we can take advantage of it, somehow. Do you have any ideas, Ewan?" the seraph asked kindly.

Ewan took a moment to process all this. "Sorry, no. In fact, I was hoping you could give me one."

Far from unfriendly ears, Ewan gave them the full account of the Raji's position, and his part in encouraging it. Query simply nodded, pressing his lips into his knuckles, but Kate rolled her eyes.

"The Director's a frapping idiot," she grumbled. "Would it kill him to cut the Sah'rassans a break?"

"He does have a valid point," Query replied. "It could pose a serious disruption to every simulation if he allows the Caitsid'h to remain beyond their time. I'm certain the Preceptor would override any resultant changes to Olenwe, for example."

Ewan blinked. "Sturilius could do that?"

"Of course," the seraph said. "For all the excitement and challenge this limited world provides, perhaps in this instance, it is unfortunate that the Earth isn't as malleable as Olenwe."

"That's it!" Ewan said, facepalming in relief.

This time, it was Query's turn to blink. "What is?"

"Rothchild won't change the rules in Sah'rassa, but the seraphim change the rules in Olenwe all the time. We could just plant a big sulianus in it and route the wind-swept Caitsid'h there!"

"Ewan," Query said, "If the Preceptor would disallow a change to the birth rates, he certainly would not approve of making a refuge in our world."

"Not to mention, you couldn't bring every Sah'rassan over," Kate added. "That'd still dork up the system."

"I know," Ewan said, "but it's the closest thing I've had to an idea in a month. Thank you both!" He hesitated. "Oh, and Query? If I do go in, would you be willing to come with me?"

The seraph grinned broadly. "Certainly! I would be concerned for your safety, otherwise."

Director Rothchild glanced up and grunted as Ewan and Tree entered his office just before noon. "You have good news, I trust? Or have the players decided to side with the Locusts and oust me for good?" he added dryly.

Ewan sighed as he helped Tree to a seat. "I've had a thought about a compromise solution," he said, "and I wanted to run it by you both before taking any additional action."

"A distinct improvement," Rothchild muttered. He placed his tablet on the desk and steepled his hands in front of him, giving Ewan his undivided attention.

"I want to create a space," Ewan said, "somewhere to divert the Sah'rassan players who've reached their respawning limit."

Rothchild's eye roll was almost exactly like Tree's. "Yes, you've made that abundantly clear. How do you propose to do it?"

Ewan took a slow breath. *Don't frap this up. We don't have any more time to waste.* "The problem from your end is that if the Sah'rassans stay overlong in the tubes, they'd take up space from new players, right?"

Rothchild nodded.

"The simplest fix would be to just create more tubes," Ewan said.

The Director shot Tree a long-suffering look.

"Love, you know we don't have the space," she said.

"There's the surface outside," Ewan pointed out.

"Even if we added new rooms and devices, it would take months, if not years," Rothchild countered. "We can't afford to wait that long."

"Agreed," Ewan said. "So, we can't make more space in the real world. The next best thing would be to make it in one of the game worlds."

The Director frowned. "You're suggesting that we create a new simulation? Do you have any idea how difficult that would be?"

"No," Ewan admitted, picturing Gabe's reaction to the idea. "But that doesn't matter. The thing is, there's already a game world flexible enough to use as a retirement home, if you will, for Caitsid'h taken by the winds. We've even made contact with it."

"Without my prior authorization?" Rothchild's voice turned hard.

"You'd already given it," Ewan said triumphantly.

"Olenwe," Tree murmured.

"The angelic realm?" Rothchild asked her. "What good will that be for the Sah'rassans?"

Come on, Tree, Ewan thought. *He'll agree, if it's your idea!*

Tree closed her eyes, thinking, but a smile crossed her lips. "The seraphim are extremely adept at molding their world to suit their interests. It would be simplicity itself for them to add a secure space for the Caitsid'h." She looked up at the cloudy sky through the windows. "One of your greatest concerns with adjusting the death rates on a world, aside from the impacts to space on the game floors, was the cultural effect on the world in question."

Rothchild sat back in his chair. "The Caitsid'h developed hardiness and respect for their desert precisely because of the conditions in their simulation. If we were to change that, we would risk undermining the very qualities which made them desirable for the war effort. But...we would still be withholding tubes from future player resources."

"We wouldn't need to route every Caitsid'h in order to buy peace with the Rajj," Tree countered, her voice gaining resolve. "What they lack is a feeling of hope." She leaned forward. "What if we routed a small fraction, perhaps two percent of such players?"

"But how would you choose who survives?" Ewan protested. "Who are we to judge?"

"I wouldn't presume," Tree said, her eyes warning him to back down. "But the Logos measures fame, infamy, and a host of other moral and character attributes. We could tell the

Caitsid'h that only those reaching a certain quality of lives can achieve the transfer."

"You would place a threshold on continued life?" hissed a voice from above them.

A piece of metal—a ventilation grate—clanged across the desk into the Director's hands, and Cerri dropped to the floor from behind Ewan's head. "That is unfair," the Sah'rassan growled. "Especially to the victims of others' cruelty."

Rothchild fixed the girl with a hard look as he quietly tucked the bent grate behind his desk. "On old Earth, people believed that only the fittest survive; like it or not, child, this belief is borne out by countless centuries of experience. If your kind are to be allowed to escape their naturally designated end, then they must necessarily be spiritually fit."

"Getting stranded in the tubes isn't a natural end!" Ewan shot back, fists clenching as Cerri growled beside him. "And what about the young, or the innocent? They wouldn't even have a chance to prepare themselves."

"Master O'Meara, I am weary of telling you that you cannot save everyone!" Rothchild snapped. "Earth is not Veridor, or Sah'rassa, no matter how much you wish it to be. Bad things happen, often without rhyme or reason, and innocents suffer the results. This world's history is written in the blood of such people, as the tides of war and famine swept over the planet." The Director regarded each of the emissaries in turn. "You have my attention, with the possibility of negotiating a truce with the Rajj. Do not waste that chance by grasping for more than I can give."

"Thank you, Grandfather," Tree said firmly. "We'll work out the details, but do we have your authorization to modify Olenwe to accommodate select Caitsid'h taken by the winds?"

Rothchild exhaled through his white beard. "Yes, you have that."

The emissaries didn't give the Director time to change his mind. Ewan tried messaging Alex, but she replied that due to the current personnel shortage, Gabe wasn't lending out any of his remaining programmers. So instead, and after an argument with Maura Pell, it was Michael Patton waiting on the bridge when Ewan arrived that afternoon with Cerri, Query, and Tree. The caretaker-turned-emissary gave them a pimply smile by way of greeting.

"Where's Kate?" he asked.

"With Sam," Ewan said, perhaps a little pointedly as Query opened his mouth.

"Ewan will accompany Quriem," Tree explained, "while Cerri and I will log into J'unai to reopen negotiations with the Rajj."

"Really?" Michael asked. "I'd have thought Ewan would go to Sah'rassa, since he, um, gets along with her better."

Cerri coughed back a laugh, but Tree's eyes narrowed. "I'm perfectly capable of dealing with that woman. Robert simply had concerns about my being confined for an extended period, should negotiation with the Lyceum become...prolonged."

"Oh, right." Michael's brown eyes drifted to Tree's belly. "I guess we wouldn't want to risk anything with the baby."

"Or her mother," Ewan added.

"Did you get the inhibitors from Medical?" Tree asked irritably.

"I did," Cerri answered, producing a handful of needles. "The shaman keeps weak locks on his elixirs."

Ewan sighed. *I'll tell Robert later.* "You going to be okay, managing both parties?" he asked Michael.

"I'll be fine," Michael replied. "If something goes wrong, I'll call Gabe."

"Try Alex if he doesn't answer," Ewan suggested, knowing it

was pointless either way. He brushed away encroaching thoughts of the last time Michael had been alone at the rail while he argued with a seraph, then let Tree stick him with the inhibitor. "But we'll be on our best behavior."

He gave Tree a kiss for luck, which drew an amused hum from Query, and Michael helped the emissaries into their tubes. The chilly wire filaments slipped into Ewan's neck and face, as always somehow finding the right nerves, and a moment later, the bridge vanished...

And was replaced by golden sky, with no land for miles.

"Oh, come on!" Ewan shouted as he tumbled backward. The sudden vertigo would have knocked his lunch free, had his feathered avatar had a stomach in the first place.

Query steadied him—without touching him—and the two turned a few circles, scouting the area. "Where are we?" Ewan called over the wind.

"Clearly, we are in Olenwe."

"I know that!" Ewan snapped, glaring at the platinum-headed angel—and realizing that he was looking instead at the vexing, dark-skinned boy he'd come to know on Earth, between the usual white-feathered wings. "But where in Olenwe? And why is your avatar all, um, humany?"

"Do you like it?" the seraph asked as he landed on a tiny sulianus that conveniently appeared below them. "Kate suggested this appearance, preferring it for its distinctiveness. Our current location was where she wanted us to...ah, please disregard that. I can transfer us to the coordinates of Sal's workshop. At least, where it was, last," he mused, before smiling brightly. "No matter; I am certain we can locate him from that point forward!"

Ewan barely had time to groan before the sky vanished and was replaced by the weirdest room he'd yet seen, even for Olenwe. Metal spheres whizzed around circular tracks set into a domed white stone ceiling some twenty feet high, above a collection of random silvery objects that he couldn't begin to recognize.

"It is good to be home," Query said appreciatively. He stretched his wings out, knocking over something that resembled a coat tree. The object gave an annoyed buzz, then melted into a puddle before flowing up into its original shape and position. The seraph took no notice, as though this was a matter of course. "I will contact Sal. In the meantime, shall we go to the landing?"

Ewan followed the boy out to a small stone balcony that jutted over the edge of the workshop's sulianus, into the open skies around. In the distance, he could see other suliana as dark flecks against the golden backdrop.

"They look like stars, only backward," Ewan murmured as he leaned on the balcony's rail.

"Like what?" Query asked.

"You know, stars?"

The seraph gave him a polite, blank look in reply.

"I guess you wouldn't," Ewan said, half to himself. "In Veridor at night, when the sun has set, the sky turns a deep blue-black. But there are stars, little pinpoints of light, scattered all throughout it. If the moon's not out, you can see millions of them, each like a little shining fire up there."

"That sounds fascinating," Query replied. "Is it a feature unique to your world?"

"No, I don't think so. I know Sah'rassa has stars, and Earth does too, although you can't see them through all the sand and dust."

"Perhaps we can find a way," Query said, absently tapping a finger to his broad lip. "I imagine Kate would be quite pleased to see the Earth's stars."

And you're all about what Kate wants, aren't you? Ewan thought. "Hey, about my sister—"

"There you are!" called Sal, as he descended from nowhere

to join them. His blue eyes sparkled as he looked Query over. "I almost didn't recognize you, Query. Are you experimenting with albedo and its effects on biomechanical functioning under a point source of illumination?"

Ewan lost the old man at *experimenting*, but Query chuckled. "As it turns out, this avatar reflects my genetic makeup on Earth, excepting the wings, of course. I've found it immersive and enjoyable to retain its use while logged in."

Sal clapped him on the back, almost quickly enough for Ewan to miss the man's hesitation. "Fascinating! Tell me, how is Earth?"

"Impressively restrictive," the young seraph replied with a grin. "So much so, that they've already decided to request dispensation from the Preceptor in order to mitigate a population overflow from one of their game worlds."

The elder's brows furrowed, and he drew up a chair—literally. "Perhaps you'd best start at the beginning."

Query pulled his own seat from nowhere, making a second for Ewan when he noticed Ewan standing helplessly. The young seraph eagerly recounted his experience of the real world, surely exaggerating the amount of time he and Kate had been spending together. But even Query had the decency to look troubled as he described the tournament and its bloody aftermath.

"The emissaries attempted to recruit supplemental forces from Sah'rassa to mount an assault against these Locusts," Query finished. "But when the natives learned of a discrepancy in respawning protocols between their world and Kate's home of Veridor, they went on strike. The Veridians did likewise, in solidarity. From what Ewan told me, the Director did not appreciate this."

Ewan grunted. "That's putting it mildly. But I think we've got a fix. Sal, how hard would it be to build a sulianus?"

"Build, you say?" Sal asked. "We would need to produce the

requisite material first, then set an agglomerational seed in order to bind the matter together...you want us to do this with machines?"

Ewan shook his head. "I think it would be okay if you cheated, so to speak."

"Ah, more's the pity. In that case, it is quite straightforward." Sal rose to his feet and pointed over the balcony's edge—and a new sulianus instantly materialized, two hundred yards away.

"Gems of old," Ewan muttered.

Sal offered him a kindly smile. "May I surmise that you're hoping to redirect some of these Caitsid'h to such a construct?"

"That's correct," Query said. "We felt it would be best for you to speak with the Preceptor, given the outcome of the four horses' last visit."

"We're not horses," Ewan said.

But Sal was watching Query, his eyes taking on a shrewd, appraising quality. "A sensible precaution. I'm sure that Sturilius and I can reach an understanding in private. In the meantime, perhaps you can show young Ewan around the local environs?"

Without waiting for a reply, the old seraph vanished, presumably transferring to the Lyceum.

"He could be in negotiation for some time," Query admitted. "Perhaps we should take his suggestion? We could use the time to practice your flight," he added mildly.

Great. Flying lessons from Kate's bonus boyfriend. "Sure."

But despite his unease at the seraphic world and its bizarre rules, Ewan's mood eventually lifted. He even managed to enjoy the company. Once Ewan got over Query's appearance—easier to do, without the pale skin and platinum hair—his constant slips into abstract speech, and his interest in Kate, the boy was fairly likable. He was also a good teacher, patiently repeating tips on efficient flight until Ewan got the hang of it.

After making a few successful up-laps past the workshop,

the emissaries struck out for a cluster of suliana that turned out to be a village of sorts. Domed houses dotted the smaller islands, with colorings as bright and varied as their neatly manicured lawns, while a stream of water emerged from somewhere inside a larger, central one to tumble over the edge, adding to the endless mist.

"I wouldn't have thought you'd need to drink," Ewan said as they flew under it.

"We don't," Query replied. "But the burbling sound is pleasing, and the mist is refreshing to fly through. You can drink from it if you like."

The villagers appeared, sometimes from nowhere, to observe the strangers. A few of them waved, but for each friendly face, Ewan saw another expression harden at his black wings.

I guess they aren't interested in my bringing more mouths to feed, Ewan thought ruefully. *Not that they'd need the food, here.*

Then Ewan saw one kid gawking at Query, not at himself. A moment later, the boy had become a striking shade of blue, with long flowing hair and pink-speckled wings, but then his parent grabbed his hand and pulled him back inside.

"Hey, Query," Ewan said carefully. "I asked Sturilius once why everyone had the same avatar in Olenwe, but I'm curious about your take on it."

Query grinned at him, seemingly as oblivious to the growing number of unfriendly looks from the remaining villagers as Kate had been with the moles. "Certainly, Ewan. Olenwe thrives on a culture of artistic expression, as you've doubtless surmised from the varied architectural and landscaping selections." He waved vaguely at the multicolored lawns. "It is commonly accepted that art is best appreciated for its own sake when separated from the artist, so we adopt a common avatar to minimize distraction. It is not unlike the Central staff's habit of wearing a uniform."

And now you're out of uniform, Ewan thought, recalling Sal's earlier hesitation. *Just by being your real self.* "Is the avatar selection strictly enforced?"

"I do not believe so," Query replied, glancing at his own body as if only just realizing why they were talking about this. His voice—singular—took on a troubled undertone. "But I do not recall anyone ever attempting to adjust their avatar in the first place."

Eventually, Query got word from Sal, and another transfer later, Ewan found himself just outside the Lyceum's effective range, facing the two standard seraphim. Sturilius regarded him with an air of cool smugness, but his silver eyes lingered on Query even longer.

Query shrank back from the Preceptor's gaze, but he didn't change avatars.

"You return to me better informed, dark horse," Sturilius said at last. "And with a more competent advocate," he added, indicating Sal.

"We've discussed your proposal with the other department heads," Sal explained, his choral voice full of eager overtones. "Anthropology is especially keen to see it enacted."

Sturilius huffed. "I still have reservations. Our world was never meant to support the dregs of another."

That's exactly what it was meant to do, Ewan thought, but instead he said, "They wouldn't bother you. I'm sure you could make it so that they don't even come near the Lyceum."

"Unquestionably," the Preceptor answered. "But as Sadalsuud mentioned, there are seraphim who may well interfere with them."

Ewan smiled. "Then don't stop them, beyond the Caitsid'h's wishes." He pointed at the Lyceum, floating lazily in the distance. "You have this huge college, but I'm guessing you're short on students. Wouldn't it be great to teach a whole new group of people all the, um, stuff you know?"

The Preceptor's scandalized expression was a perfect copy of the Director's. "Not only do you want us to accept these alien creatures into our world, you ask that we spend precious time *teaching* them?"

"Only if you want to," Ewan replied.

"I'd like that!" interjected Sal. "Now that Query's gone to Earth, I've got far too much downtime on my hands. I'll tell you what, old friend. How about you let me be in charge of this retirement park, and if any promising candidates emerge, I'll forward their profiles to you."

The Preceptor regarded Ewan—or rather, his black wings—for a long time, even by Olenwe's standard. "I fear the intrusion of Earth's limitations. Already, the Harbingers bring the victims of death." He fixed his gaze on Query, his frown deepening. "Wings of white, for the one formerly of our own," he mused sadly. "What madness and disease will the white horse bring home to us?"

"Sturilius," Sal said gently. "You know we don't truly exist in a vacuum. Much better to help these other people keep us safe and keep the worst at bay. As for these newcomers sullying Olenwe, I think we've got a unique opportunity to show off. What better way to improve their world, than to teach them how wonderful ours is?"

Sturilius sighed, and after another long, judgmental silence, his chiseled resolve faded. "Very well. I'm assigning the construction and administration of this experimental zone to the department of practical mechanics. They'll be your problem, Sadalsuud."

Ewan couldn't be sure how long it took Sal and Query to assemble the new land: essentially a blank field covered in high grass, slightly darker than the golden sky. The seraphim worked tirelessly, and without eating or sleeping to distract them, the only in-world measure of time Ewan had was the lazy drift of clouds and other suliana on distant currents.

There wasn't much he could do to help, beyond take the occasional image and pass it to Tree and Cerri. Amad'hi demanded a full description of the new Caitsid'h afterlife, which meant that Ewan had to wrangle one from seraphim. The sulianus existed in something Sal called "a topological nook in the corners of the attitudinal dimensions," which apparently meant that it didn't actually occupy any space in Olenwe itself...Ewan didn't bother translating that for the Rajj, but he did discover how a traveler walking in a straight line across the ground would return to his starting point. But if one simply flew up—which the Caitsid'h would not be able to do, at least not at first—the whole thing appeared to be nothing more than a regular sulianus.

Sal had a good laugh, watching Ewan repeatedly leap off, land, and run around. "Try not to think about it too much," he suggested.

Instead, Ewan focused on finding an appropriate name for this strange and wondrous place. Veridor didn't have any tales of an afterlife; everything and everyone stayed contentedly in the Logos's cycles. He didn't know anything about Sah'rassa's traditions, but since the Caitsid'h weren't going to be staying in Sah'rassa anyway, that was probably for the best. No, what he needed was a good, earthly name, for a place that boasted fields of gold, a land without suffering or want.

By the time Tree's party transferred to Olenwe for an inspection, he'd found one.

"Welcome, O Rajji, to Elysium," Ewan said formally to all forty of the Caitsid'h leaders when they appeared. They were an intimidating group: women of all stripes and ages, silently assessing their new custom-built afterlife. Lionesses weaving through the tall grasses, their different appearances as striking and pointed as seraphic uniformity.

Tree, in her human avatar, came over to give him a hug as the Rajji fanned out.

"Everything go okay on your end?" Ewan quietly asked his wife.

She slumped in his arms. "They're exhausting. They spent as much time posturing among themselves as they did trying to wrest concessions from me."

"I guess you know how your grandpa feels with the chiefs," Ewan teased, smiling as Cerri'dah led Amad'hi away.

One of the other Rajji looked up, then gave a shout as a team of eager anthropologists descended from the sky. Sal quickly intervened to make introductions, and before long, there was a seraph for every trio of Caitsid'h, asking at least as many questions as they were.

"The Moon is missing," said one woman, her auburn fur streaked with golden stripes.

"Ah, yes. Sorry about that," Sal replied. "Not knowing what moons look like, I had trouble approximating it."

"You could go see it for yourself," Ewan called. "I'm sure we could get a transfer."

"I say you should leave it be," said another Rajj, a middle-aged woman with sand-tan fur and white spots on her face. "It will discourage our warriors from being careless, to know this world is unlike home." Several of the other leaders echoed agreement.

After everyone had the chance to explore, the party regrouped. Ewan found himself looking into forty pairs of inscrutable eyes. "So, um, what do you think?"

"We can make it however you like," Sal added. "It's easy enough to expand. Buildings, mountains, lakes. Trees, too."

"I think it will do, for now," Amad'hi said. She regarded her sisters, receiving nods of approval. "At the least, it is far better than the fate my own son and granddaughter met. Or your son," she added to Sashi, nearby. "Thank you, Ea'win Omi'ra, for your efforts. And you, Tri'ana Omi'ra. You have fought for the Caitsid'h to create this place, so the Caitsid'h will fight for you once more." She hesitated, watching Cerri'dah's ears twitch as a butterfly fluttered past. "Perhaps one day, you can make your Earth grow things as well. Then no one will need the wind to take them anywhere."

"I hope so," Ewan replied. He sighed in relief…and regret. *In the end, that's the only solution. I love being logged in, even here in Olenwe, but we can't afford to stay. None of us can. The real world's problems need our attention more, and we're late as it is.*

He bowed to the assembled Rajji. "In the meantime, thank you for the gift of your people. They will fight for us all."

27

MAIDEN FLIGHT

WITH ELYSIUM'S FOUNDING, BOTH SAH'RASSA AND VERIDOR resumed sending players, transforming the once-frozen winter dam on logouts into a rushing spring brook. As the months began slipping past, Ewan decided it was easier to mark time by the three-week periods it took for each cohort of players to make the transition to Earth.

They came, in numbers Ewan had only dreamed of a year ago: wave after wave, a hundred at a time. Alice Spencer's staff did Gems knew what to rush food production, which at first consisted mostly of worms, but the burgeoning population pushed the kitchen to the limit, even with the help of volunteers like Tricia O'Meara. The Centrals lost in the tournament attack couldn't be replaced, of course, but Ewan and Tree did coordinate with the players' leadership to make sure that enough support staff came out alongside the eager warriors.

The Director's army was growing, by leaps and bounds. All it needed was a target.

But the Locusts remained as invisible as they had since the

tournament, despite the Centre's efforts—which admittedly weren't well-coordinated. Following Rothchild's orders, Gabe eventually reached out to Ewan and Rocco to direct Sah'rassan reconnaissance parties to other known military installations. The programmer never apologized for his outburst on the bridge, nor did he acknowledge Ewan's success in Olenwe, but he did nerf his anger back to a brooding simmer as he waited for the players' next insane gambit.

For his part, Ewan was tired of trying to make peace with his former friend, only to have it blow up the next time disaster struck.

In the meantime, the Director tasked Engineering with getting his new forces the finest gear possible—including sailcraft. Ewan wasn't sure whether Query or Kate was more enthusiastic as they briefed the military leadership on their invention-in-progress, but Sam loomed behind them, the only dour face in the room as the other chiefs quickly grasped the potential of a flying weapon.

When Ewan got a message from the mole one early March morning, asking for help with "Kate's project," he sighed and passed his tablet to Tree. She levered herself up to sitting, then leaned into him for a hug.

"I didn't think it was ready to fly," she said.

"I doubt Sam thinks so, either," Ewan replied. "He probably just needs a friendly ear."

Tree nodded, then handed him the tablet so she could rub the sleep from her baggy eyes. "I've got a prenatal checkup with Angela this afternoon; I'll let you know if anything comes up." She glanced down at her now-massive belly, then made a disgusted sound. "Ugh. I look like a loaded camel."

"No, you don't," Ewan said. "If you'd quit slouching, you'd see that."

"You try hauling the baby everywhere and see if your back

stays straight," Tree grumbled. "Surely, she was supposed to come out by now!"

Ewan gave her a sympathetic hand squeeze. "You going to be okay?"

She equipped a smile and kissed his cheek. "I'll be fine. Go on, and say hello to the others for me."

After a quick shower and change into the now-standard armor for surface work, Ewan went to the dining hall. Kate and her boyfriends were in line, each studiously ignoring Tricia's disapproving eye.

"Hey, Mom," Ewan said quickly as the others retreated. "Are you going with Tree to her checkup later?"

"Yes; she asked me yesterday. I still can't get used to all of the equipment the healers use here," Tricia replied, still watching Kate's herd. "They act as if pregnancy was an illness instead of a blessing."

I'd say they see it as both, Ewan thought. "They're just being careful. But thanks for being there."

Tricia handed him a tray, heaped higher than he'd seen in a while. "Of course, sweetheart."

Sam made room for him at the table a moment later, picking at a similarly massive meal. "Thanks for coming," the mole grunted.

"Sure," Ewan said, bracing himself. "How's it going?"

"We are on schedule," Query said, pushing his glasses up on his nose. "Although our efficiency would be greater if we didn't waste time confirming known material properties before installation."

Sam's forearms bulged, and his spoon groaned. "I keep telling you, Twiggy. Wastes material's been weathered for centuries. You can't make assumptions about its integrity."

"I am well aware of the questionable integrity of surface resources," Query replied, his brown eyes flashing.

"The important thing is, we're getting it built," Kate said irritably, forcing the boys into silent glaring. "Karl let us convert one of the spare ag buildings into a test hangar," she explained to Ewan. "We've gotten most of the hull built, but Mule here thought we could use a hand rigging the sail. The other moles are all tied up, making 'roos and buildings. By the way, where's your shadow?"

"Cerri?" Ewan asked. "She and Rocco took the latest greenhorns on an orientation patrol; they'll be back in a couple of days."

After breakfast, Ewan followed the others out to a building half a mile southeast of the Centre. The roof was nothing more than canvas, flapping in the wind. As he stepped inside, thinking about vehicles in general, Ewan found himself remembering the icy boat Tree had fashioned in Veridor, the one that carried them safely—more or less—out of the Argenone Mountains. But where that vessel had graceful curves and a sense of delicate purpose, the hulking mass lurking in the building was less like a ship and more like the victim of a game of tug-of-war. The sail, neatly folded in a corner, bore the same labyrinthine patterns as its counterpart in Olenwe had, but the main body might as well have been a miniature camel: solid, angular, and studded with rivets, about twenty feet long and twelve feet across.

The name *Red Horse* was painted above the entry hatch.

"Wow," Ewan said, for lack of anything better to offer.

"This is merely a prototype," Query replied, his voice thinner than usual behind his mask. "A proof of concept, to demonstrate to the Director and his chiefs before manufacturing larger varieties."

Ewan blinked. "You're going to make them even bigger?"

"Of course," Kate said, pushing past him with an armful of steel cable. "Baldy wants these things to carry troops."

"I sympathize, Ewan," Query said as he began arranging the

sail. “By all appearances, the cabin is ungainly and excessively heavy, even for a prototype.”

Sam thumped the hull. “That excessive weight’s called armor, Twig. It’s the only part that’ll keep the Locusts from blowing this thing out of the sky, assuming your tissue paper can get it up there in the first place.”

“I assure you, it will do the job nicely,” Query said, handing Kate a corner so they could spread it out behind the body. “The foil is indeed thin, but it will be electromagnetically reinforced by the very particles that buffet it. Its light weight makes it an exceedingly efficient component of the vessel, in compensation for your factors of redundancy.”

“They’re factors of safety!” Sam snapped. “Kate, you tell him! My brain’s not lofty enough to reach his giant ears.”

“Sam’s right,” Kate huffed, lugging her end of the sail up a scaffold to clear the cabin. “We’ve only been in the first few hundred yards of air on our gliders. The winds might get a lot rougher once we get higher.”

“A few hundred yards?” Ewan repeated. “On those flimsy little backpacks?”

Query ignored him. “That is the purpose of today’s test flight, Kate. Lacking simulation capabilities, we need to collect atmospheric data manually.”

“Test flight?” Ewan and Sam said at the same time.

“Of course,” the seraph answered, as he pulled his own end of the sail over the cabin. “Did Kate not tell you?”

“There’s a lot she isn’t telling me, anymore,” Sam growled.

“Where are you going, Mule?” Kate asked as he yanked his mask off and stomped into the hull.

“To make sure the damned bolts are tight!” he shouted back.

Now I know why he needs help, Ewan thought grimly. Sighing at the prospect of talking up his little sister’s boyfriend to her,

Ewan moved around to where Kate was attaching the sail to massive hooks on the cabin.

"So," he said. "Sam and Query."

"Don't you frapping start with me," she warned, waving a wrench at him. "I get enough from them and Mom, as it is."

"And rightly so!" Ewan scolded as he climbed up to keep the cable taut. "I thought you and Sam had a good thing going."

"We did," Kate said, grunting as she bent the cable into a clamp. "But he's limited, E. Take flying. He can't hack the idea, much less the practice."

"Yeah, well, he wasn't a natural-born seraph," Ewan countered, suddenly wondering what game world Sam would have been born into. "You've got to cut him some slack."

Kate forced the clamp shut, then huffed into her mask.

"You know he's jealous of Query," Ewan pressed quietly, following her across the roof to the next cable.

Growling, she grabbed a new clamp from her belt. "This isn't Veridor. I can choose who I want to spend my time with, and how I spend it."

Ewan passed her the cable, but he didn't let go until she'd looked him in the eye. "You know it's not right to play them off against each other."

"But how else can I know which one to choose?" Kate jammed the cable through, then started wrenching it closed. "I'm so confused! Sam's been good to me, you know? Always encouraging, always helpful. He helped me get my feet back on the ground, after Dad died. But he'd try to keep me there, grounded, if he could. And Query? He's a beanpole, but he's cute, and imaginative, and the way his eyes light up when he gets one of his ideas..." She sniffed, and Ewan's heart twisted as she brushed a tear away. "He's about to help me fly, for Gems' sakes! But he's so out there that no one understands him." Her voice became a frightened whisper. "What if he decides I can't understand him, either?"

Ewan sighed and pulled her into a hug. "They're both good guys, K. I've seen how they look at you. You just need to let one of them down gently, that's all."

"Easy for you to say," Kate grumbled. "What would you do if you had two Trees to pick from?"

"Probably get shot," Ewan replied, drawing a chuckle from her. "Or zapped."

After several hours' work and continued snarking between Sam and Query, the seraph eventually decreed the sailcraft ready for a test flight. "Who would like to come aboard?" he asked cheerfully, wiping the sweat from his brow.

"Count me in!" Kate said.

"I'm coming too," Sam said firmly. "Unless you think I'm too heavy. I wouldn't want to break your little toy."

"Not at all," Query replied with a cool smile. "Your bulk would doubtless help me assess the sailcraft's performance under extreme conditions."

Ewan stepped between the boys as Sam raised a fist. "In that case, I'll also tag along."

"Wonderful! Follow me, please." Query strode into the vessel, turning right to reach the little enclosed cockpit. There were only two seats, positioned side by side; Query and Kate took them, hanging their masks on the armrests. Sam stood behind Kate, but he was twisting his own mask like it was the seraph's neck.

Ewan gave the big guy a reassuring pat on the back, but he couldn't find anywhere to hang his mask, much less anything like a handhold.

Query flipped a switch, and the consoles in the front lit up. "Wiring test successful. The magnetic repulsor should achieve full power in approximately forty seconds. Ewan, as this is your first visit to the helm, let me acquaint you with the controls. This throttle here controls the repulsor's output." He patted a short lever on his right. "And the gimbal will respond to inputs from the yoke, like this." He gripped a larger stick, equipped with a pair of handles, and gave it a light twist.

The craft shook.

Query frowned. "Hmm. That could be troublesome."

"What could?" Sam asked suspiciously.

"Most likely nothing," the seraph replied, drawing a look from all three of the others. "I suspect we simply experienced minor electromagnetic interference from the main hull. When we go to full power, the redirected force to the sails should override such tremors."

Ewan swallowed, wishing again that he and Sam had chairs as Kate quietly strapped herself into hers. *Query obviously wasn't expecting anyone else to tag along!* He glanced at Sam, but the mole was clenching his jaw, determined to stay aboard.

"The batteries are fully charged," Kate said, checking a meter on her side. "We'll lose charge rapidly, but hopefully the static routers will compensate."

"Keep me apprised, just in case," Query answered. He placed his hand on the throttle. "Shall we?"

He pressed the lever forward, and Ewan's skin tingled as the repulsor thrummed to life in the rear bay, sending a buzz throughout the vessel. Sam grunted in surprise, then slipped back toward the wall. "Hey!" he called. "My leg's getting yanked!"

"Ah. It must be the metallic components in your prosthesis," Query said without concern. "I expect you will be unharmed if you hold still."

"That's easy enough," Sam grumbled, trying to pull himself free. "I'm pinned to the wall!"

"At least you have a safety harness now," Ewan offered with forced levity.

"Deploying the sail," the seraph declared, ignoring them both as he opened the throttle even more. Ewan heard a scraping, crunching sound above them, then saw the canvas roof fly away as the sail's forward edge leaped past it a good thirty yards.

Kate let out a whoop as Query pulled the yoke back, but it was lost in the noise of the sailcraft smashing forward—through the wall—as it leaped into the air.

Ever since logging out, Ewan had maintained a healthy fear of the Centre's elevators, respecting that they might somehow break and send him careening down into the depths. Ten seconds into the *Red Horse's* maiden flight, Ewan was praying for the safety of a fixed cable and enclosed shaft. The sailcraft pitched and swerved, swinging precariously from its cords, and Ewan gripped the back of Query's chair with white knuckles, regretting among many things the large breakfast he'd eaten.

Query kept a sharp eye on the vessel's radar, periodically looking up to make sure that the sail was still attached.

"Why is it shaking so much?" Sam shouted, though of all of them, he wasn't sliding around.

"The wind is considerably stronger than we projected from the speeds recorded at our gliders' altitudes. I believe I can compensate." The seraph wrenched a lever around, and the shuddering decreased—slightly. "There."

"What did you do?" Ewan asked.

"I adjusted the morphological characteristics of the sail's aft section," Query answered.

"You what?"

"He changed the shape," Kate translated, grinning. "Now we've got a bumper on the back of this carriage."

"This is effective," Query mused. "Unfortunately, it will only help us while we travel with the prevailing winds."

"What happens when we turn around?" Sam asked.

"We will be flying into the wind," Query answered simply. "I am hoping that the sail's structure can be adjusted to compensate."

"You're *hoping*?" Sam exploded. "You've got us up here a mile in the air, and you don't know how to get us back?!"

"This is a test flight, after all," Query replied tersely. "How one could anticipate every potential setback is beyond me."

"But are we going to be okay?" Ewan asked. He looked to Kate for a realistic answer, but her expression was as nervous as he felt.

"Q," she said, "tell me you can land this thing."

"Theoretically, yes. And without question, we will reach the ground eventually. The only variable is at which vector we will descend."

"What?" Ewan said, hoping he'd misheard.

"He said we're going to crash!" Sam growled.

"Okay, Query, I think we've got some good data," Kate said quickly. "We know we need a way to tack into the winds."

"Quite so," Query agreed. He turned around and finally noticed how pale his passengers' faces were. "Shall I take us back?"

"Yes, please!" Ewan yelped, grateful that *he* didn't need to act tough to impress Kate.

"Very well," the boy replied. He turned the yoke, and the craft shuddered as the repulsor turned with it. Sam slid too, as his leg dragged toward the far wall. The sails changed shape, but as they turned broadside to the wind, the consoles on the front blinked and sparked.

Query tsked. "We're getting interference from the sand—"

There was a series of loud, shuddering pops. The consoles went blank as the sail flew out in the direction of the winds, only half attached. Ewan's stomach flew into his mouth as the *Red Horse* slipped out of the sky, dragged on by the winds as it fell. He got a reassuringly panic-inducing sensation of being weightless as the floor fell slowly out from under his feet, but soon enough it slammed up into him, as the ship hit the sands like a meteor. Metal wailed as it crunched and snapped, they rolled sickeningly...and when the hull finally skittered to a stop, Ewan could just glimpse the silver sail escaping into the storm before he blacked out.

A sharp scent stabbed him awake again. Consciousness brought a crushing, throbbing pain in his legs. Not far away, Sam and Query were shouting at each other. Ewan opened his eyes to see Kate hovering over him with a foul-smelling cloth. "Ewan! Oh Gems, I'm so sorry! Can you hear me?"

"Yeah," Ewan said, though his voice seemed to come from a few feet away. He leaned his head up with a wince, reassuring himself that the rest of his body was there and not just a mass of pain, then flopped back down again. "What happened?"

"We crashed," Kate answered, her voice mortified and embarrassed. "The shear force in the wind was too strong for the cables, and the sail broke off."

"Are you okay?" Ewan asked automatically.

She laughed, bitterly. "Yes, I'm fine! The safety harness and the sands broke my fall. Query's okay too, his pride's injured more than anything else, and Sam's safe enough. He got a knock to the head, but the repulsor kept his leg fixed to the wall until the generator broke."

Ewan tried to chuckle, but it came out as a strained cough. "Must've been bad, if you think Sam's thick head might take damage."

She grimaced. "E...I think you broke your legs."

Ewan tried to move his right leg and received a dizzying pain. "Ow. I think you're right," he gasped. To his surprise, he thought of Gabe getting shot at Fort Gilmer. *Nerf it all...have we ever logged out a player who didn't get people maimed or worse?* "What's the plan, now?"

Kate glanced over her shoulder at the others. "You were unconscious for about twenty minutes. Sam radioed the Centre; they're sending a rescue party out now. So, we're waiting for them—knock it off, you two!" she yelled.

"You're defending him?" they both shouted at the same time, then glared at each other.

"Clearly, you did not stress the limitations of the steel construction in the design phase," Query sniped at Sam.

"Don't blame this on me! The hull's durability is the only reason we're even alive right now!"

Query scoffed. "The fall was only five hundred meters."

"Five hundred meters?!" Sam bellowed, double-facepalming before flinging his massive arms wide. "This isn't your weird painless game, you idiot! Even a drop of twenty feet could kill us out here! Or weren't you paying attention during the tournament?"

"Guys, I said to knock it off!" Kate barked. She stalked toward them, reducing their argument to snarling. "Honestly, we were all at fault. Query, Sam's right. You've got to remember that the rules out here are solid. We need to build with a better factor of safety."

"We shouldn't be trying to fly in the first place," Sam grumbled. "We're not meant to be."

"Blast it all, we can do anything we dream of!" Kate snapped. "Why can't you use your imagination more, Dad—Sam! I mean Sam!" Face going sheet-white, she reached out to her boyfriend.

But Sam pulled back, watching her with such loud hurt that Ewan forgot his own pain for a moment.

"Sam, I'm sorry," Kate said, her voice shaking now. "You know I didn't mean it."

"I know you miss your father," Sam said stiffly as blood trickled down his forehead. "But we agreed that you would treat me differently."

"You're right, I will," Kate blurted, pleading. "It was just an accident. It won't happen again."

"No, it won't," Sam said bitterly. He stood taller, swaying and drawing Ewan's attention to the twisted metal of his leg—the leg Kate had made for him. The mole's voice quavered as he spoke. "We should take some time off. I need to think, and we all know I can't do that as quickly as Twiggy."

Without waiting for a reply, Sam turned and began half trudging, half limping across the dunes in the direction of the Centre, leaving Query and Kate to stare at each other while Ewan blacked out again.

28

THE ARRIVAL

ROBERT NICHOLS SIGHED AS HE REVIEWED THE SCAN OF EWAN'S legs, then showed him the image. A network of dark lines wove across the white bones, giving them the appearance of a tile mosaic. "O'Meara, you are the single most injury-prone person I've ever encountered."

Ewan sighed, too. "I didn't think it would be so dangerous."

The chief arched an eyebrow at him. "Getting flung through the air without so much as a safety harness? Dangerous? I believe *didn't think* covers it nicely."

Tree gave Ewan's hand a squeeze, mercifully not piling on in public. "Will he recover?"

Nichols sniffed. "He'll be fine. The osteotic supplements he received during his initial rehabilitation are stronger than the average bone, though they cannot heal in and of themselves. Miraculously, there aren't any full breaks, so we needn't worry about that." He turned to Ewan. "I'll give you a series of injections and keep you immobile for a week, to ensure the bone reconnects properly. A month would be preferable, frankly. Repairing bone isn't as simple as reinforcing it."

Ewan swallowed. "How am I supposed to sit still that long?"

Nichols adjusted his glasses, not suppressing a dark smile. "It'll be into the shocky with you. Then we'll reevaluate your condition."

The next week confirmed Ewan's long-held suspicion: three months in wheelchairs and crutches were far more comfortable than sitting in Kate's infernal contraption. The needles in his legs made him itch horribly, and his back felt like it had to pop every few minutes. Nichols sedated him for most of it, partly for mercy, but mostly to shut Ewan up.

When Ewan finally escaped Medical, he was back in a wheelchair, with strict orders to stay off his feet for at least another two weeks. As he rolled home beside Tree in the halls, every heavy step she took drove his own guilt higher.

What a pair we make, he thought ruefully. *She's the one who ought to be getting a ride.*

They took the rest of March off, leaving recruitment and war meetings to Al'Dashan and Rocco. Cerri made herself scarce when they started swimming more to take advantage of the dis-encumbering perks of the water, but when Lucia haunted the pools a little too much for Ewan's sanity, he and Tree also got into the habit of taking long walks on the game floors. The silence and darkness were refreshing, and the constant, low-level thrum of the massive electric grid that kept the game worlds alive gave Ewan the clear impression that the baby wasn't the only one in a womb.

As if the Mother Herself was waiting for the big delivery day, too.

Tree got her first contractions right after Ewan upgraded from the wheelchair to crutches. He'd called his mom and Lucia in a panic, then cleared a wide path to Medical, only for the older women to explain that sporadic contractions were perfectly normal, even months ahead of labor.

"You're just warming up, honey," Lucia assured Tree. "Stretching, before the big event."

"Will giving birth be like that?" Tree asked. "It felt like something had gripped me from inside and wouldn't let go."

Ewan's gut automatically clenched, determined to stay right where it was. "Gems," he muttered.

Tricia offered Tree a sympathetic smile. "My experience was that labor was far more intense. As if someone was pulling me inside out, each tug coming faster than the last."

Tree paled, but Lucia shot her a wink. "Lucky girl; that sounds intense. You can expect to feel contractions from here on in. When they start happening every few hours, you'll know you're close."

Frapping hell, Ewan thought.

Tree shuddered. "I can hardly wait."

Ewan got back on his feet as April began, then spent the first half of the month catching up. Al'Dashan reported that he was pulling greenhorns from J'unai faster than Paul could send replacements. When Amad'hi complained, Rocco suggested recruiting from the Nightpaws, the thieves' organization that Cerri joined after Hara'noh's death. The Nightpaws' A'Meer had been willing to send help, so long as his people had a crack at Elysium—and so long as Amad'hi let him set up a headquarters in J'unai for "brokering of services" with the Rajji. Rocco assured him the trouble was worth it, though: the Nightpaws were excellent spies.

But the Locusts' threat seemed distant again, at least with a baby on the way. On the third Sunday of April, Lisa Deering organized a baby shower in the dining hall. Ewan could hardly recognize the room as he and Tree entered. Soft, fluffy bunting and tablecloths crowded the space, vaguely reminiscent of Olenwe's misty sky, only pink instead of gold.

"They're here!" Lisa called.

They certainly are, Ewan thought, smiling at the friends and family present from across four worlds.

He helped Tree to the seat of honor, at the center of a table along the far wall. Carmine Rothchild met them, holding a bowl of peas. "These are from the surface," he announced, regarding the crowd before offering Tree the bowl. "The first fruits of our restorative collaboration between players and the Central staff, to nurture an even more promising collaboration. Please accept this gift, from one Mother to another."

"Thank you, Grandfather," Tree said, taking the bowl as if it were epic treasure. Rothchild extended a hand to Ewan; after deflecting a memory of the Director arguing against the baby's very existence, Ewan shook it.

Time to move forward.

"Thank you, all of you," Tree said as Rothchild took a seat, leaving her in the commanding position for the afternoon. Ewan sat beside her as she wiped a tear from her cheek. "Even though the Earth isn't the most beautiful place to raise a child—"

"We're working on it!" Kate called out, prompting a laugh.

Tree smiled. "Yes, we are. Nothing in this world comes without cost. For centuries, we have all paid that cost, each in our own way. Divided, jealous, each of us fiercely guarding our own fragment of that whole we share. But we live now in a moment where all those efforts, all those sacrifices...we must persist, never faltering. Help me make this world a home to be proud of. That our children can be proud of."

"Hear, hear!" boomed Al'Dashan, his arm wrapped around Lucia's waist. He raised a cup. "To the young mother!"

The others joined the toast with varying degrees of confusion, but when Lisa and Tricia emerged from the kitchen with a massive cake, everyone knew what to do.

Shortly after the cake made the rounds, people began coming up to give their congratulations—and gifts. Tricia gave her son and daughter-in-law a woven bassinet with a soft green blanket for the baby, skillfully handcrafted. "I kept it neutral, since we don't know the baby's sex, much less their gender," she explained, eying the pink decorations with an amused smile. "Ewan had a blanket just like this in Veridor. I couldn't log that one out, so I thought making a new one would be the next best thing."

"Thanks, Mom," Ewan said. *This thing's like a knapsack,* he thought as he rubbed the fluffy cloth between his fingers. *Was I ever that small?*

Sam and Kate came next, holding a little plush aurochs. "We'd made it last month," Sam said, studiously avoiding Kate's eyes. Query, looking as awkward as the other two, gave Tree a set of silver chimes, assuring her that the harmonic relationships between the slender rods would induce sleep for the baby. Lisa gave them a set of plastic blocks, and Lucia gave Tree a breast pump, to help Ewan take on bottle-feeding duty.

Almost everyone gave them diapers and towels, too. When Ewan wondered aloud how much mess they expected the baby to make, they laughed.

Rocco gave them a plastic figurine of a Ta'anin, thanking the moles for helping him make it. "It will guard the kitten's room and be her mount when she journeys to Sah'rassa," he said. Al'Dashan similarly gave them a rocking horse, acknowledging it would be a while before the baby was leveled enough to use it. Robert Nichols gave them a collection of vitamin supplements, some for the baby and some for Tree, and Angela laughed as she handed the couple a schedule for postnatal health checks and measurements.

As the guests continued coming and the presents began to pile up, Ewan shook his head. *The baby's got more stuff in the real world than I do, and she isn't even born yet!*

Cerri was one of the last people to approach. Locking eyes on Ewan, she produced a small stringed instrument that resembled a lute, perhaps a bit wider, with a shorter neck and no frets. "Ea'win Omi'ra, this is not your fragile guitar."

Ewan suppressed a grin at the non-apology. "I can see that."

"It is an oud," she said seriously. "My father used to play for Hara'noh and myself when we were kittens." She thrust the instrument at him, and Ewan took it gently from her. He strummed it experimentally, then winced at the discordant sound, prompting a mix of yowls and laughs from the Sah'rassans.

Ewan tinkered with the oud over the following weeks, getting the hang of it with help from Cerri. It lent a fresh, exotic feel to his favorite songs, and the apartment's atmosphere brightened with renewed music. He pranced around the nursery, dodging the cluttered toys around the mountain of diapers, while Tree sat in her soft chair, smiling and telling the unborn child how her daddy looked silly but was really sweet.

He spent extra time relearning the Veridian birthday song, expecting to need it soon. As the days went by and Tree remained merely pregnant, Lucia began marking their passage on the calendar in the players' neighborhood, bringing jovial sighs as the early betters missed their marks. She gave a pout of her own when the 28th passed, and late that evening she resignedly drew a big X over the date. "You're past due now," she informed Tree. "How are you feeling?"

"Overdone," Tree said with a grunt. "But I'll manage."

"We'll give the little one a couple more weeks to decide," Lucia said to them both. "Then we'll haul him out, one way or another. In the meantime, you should take longer walks, and be especially intimate." She winked at Ewan. "It will help Tree's body warm up, and maybe the baby will decide it wants some privacy!"

Sure enough, two days later, Tree stumbled to a halt on the game floors.

"Is it starting?" Ewan asked nervously.

"I don't know," she said, closing her eyes to focus inside. "But it feels different than before."

They finished their lap and rode back up to the residence

halls, but Tree's contractions started coming in with increasing frequency—and urgency. After one especially long one that had her gripping the sheets, she said, "Love...you'd better message them. Now."

"Okay," Ewan said, pulling out his tablet. "Mom's at work but says to let her know when your water breaks. Lucia's going to start preparing things in Medical." He sighed inwardly, reading the rest of the message. "She also says now is the time to help get things, um, moving."

Tree sighed too, but she was looking at her swollen body again. "I don't know what you see, anymore."

"I see the most beautiful woman in any world," he said sincerely.

She huffed, but she did smile. "Then you're not looking. Come here."

They stayed in for the remainder of the evening, stocking up on rest while they could. As Ewan watched the clock to time Tree's contractions, he found himself fighting down a sensation of hurtling into the unknown. Was this their last night together, alone? Could they maybe squeeze in one more walk? Would they ever sleep again?

What were all those diapers for, really?

By eleven o' clock, Tree was having her contractions about twenty minutes apart. After a particularly intense one that left her gasping, Ewan helped her get dressed and knocked on Tricia's door. He tried Cerri's door too, but the Sah'rassan girl didn't emerge.

So Ewan rolled Tree to Medical in a wheelchair, but she didn't object, already focusing on the activity inside her, tuning out the rest of the world as her body geared itself up for the work ahead. It reminded Ewan of the players' tubes, blocking anything irrelevant to the work at hand, filtering attention and even sensation down to the most important parts.

Remembering how Tree held his hand all through his log-out, Ewan reached forward and squeezed her shoulder. “Hang in there, love. I’m still with you, all the way.”

When they arrived in Medical, Nichols came from his office to meet them. “We’ve got Room Three ready for you. Per Treanna’s insistent request, Madame Howe will be directing the delivery, but Angela will be assisting her.”

“I’d like to assist as well,” Tricia said. “With your permission, Tree.”

Tree curled up around another contraction, but she nodded.

“Very well,” Nichols said. “I’ll be standing by, should the need arise.” He stifled a yawn, rubbing his eyes behind his glasses. “Your baby seems perfectly normal. Already, it shows no consideration for the schedules of others.”

Ewan felt the unknown lurch a little closer as Tricia chuckled. “It takes a village to raise a child, as the old saying goes,” she said, patting Ewan’s arm. “You’ll have help, sweetheart.”

“Bring her in!” Lucia called from the room.

Ewan obeyed, helping his wife to the bed. It was set in a reclined position, with two large pads out for Tree to spread her legs onto, each covered in a fuzzy cloth. Lucia’s manner was all business. She slipped Tree’s dress up and off and directed Angela to give her a blanket, then told Ewan to start leading Tree through the breathing exercises they’d practiced for months. The midwife settled onto a stool between Tree’s legs and equipped a thin glove with a snap. Ewan gasped when Lucia placed her entire hand into Tree’s body, but Tree either didn’t notice or didn’t care.

“You’re doing fine, honey,” Lucia said. “Already at four centimeters.”

“How wide does she need to get?” Ewan asked, as Tree crushed his knuckles for another contraction.

"Ten centimeters," Angela replied, swabbing something onto Tree's thighs.

Ewan vividly recalled the ball Lucia had shown them during their first prenatal session. *Mother of all, how do women survive this?!* "What should I do?" he asked weakly.

"Keep talking to her!" Lucia ordered. "Make her happy, honey; this is your big chance."

Ewan took Tree's hand in both of his, partly for the gesture and partly to relieve her grip. "I love you so much, you're amazing!"

Tree gave a cry as another contraction shook her, grinding both of his hands anyway. "You. Are never. Touching me. Again!" she panted.

Tricia laughed when Ewan winced. "Don't worry, dear. I said the same thing to your father, but we ended up having Kate too."

Ewan soon lost track of time as the world throbbed around them, measured now only by the spacing between Tree's contractions and the dilation status updates from Lucia. The midwife ordered Tree to relax and ignore her body's insistence to push, reminding her that pushing before she was dilated enough would only make things more difficult. Tree continued to cry out, and Ewan kept coaxing her to breathe, promising whatever crazy things he could think of to make this pain up to her.

How was any of this normal? Why did the Logos, the Mother, whoever, *design* people's bodies to split apart to produce a child? In a dim, distant part of his mind, Ewan understood that he and Tree were now initiates into one of the strangest miracles of any world. He tried to comprehend what she was feeling...but he couldn't.

He asked Tree several times if she wanted something for the pain, but she clenched her teeth and shook her head, refusing to risk a drug affecting the baby. Between contractions, her head flopped back, alternately pale and flushed but always drenched with sweat, with her eyes rolled up into her head. But she continued to smash the bones in his hand, as though by compressing him hard enough, her body would open up for the baby. As he wiped her brow and tried not to notice the trails of blood wending around her thighs, Ewan had the overwhelming conviction that Tree was the bravest and toughest person he'd ever heard of.

"Okay, Tree, you're at ten! The next time you feel it coming, I want you to push!" Lucia commanded, her eyes bright with excitement. She flashed a mirror to show Ewan Tree's progress, and he nearly fainted from shock at the bloody, scruffy head of hair peeking out.

Tree gave a scream of agony, and Ewan breathed hard, as much to calm himself as to remind her to join in. "Almost!" Lucia said. "That's my girl; you just keep doing that, and it'll come!"

"Get this thing out of me!" Tree snarled between contractions. When the next push came, Ewan sent every ounce of his love and support into her hand, praying for the baby to cooperate and come out already.

After what seemed an endless cycle of pushing and yelling, at last Tree succeeded. With a horrible squelching sound and the appearance of her belly being sucked dry, the baby came sliding out into Lucia's waiting hands.

"You did it!" Ewan exclaimed, not even knowing to whom he was talking, anymore.

Tree flopped her head toward him, her eyes glazed and her mouth hanging open.

He planted a huge kiss on her sweaty forehead. "That was amazing. You're amazing."

"Come here, Dad," Lucia called.

Dad. That's me, now!

Ewan carefully pried his fingers from Tree's grip, noted with relief they were still attached to the rest of him, and went to his child. Angela toweled the baby clean with an expression somewhere between awed and wistful, then returned it to Lucia —who gave it a light swat on the bottom.

The newborn bellowed a cry that made them all jump.

"Well, she's got a good set of lungs on her," the midwife announced.

"She?" Ewan asked.

"Yes, 'she'! Dear Mother, I thought you'd know a female when you saw one by now!" Lucia laughed, then rested the baby into a blanket Angela had made ready. Sure enough, it was a girl, her anatomy flushed in sympathy with her mother's. A thin cord of flesh connected her to something still inside Tree.

"Here," Angela said quietly, handing Ewan a pair of surgical scissors. "Go ahead and cut the umbilical cord. Treanna still has to birth the placenta."

As though he was in a trance, Ewan snipped the little cord a few inches from the baby's—his daughter's!—belly, then stepped back carefully as Lucia took her seat between Tree's legs.

"Okay, Tree," Lucia said. "The hard part's over. Now, push again."

Ewan brought the baby girl around the bed, fearing he'd somehow hurt her. *She looks so gray and squashed,* he thought. *I guess that's normal, considering what she just went through.* The baby's eyes were closed as she bellowed, a shrill, piercing yell that made Ewan's brain shake from a foot away. He put a finger to her cheek, now turning purple from the crying, then touched her tiny hand as it waved vaguely from the blanket. Her fingers latched closed around it with surprising force. "You've got your mom's grip!" he laughed.

Then she opened her eyes and looked right at him. They

were a startling deep blue, almost black, like the night sky just before the dawn.

"Hi," Ewan said, heart soaring. "Welcome to the real world."

Tree grunted, and in the corner of his eye Ewan saw the placenta slip out of her and into Lucia's hands, a grayish blob of flesh. "All done!" the midwife said happily. She handed the placenta to Angela and began wiping away the mix of bodily fluids spattered all over Tree's body and the bed. "Well done, honey. You're a true woman, even more than I am."

Angela huffed. "Not every woman has a womb, Lu. You know that."

"But the Mother does," Lucia countered with pride. She beamed at the child in Ewan's arms. "And it's healing, after all this time. The little one's proof of that."

"Whatever the case, I'm proud of Treanna," Tricia said gently but firmly, cutting the debate short. She smiled at her daughter-in-law as she moved to dry her face. "You managed it all at such a young age, and in this world, no less." She waved Ewan over to them. "Would you like to meet your daughter?"

Tree nodded, biting her lip as she reached out to the bundle in Ewan's arms. She took the baby and held it, automatically moving her own blanket out of the way to expose a breast. "Hi there," she cooed, making Ewan's heart soar again to see them together. "You did great, too." As she held the newborn up and coaxed it to try and latch onto her nipple, she gave Ewan an exhausted, grateful smile. "So did you, love."

Ewan grinned. "You did all the hard work, this time."

Lucia and Angela joined them, toweling their hands. The midwife tickled the baby's cheek, then hooked a finger into her mouth right beside the nipple until the baby grabbed both, making Tree jump and gasp. "There you go!" Lucia giggled, looking as happy as Ewan had ever seen her. "What are you going to name her?"

Ewan and Tree exchanged a glance, as if both of them had

only just realized they'd forgotten to come up with any. "How about Hope?" he asked. "The real world needed hope, and now it has some?"

Tree snorted. "You are not naming our child after the *Esperanza*!"

"Good point," Ewan admitted, though he privately thought the hurtling-into-the-unknown feeling he'd had earlier was a pretty good fit for their old ice boat.

Stalling for time, he glanced at the clock on the wall. It was six-thirty in the morning on the first of May—he'd won the bet! Somewhere out there, in the unknown beyond the storms, the sun would just be rising...

"How about Dawn?" he said.

"Dawn O'Meara," Tree murmured. "Would you like that?"

In reply, the baby girl clamped harder onto Tree's nipple.

Tree gasped but smiled, and Ewan leaned over to give her a soft kiss, wrapping his arms around his new little family. Tree leaned back into him, resting as their baby hungrily suckled. "Yes, that's perfect," she said. "Dawn has come to Earth at last."

29

SACRED BLUE

EWAN WHEELED HIS FAMILY HOME THREE DAYS LATER, WITH TREE sheltering Dawn in her lap as people stopped them to offer congratulations and try to catch the baby's attention. Dawn responded with about as much sociability as her mother, though, so Ewan did most of the thanking and handshaking.

When they finally reached their apartment, Ewan took them straight to the nursery. He helped Tree settle into the nursing chair, then wrapped Dawn up in her green blanket—no easy feat, since Dawn was determined to stay clamped onto Tree's breast.

Ewan chuckled as he stood back to assess his work. "She looks like a bean wrap."

The baby grunted, and Tree smiled as she stroked the patch of dark hair on her wrinkly, tiny head. "She has your hair."

"Maybe," Ewan said. "Though Lucia said that might change over the next year. Eyes, too." He reached for his daughter, but she ignored him, suckling away and snorting like an aurochs. "Um...is there anything I can do?"

"I don't think so," Tree replied, wincing when Dawn bit. "Hand me my tablet?"

He fetched it for her, then hung around, looking for something to do while Tree read up about nursing and recovering from delivery. It was easy to feel like he was intruding on snack time, just sitting there and staring as his wife read and the baby tapped out one breast, then started on the next.

I guess that's what they're for, Ewan thought, with a little embarrassed envy.

He eventually started bringing Dawn's toys to her, telling her about each one. He put the little roaring Ta'anin up on a high shelf, where it could survey the room. The rocking horse found a place by the chair, and the plush aurochs went into the bassinet.

"Ewan, I think she fell asleep!" Tree whispered.

He looked over to see Dawn's eyes closed, her tiny hand dug into Tree's breast. She was still sucking, but only slowly now.

Can babies nurse in their sleep? Ewan wondered. He'd have to ask his mom when she got home—which reminded him that Tricia would be returning to Veridor soon, now that Dawn was fully spawned and her stuff had overrun the room.

The thought came with a mild sense of panic.

Tree rose and gently placed Dawn into the bassinet. When the newborn cried, Tree froze as though she'd disturbed a mob, but after a moment, Dawn settled down. Tree shifted the aurochs to the baby's feet, placidly watching over her. Then she looked at Ewan, her brown eyes all the private message they needed. He gave her his best rakish grin, then led her tiptoeing out of the baby's room and into theirs.

The moment she hit the mattress, Tree was passed out as well. Ewan lay in bed for a little while, struck by how much roomier it felt now that Dawn had her own space; then he kissed Tree's brow and slipped into the living room to give his wife space, too.

The next two weeks passed in a blissful, sleepless haze.

Tricia moved her bed to the couch, but she spent most of her off-duty hours gushing and fussing over Tree and Dawn in the nursery room, with such equal intensity that Ewan couldn't help laughing. Everyone who stopped by on business—or whatever pretext they could cook up—wanted to take pictures. Dawn didn't appreciate this, preferring to stay attached to Tree's chest under her nice, warm blanket. At night, the baby cried every hour or so; by the end of the first week, Ewan wondered if they shouldn't have kept Dawn in their room after all. He spent as much time retrieving the baby as he did rubbing Tree's feet, now sore from all the pacing she did to soothe Dawn back to sleep.

Lucia came by every few days as well, to nurse the baby and give Tree a break. Seeing Tree nurse had helped Ewan get used to the exposed-chest routine, which made it much easier to instead see Lucia's warm, grateful smile as Dawn suckled away. That said, he tried to make himself scarce for those visits, especially after the time Tree stepped out of the bedroom and sniped about how nice it was not to be needed by anyone.

At least there was plenty to do, out of the house. For the time being, Ewan was the acting Chief Emissary, which meant he got to do all the explaining for his fellow players when Rothchild called him in for reports. Despite the *Red Horse*'s disastrous first flight, the Director had taken the view that it had flown, however briefly. He had Kate, Sam, and Query working exclusively on the sailcraft's redesign, which meant Ewan spent most of his time navigating their broken love triangle. Little things, like reminding someone that cracking a beam over someone else's head wasn't a valid material stress test—and warning them not to try it.

But eventually, the *Red Horse 2* began to take shape…and as the frame slowly came together, so did its creators. Sam explained his continued presence to Ewan by saying he was the only Engineer Karl Taylor could spare, now that that Rothchild had ordered a staggering twenty new armadillos to support the ever-increasing player contingent. But Ewan didn't miss the way the mole's eyes lingered on Kate when she wasn't looking. Or how he watched Query as if expecting the seraph to endanger them all at a moment's notice.

For Query's part, the wind had apparently gone from his sail after the first crash. He covertly watched Kate as often as Sam did—albeit with far less subtlety—but despite Sam's separation from Kate, she wasn't giving Query any extra attention. If anything, she'd started treating both boys with an entirely un-Katelike aloofness, so much so that Ewan gritted his teeth and spent more time with "Twiggy" to make up for it.

"This time around, I will take full advantage of the increased winds in the middle altitudes," Query explained one afternoon, as he fiddled with a control knob in the rebuilt cockpit, more like a camel's cabin, that now sported four chairs, all with five-point safety harnesses. "We can still employ the fundamental mechanics of the electromagnetic sail and repulsor, but our previous experience indicates that we will gain more effective control from adjusting the morphological—sorry, Ewan, the shape—of the sail to accommodate the prevailing winds. After a thorough review of the concept of tacking in naval vessels, followed by extensive testing in my workshops back home under comparable simulated conditions, I believe I have the principles down."

"Okay," Ewan said, for lack of a better response. "So, um, how do you steer?"

The boy smiled. "With respect to the pilot's interface, operation will largely be the same as before. I've programmed the controls to reflect the function of aircraft, as used in the Earth simulations. If I pull the yoke backward, then the sail will move like this." He cupped one long-fingered hand palm-down, then arched it into what Ewan would have called a normal sail's shape. "In this configuration, the craft would gain altitude. Pressing the yoke forward will flatten the sail and take you into a dive, albeit far gentler than the last time," he added. "The central computer adjusts these basic modes to current wind and static readings, regardless of intended course."

"What's that mean?" Ewan asked.

"You can fly into the wind now, albeit considerably more slowly than flying with it. Would you like to try?" Query asked hopefully.

"Flying?" Ewan resisted the urge to glance at the exit hatch. "Um, yeah, when you're sure it's ready. And when Kate's sure, too. And Sam."

The seraph's smile faded, then went belly-up at the mole's name. "A reasonable request. I will get what approval I can."

When Dawn was three weeks old, enough to recover from the exertion of being born, she suddenly decided she'd had a good nap and was ready to go for real. Unfortunately, no one knew where she wanted to be going, which meant Ewan and Tree got dragged into a tortuous guessing game with their tyrannical referee. That ear-splitting cry could mean anything, and it often did. The sleepless parents settled into a routine of bouncing, diaper changing—running through their stash with alarming speed—and, when all else invariably failed, nursing.

Not that Ewan could get involved with that one. The one thing Dawn was emphatically clear about was that the bottle was *not* Tree's breast, regardless of what they put in it. The first time he'd tried, Ewan spent a good ten minutes trying to wedge the rubber nipple in Dawn's mouth, which should have been easy since it was open and howling. But the baby would turn her head away, and when he tried Lucia's finger-hooking trick, she clenched her little lips shut, scrunched her face until it turned purple, and made such awful grunting, gagging sounds that Tree came in to make sure she was still alive.

At which point Dawn demanded that Mommy nurse her properly.

As May ended, Ewan became convinced that no one was truly an adult until they'd been woken for the fifteenth time in the dark of night by a screaming baby—and realized that dealing with it was up to them, and them alone.

Unsurprisingly, Cerri made herself scarcer by the day. On the odd chance she was in the living room, she still would instruct Ewan on his mistakes with the oud, but every time Dawn cried, the Sah'rassan girl would flee into her darkened room like a teenager.

The one grim consolation Ewan got was that Dawn also rejected "Aunt Lucy." But that only meant that Tree was locked down even more, which added to her misery. Even when Ewan insisted on taking her out for escape dates—like going for walks, or to the dining hall, or eventually just stepping out of the nursery room—she spent the whole time fretting and berating herself as a mom.

When Ewan finally started getting a full night's rest again, it was because Tree started sleeping in her chair instead of coming to bed.

So, as the second week of June came and Query invited him to fly, Ewan guiltily accepted. On a particularly warm afternoon, he stepped onto the sand and into a strong wind, as though Mother Earth was hoping to see the *Red Horse 2* take flight as well.

Just bring us down in one piece, he thought at Her.

The respawned sailcraft was out in the open, its massive sail furled tightly against the gusts for the moment. It was bigger all around, maybe thirty feet long and half as wide. The steel hull had a sleeker, more elegant cut to it, but it still looked capable of punching through anything unfortunate enough to be in its way. Ewan couldn't help noticing a pair of machine guns peeking forward from the underbelly, driving home how much closer Kate's team was to a production run.

Sam greeted him at the hatch, bearing both the craft's name and the Centre's insignia: an image of the Earth in the Mother's hands. "Hi, Ewan—are you all right?" the mole asked.

"Yeah, I'm fine. Why?"

Sam furrowed his brow. "You look like Tree gave you two black eyes."

Ewan rubbed his face and dredged up a smile. "She didn't, but Dawn's giving them out to anyone who can hear. So, you think this bucket's going to fly today?"

Sam snorted, almost exactly like an aurochs. "It flew just fine, last time. Getting it to land, that's the trick. How are your legs?"

"Pretty good," Ewan replied, jogging in place to both demonstrate and wake himself up. "They're mostly back to normal, although they still jar a fair bit. I was lucky I didn't lose them—oh, Gems. I'm sorry."

"I keep telling you, it's fine," the mole said gruffly. "People make mistakes, right?"

Something in Sam's tone warned Ewan he was talking about someone else.

"Come on," Sam said after a moment. "At least Twig put seats in there for us, this time."

Ewan followed his friend inside. Having worked on the cabin with Query last month, he knew the basic layout, but just as he'd discovered with the bridge a year before, the real thing was something entirely different. The consoles, now lining the front three sides, were alive with lights and gauges. Warm air blew in from above through ductwork lining the outer wall, and the repulsor, secured in the back room, hummed in anticipation.

Query rose from his chair as Sam took his own, opposite Kate. "I am pleased you could join us," the seraph said. His black hair had filled out but was cropped close, giving his head an oddly ball-shaped appearance. "I believe you will find this flight to be far more satisfactory. Hopefully you can report our success to Director Rothchild."

"Yeah, I hope so," Ewan said, taking the seat next to Query. "Oh, when did you add a second yoke?"

"Kate suggested the modification," Query said. "Partly for instructional purposes, and partly for redundancy. Should the pilot become incapacitated, the copilot may still operate the sailcraft."

"Why—" Ewan began, before catching himself with a mental slap. *Wake up, player! You may be a dad now, but that's all the more reason to learn to fly this thing*. "Never mind."

Query nodded, for once seeming to register the military implication as well. "Both the pilot and copilot seats are fully flight-capable. The yokes are synchronized, so any actions taken by one person will be felt by the other. Additionally, the sail's current configuration may be locked in by depressing this lever, one beside each yoke, to enable semi-automatic flight for short periods. Well, then. Shall we?"

He flicked a switch, and the sail flew out above them. This time, it was four-sided, with the corners turned like a diamond to extend at least fifty feet beyond the front and back of the sailcraft. The repulsor's hum turned into a buzzing rumble, and when the yoke pulled back in Ewan's hands, the *Red Horse 2* soared with the wind, leaving Ewan's stomach on the ground.

The ride was smoother, much smoother than before. The repulsor's vibration faded into the background, and Ewan peered forward to see how the sail changed its shape to match Query's movements.

“Operation is within expected parameters,” Query announced, sounding pleased. “Consistent with test runs in Olenwe.”

“It feels luxurious,” Kate agreed.

Ewan turned to see both her and Sam walking to the front. “Hey, your leg’s not stuck!” he blurted.

“Not this time,” Sam said with a chuckle. “Twiggy put in some kind of EM shield for the cabin. The sail can feel the repulsor, but we won’t.”

“We’re stable at five hundred meters,” Query reported. “Increasing altitude to one thousand.”

The flight continued with little more than the occasional shimmy from the wind at their backs, and Ewan eventually realized that he was enjoying the experience. The storm whipped around them, but the redesigned sail held its shape, deflecting excess energy in the form of lightning that streaked down to the hull’s roof.

“I’m glad we’ve got that shield,” Ewan said, mesmerized by the display.

“Indeed,” Query replied, smiling. “But those electrical arcs are part of the design. Static generated by the sand against the sail is absorbed into the batteries, greatly extending our effective range. As long as we fly in the storm, we should be able to move almost indefinitely, although naturally I wasn’t able to test that theory until today.”

“Incredible,” Ewan murmured. “You’ve made perfect use of this world’s worst environment.”

The seraph dipped his head. “Thank you. One thousand meters, all systems nominal. Would you like to try flying her yourself?”

Ewan grinned, but he hesitated. “As long as you don’t think I’ll crash us.”

“I think we will be fine. Besides, you cannot ‘crash’ us more than I did on my first attempt. Now, grip the yoke in both hands…"

Incredibly, and as a testament to Query's design, it only took about five minutes for Ewan to get the hang of flying the sailcraft. He wheeled them about with a whoop, marveling at how the sail automatically shapeshifted into the best form for flying into the wind. Laughing, he said, "I never would have believed two years ago that I'd be flying something like this over an alien world!"

"It's a good thing your Tree-elf stumbled into ours," Kate agreed, reaching forward to squeeze the seraph's shoulder. "Angel Boy, you are something else."

Query started at the contact, but he was beaming. "Thank you. I do apologize for the mishaps of the first flight."

"Apology accepted," Kate replied, as though she'd been the one who had her legs broken last time. "You actually built a working flying machine, and in only three months!"

Sam grunted, and Query shot him an embarrassed smile. "In fairness, we all built it together," the seraph said. "And three months is far slower than the two days for my first model from home. But…I have come to appreciate that the slow way is often the best way on this world."

Sam watched him a moment, as if expecting the comment to be a joke, but no one laughed. "So, Twiggy," he said, "You said we'd have power as long as we flew through the storm, but when would we not do that? Unless you're planning on flying out over the oceans?"

"You aren't thinking three-dimensionally," Query answered. "We can simply climb higher."

Ewan's palms began to sweat on the yoke. "Wait. You mean we can get above the storms?"

"In theory, yes. As I have yet to fully assess the wind velocities in the upper troposphere, it is possible our modifications will be insufficient to the demands of the higher altitudes."

Ewan barely heard him. *What would the others think if we brought back a picture of the Earth's sky? Its real sky?* "Does this boat have cameras on it?" he asked, his voice trembling.

"It has a wide array of imaging capabilities—" Query began.

"Yes," Kate said, her own voice resonating with Ewan's growing excitement.

"Sam?" Ewan asked, turning back to the mole. "What do you think? Worth the risk?"

Sam's eyes were distant, but his knuckles were white. "I think it is," he whispered.

Ewan pulled back on the yoke. The headwind caught them and flung them high, higher than ever. His ears popped, multiple times, and Query took notes on adjusting the cabin air pressure system to accommodate. The electric arcs got thicker and nastier, sometimes spidering across the viewscreen, or alarmingly, making the sail go limp in spots, but the batteries' renewed charge always filled them back out. The *Red Horse 2* was built for this chaotic, swirling world, giving back everything it took as Ewan breathlessly wrestled the wind for control.

And then, so suddenly that he couldn't register when it happened, the sailcraft shot out above the clouds, wobbling as the sandless winds caught it.

"Dear Mother," Sam whispered behind him as the craft stabilized. "It's so clear!"

Off the right side, ahead of the sail's curved surface, the sun —the true sun—was shining, a brilliant disk of yellow-white that made Ewan squint. Everywhere else was an infinite blue, not a cloud to be seen. *Because we're above them*, Ewan thought in awe. He gazed into that blue, the color he loved so much, tears rolling down his cheek to splash onto his hands as they gripped the yoke.

"It's just like home," Kate murmured, leaning over Query's shoulder.

"Are we taking pictures?" Ewan asked.

"I'm bringing all sensors online now," Query answered. "But as a precaution, it may be prudent to use your tablets as well."

All four aeronauts took as many pictures as they could, speaking in awestruck, reverent murmurs. Any player back home would have laughed at them, taking so many images of a featureless blue sky. But in the Centre, those pictures were proof: proof that humans had once again felt the sunlight on their faces, seen the light which patiently waited to warm Mother Earth again.

"I was wrong," Sam said, crying freely. "We *were* meant to fly!"

It was with great reluctance that Ewan brought the *Red Horse 2* back down into the howling sands. Out in the open, the batteries depleted with disappointing speed, forcing the crew under cover well before sunset. They returned to the Centre in silence, each holding onto the feel of the experience in their own way.

The word that kept coming to Ewan's mind was *religious*.

It was past ten o'clock when Ewan made it back to his apartment. Tricia was asleep in the living room, her careworn face relaxed in the comfort of her dreams. Ewan slipped quietly by to Dawn's room, finding Tree passed out in the chair with the baby attached to her chest in the soft glow of the night light. He stood there a long moment, his heart filling to bursting as he looked at the two of them, listening to Dawn's wheezy little breaths as she slept with a nipple in her mouth. He blew a kiss to his daughter, not wanting to risk waking her, then gently wiped the drool from Tree's open mouth.

She gave a start and snorted, then opened her eyes. "Love," she murmured. "Is it morning already?"

"No, we've got all night," he whispered.

Tree smiled, blearily. “I think she’s finally asleep.”

In reply, Dawn coughed and hiccupped, then fussed as she stared up at her parents with wide, unblinking eyes. Tree groaned, and Ewan gave her a kiss on the cheek as she let her head flop back. “Argh, my bottom is numb! How can it be so sore and still go numb?”

Ewan chuckled in sympathy. “Do you want me to take her?”

“No, it’s okay.” Tree sighed, giving Dawn a pleading look so full of exhaustion that Ewan nearly took the baby anyway to order his wife to get some real sleep. Tree turned back to him, and her expression suddenly became alert. “How was the flight?”

“Incredible,” he said, pulling out his tablet. “There were no problems. In fact, I brought you a little souvenir.”

Tree’s eyes widened almost as much as Dawn’s when she took the tablet. “Mother of all.”

“Yeah. I took us up over the clouds. The sky up there is so clear! I wish you could’ve come and seen it with me, but I did the next best thing I could think of. Hey, are you okay?”

Far from smiling, Tree sniffed, blinking away tears. Her voice was heartbroken as she snuggled Dawn up to her breast again. “I should have been there with you…I’m sorry.”

Ewan’s heart broke with her. “Hey, I’m the one who’s sorry you’re cooped up in here. I’m not trying to have any adventures without you or anything, so if you don’t want me to go up again—”

“No.” Tree gave him a firm look, then smiled sadly. “No, love. I want you to get out there and bring back more pictures. Show me what’s happening outside, so I can feel like I’m there with you. One day, we’ll go out again, just the two of us.”

“It’s a date,” he promised, holding his breath as Dawn’s eyes closed again. “Here, let me take her. You get some rest.” Not waiting for an argument, he reached out and scooped his daughter up, cradling her in his arms. She snuffled and fussed, but her eyes never opened, and after a moment, she rested her tiny head against Ewan's shoulder.

"Go on," he whispered. "We'll be fine. I'll catch you up when I can."

Tree stifled a yawn and gave him a kiss. "I don't deserve you." She slipped out of the room, pulling her robe around herself as she left.

That makes two of us, he thought gratefully.

He walked around the room with Dawn for a few minutes, waiting to see if she was really asleep. When she didn't stir, he tried setting her into the bassinet—but as he lowered her in, her head fell back and she woke up screaming.

"Oh, frap! Shh, shh," he pleaded, hoisting the baby back up against his shoulder. "Don't wake Mommy!" He cast about the room in desperation, then grabbed his tablet from the arm of the chair. "Here, Daddy's got a present for you!"

He sat down, holding Dawn against his chest. The baby leaned in to suckle and cried again when her lips found his sand-beaten armor instead of Tree's breast. Ewan quickly turned the tablet back on and held it up, still displaying the picture he'd taken of the sun. He wiggled it to get her attention.

Her wide baby-blue eyes fixed onto the screen, and she began grunting and wiggling so hard that Ewan nearly dropped her. Her little arms waved around, not coordinated enough to reach yet, but he scooted the display closer to her. She stared at it, cross-eyed and open-mouthed, and Ewan laughed.

"That's the sun, Dawn! Daddy saw it today, flying way up high in the sky like a Ta'anin. Or an angel," he mused, glad to finally have a good experience to go with the image. "Did you know you're named after the sun?" he asked, smiling when she grunted again. "Your aunt Kate is working to make it so we can all see the sun one day. We all are," he finished softly.

He sat with his daughter, flipping through the pictures until her eyes got heavy and slipped closed again. This time, he waited a good twenty minutes before daring to move, and when he set her down into the bassinet, she mercifully stayed asleep. Ewan smiled again as she twitched her little lips—in some dream of nursing, no doubt—then he slipped quietly out of the room to join his wife for some much-needed rest together.

30

DARK HORIZON

WHEN EWAN WENT TO PICK UP BREAKFAST THE NEXT MORNING, the dining hall was unrecognizable.

Someone had knocked out the wall separating the dining and serving areas, leaving something resembling a bar. The tables and seats were rearranged, breaking the utilitarian long rows into more sociable clusters and islands with white, puffy napkins sprouting from their centers. And Centrals gathered in confused, excited pockets to point at the walls—now ringed with a breathtaking, familiar panorama of blue, complete with the brilliant sun to the south.

"What do you think, Ewan?" Lisa Deering called from the bar, once he'd taken it all in.

"I think Sam must've told someone the moment he got in," Ewan replied, grinning broadly. "It looks almost as good as the real thing."

Lisa clapped, then remembered to put down her serving spoon. "Yes! I've asked Chief Spencer if we can rename the dining hall as the Blue Sky Oasis."

Ewan chuckled, wondering if Alice Spencer had even

gotten warning about her hall's overnight re-spec. "Sounds like a good tavern name to me."

"That's just what I was thinking!" Lisa beamed at him as she passed him a handful of bags. "I wonder if I could get Outfitting to make uniforms like Tina's, in Veridor."

Quickly banishing the image of his mom in a skimpy barmaid's outfit, Ewan shrugged. "I guess it can't hurt to ask."

Not that he mentioned the possibility to Tricia when he returned home. Dawn was in a forgiving mood, letting Grandma bounce her on one knee and giving Ewan and Tree the chance to share breakfast in the living room.

When the baby gave an especially delighted squeal, Tree leaned into Ewan's shoulder. "It's moments like this that make it all worthwhile," she said quietly.

"Yeah," Ewan agreed, chewing as his eyes strayed to Cerri's door. "Hey, has Cerri come out yet?"

"No. Why?"

"I don't know...I guess I haven't seen her much recently." He flashed Tree a grin. "Maybe I'll go check on her, make sure she's not trapped in there or something."

"By all means," Tree said. She stood, then gave him a lingering kiss that made his blood surge before giving him a look he hadn't seen in way too long. "You know where to find me, as long as Grandma can keep Dawn busy."

She half skipped, half stumbled to their room.

Ewan resisted the temptation to charge in right after her. He quickly finished his bean wrap, then knocked on Cerri's door. "Cerri, are you in there? I brought some breakfast for you."

There was no reply.

"Cerri? Are you in there?"

Still nothing.

Preparing to duck, Ewan pressed the door open.

The room was in total darkness. Turning on the lights revealed a space that looked even messier than Kate's...almost ransacked, even. Clothing and boxes were scattered all around, leaving a little nest in the center of the bed. Lying on the floor next to the wall was a metal ventilation grate—and a twisted bedsheet hung from the corresponding duct.

Ewan groaned, then climbed up and stuck his head in. "Cerri, get back here!"

Silence continued to answer him. Grumbling to himself, Ewan put the girl's food on the bed and left, deciding not to mention the absence to Tree and spoil her good mood, but his own was slipping.

She'd better not be spying on the Director again, he thought irritably.

The next morning, Cerri came to get breakfast with him. "Why were you intruding into my chambers?" she hissed as they walked to the Oasis. "I did not give you permission to enter."

"You hadn't come out all morning. I was worried about you," Ewan whispered back, glowering at her spotted face as she stared fixedly ahead. "You know you're not allowed to climb around in the vent system! If someone caught you spying—"

"You have given your promise to rescue me," she reminded him haughtily. "Unlike you, I am not distracted with a kitten. I will repay my life debt."

Ewan blinked. "What? How would crawling around the vents help me kill Frasier? He's nowhere near the Centre!"

Cerri dropped her voice to a mutter, so only he could hear. "When Bri'jash devised my sister's death, he did not sully his own hands."

Ewan's neck prickled, as if he was in his Caitsid'h avatar. "You think Frasier had help?"

"Of course he did. The man with long hair and the security guard have already helped him, have they not?"

"Yeah, okay, but they're gone too." Ewan gripped her

shoulder, partly to steady himself. “Cerri, are you saying you’ve caught someone here, in the Centre? Helping Frasier?”

In reply, Cerri simply gave him an even, amber-eyed stare, then entered the dining hall.

Ewan decided not to mention this development to Tree either, but that afternoon they both received a message from the Director, summoning him to an emergency war meeting. Tree’s eyes narrowed as Dawn had her own late lunch, but all she said to Ewan was, “Go on, love.”

When Ewan stepped into the Director’s office, he found Gabe, Nathan, Al’Dashan, and Rocco already waiting. “Thank you for coming,” Rothchild said neutrally. “I trust your family is well?”

“Yes, sir,” Ewan answered. “Sorry for my delay, and Treanna’s absence. She sends her regards.”

Rothchild nodded as Ewan took a seat. “Thank you. Unfortunately, we are not here to discuss the baby today. Master Rocco, now that we’re all here, will you give your report?”

The Sah’rassan loomed over the desk as he stood, dimming the weak light further. “We sent two of our finest spies, Nightpaws both, into the Locust village one moon ago,” he said. “They have watched the enemy, but they found no trace of a mysterious weapon. Until this morning.”

He connected his tablet to the ancient desk, and an image appeared over the scarred wood.

Ewan’s blood chilled as he regarded some kind of bomb. Without anyone in the image to give a sense of scale, he couldn’t guess at its size, but it was black and shaped like a typical Central rocket. Written across the casing at the top were the letters E-M-P, with smaller, illegible text below.

For a long moment, the room was silent.

“An EMP,” Gabe whispered. “They’ve done it.”

"Done what?" Rothchild asked. "Is this their weapon, Reid? Do you know what it is?"

Gabe huffed, blue eyes glinting as he turned to the Director. "Oh, yes. This device was in my initial report to you, part of an inventory of weapons historically employed by the Terranovan militaries. Electromagnetic pulses, or EMPs, are a variant of tactical nuclear weapons, especially favored in the post-Rapture resource wars as a way to disrupt enemy communications. I listed them as a high-level threat to the Centre, as you may recall," he said pointedly.

Rothchild said nothing.

"What are nuclear weapons?" Al'Dashan asked.

"I believe you're asking how much damage they can inflict," Gabe answered. "The details of their operation are beyond your capacity. Beyond anything your worlds can conceive," he added, regarding Rocco as well. "Suffice it to say, our ancestors devised bombs powerful enough to convert a city to toxic ash in seconds. They even built delivery systems that could employ such weapons against any location on Earth, in the time you take to log in from the bridge."

Ewan let out a breath he hadn't realized he was holding. "This is what you were looking for at Fort Gilmer. Wasn't it, Gabe? Something the Locusts could shoot at us, and it would be over?"

"Not in the sense you're picturing, O'Meara." Gabe's eyes hardened even more. "Most EMPs were designed to explode in the sky, not on the surface." He turned to study the image. "This one's mounted on a rocket—you can see the thrusters at the base, there—to give it sufficient altitude. Detonated high enough, such a device would unleash a cascade of electromagnetic waves that pass through organic material harmlessly, but everything with an electronic circuit would be disabled, if not destroyed."

Ewan's blood froze. "But everything in the Centre has electronics!"

"I'm aware of that," Gabe replied, his voice taking on a deadly edge. "That is why I listed such weapons as a high-level threat in my initial report. If successful, the Locusts would leave the Centre's infrastructure intact, with all its food and staff ripe for the taking, while at the same time rendering us defenseless —to say nothing of the effects on the game floors."

"Dear Mother," murmured the Director. "It would kill every player."

"Precisely," Gabe said. He leaned back in his seat.

"What do you want to do?" Nathan asked, to no one in particular. "My defense corps is still active, for now. We're ready to face the attack."

"As are we," growled Rocco, regarding the black tube for the sleeping Ta'anin it apparently was.

"The Ether Corps is ready, too," Al'Dashan said.

Ewan opened his mouth, but the words jammed in his mind. *Why?* he thought. *Why did the people of old Earth build such a horrible thing? How could they have just left it lying around?!*

But Gabe's fey laugh made Ewan's skin crawl. "You don't understand at all. I've been telling you for months; we can't afford to *wait* for an attack! An EMP's effective range is hundreds of miles. We'll be lucky if they can't launch it from their base!"

For what seemed like forever, the only sounds in the office were Gabe's exasperated sigh and the trickle of sand against the windows.

"Could we set it off in the ruin?" Nathan asked eventually. "That might cripple the Locusts for a follow-up assault."

Gabe shook his head. "They've proven extremely adept at scattering and regrouping. Even if we managed it, the survivors will doubtless find another EMP. And we wouldn't know until it was too late."

At last, Ewan found his voice. "The Locusts are coming for us. They'll use that thing to wipe out our electronics, then move in for the kill. Right, Gabe?"

The programmer nodded, his smile grim as he looked at Ewan—really looked, for the first time in months. "Now you're seeing it."

Ewan closed his eyes, wishing he couldn't see it quite so clearly. "So let's disable this one, but quietly. We can meet them in the Wastes, catch them by surprise when our forces keep fighting. They won't have a chance to regroup."

"Agreed," Rothchild said, though his voice was still troubled. "Master Rocco, can your people disable the EMP?"

"Perhaps, if they were given instruction." The Sah'rassan glanced at Gabe. "Is that possible?"

"Possible?" the programmer repeated. "Certainly. But do any of us wish to risk a miscommunication on this? No, I didn't think so," he said softly into the silence that followed. "I'm the one who's familiar with the weapon. Given an evening, I can learn enough to disarm it."

"You would be putting yourself at extreme risk, Chief Reid," the Director warned.

"I know." Gabe's jaw clenched. "But I would rather die fighting than sit idly while the Centre I knew is dismantled around me. I will go, with your permission, Director."

"Very well," Rothchild said. "How do you propose reaching Ruin 7?"

"He could take a 'roo," Nathan suggested. "He could get there in a long day, and the rest of our military can follow up in the new armadillos."

"If the Locusts are coming, it's a good bet they'll have scouts," Al'Dashan pointed out. "Gabriel may be captured, and the Locusts would launch their attack immediately."

"We'll take the *Red Horse 2*," Ewan whispered.

Goosebumps tickled his shoulders as he pictured the

mission in stunning detail. An epic quest in the real world, taking out the Diamond Lord and the Locusts in one stroke. Ensuring his family could grow in safety. “The winds are mostly from the south. I could get us to the Memorial in a matter of hours,” he said. “Gabe and I could slip in with a couple of warriors, under cover of darkness if we left tonight. He could study on the way. We’d be in and out, and the Locusts would move ahead to engage our main force, never the wiser for it.”

Ewan opened his eyes again, to find Gabe watching him closely. “I know how you feel about players, Gabe.” *I’ve felt it, too*, he thought, remembering the Mother’s Children at Fort Gilmer. Paul’s corpse humor in J’unai. His own legs, broken by Query’s reckless test flight. “Let me make it up to you,” he said quietly. “Trust me, one more time. We can fix this, together.”

“Very well,” Gabe said after a long moment. “Once more, O’Meara.”

Rothchild cleared his throat, drawing the others’ attention. “Then we are agreed. Emissary O’Meara and Chief Reid will undertake a mission to covertly disarm the EMP tonight. We will engage the Locust Nation in the Wastes the following afternoon, and destroy them utterly.” He stood, and the image of the weapon vanished as the others stood as well. “Chief Sanderson, Master Rocco, Master Al’Dashan: see to your troops. Call up every player who has previously been logged out, for emergency rehabilitation. They will guard the Centre when our main army embarks. By the end of tomorrow, this war will be over.”

Two hours later, Ewan equipped his weapons and armor, then slipped into Dawn’s room. Tree was asleep in her chair, with Dawn suckling away in her lap.

"Tree," Ewan whispered, shaking her shoulder gently. "Love, wake up, please. I need to talk to you."

Tree's eyes opened, but when she saw Ewan's gear, she sat up, ignoring Dawn's bleary protests. "What is it?"

"The Locusts have their weapon. It's something bad enough to kill every player in the tubes and break every machine in the Centre." Tree's face paled, but he went on. "They only need to get within a couple hundred miles to use it."

She considered this, looked at the baby with a sigh, then said, "What's our response?"

Ewan bit back a sigh as well. *Love, you'd have been my first pick to come with me, otherwise.* "We think we can disarm it so that the Locusts won't notice, then lure them into an attack."

"You're going to disarm it?" Tree asked, her voice incredulous.

"Gabe will," he amended, ignoring her usual narrowed-eye reaction. "I'll fly him over there. He's been researching these weapons for months. If anyone can do it, it'd be him."

"Of course it would." Tree sighed, then gripped Ewan's hand. "Love, be careful. You've seen how self-serving Gabriel is, and I can't be there to protect you. He wouldn't hesitate to sacrifice you if he thought it would help the mission."

Just like he tried to do with Cerri, Ewan thought, but he only smiled sadly and squeezed her hand back. "Frasier's found a way to destroy everyone and everything I love. I can't let him get away with it. I'm not planning to die, but I will if that's what it takes to protect you."

Tree bit her lip. "Love..."

He tried not to hear the pain in her voice. "You once told your grandpa how critical Centrals were, that we couldn't afford to lose them like we lose players. Well, I've seen that firsthand now, and Gabe's probably the smartest Central we've got. If anyone's going to get sacrificed—"

Tree pulled him down, silencing him with a hard kiss over Dawn's protest. "I don't care. Sacrifice him first."

When he could breathe again, Ewan offered, "How about I just promise to come back safe and sound?"

"I'll hold you to it," she warned, looking ready to wreck death itself if he didn't. "Ewan, I love you."

"I love you, too," he said, smiling for the first time since the news broke. Dawn gave an annoyed grunt, and Ewan stroked her scrubby hair. "And I love you too, Dawn."

They held each other close, letting the embrace speak for them, and far too soon, Ewan's tablet beeped with a message from Kate.

"It's time," he said with a sigh. He kissed Tree once more, then took a step back and held up the tablet to take a picture. "Smile?"

Tree rolled her eyes at him. "I'm a mess! I haven't brushed my hair for a week."

"I don't care. You're what I want to see." Ewan blew her a kiss, and the tablet's flash lit the room momentarily as the device captured the image. Dawn cried in protest, then went back to nursing. "I'll be back in a few days," he promised. "I love you," he said again, to leave her with his best.

"I love you, too. Good luck."

Ten minutes later, Ewan's party boarded the *Red Horse 2*, already made ready by Kate's team. Sarah Duncan had volunteered as soon as Al'Dashan announced the mission, and Bach'an joined on just as quickly, if only to keep Sarah company. They saluted Ewan, fists thumping against their black armor, then hurried inside.

"Are you ready?" Gabe asked, checking his rapier and pistol. "One way or another, we're going to finish this."

"We're on the same page," Ewan assured him, checking his own swords. *Friends or not, we can still make a good team.*

"Frasier's not going to know what hit him. And Gabe? Thanks, for trusting me."

The programmer offered him a thin, weary smile. "Just prove me right, O'Meara."

Gabe went inside, and Ewan took a moment longer to tell Kate to watch over their mom, just in case. Then he slipped into the sailcraft and took the pilot's seat.

A moment later, the party vanished into the darkening sky.

31

DOWNDRAFT

The endless sands faded to black outside the main window, punctuated only with the occasional arc of lightning flickering across the sail. No one spoke, leaving Ewan alone with his thoughts as his blood quickened.

Two years. Had it only been that long since he'd met Tree?

Before she appeared in Whitehaven, Ewan had been so sure about his future. Six years of relentless leveling, trying to outdo Old Max. Yearning, in the depths of his heart, for an epic quest to boost him into glory. And now, the Hero of Veridor was about to strike a final blow against the hated Diamond Lord, by leading an allied party from three worlds in a flying chariot built by the mad ingenuity of a fourth.

As he gripped the yoke and held it firm against the storms' wrath, Ewan smiled.

"O'Meara," Gabe said, bringing Ewan back to the present. "Perhaps you should teach the rest of us how to fly this transport."

Ewan's smile faded, but he nodded. "Fair enough. It's actually easy, since Query rigged the controls to adjust to the storms outside. All you really need to know is to pull back to go up and slow down, and push forward to go down or speed up. Want to try it?"

Gabe was a quick study, and before long he'd mastered the basics of flying the *Horse*. "Thank you," he said, chuckling. "Now I understand how you managed to fly over the storm with minimal experience."

"Do you think we could do that?" Sarah asked hopefully. "I know we're on mission and all, but I'd love to see it."

"Sure," Ewan replied, his grin returning. "Who knows? Maybe we can make better time without the sand knocking us around. Hang on!"

He pulled back on the yoke, and the *Red Horse 2* began climbing. It was easier than the last time, though Ewan didn't know whether it was because he'd already done it once before, or if it was because the winds were at his back now.

As before, the controls jerked free as the *Horse* burst out of the clouds, but Ewan wasn't prepared for the night sky. It was even more awesome than the day's, dotted with countless stars as the rising moon's light glowed from the swirling cloud tops.

The same stars, he thought reverently as he recognized his childhood constellations. *The Sah'rassans have it right: all our worlds share the sky.*

Ewan leveled the ship, allowing Bach'an and Sarah to make their way forward. "What do you think?" he asked Gabe, seated beside him.

The programmer's face was pale, eyes as wide as if he'd seen a ghost. "It's beautiful...a beacon of hope for everyone," he murmured, voice trembling, before he collected himself back to his usual confidence. "And nearly as perfect as what we've programmed for the game worlds. Here," he said, vacating his seat to give the others a better view.

"It's just like home," Sarah whispered as she took the copilot's seat. "But these are the real thing, aren't they?" She beamed as she looked out, entranced. "They're breathtaking."

"Ea'win Omi'ra, the Moon is behind us," Bach'an said. "Let us turn to see it, for it has missed Bach'an."

Ewan chuckled. "I think we can spare a moment." He wheeled them around to the right, causing the moon's light to glint off the sail's leading edge as it morphed into the new course. As Ewan leveled off again, the moon itself came into view, shining brightly just over the eastern horizon.

"I have missed the Moon as well," the Sah'rassan man murmured, leaning over Ewan's shoulder to get the best view. "It is good to see—"

He grunted, then coughed, and something hot and wet splashed across Ewan's left hand.

Blood.

Ewan shouted and whipped around, just in time to see a rapier's point withdraw into the Sah'rassan's chest. Bach'an's eyes bulged in shock, and he fell forward onto Ewan, pinning him over the safety harness, his massive scimitar uselessly sheathed on his back.

Sarah turned as well, only to be impaled through the gaps in her armor by the rapier's precise thrust. She cried out in pain, then slumped back into Gabe's seat as the programmer inspected his blade.

"Gabe!" Ewan shouted, trying to push Bach'an's body away. "What in blazes are you doing?"

But Gabe turned and planted his boot in Bach'an's back, holding him in place. Then he smiled at Ewan...an expression so cold and triumphant, that Ewan froze where he was.

"No," Ewan whispered. "You can't be. How could you work for Frasier?"

Gabe tsked, then pressed his rapier's tip into Ewan's throat around Bach'an's corpse. "Please, O'Meara, give credit where it's due. I agreed to teach you, after all, and this lesson's been far too long in the making."

The words echoed through Ewan's mind, ricocheting like bullets. "Teach me? About the real world?"

Gabe's smile broadened. "So you were listening, player. Recall, then, what I once told you. How the real world is cruel and harsh. How it will crush anyone who pretends otherwise."

At once, Ewan found himself in his worst memories: Whitehaven's square, with blood and fire and rubble all around him. And a pair of icy, murderous eyes piercing his soul as their owner uttered those words with all the hate the real world could offer.

When Ewan could speak again, his voice rasped. "It was you...all along...you're the Diamond Lord!"

Gabe's eyes glittered as he took a slight, mocking bow. "At last, you understand."

Fire surged through Ewan's blood. Roaring, he shoved Bach'an's body at Gabe—at his enemy—but the programmer-Gem struck Ewan across the face with the pistol in his other hand. Ewan's world exploded in pain and his vision blacked out, but he held on desperately, using the rage of betrayal to stay conscious long enough. He felt Bach'an's body being dragged off him, and he reached clumsily for the catch on his safety harness, but Gabe struck him again, and the world vanished altogether.

When he came to, Ewan immediately tried to leap to his feet—but he couldn't move.

"Fair warning," Gabe said pleasantly from Ewan's left, now sitting in the pilot's seat. "I've tied you tightly enough that if you're not careful, you'll lose your hands."

Ewan cursed and shook his head, clearing the spots from his vision. The *Red Horse 2* was back in the storm. The cabin lights were dimmed, and only the occasional burst of static lightning interrupted the outer darkness through which they were descending. He tried to spin around, to kick Gabe, but his legs were bound behind the pole supporting the chair, and he couldn't reach the floor to pivot.

"Where are the others?"

"I moved them to die in the back room," Gabe replied. "Players were never meant to be seen."

"You murdering, nerfing—"

Gabe spun him around in a wrenching, dizzy circle that crushed his wrists and left him gasping. "I didn't murder them; you did. You distracted them with the promise of something to which we have no right to aspire."

"You bastard!"

Gabe spun Ewan again, adding a lurching queasiness to the pain.

"Why did you leave me alive?" Ewan gasped.

Gabe stopped him and leaned in, pressing his forehead to Ewan's. "Because you have incensed me, and I intend to take my revenge before I allow you to die. As I told you in Whitehaven, killing you isn't enough. Not anymore. I have to kill your spirit first." He spun Ewan again. "Tell me, player. How best to kill hope?"

"What?"

Gabe hauled him to a stop and punched him in the face. "How best to kill it? Come now, O'Meara."

Ewan spat blood but missed Gabe's face. "I don't know!"

"It's simple." Gabe smiled, in the casual, easy way Ewan used to think was sympathetic. "You let the subject gather as much hope as he possibly can, then show him how false it was."

Dark clouds swam through Ewan's mind, agitated by nausea and laden with pain. "You didn't let me gather anything," he coughed after a moment.

"Then let the lesson begin," Gabe said, his voice eager. "In the spirit of bonding, allow me to first demonstrate with my own experience. Did I ever tell you why I became a programmer?"

Ewan tried to move his hands, but all he got was more pain. "No, and I don't care."

"Liar." Gabe's eyes flashed. "Don't let your own poor judgment distract you from the lesson. Like every other member of the staff, I was forcibly taken from the game worlds, per the Centre's farsighted policies. Snatched, if you will, from my true mother's arms before she could welcome me into her fantasy." He laughed softly, nostalgically. "I was a precocious child. Driven by a burning curiosity, a hunger to learn everything. You know the feeling, don't you, O'Meara?"

Images of long nights in the woods formed from the dark mist in Ewan's mind. Countless deaths, chafing against the Church and its meddling.

Gabe smiled again. "It didn't take me long to learn of my abduction—adoption, that is. I can't tell you how relieved I was. My foster parents never gave me the attention I needed, too busy with their Central lifestyle. You know the one."

"The one you live?" Ewan countered, remembering Gabe with Frasier's wife.

Gabe's smile faded. "Indeed. Imagine my astonishment when I learned my true parents were players. I was only seven at the time, much younger than most children are when the grim truth is revealed to them. I was elated to discover that I would have been a favored son of Galaxia, no less!" The programmer's voice dropped to a malicious hiss. "I knew my purpose, then. Not the bland existence of Earth, but the endless stars of my home world. I would bridge the gap and claim my birthright. Alight with hope, I learned to hack into the Logos, to observe my parents in secret." He paused, waiting until Ewan looked into his icy eyes again. "Do you know what I found, O'Meara?"

"I don't care," Ewan lied, furious with his own rising curiosity.

Gabe gripped Ewan's jaw, threatening to break his teeth. "I discovered that far from mourning my loss, they *celebrated* it. They were thrilled for their son to be a sacrificial lamb, cast off to a life of misery and servitude on a dead world!"

Gabe punched Ewan in the belly, then spun him an especially long time. "That was the reward hope held for me, O'Meara," he snarled as he slung Ewan's chair, again and again, until Ewan vomited. "That is what the game worlds are, player. False hopes. Every one a lie, pleasant only because they ignore the truth of this world at our expense!"

The chair stopped spinning, but it took Ewan minutes to stop the world from spinning as well.

Gabe continued, his voice bitter. "I decided then that I would master the worlds, rather than let myself be their victim. I apprenticed ahead of my time. It's laughably easy to shine in comparison to the apathetic staff, isn't it? At ten, I was a full-fledged programmer; at sixteen, I was a chief." Gabe's eyes glittered as he licked his lips. "My passion caught attention, and I was adored and admired by everyone...especially the women. My adopted parents had already taught me exactly what relationships were worth, but once I understood the pleasure to be had, I decided to master that sphere as well. You know, O'Meara, I don't think there's a woman in the Centre I haven't bedded."

A rush of defiance steadied Ewan's lolling head. "Tree would never have chosen you."

For a long moment, Gabe simply stared at him. Then the programmer chuckled, then laughed, his voice rebounding off the cabin walls as he threw back his head. "She never told you? Your whore of a woman sold her body to me for the very privileges she needed to sneak into Veridor in the first place.

She followed me straight to my bed at the mere suggestion of it!"

Ewan's heart stopped beating, and the world narrowed until all he could see was the dim outline of the programmer, laughing hysterically. "You're lying," he growled. "Tree would have told me! She only ever let someone kiss her, once."

Gabe leaned back in his seat, grinning in a shock that somehow mirrored Ewan's. "Annie is so precise, isn't she? So good at telling the technical truth. I admire that. Yes, O'Meara, I only kissed her once, because I was busy with the rest of her. Tell me, does she still moan when you tickle the little mole on her left thigh?"

Ewan struggled to breathe. "How—"

"I told you, I was there." Gabe slapped Ewan across the face, playfully, then laughed again. "I can't believe she never bothered to tell you, or that you never asked why she hated me so much! Your own wife has proven less honest than the man who betrayed you. Tell me, what's it like now, lying with her? I expect the birth stretched her out horribly, not that you'd know the difference."

"You nerfing bastard! You have to be lying!"

Gabe grabbed Ewan's face again and held his eyes open, locked onto his own. "O'Meara, I'm telling you honestly that I bedded her before she ever knew you existed. You know how Annie is. She'd do *anything* to accomplish her goals."

He licked his lips, and Ewan vomited again, trying out of spite to hit Gabe with it. But the programmer was too fast, spinning Ewan around and punching him in the back of the head. "Still," the programmer mused, "had I known the trouble that bitch would cause, I wouldn't have given her the privileges to sneak into the games." He whispered into Ewan's ear. "At the least, I would have revoked them after taking my pleasure from her.

"But I digress. Indulge me with your attention, player, and I will tell you the story of your gathered, false hopes." Gabe swung Ewan around again, then sat back in his chair, keeping one foot against Ewan's leg to turn him side to side. "You see, Annie never told me why she wanted those privileges, and several months passed before I noticed she wasn't taking meals with the rest of the staff. When I checked the logs, I saw that she'd slipped into Veridor. I didn't know what she was playing at, but I assumed it had to do with the Locust attack. Annie was quite passionate about that, deliciously so. And as she hadn't told a soul about our private bargain, I decided to have some fun with her again.

"By then your Church had lost interest in Annie, so I spurred them into action, using an avatar of the old game masters and a private tube from one of the Centre's many defunct bridges. For good measure, I even located Annie's tube and routed a baby to it. When that stupid boy Michael found her on the game floors hardly a week later, I was there when Rothchild had her hauled before the chiefs. She went on interminably about players and their usefulness. About you in particular," he sneered, looking Ewan up and down. "I admit, her poor taste offended me. When she described your location, I returned to the game and ordered the Church to meet you in that coastal city. What was it, End of the World or some such nonsense?"

He paused, waiting for Ewan to speak, but Ewan's voice was gone, along with his heart and gut. The programmer's eyes were an icy basilisk, holding him in place so the predator could savor the meal.

Gabe's smile thinned. "She surprised me by managing to log you out. It was a loophole, granted by her caretaking privileges, and one I closed soon after. I toyed with cutting your life support in Medical, but Annie never left your side." He huffed. "I wasn't concerned. I was busy securing the Director's confidence with Terranovan upgrades to the camels, and you were a vegetable. It was a matter of time before Rothchild returned you to the game floors or recycled you outright. But then you had to go and open your eyes."

He leaned forward and punched Ewan in the face again.

"Annie kept you locked in her room after that. I didn't expect you to last a day when she finally trotted you out like the freak you were, but I underestimated you. After you laid Harper out, I decided that perhaps she had been partially correct, that maybe you had something worth learning before I got rid of you. So I volunteered for your combat training. I learned everything you had to teach me—it only took a week or two, mind you—and then I defeated you in the tournament."

Ewan finally found his voice. "You lost."

Gabe boxed Ewan's ears with a snarl. "Only on a technicality! You used the rules of the game to save yourself, but I am the game master. I make the rules, here! In a real combat situation, you'd have died after I'd gotten up to stomp your heart into the dust. But after that, you were the Centre's new...what did you call me? The golden boy?" Gabe scowled. "I realized that I couldn't count on the staff at large to reject you anymore, so I arranged a scouting mission to the Wastes, for parts we didn't need. I encouraged you to lead us there, and lo! your pathetic swords were no match for the Locusts. Your ineptitude nearly got both Draper and Sanderson killed. It *did* get Harris killed, didn't it? That was when Frasier joined my cause."

A pang of guilt bubbled up through the pain, causing the dark cloud in Ewan's mind to take the shape of Maria Harris, dying in the camel's turret.

"When you managed to capture one of the Locusts, I made friends as quickly as I could with him. They're my people, you know," Gabe added. "They understand the real world. They stare into the face of despair every day, and like me, they take what they can as the world dies around us. I allowed your captive to escape, to tell his kind they had an ally in the Centre."

The dark mist revealed a Locust warrior, bursting from Gabe's turret and sprinting across the camel's roof to freedom. "You traitor," Ewan rasped.

Gabe shook his head, eyes glittering. "I'm preserving the natural order, player. I'm the only thing protecting my dead, broken world from your optimism. The staff were angry about your failure in Ruin 7. I did my best to fan the flames, but too many people had already accepted you, felt the stirrings of hope that you infected us with. Particularly the Director, who knew a tool when he saw one. No, I had to get rid of you myself, but I needed to do it in such a way that you'd recant your errors to the staff. Then everything would have gone back to normal, and I would have resumed my rightful place at the pinnacle of the bone pile.

"So, I made one last-ditch effort to destroy you. I refurbished a bridge, then used it to show you I'd had your family arrested. You always were soft on family," Gabe said, tsking. "You never learned how worthless they really are, abandoning you in your hour of need." He leered around the empty room. "Or lying to you about their pasts. I knew you would go running back to your game if your family was in danger, and I followed you in and deleted them in front of your eyes. You should have seen your face, all broken and despairing," he murmured. "Just like it is now. You understood, then, that this world and all its true children will gut your ideals and leave you begging for death."

"But I won that fight," Ewan whispered, numbly.

"You bought yourself time," Gabe corrected. "Every hollow victory you've achieved has only made this day all the sweeter. Every time you overcame my efforts, you sowed the seeds of your future despair. Hope cannot endure forever, and all things must end. Life has but one purpose, O'Meara: to die." He leaned forward and patted Ewan on his swollen cheek, each tap another jolt of pain. "If only you'd embraced that truth, we wouldn't be here now."

Ewan struggled against the fog pulling at his mind. "What did I ever do to you?" he whispered. "I was only trying to help."

Gabe twisted his ear, hard enough to tear the top. "Aren't you listening, player?" he snarled. "The Centre can't afford your lies. Even if by some miracle you changed this world, you have no idea what horrors would rush in to take its place!"

Settling back again, he continued. "After Whitehaven, I threw myself into the effort of breaking your spirit in the real world. Your father's death was convenient, certainly, but your sister and mother kept you going. Rothchild was after the Diamond Lord to keep you pliable, so I changed tactics, pledging to help you hunt me down." He laughed, spinning Ewan again. "I wonder, O'Meara, why that took so long? With so many players now alive and well in the Centre, I had little choice but to call on my allies in the Wastes. I assigned Frasier to the communications array, and he sent the Locusts to find the EMP as a weapon of last resort while I continued to work quietly, turning as many staff as I could against the players. You made it easy for me, you and your woman. To think, you would get Annie pregnant against all expectation! The ultimate in false hopes for the future!"

Gabe struck Ewan again, this time between the legs. Ewan cried out, trying to double over, but the bindings held him tightly.

Gabe sighed contentedly. "I gained many followers, on account of your little spawn. In the meantime, I helped the Locusts advance, directing them to our weakest patrols, joining in the battle myself when my duties allowed. I've enjoyed watching your countrymen die a real death out here, O'Meara. And I could barely keep myself from laughing when you brought that pathetic little girl from the cat world! It was as though you were trying to make a case for banishing the players. I helped you make it, using that Veridian priest and your own distraction to recruit the worst your world had to offer. And when their fervor became inconvenient, I arranged for Coley and I to feed you to the Locusts."

Ewan's heart twinged, coming back to life at the image of Patrick Lee and the others. "I thought you were the victim," he rasped, struggling to talk around his swollen tongue.

"I *am* the victim," Gabe said coldly. "I am the hero. Your players exceeded my wildest expectations, and only through sheer luck did I survive your foolish sentiment in rescuing that cat girl. After that, I had to sacrifice Frasier. You were so determined to see him burn, O'Meara. So certain you were right." He spun Ewan again. "Tell me. Do you feel you're right, now?"

Let it stop, Ewan thought, but he couldn't ignore Gabe's voice, or its venom.

"That imbecile from Olenwe, the one bedding your sister, almost offended me more than you do, O'Meara," Gabe said. "It took him almost no time to solve Rothchild's imaginary food supply problem, which forced the Director to take the players' side and hope for the best. You see, O'Meara? Hope, distracting the Centre from its core mission. Playing those politics netted me a few more followers, but the damage was done. Live or die, your kind had made too many changes for the Centre to recover to its former self.

"So, I committed myself to excising your cancer with the EMP. When the Locusts were somehow outclassed by your Sah'rassans in their own Wastes, I arranged their raid to retrieve Frasier and coordinate their search. When they found one, I nearly ordered the attack then and there...but I saw the potential of this flying machine." Gabe ran his fingers across the yoke with a lover's touch. "The perfect delivery method for my weapon, and crafted by my prey, no less. I told my people to wait in Ruin 7, that I would personally bring to them the very tool we needed to finish the Centre off. Once you'd proven yourself capable of flying it, I had the Locusts let slip the EMP's existence to your spies. They dutifully reported back to Rothchild, and you didn't even hesitate to volunteer! Your eyes were so full of hope, O'Meara, it was all I could do to keep my hands off your throat in the Director's office." Gabe reached out and crushed Ewan's neck, his smile broadening. "And you so obligingly taught me how to fly, tonight. The least I can do is teach you how to fall."

He released Ewan and turned to check the *Horse's* progress.

Ewan gasped, floundering in his dark sea of pain and betrayal—and realized with horror that it wasn't Gabe's betrayal that hurt him the most. Everything the programmer, the Diamond Lord, said had the hard ring of truth in it. Twisted, but true. And now Ewan's hopes were laid bare: never truly his, but a knife's edge he'd only stayed on through blind luck.

And now there was nowhere to go, but down.

Tree...why didn't you tell me?

"You know I'm right," Gabe said quietly. Sympathetically. "I'm telling you the truth, when no one else would. Can you see now, how cruel and harsh the world is? Don't bother fighting it anymore. As your worst enemy, I won't lie to you."

The words pounded through the pain, each burying Ewan a little more. "What are you going to do now?" he asked, his own voice distant. "What happens next?"

"I'll use the EMP on the Centre and wipe out your race, once and for all. We've indulged your fantasies long enough, wasting our time and resources for millennia to keep your kind alive for a world in which they have no place. Mother Earth is barren, O'Meara. She has no room, or forgiveness."

Things can't get any worse, Ewan thought. "You're going to help the Locusts destroy the Centre?"

The Diamond Lord chuckled. "Of course not. The Locusts are useful, but they don't see the Centre's true value: its stability. Rest assured, player, the Locusts will not enter it."

"But how will you stop them?"

"I've told you before; I have friends among the staff. It's been difficult and frustrating, but I've assembled a loyal army, capable of wiping out the Locust rabble. You drove them to me, you know. Every time you inspired hope in some people, you shattered it in others. Take Sanderson, for example."

Ewan's heart twisted again. "Nathan?"

Gabe nodded. "He's a perfect example of why you need to be destroyed. That boy had a comfortable life, picking at the ruins. Then you inspired him to be more, even as you worked to render him obsolete. That boy believed in you, but you let him down, like you have every person who sees the world for what it is. Nathan knows now the only way to keep his position is to destroy the players who would usurp it. When the battle comes tomorrow, Sanderson and those like him, the victims of hope, will turn on the players and sympathizers before eliminating the Locusts. Then they'll follow me back to the Centre, where the EMP will regrettably have already been detonated. We'll be too late to save the players, but the survivors in the Centre will welcome us with open arms—and legs." He shot Ewan a lecherous grin. "Life will return to normal. Even better, in fact. We can glide gently down into oblivion, along with the rest of the planet, without struggling or even caring in the end. A perfect finish for the human race, our just reward for the damage we've done."

It's worse, Ewan thought despondently. Mustering what little fight he had left, he said, "What about Tree, and Dawn?"

Gabe's smile somehow turned even more malicious. "I'll make sure Annie forgets you soon enough, even if birthing makes her a worthless mate. As for the brat, perhaps I'll raise her myself. It's my right as a Central, after all. Yes...when her own turn comes, I'll be the one who tells her how her player father gave up and left her to me."

Ewan tried desperately to lunge at Gabe. The cords dug into his wrists, slicking them with his blood, and he wrenched himself forward, yelling and cursing and crying. Gabe flinched in surprise, but then he merely turned his attention back to the controls, while Ewan fought the barbs in his heart and body until he lost consciousness.

32

FORSAKEN

"GET UP, VEGGIE!"

The words, rough and gloating, trickled through the blackness. Ewan tried to ignore them, but a pair of equally rough hands grabbed him by the shoulders. Pain blossomed through him again as the voice's owner threw him from the chair, then dragged him outside.

Sand and rubble scraped Ewan's bruised face. He turned as best he could, forcing his sluggish body to respond. Opening his eyes, he saw his ankles in Jeff Harper's grip as the former security guard cursed his way across the broken pavement of the Memorial. Ahead, at least fifty robed Locusts stood in the darkness, their scarred faces dimly lit by the odd flashlight. But they paid Ewan no mind, too busy watching an altercation brewing in their midst.

"You promised us the right of salvage," snarled a voice, guttural and male. "But we found no bodies on the flying machine."

Gabe's voice answered, impatient and dismissive. "The fate of two players' corpses is of no interest to me, Awa. If your people couldn't be bothered to collect them before your rivals did, that is your own problem."

"Then I challenge the other alphas!" Awa bellowed. The other Locusts shifted back, making space, and Ewan saw a monster of a man, barrel-chested and easily six and a half feet tall.

What are they eating out here? Ewan wondered dimly.

Awa glared around the group, brandishing a makeshift concrete club. "Who dares to steal from the Lynx?"

"We need not take what you would freely throw away in time," said another man.

Awa started for the man, club raised. His target stepped forward, backed by two others drawing weapons as they went —but a different gun spat into the ground between them.

"That's enough!" Vincent Coley growled, taking aim at Awa's head with a rifle as he emerged beside Gabe.

"Contend with it on your own time, Awa," Gabe said coolly. "By tomorrow night, you'll have more bodies than even your appetite can manage." He turned away from the Locust. "Status report."

"We've got the EMP ready for transfer," came James Frasier's thin voice. He smirked at Awa. "Now that the rear cabin's been aired out, installation should be simple."

"Get on it," Gabe ordered. "Draft whoever you need to help."

A disgruntled murmur rippled through the Locusts, and the man who'd stood up to Awa stepped forward again. Coley locked onto his head, but Gabe beckoned the man to him.

The man didn't move. "I do not recognize you, settler," he said calmly. "Who are you, that acts as if the Twice-Forsaken are yours to command?"

"I am their chief," Gabe replied, indicating Coley and Frasier, and Harper too, as the thug finished dragging Ewan into the ring. "And I am the Diamond Lord, to hapless creatures such as that. I already command you. It was by my information that you've held your own territory against the settlers and their pets. It was by my direction that you located the EMP we will use to annihilate them."

The alpha was still, but the challenge in his voice was clear. "It was your direction, then, that led us to starvation while you play your games. We should have struck tens of days ago."

More murmurs from the ring, mostly in agreement.

"I assure you, the wait will be well worth the pain," Gabe said quickly, addressing the group. "Now the sailcraft is finished, and it is ours."

"Far easier for you to wait in your comfortable fortress!" a woman called. "We have lost many children."

The murmurs became grumbles.

"And you will lose far more if you do not unite under me, this instant!" Gabe snapped. "Even now, the Centre's Director sends his army. An army of players like this one." He stepped on Ewan's head, grinding the side of his face into the sand and rubble. "Five hundred players, each with a lifetime of combat experience, much better fed and armed than you. Millions more wait underground, an endless tide that will sweep through us all. You know what they're capable of; you've lost enough battles with them. Now that they know of your existence, they will never stop hunting you!"

Ewan tried to push up, but Coley's gun jammed into his neck.

Gabe stepped away, pacing around the ring. "I alone offer you the chance to eliminate the player threat, to prove your mastery." He pointed at Awa, then the challenger man. "You are weak. Fighting each other, and for what? Corpses in the desert, while the spoiled children of the Centre feast?"

"Your settler names mean nothing to me," the challenger said.

"Then I will use yours. You know the Great Mother as I do. Return with me, and let her true children claim what is theirs. I will bring you to the promised land!"

Many of the Locusts drew a sharp breath, but the challenger held firm. "You are not Twice-Forsaken."

"No," Gabe whispered, the malice in his voice almost tangible as he returned to face the man. "I am Thrice-Forsaken. Cast out, not only from my domain and my home in the Centre, but from my dear mother's joyous arms. I am her gift. Her sacrifice, born to rule you." He towered above the challenger, one hand on the pistol at his side. "Follow me to the last remnant of our storied past, or kill me and die tomorrow like the animal you are."

Do it, Ewan pleaded silently. But even as the thought formed in his mind, he pictured the coming day's battle. Without the Diamond Lord to rally his Central loyalists, the Locusts could win in the confusion. They could roll straight into the Centre, EMP or no EMP, and slaughter everyone.

Nerf it all...we still can't afford to sacrifice him!

The Locust man apparently reached a similar conclusion, because after a long, tense moment, he slowly went to his knees. "As alpha, I have the mastery of the Bear Clan. We will follow you."

One by one, nearly three dozen Locusts—other alphas—came forward, pledging loyalty to their new lord. Ewan could do nothing but lie there on the ground, still pinned by Coley's gun.

Until Harper came back for him. "Director," he called, scruffing Ewan by the collar. "Where do you want this trash?"

Gabe didn't even turn around. "Secure him for the night. I have more to teach him, tomorrow."

Ewan barely felt the trip, despite being dragged over even more rubble. He barely noticed when Harper took him into a half-collapsed building and tied him to the remnants of a wall, hanging him up by the wrists. He did notice, however, the corpses on either side of him. Another surge of dread took him, but when he looked more closely, he realized with a pang that the bodies weren't Bach'an's or Sarah's.

Harper saw his gaze and laughed. "Like your roommates? Effing spies. I prettied them up myself last night, once Reid told me where to find them." He gave Ewan a broken-toothed grin, then slugged him in the gut before leaving.

Ewan's night passed in half-conscious agony, until his body gave up on telling him how hurt it was and went numb. It wasn't unlike limbo, Ewan decided. A chance to do nothing but reflect on the choices he'd made, the mistakes that led him to his death.

And every other player's, he thought bitterly. Millions of them, waking up in the morning with no clue about what was coming. Not knowing their delusional worlds would vanish to blackness, leaving them to die in confused panic as the life support failed.

No warning. As an emissary, he should have warned them.

He told himself that his friends in the Centre would resist, but it was a hollow hope at best. Most of them wouldn't even see through Gabe's treachery, believing that the programmer had fought bravely but failed to stop the EMP. Tree wouldn't be fooled for a minute, but what good did that do? She'd known Gabe's nature, if not the depth of his hate, but even at the end, she'd told Ewan nothing of use. Faced with embracing Gabe or letting Dawn die...Ewan knew full well what his wife would choose.

Survival. No matter the cost.

I never should have helped her, he thought despondently. *We'd have all been better off.*

Soft footsteps approached. Ewan resigned himself to another dragging, but instead he got a firm tap on the forehead.

He turned away, but the tap repeated, insistent, until he opened his eyes.

A Locust, the man who'd challenged Gabe earlier, regarded him from a foot away. "I would speak with you," the man said quietly.

Ewan tried to sigh, but it came out as a strangled cough. "I have nothing to say to you."

"I disagree. I wish to know why this settler lord hates you so."

"I wish I knew, too."

To his surprise, the man cut the cables around his wrists, then eased him to the floor. "I am Kadh, Alpha of the Bear clan. Who are you?"

Ewan gathered his senses, fixing on Kadh's foul breath and the rounded scars across his face. *Like the Sah'rassans' paint.* "Ewan. Ewan, from Veridor."

"Veridor," Kadh murmured, testing the name. "I do not know it. Is it a settler clan?"

"No, or yes, I guess," Ewan answered after a moment. "Veridor's a simulation."

"I do not understand."

"A simulation," Ewan repeated wearily. "It's where the players live."

"The settlers' vast army?" The man frowned. "You are a warrior, then?"

"Yes," Ewan whispered. "I was a warrior."

"Tell me how these players live in simulations," Kadh insisted. "Are they ruins, like this place?"

Ewan shook his head, barely moving before the pain redoubled. "Not at all. They're entire worlds, full of green things and clear skies."

Kadh leaned back, exhaling sharply, his foul breath flooding Ewan's nostrils. "The Great Mother took away such places many, many tens ago. What you speak of, it cannot be real."

"Of course it's not real!" Ewan snapped, laughing bitterly. "None of the game worlds are! They're fantasy, and fragile, and you're going to destroy them all!"

"And you are here, to claim right of possession?"

"What?"

Kadh's head tilted, his scarred expression uncannily like a puzzled bear's. "Among the Twice-Forsaken, no clan may intrude upon the resources of another. We claim the right of possession, so others know there is nothing to share. If no one occupies a place, then others may take it."

Ewan tried to think about this, but all he could get was an image of the Locusts shooting each other over cans of food. "It's something like that, I guess. Players haven't been to the real world for ages."

"Why not?"

"Because it's broken!" Ewan snarled, before lapsing into more coughing. "That's the whole frapping point of the Centre. Someone built it during the Rapture, to let everyone ride out the Wastes. Everyone was supposed to hide in the game worlds, until Earth was safe to live on again." He sighed, a ragged shudder. "As if that could ever happen."

"The promised land," the alpha murmured, a hungry light in his eyes. "Your Centre, it truly is the promised land?"

Ewan hesitated. "I guess that's what Gabe called it," he admitted. "But that's probably a lie. What is it?"

"Many tens ago, our ancestors lived on a green world, such as yours." Kadh spread his arms wide. "When the Great Mother punished her children, they created a refuge. A hidden place, where the water flowed without poison, where the sky was good to breathe."

"The promised land," Ewan said quietly. "But you didn't get to come, did you? You got...forsaken."

A door slammed nearby, making them both jump. Kadh pulled his hood up and disappeared into the darkness of a corner, leaving Ewan alone as Jeff Harper approached. For a moment, Ewan toyed with fighting back, but it was pointless. He didn't know where the EMP was, much less how to disarm it or even set it off.

I'm just an ignorant player, and now we're going to die for it.

"Trying to run away?" Harper growled, eying the broken bonds before kicking Ewan in the chest. "Not on my watch, worm. Reid wants you in the air with us when we use the imp."

"It's EMP, you idiot," Ewan whispered, earning himself another kick.

He squinted as they emerged, more against the sand than the dim morning light. All around him, Locust warriors were gearing up, climbing into dozens of repaired old-Earth transports. Preparing, for their glorious defeat at Gabe's hands.

A baby's cry jolted Ewan fully alert. He twisted in Harper's grip, afraid he'd heard Dawn—and saw a couple of women, each holding an infant to their scarred breasts.

How? he wondered, losing the view when Harper shoved him through the sailcraft's hatch. *How can these people have kids normally, when no one in the Centre could manage it? What kind of childhood do they have in the Wastes?*

What right of possession do the players and Centrals really have?

He just got a glimpse of the EMP, secured next to the repulsor, before Harper picked him up and shoved him into the copilot's chair.

"Good morning, O'Meara," Gabe said pleasantly from beside him. "Are you rested and ready for today's lesson?"

Ewan sighed and braced himself for the day's torture, too despondent to fight back anymore. He buckled himself in before Harper could bind him, then faced forward to see the inevitable end of his hope.

You promised me you would come back safe and sound. Tree's voice drifted through the back of his mind. *I'm going to hold you to it.*

"It was another lie," he whispered, as the hatch closed and Gabe took them aloft. "We just keep lying to each other. I'm sorry, Tree."

33

THE STORM BREAKS

THE FLIGHT DRAGGED ON, SEEMINGLY FOREVER. THE *RED HORSE 2*, the harbinger of war, pressed mulishly into the constant headwind under the Diamond Lord's direction. The Locusts had moved ahead on the ground, whether to thrash the players or to get breathing room from their new master, Ewan wasn't sure.

Coley and Harper kept their positions in the cabin, pretending to operate the *Horse's* sensors but really keeping guard on Ewan, just in case. They needn't have bothered; Ewan sat there, bound by the dead weight of his heart. He gave no outward reply to Gabe's digs about Tree, but each scandalous detail the chief described painted a devastatingly real picture in Ewan's mind—to the point where he couldn't even think of his wife without automatically picturing Gabe with her, taking her while she watched Ewan with disappointed acceptance.

What are you looking at me for? he thought bitterly. *I'm not the one who could help you. I never was...and you knew it.*

"You're far more fun to have around, now that you're broken in," Gabe mused after a while. "Now, pay attention. What do you see on the radar?"

Ewan obediently looked at the screen, finding at least a hundred contacts in a writhing scrum. "A battle."

"That's right, player," Gabe lilted. "Your next lesson is at hand. Let's get closer. It will be perfectly safe: each side thinks we're with them. Let them draw hope from our divine intervention!"

He took the *Horse* down, laughing softly to himself. The dust thinned, and the radar was replaced by a camera feed from under the hull, the colored blips replaced by killing, dying people. Central armadillos rampaged across the sandy field, trading fire with four times as many Locust tanks—and the captured 'dillo, now painted red. The 'roos and more nimble Locust transports wove between them, guns ablaze, shooting into and running down ground forces to stain the dunes.

Ewan winced as a pair of tanks rammed into a 'dillo, tipping it, then fired into its underbelly at point blank. The resulting fireball seared the air, rattling the sailcraft and forcing Gabe to swerve aside. Fighters on both sides raised their weapons in a cheer as they flew past, before turning back to the bloodbath.

"Isn't it beautiful?" Gabe asked softly. "The way we murder each other over the Mother's corpse? Do you see, O'Meara, how our inevitable fate is to kill ourselves off?" He sighed, and Ewan looked up, trapped by the sudden sadness, the weariness, in the programmer's icy eyes. "You understand, don't you? It's a mercy to speed it along. We must end humanity's lingering death in the Centre, and with it, the misery every waking soul endures to preserve an impossible dream."

Gabe activated the communications array, and static crackled into the *Horse's* cabin. "The Diamond Lord descends on a path of fire," he announced, giving Ewan a wan smile as his amplified voice rang out over the Wastes. "He calls upon his people. Who will follow him?"

In answer, the roof hatches popped open on half the armadillos, and white banners rolled down their sides. They wheeled about, plowing through their own ground forces—players, all—and obliterated the 'roos, catching the Sah'rassan pilots by surprise.

A trickle of defiance crept into Ewan's voice as the still-black transports regrouped, forming a defensive ring. "You didn't get all of them," he murmured.

"I didn't need to," Gabe answered smugly. "Sanderson was careful about his assignments. Those vehicles have no one worth keeping aboard." He chuckled, the fingers of one hand dancing across a console as he brought the *Horse* about for another pass. "Even I can be inspired by your fellow players' actions. Do you recall what they did to that armadillo at the fort?"

Ewan watched in horror as the players' 'dillos suddenly went berserk. Guns locked onto targets at random, spewing fire in all directions, and the behemoth vehicles turned drunken circles, colliding with one another.

"Your kind only knows how to leech benefits from the system," Gabe said. "Look now at what a master does with it! Adjust a line of code, and left becomes right. Disable a subroutine, and a friend becomes a deadly liability. Let's listen in, shall we?"

He swept a hand over the console, and Nathan's voice tore through the cabin. "Gunner, target 'Dillo 3; it's got the most Veridians. Fire!" Below, a rocket flew from one of the white transports, pummeling one of the disoriented victims. The 'dillo rocked, smoking, and its crew fled—only to be cut down by friendly fire.

"Good shot, Amy," Nathan said. "Target 'Dillo 6—"

"What do you think you're doing? That was one of ours!"

Dread uncoiled in Ewan's gut, leaped up his spine as he recognized that voice. The voice of a big young man who'd once fought alongside Nathan and Gabe to knock Ewan senseless.

“Sam,” he whispered.

“That ‘dillo wasn’t one of ours,” Nathan answered Sam. “It never was.”

“Are you frapping crazy?!” The dread grabbed Ewan’s throat, allowing him only a strangled cry as Kate joined in. “Those Locusts are shooting at us!”

“Not anymore,” Nathan said, his voice a younger copy of Gabe’s confidence. “They know what side we’re on—at least, they think they do. Sam, the time has come! The players are the real enemy. They’ve taken our food, our jobs, and our pride. You know it better than anyone, thanks to *her*.”

Ewan finally managed to shout at the console. “Sam, please!”

Gabe chuckled. “They can’t hear you,” he said to Ewan. “We are but ghosts in the wind.”

A click sounded from the speakers—the sound of a gun being armed.

“Kate,” Sam said slowly. “Get out of here.”

“Don’t do it! They’ll kill you!” she yelled.

Nathan’s laugh was incredulous. “You can’t be serious! You’re going to let her run back to that idiot player?”

“Yes,” Sam replied, his voice steady. “Because that’s what she needs to do.”

“Sam!” Kate screamed.

“Kate,” Sam said, “you pushed me to think big and dream big, even when I thought I couldn’t. I can never thank you enough for that. I’m glad I was there for you when you needed me...but you don’t need me anymore.”

“That’s not true!” Her voice was breaking, pleading. “I need you more than ever!”

“Kate, he can give you the sky. I want that for you. I want you to be happy.”

“No, Sam, I love you! Don’t do this!”

"I love you too," the mole replied sadly. "So does Twiggy. Tell him I said he'd better take good care of you, okay?"

Gunshots sounded, and Kate's anguished cry pierced the *Horse's* cabin, tearing the speakers as if the sailcraft was crying in sympathy for its creators. For its dead father.

Ewan saw a red-haired, black-armored figure race out onto the sands.

Nathan's 'dillo turned, locking onto her.

And Ewan's defiant spark, smothered the night before, flared to life again. Heart pounding, Ewan grabbed the copilot's controls and wrenched hard, putting the *Red Horse 2* into a steep bank that sent Coley and Harper flying into the wall. Kicking at Gabe to spin him in his seat for a change, Ewan plunged the sailcraft into the 'dillo, smacking it broadside across the top with a horrible crunch. The *Horse* bounced up, its sail undamaged, but the 'dillo toppled.

The controls flew out of Ewan's hands as Gabe took them about. Snarling, the Diamond Lord fired the *Horse's* guns at Kate as she fled, but Ewan punched him, knocking his aim wide. The two fought for control, trading blows as the sailcraft careened through the chaos—but Harper's meaty hands grabbed Ewan's shoulders. The thug spun Ewan around and drove a knee straight into his chest.

Ewan cried out, winded. Harper kneed him again, then gave him a hard punch to the face. "You're not going anywhere, worm!"

"That's enough!" Gabe snapped.

Harper punched Ewan one more time, then stood back, panting as he licked Ewan's blood off his knuckles. "Just like your grandpa, veggie."

"It seems O'Meara is eager for his next lesson," Gabe growled, wiping the blood from his nose as Harper and Coley tied Ewan up again. "Check for any damage he may have caused, and prepare the EMP for launch."

The goons disappeared into the back. Ewan tried to twist around to kick Gabe again, but the programmer merely regarded him in amazement.

"You truly haven't given up, have you?" Gabe released his harness and stood, shaking his head in disgust. "Were you inspired by Draper's self-destruction? A little too familiar for you, perhaps, that soft spot for faithless women?"

Ewan took a shaky breath, around the resentment burning in his soul. *If Sam can forgive, then so can I!* "That's not going to work on me again, Gabriel," he said, trying desperately to assure himself it was true.

Gabe threw his head back and laughed. "Now you even sound like Annie! But you know, all it takes is one taste. You've seen how passionately she reacts to me, even now. Do you think you can embrace her again, without thinking of me?" His voice became a whispered hiss. "Do you think she does?"

The image of Tree and Gabe reformed in Ewan's mind, more painful than anything Harper had dealt. "No," he whispered.

Gabe sighed, and his voice became almost pitying. "Don't take it personally, O'Meara. Your entire family may be worthless, but all families are. Your father lacked the wherewithal to even live in the real world, your mother feeds the very people who want you dead, and your sister's as great a whore as your wife. And you, with the blood of millions soon to be on your hands, all because you wouldn't bow to your mistakes." He shook his head. "One can only wonder what disasters your spawn would have caused, without my intervention."

Ewan tried uselessly to lunge at him, but Gabe smiled sadly. "I warned you. There's no magic, no miracle to save you," he said, gesturing to the empty cabin. "In reality, you're on your own."

"Ea'win Omi'ra's family will never desert him!"

A clang sounded from behind Ewan, followed by a piece of metal flying across the room. Ewan just caught Gabe's bewildered expression before a red mist exploded into the chief's face. The Diamond Lord howled, clutching his eyes as he stumbled back, tripping over his chair.

Elated but stunned, Ewan gaped as Cerri stepped to his side, a spray bottle in one hand and claws on the other. Her amber eyes watched Gabe as she glowered. "You complain like a kitten. *I* have been rejected by my families thrice before, but I have enough sense to make a new one for myself instead of harming another's."

"Cerri," Ewan blurted, still trying to process. "How did you—where did you come from?"

The Sah'rassan girl glanced down at him, offering the barest hint of a smile. "'How' is with this pepper spray, which Kai'tah and Tri'ana Omi'ra made with the girl who gave me fish. 'Where' is from the ventilation duct." She pointed up behind her. "It was difficult to hide Bach'an and his human in there. It is fortunate that he volunteered instead of Rocco."

Ewan suddenly realized he was laughing hysterically.

Cerri tore the ropes binding Ewan; then she advanced on Gabe, her lips pulled back in a snarl. "You are the killer of Ea'win Omi'ra's father," she growled, slashing him across the face as he tried to stand. "And you are no better than the sh'takhi who called the winds to Hara'noh." She turned to Ewan. "My debt is paid."

"A hundred times over," Ewan agreed. Half afraid he was dreaming, he reached for his swords and found empty space. "Do you know where my weapons are?"

"They are in the back." Cerri snatched Gabe's rapier from his belt, then tossed it to Ewan. "Will this do?"

Ewan gripped the hilt—Kate's work—with grim satisfaction. "It's perfect."

He hefted the blade, lining up on Gabe's heart, but then the back door opened.

"Sir, the imp's loaded, just like you—what are you doing here?" Harper asked blankly.

Without thinking, Ewan spun and hurled the blade, aiming for the chest. It sank into Harper's eye instead, and with a final grunt of bewilderment, the thug dropped to the floor.

"Coley's back there, too," Ewan said quickly. Cerri nodded and slipped into the back room, hot sauce spray at the ready. Ewan laughed in grateful disbelief as he moved to Harper's body and pulled the rapier free...

Gabe shot him in the back.

The armor held, but Ewan still dropped. He rolled away, narrowly avoiding a follow-up head shot, then swung for Gabe's knees. Gabe leaped over the strike, laying suppression fire as he made for the hatch. He snatched a parachute pack and first aid kit from the wall, then turned to Ewan. "You're too late," he snarled, spitting blood as it poured from the four gashes running diagonally across his face. "I armed the EMP; it'll launch in less than three minutes!"

He jammed the hatch release, and it opened with a snapping hiss. Ewan threw the rapier at him, but the blade hit him sideways. Gabe stooped to pick it up, looking up to give Ewan one last taunt—but Vincent Coley came stumbling out of the back room, screaming curses as he wiped his eyes, with Cerri hot on his tail. She shoved the scout into his Diamond Lord, then leaped neatly aside as the two men toppled out.

"Cerri'dah has bested you!" she taunted, before turning to Ewan with an impish smile. "Even if it was a 'cheap shot.'"

Ewan huffed a laugh, grimacing as he stood. "It was a legal move. Let's just hope that sand isn't loosely packed."

Then, in the relative calm, he heard the pilot's console beeping.

Ignoring his body's protests, Ewan ran to the chair and

pulled up the map. "Frapping hell. We're too close to the Centre!"

"Can you disarm the weapon?" Cerri asked, following him.

"I have no idea how. Gabe didn't tell me anything." A mix of sweat and blood trickled over his eyes, and he smeared it away with the back of his hand, realizing it was shaking as the only feasible plan formed in his mind.

He didn't know how to disarm old Earth weapons; he was just a player.

But he knew how to fly.

His heart froze, considering, then churned its agreement. *My family's given everything they have to help me. Now, it's my turn.*

Ewan wheeled the *Horse* to the north, diving low over the dunes and picking up speed. "Cerri, you have to jump off. I'm going to take this thing as far as I can, but you have to tell the others. Tell them the truth about what's happened!"

Cerri regarded him, amber eyes unblinking.

He pushed her toward the door. "Go! Tell Tree I love her... and that I'm sorry I couldn't keep my promise."

She said nothing, then turned and raced to the hatch.

Ewan counted to ten, then yanked back on the yoke. The *Red Horse 2* shot into the sky, boosted by the tailwind to a nerve-wracking speed that wasn't nearly enough. He willed the sailcraft to outpace the winds, praying to the Logos and the Mother with all his pounding heart. The battle below whipped past him on the radar, and he put everything he had into flying up and out: the dark horse, racing to save the Centre from starvation for the lack of power.

He burst once more through the clouds into a brilliant blue afternoon, completely cut off from the chaos on the surface. He squinted as he checked the radar, exhaling as he saw he'd made it to three hundred miles from the Centre. Now all he could do was wait and pray that Gabe had honestly estimated the EMP's range.

Mother knew, he'd been honest enough with the rest.

A roar erupted from the rear cabin, and the *Horse* rocked, nearly shaking Ewan from his seat. The EMP tore through the roof, and the yoke tried to leap with it out of Ewan's hands, before the sail went limp. As the vessel pitched backward, Ewan saw the Diamond Lord's weapon streaking up through the sky, a column of fire and smoke tearing into the pure blue he loved so much.

"Thank you," Ewan whispered to that blue.

In answer, the sky ignited, as though a new sun had been born above him. Ewan cried out, throwing up his hands against the dazzling brightness as it seared his eyes even through his fingers. All around him, the cabin crackled and sparked as the controls overloaded, and the *Red Horse* 2 gave a satisfied shudder before sinking gently back down into the clouds, its sail turned into a parachute.

"It's done, then," Ewan whispered, throat burning and still seeing nothing but the intense light behind his eyelids. He thought of the picture he'd taken, only the night before, but he couldn't find his tablet. "Tree...it's for the best, this way. Players dying, so you can live. Tell Dawn I love her." He drew a deep shuddering breath, dredging up what joy remained from his broken heart. "And I love you, too, even now. Especially now. Remember me like that, okay?"

Then, giving in to exhaustion at last, Ewan let himself slip into oblivion as the flying machine took him back down to Earth.

34

AFTERMATH

DARKNESS, UTTER AND COMPLETE.

Ewan woke to a dull, thumping rumble, vibrating through his battered body from the floor and the wall behind him. He tried to open his eyes, but his eyelids wouldn't budge. Every part of him, inside and out, ached and burned. Gingerly, his arms throbbing as he raised them, he traced his fingers across a bandage that seemed to wrap around his entire head.

"Be at ease, Ea'win Omi'ra." Cerri's voice spoke from his left, soft and calm. "We are returning home, now."

Ewan tried to speak, eventually managing more than a scalded croak. "Cerri?"

"I am here," the Sah'rassan girl replied.

Am I dead? he thought, before trying, "Am I dreaming?"

"No. But the dream worlds are safe, thanks to you."

"What?" He coughed, hard, and she thrust a bottle into his hands.

"Drink, Ea'win Omi'ra. Do you not remember the past hours?"

Ewan drank deeply, then nearly spat out the bitter, stinging stuff. "I'm starting to. I seem to remember telling you to go and warn the others what happened. Why didn't you?"

"Because the winds were calling you. I knew you would ride them until they took you, so I stayed on the flying thing. Tri'ana Omi'ra would not be pleased if I allowed you to die, and I did not wish to owe another life debt."

"You should not expect Cerri'dah to do as you say," came a deep, amused voice, in front of Ewan. "Especially if what you say is foolishness."

"Rocco?" Ewan asked, frowning despite the pain. "How did you get on board—we're on a camel!"

"That is correct," Cerri said, pressing the foul drink at him again.

"But...how did we get here? The EMP broke the *Horse's* sail."

"It didn't break, E." Kate's voice came from Ewan's right, flat and exhausted. "We redesigned it to be resilient, remember?"

"I took cover in the vents," Cerri said simply. "When the shaking stopped, I did not hear you speak, so I came out. You were lying on the floor, as though dead. So, I brought us back. The flying boy made his machine easy to learn."

Ewan tried to picture Cerri, of all people, flying the sailcraft. He shook his head, which sent a searing pain through his skull. "But everything on the *Horse* was electronic. How did you manage?"

Kate gave him a halfhearted thump on the leg. "Query shielded everything from electromagnetic interference, after Sam..." She shook, trying without luck to stifle her sobs. "Sam told him to."

Ewan gently reached around to give his sister a stiff, sore hug, bumping into someone pressed up against her other side. "Then I owe them both. But where are we now?"

Footsteps approached from the left, tired but harried, stopping in front of him. "You're aboard Camel 5, O'Meara, along with half of the survivors."

"Robert?" Ewan looked up pointlessly at him. "Is that you? What do you mean, half?"

"I mean precisely what I said." The medical chief sighed. "We knew the battle was over, for better or worse, when power in the Centre flickered. Don't worry," he said quickly, as Ewan stiffened. "No one in the Centre was harmed as a result of the EMP. Staff, or player."

Ewan exhaled, letting some of the pain go. "Thank the Mother."

Nichols sniffed. "From what Cerri'dah has been incessantly telling everyone, it is you we should thank. Once again, you risked your life to protect us all."

It wasn't risking, Ewan thought automatically. A hollow feeling, one he'd been able to ignore in the heat of the moment, began to gnaw at his heart. *I knew I wasn't coming back. And Tree's going to know it, too.* "Yeah, I guess I did."

Nichols hesitated, seeming to sense Ewan's mood. "Additionally, both you and your family continue to strain the limits of what medicine can do. Cerri'dah, I wanted to inform you that both of your other charges are stable. Only time can tell what level of neural damage they suffered."

"Charges?" Ewan repeated.

"He is referring to Bach'an and his human," Cerri explained. "I told you, I hid them in the vents."

Ewan tried to pass a hand through his hair, but it was wrapped up. "But...I saw Gabe kill them."

"But *I* had elixirs," she replied proudly.

"Your young friend made pioneering use of the metabolic inhibitors she stole from Medical," Nichols explained, his tone more impressed than admonishing. "Through regular overdosing, she managed to slow their heart rates long enough for me to get to them. Frankly, it's a miracle they're alive, but they are. In fact, due to the onboard shielding, they suffered far less irradiation than you did."

Ewan half laughed, half coughed. "Yeah, I guess I took a real beating. Thanks for patching me up again."

Nichols hesitated again. "Don't thank me yet. The EMP's detonation inflicted massive damage to your retinas. I've done what I can to minimize stress to them, in transit."

"My eyes…" Ewan's voice faltered as he remembered the intense brilliance through the glass, the man-made sun—all too close.

And he'd looked right at it.

He swallowed, but his stomach only tried to send it back up. "When will we know?"

The doctor's voice was sympathetic, which only made it worse. "I'll run a full scan, as soon as we return to Medical."

"Yeah. Thanks."

The footsteps receded as Nichols made his rounds through what Ewan now realized was a camel packed full of the injured—probably the dead, too. He sat there, trying to understand what he'd learned, but it was as if Nichols had wrapped a bandage around his future as well, making it impossible to see.

Kate shook against him, more than the camel could account for. He gave her another hug. "Hey," he said, trying to make his broken voice gentle. "Do you want to talk about it?"

She took a ragged breath. "I don't know how to tell you this. Sam's…he's…he's gone." She shuddered.

"I know," Ewan answered, heart burning. "I heard everything from the *Horse*. He was very brave."

"He was a frapping idiot!" Kate cried. "He left me, E, just like Dad! They both took the easy way out, letting someone else kill them. They left me behind, alone."

Ewan's skin prickled at how near her words were to Gabe's, cursing his own abandonment. "Kate," he said carefully, "I know for a fact that Sam loved you. Dad did, too. I'm sure they wouldn't have left you if they'd thought there was any other way. They died to give you the chance to live, and they left their love with you. As long as you remember that, they'll still be alive inside you."

"Yeah, well, what do you know about it?" she grumbled.

He forced a chuckle. "You're joking, right? I know more about dying than anyone."

Except how to do it right, he thought automatically.

Kate huffed out something that could have been a laugh.

Ewan sighed. "I'm sure Sam thought he was saving you from having to choose between him and Query."

Kate sighed too, leaning into his shoulder. "That frapping idiot. Now he's in the way. How can I look at Query, without feeling like Sam didn't set us up?"

Ewan was grateful for the bandage, hiding his own tears as he thought of Tree and Gabe. "I don't know. But don't trick yourself into thinking he gave up on you. Sam was family. If I've learned anything in the past day, it's that family never truly leaves you."

"Yeah," she mumbled. "It just hurts."

"I know, K. I know." Ewan tilted the top of her head toward him, gave it a kiss. She didn't even protest. Trying to believe his next words himself, he added, "But the hurt's proof you can still feel, and that means you can heal again."

"Maybe…but I want revenge, too. Nathan's got to go down."

Ewan tried to blink. "Nathan? I thought I took him out with the *Horse*."

"No," Kate said bitterly. "When the EMP blew, everyone quit fighting. Even the wind stopped, like the bomb blew it back, and there was a touch of daylight on the ground. I looked, just like everyone else, and someone dropped out of the sky, on a parachute."

Ewan drew a sharp breath. "Gabe."

Kate shrugged against him. "I guess so. He landed right in the middle of the field. Next thing I knew, the Locusts and the player-haters were all running over to him. Nathan crawled out of his wrecked 'dillo. I went after him. Even got a shot or two in, but it didn't stop him." She bellowed in frustration. "Nerf it all, my own armor saved the little scrub!"

A chill crept up Ewan's spine. "Surely someone else went after him. Why didn't you all attack?"

"E, we were wiped out! Al'Dashan rallied the players to him, but we weren't in any position to fight. There were too many people in the enemy group, and we had too many wounded, not to mention half our weapons didn't work anymore." She barked a laugh. "Apparently the other guys thought the same thing, because they made no move to attack us, either. A few hours later, two camels came to the battlefield, to pick up the survivors."

Half of which are on this camel, Ewan remembered, with rising anger. "Where's the other camel?"

"The Locusts went all invisible in the sands. When the camels showed up, one of them automatically went straight to Nathan's group. They climbed right on board, then kicked out the drivers before hauling the Locusts up with them." Kate made a disgusted sound. "They're long gone."

And just like that, Gabe's still out there, Ewan thought. *Plotting Gems know what disaster for us, next.* He released Kate and grabbed his own wrists to control his shivering, as she fell silent and eventually went to sleep.

All I've done was buy us time...raise our hopes that much higher, for him to crush.

They reached the Centre after dark. Ewan let Kate and Cerri guide him to Medical, while Rocco assured him that he and Al'Dashan would provide the Director with a full report on the ground conflict. Ewan moved stiffly through his personal darkness, disoriented as someone put him on a gurney; after a moment's wheeling, he felt the elevator floor shift under his back.

Thank the Mother they still work, he thought with a shudder.

He hadn't been in his Medical bed for five minutes when he heard her voice. Full of fear and pain, as if she'd already guessed the worst. As if she hadn't already known the worst.

All his own pain, all his anger—everything he'd managed to push away, long enough to die for her—came roaring back.

"Ewan!" Tree cried. "Oh, love, what happened? Robert, is he awake?"

Ewan stiffened when her hand gripped his. "Wide awake," he rasped, as fury surged through his heart. "It was Gabe. He was behind it. All of it."

He didn't need to see her face; her sharp breath told him everything. Confirmed everything. "Ewan…you have to know—"

"Robert," Ewan called, far more harshly than he'd expected. "I'm ready for that scan, now."

"Scan?" Tree asked, her voice more hurt by the second. "Love, what happened?"

Ewan ignored her. "Robert!"

"Very well," Nichols replied, his voice getting louder as he neared. "Tilt your head forward, if you can."

Hands—Tree's hands—tried to help, but Ewan shook her off with a pained grunt. She took his hand again. This time he squeezed back, thinking vindictively of how she'd crushed his fingers when she'd been the one in the bed.

The bandage came off, one lap at a time. "All right," Nichols said, unable to keep the edge from his tone, either. "Look at me."

Ewan opened his eyes. Nothing changed.

"What happened?!" Tree's voice was anguished, now. Her fingers gripped his face, turning him to her. "Ewan, what's wrong with your eyes?"

What little hope he'd held onto turned to ash. "Robert, are they open?"

Nichols turned his head again. Ewan felt a dot of heat on each eye in turn, but the blackness remained. "Yes. Can you see anything?"

"Nothing whatsoever."

Nichols sighed. "I'll get the imager."

"For Mother's sake, love, what happened?!" Tree pleaded as Nichols left.

"I'm blind." The words were heavy, final. Unforgiving. "I saw something I shouldn't have, and now I've paid for it."

Tears, her tears, splashed onto his hands. "No! You can't be—"

"I've been blind all along!" Ewan snarled, savagely imagining her guilty expression before taking a shuddering breath. "It was about time my body caught up."

Tree fell silent after that, aside from quiet sobs.

Nichols returned before long, pressing something cold and rubbery around each of Ewan's eyes. "Your retinas are burned completely through. There's not any healthy tissue left to stimulate even partial regrowth." The doctor's hand gripped Ewan's shoulder, transferring a fresh dose of guilt and sympathy that may as well have been poison in Ewan's veins. "There's nothing I can do. I'm sorry, son."

Ewan jerked his shoulder free. "I'm not your son!"

It took Nichols a moment to speak again; when he did, his voice was tight. "Be that as it may, you're in my care. I suggest you reflect on that, and have the grace to be silent if you cannot be civil to those who care about you."

Ewan sullenly took his advice, saying only what was required of him as Nichols cut off his armor and treated the rest of his wounds. Aside from his eyes, his skin and throat were scorched by the EMP's radiation, and he had dozens of bludgeoning injuries to his head and body, ranging from massive bruises to a broken rib. Every discovery sent Tree deeper into her misery. Ewan lay back, enduring it as best he could as he tried to come to grips with the maelstrom raging within him.

When Nichols eventually released him with orders to come in tomorrow for follow-up treatment, Ewan still didn't know what he felt.

Tree led him out to the hall, saying nothing. Ewan let the silence hang, focusing his other senses on the walk. As a boy, he'd loved the darkness of Veridor's caves. Found it soothing.

You'd better get used to it, he told himself grimly, as he refused Tree's help and bumped into one corner after another.

At length, they passed through their apartment door to the scents of home: diapers and breast milk. Dawn was in her room, fussing at Lucia as the nurse babbled nonsense at her.

Ewan groped his way to the couch and dropped onto it, then immediately wished he hadn't when every inch of him howled in pain.

Tree sat next to him. Waiting.

We might as well get it over with, he thought. "So. We need to talk."

Her voice was hollow. "We do. About Gabriel's actions, both now and then."

Ewan clenched his fists. "You told me he only ever kissed you. Once."

"He did. That was how I knew it was wrong, although I expect he focused on...other aspects of the encounter."

"You think?" Ewan snapped. "Nerf it all, Tree! I need to know the whole truth, and I need you to tell me, because right now I think frapping Gabe's been more honest with me than you have!"

She stiffened, and for a moment Ewan thought she would leave after all, but then she took a deep breath. "Fine. It was the night before I first logged into Veridor," she said, her voice strained but resigned. "The Locusts had just destroyed the first camel. I was furious with Grandfather for his inaction. I had to do something, and I had the epiphany that if no one in the Centre knew how to fight in its defense, then the players might.

"That meant I had to get into the simulations. I had some access as a caretaker, but I couldn't log in. So, I went to Gabriel. He modified my account on the spot without any questions, but when I asked for full privileges—the kind a game master would have, I suppose—he demanded to know why I wanted them.

"I told him it was a secret, but that by helping me, he would be helping the Centre. He was always ambitious...I knew he wanted to be the Director one day, so I told him the less he knew, the better." She paused, taking a long breath. "He suggested that we discuss the matter more privately. I knew what he meant—"

"And you said *yes*?!"

"Yes, I did!" Tree snapped. "Ewan, I was raised in the Centre! I was of age, and I decided its defense would be worth the price."

"The price." Ewan huffed, comparing her story with Gabe's version—the only thing he could see clearly, anymore. "That's not how *he* put it. You're telling me you felt nothing for him?"

Tree shifted, turning, so they could stare out into the void, side by side. "I would be lying if I said no," she admitted. "But you have to understand, love. He wasn't like anyone else on the staff."

"Yeah. He tried to kill us all," Ewan growled.

She made an exasperated sound. "If you want the truth, then listen. Gabriel was the only other person I knew who'd read the stories of Old Earth. He was brilliant, driven, focused. His determination was like yours, that drive I love so much about you."

"I'm nothing like him!" Ewan spat.

"Not in the ways that matter, no," Tree said irritably.

"This frapping well matters to me!" he shouted.

"Then shut up and listen!" Tree shouted back, breathing furiously now. "He led me to his room. He walked so quickly, I had to run to keep up with him. He never once held my hand. When we arrived, he told me to get undressed, to get into his bed." Her voice tightened, struggling to stay even. "He climbed on top of me...he touched me. But when he kissed me..." She shuddered. "It wasn't at all like the first time you and I kissed. I knew then that I couldn't go through with it. I told him to stop, but he didn't. So I slapped him and fled, and I've regretted my decision ever since."

Ewan lowered his face into his hands, scrubbing his eyes as if that would help. Her story fit, well enough, but knowing it didn't make the pain, the disappointment, any less.

Tree continued, her voice settling into a dead monotone. "The following day, I logged into Veridor. Without the additional privileges, I wasn't able to persuade the Church. They attempted to arrest me...they chased me, straight to you."

Ewan stared blankly toward the floor, searching in vain for anything to reorient himself.

Why, exactly, was he angry? The thought of Tree with another guy made his stomach clench, especially with Gabe's narration gleefully whispering the details in his mind. But Tree was right: born and raised in the Centre, it was a wonder she'd only had the one lover, even at her age. No, it wasn't what Tree had done in the moment; it was how she'd handled it afterward. Months, years even, of letting him buddy up to her ex without a word. All the scorn she'd heaped on the other Centrals' relationships, all the possessive blasting she'd given him...now it made a perfect, infuriating sense.

But what hurt most of all was that after all they'd been through together, she still hadn't trusted him enough to share something so important to her. Instead, she'd kept it a secret, known only to her and Gabe.

She let him in, where she shut me out.

Ewan sighed, then forced himself upright again. "Why didn't you ever tell me? You knew how I felt about the jerk who made you cry."

"That's precisely why I didn't tell you," Tree said bitterly. "Gabriel may have been despicable, but he was useful. He had skills and power we needed. I couldn't risk losing that by turning you against him."

"Tree, he murdered a hundred people last year, and almost killed everyone today!"

Tree huffed. "How could I have known that, back then? I knew he was grasping and manipulative, but I had no idea how violent he would become."

"You keep me in the dark again and again, but you call *him* manipulative?" Ewan said in disbelief, yanking on his hair. "You should have warned me! So what if he didn't help, after the thrashing I'd have given him? We could have found another way!"

"The only way you've found all year leads straight to the game floors!" Tree snapped. "I've lost count of all the times I've begged Grandfather to be patient with you, and it's barely been enough to keep you here with everything that's happened. How long do you think you'd have lasted, if you assaulted Gabriel?"

"Long enough to kick his ass," Ewan growled. "You should have trusted me!"

"How can I?" Tree's voice became shrill. "How can I trust you to respond appropriately, when you're so impulsive and there's so much for us to lose?"

She gripped Ewan's wrist, but it only reminded him of Gabe doing the same thing months ago. Warning him to be civil, just long enough to see the Diamond Lord's grand reveal. Until Gabe had wrung every bit of value from him.

"So much for your promise to keep no more secrets," Ewan snarled. Ignoring his body's protests, he wrenched his arm free and stood up. He stalked for the door, but he immediately tripped over the couch's arm and landed hard on the floor.

Tree was there in an instant, but he refused her belated help. "Ewan, please don't go!" she pleaded as he got up again. "I need you! Dawn needs you!"

"So I'm useful, like Gabe?" he hissed over his shoulder as he found the door. "Between the two of you, you've used me up. But I guess that's what Gems do best with players, isn't it?"

He stormed out, then crashed into the opposite wall. Swearing, he turned and moved up the hall, keeping his fingers against the cold steel.

He'd made it as far as the corner before someone ran up behind him. "I don't want any help!" he growled.

A hand grabbed his and spun him around with surprising force. "You need it anyway, honey," Lucia said, her tone not brooking any argument. "Come back home." She locked an arm around Ewan's waist, then marched him back to the apartment.

Tree was in Dawn's room, sobbing.

"We can do this here, or in your bedroom," Lucia said bluntly. "What's it going to be?"

Ewan was tempted to say the bedroom out of spite, but he couldn't bring himself to do it. "Here," he growled, letting Lucia guide him back to the couch. "What do you want?"

"To help," she said again. "I thought you might appreciate the voice of experience."

Ewan scoffed. "Yeah, you'd be that, wouldn't you?"

"I would," Lucia said firmly. "Which means you'd be mistaken to ignore what I have to say. Now, tell me why you're upset."

Ewan threw his hands up, wincing when he smacked the table. "Where do I even start? I just found out my wife's been letting me in less than the jerk who murdered my father."

"She never let him in," Lucia said evenly. "She told me that much."

"Not like that!" Ewan snapped, even as part of him darkly wondered if Tree was still holding back, out of some twisted sense of mercy. "She won't tell me the important stuff until it's too late. Every time I learn her secrets, it's a frapping disaster."

"If that's the case, I don't blame her for keeping them," Lucia said wryly. "Honey, she's scared. You're her world. From the moment she brought you here, she's done nothing but help you."

Before that, even. Ewan's heart burned as he thought of Tree crossing the Veridian wilderness with him, using her magic to keep them going. All the months she spent after logging him out, patiently taking him from tube-bound player to human being. All those secret meetings she had with Rothchild.

"She needed me for the war," he said mulishly. "She'd have done it for any other player."

"Would she have borne a child for any other player?" Lucia asked cuttingly. "Could she have, even?"

"I—I don't know."

Lucia sighed. "You may not be able to see anymore, but I can. I was watching you both when Dawn was born. You and Tree share a deep connection, something truly special."

Ewan grunted. "Some connection we've got, if she followed Gabe to bed."

"Ah...and you've never gotten worked up over a woman you hardly knew, just because she came on strong?" Lucia asked, her voice turning pouty.

Ewan's skin itched. "You know I have. But you forced that on me. I wasn't interested."

The older woman leaned close, the pout dropping to a throaty whisper. "Your body was. And what about all those times this past year, honey? Do you think I didn't notice the way you looked at me, when you and Tree came to the nursery?"

"That's not fair!" Ewan sputtered, but the itch blossomed into guilt. "I...I didn't know how badly you'd wanted a baby."

He could feel Lucia's eyes, burning into him. Her breath, hot on his neck. "And if you'd given me one, there'd have been no pleasure in it, for you?"

Ewan tried to ignore the blood rushing through his body, proving her point to his shame. "That's not the same! I was with Tree."

"And if you hadn't been?"

He tried to think of anything else, but Lucia was pressed against him. Impossible to ignore. "I don't know. Maybe. But you probably wouldn't have taken no for an answer."

Lucia leaned away, her voice turning sympathetic. "Probably not," she admitted. "Do you think Gabe did, with Tree?"

"No." Ewan sighed in relief, though his heart was still racing. "Tree said she ran away."

They sat for a long moment, listening to Tree cry in the other room. "Tell me," Lucia asked gently, "have you ever forgiven yourself about me?"

Ewan shook his head. "Tree forgave me...that was good enough."

"There you have it. Tree hasn't forgiven herself about Gabe, so you've got to be a man and forgive her instead."

"What if I'm not man enough?" Ewan whispered.

He nearly jumped out of his skin when Lucia gripped him. "Trust me, honey. You're man enough." Chuckling, she let go.

Ewan's face burned, but not at all from his injuries. "Please don't do that again."

"Go in there and make up with your wife, and I won't have to," Lucia said firmly. "If you don't, I'll remember what you said about helping me."

Ewan groaned inwardly, but underneath it, he felt a smile trying to break out. "I hope you can find someone, someday. It just won't be me."

"I know," Lucia said, her voice wistful but satisfied. "Go on, honey. I'll follow you in a minute, to get Dawn."

"Lucia...thanks."

"Any time," she said sincerely. "That woman is your world, as much as you're hers. Take care of her."

"I will." Ewan's heart was still broken, and he and Tree had a ton of work ahead of them. They needed each other, to see what the other couldn't. To keep the communication lines open, especially now. If they didn't, they wouldn't stand a chance against Gabe's poison.

It'll be hard, but we've got to trust each other.

Bracing himself, Ewan felt his way over to Dawn's room, reaching out blindly for his wife so they could face the future together.

EPILOGUE

Ewan picked up his oud, ready to try again.

When the Dawn marches over the fields and farms,
The horses and aurochs will play.
They'll frolic and dance where the grass is warm
And sing out in joyous refrain.

"That does not rhyme," Cerri said from the living room.

Ewan ignored her, moving straight into the chorus.

And the Dawn keeps on marching all over the world.
She chases the darkness away.
And although she moves on as the blue skies unfurl,
Her passage will brighten the day!

Dawn squealed, then grunted like her plush aurochs. The one they'd named Sam.

"Well, I'm glad *you* like it," Ewan said.

"We all love hearing you play," Tree chided.

"Tri'ana Omi'ra is correct," Cerri added, her soft footfalls coming to the baby's doorway. "Your music is almost acceptable. In time, you may yet be able to play a Sah'rassan melody."

"I think I'll stick with the Veridian ones, for now," Ewan said. "I haven't written a song for years. I've got verses for the ocean, jungle, and farm, but I still need something for towns and mountains."

"You'll get it," Tree assured him. "Next time we log in to visit your mother, we should stop by the Argentine pool. We can watch the sunrise from there."

"I'd like that." Ewan smiled, and not only at the thought of their special place. By a miracle of the Logos, the wires in his tube made contact behind his eyes, deep enough to get around them.

In the game worlds, he could still see.

Tree had taken full advantage, collecting thousands of images to share with him there. Thanks to her effort, Ewan had watched Dawn's dark hair transform to a light copper, somewhere in between Tree's and Kate's. And though his own eyes were now a red-flecked mix of gray and pink, his daughter's were a vibrant, spring green.

"Love," Tree said, drawing him back to the blackness. "It's almost time for the activation."

"Yeah," Ewan replied, trying to keep the disappointment from his voice as he set the oud aside.

Tree heard it, anyway. "I'm sorry. I know it won't be the same for you."

"It's okay," he said as he dredged up a smile. "I've already seen it. Want me to carry Dawn?"

"No, I've got her—" Tree grunted, followed by stumbling footsteps. "You've gotten so big!"

Ewan held out an arm to steady her, and Cerri pressed his sword cane into his other hand. A gift from Kate, to feel his way forward—and whack anything that tried to stop him.

Not that anyone lets me fight, these days, he thought sadly.

In the four months following the Battle of the Wastes, Ewan had done his utmost to compensate for his blindness. He sparred relentlessly with Cerri and Kate, then Al'Dashan, once the captain—colonel, now—had recovered from his own injuries. It was lopsided combat to say the least, but it gave Ewan an excuse to hear the Veridian warrior's perspective on the war effort, now that Al'Dashan and Rocco jointly led the Central military while Ewan sat in the dark at home, writing nursery songs and treading eggshells with Tree.

The week after the battle, the Centre sent a mop-up force to the Memorial, but the Locusts were gone. Ewan's one major contribution there was telling Rothchild and the others what little he could remember about his conversation with the alpha, Kadh—which amounted to saying the Locusts had obviously survived this long by not staying put. Ewan also told them about the Locust babies he'd seen, raised openly in the Wastes, but no one had an explanation for that, either.

Evidently, though, the Central deserters wanted more comfort than their nomadic allies could offer. One month after the battle, the stolen camel rolled up under a false ID code, long enough for the people inside to gut one of the agricultural buildings on the perimeter.

"We are at the elevator," Cerri warned quietly. "Be wary of the threshold."

A short ride later, Ewan found himself pressed into a gathering crowd, some of them donning masks for what would hopefully be the last time as they made their way outside. Ewan declined, as did Cerri. Dawn followed suit, throwing a fit as Tree wrangled her into a tiny version.

They continued, swept up in the growing river of people making its way to where the grandstands had been. After tripping his fifth victim, Ewan tucked his cane under his arm and let Tree and Cerri lead him.

If Kate and Query pull this off, it'll be a bigger spectacle than anything I ever concocted.

"The Caitsid'h say the world is made of two elements," Cerri observed sagely as they walked. "The sand, and the sky. After today, I think the Earth will be the same."

"Yeah," Ewan said, "but hopefully not forever. I like to think there's room for more in the real world, you know? With a little luck, maybe we can make it as green as Veridor."

"And with a lot of work," Tree added.

They eventually came to a stop in the midst of an eager—and friendly—crowd. Gabe's treachery had flushed out the player-hating Centrals, allowing the remnant to properly welcome the Veridians and Sah'rassans still pouring in. Each culture was certainly still its own, but together they had started becoming something greater, building onto the best each one had to offer.

Ewan logged in as often as he could, to help vet every new recruit.

The Logos's chime rang out through the dust, followed by the Director's resonant voice. "My dear friends," he announced. "People of all races and worlds. We stand here on the surface today, to bear witness to a miracle born from human ingenuity and the resources to manifest it on the Earth. Before we begin, however, please join me in a moment of silence to honor the blood and sacrifices of those who made this day possible."

Ewan fought back a sudden flood of tears as he heard the rustle of hundreds of heads, bowing in memory. He thought of Patrick Lee, so young and eager, never knowing he was a pawn. He thought of Jennifer Tilley and her husband, dying as they shielded their son near the very spot he now stood. That made him think of Kyle—which made him think of Bach'an, too. The two of them had bonded, playing hours of ping pong in the gym until Bach'an's severed back gave out for good. Now they were in Sah'rassa together, acting as Amad'hi's in-game Claw and personal assistant. Sarah Duncan went to see them often, but thanks to Nichols's surgery, she still served in the Centre as one of Al'Dashan's lieutenants.

But, more than anyone else, this day was meant for Sam. Ewan gave it up, letting the tears roll from his dead eyes as he thanked the big guy with the furrowed brow and easy smile, for saving his spirit.

Rest in peace, my friend. I hope you're in a better place.

"Thank you," Rothchild said quietly. "From the moment Chief O'Meara logged out our first heroic player, the bounds of the possible have continued to make way for our inspired purpose. Now, over two years later, we are assembled to witness a remarkable feat, unmatched by any in Earth's history. Please join me in recognizing the ingenuity of Quriem, the craftsmanship of Katrina O'Meara, and the dedication of the late Samuel Draper, without which the other two assure me this wonder could never have happened."

The crowd applauded, until the Director cleared his throat. "Now, I am told by the designers that the effect of the scrubbing network will be almost instantaneous, once it is activated. Are you ready, Miss O'Meara?" he asked, pausing to listen to Kate's answer over his radio. "Then let us part the curtain of sand above us, at long last!"

The hairs on Ewan's neck tingled, and a moment later he felt a rush and pressure as the *Red Horse 2* soared past overhead.

"That felt close," he muttered, passing a hand through his hair.

"Oh, they cleared the Towers by at least fifty feet," Tree said lightly, as Dawn babbled.

As usual, Kate and Query had tried to explain to Ewan how their latest invention worked. As usual, he hadn't understood most of it. The moles had put up an array of scrubber platforms, apparently like some epic version of Kate's static-wild hair, which generated an electric field, but not one strong enough to hurt anyone. Somehow, this field was supposed to make the windblown sand stick together, which meant it would be too heavy to stay aloft. The scrubbers were powered by wind turbines, which would theoretically work just fine in the clean air they were helping to create.

It all sounded very neat. Exactly the kind of thing that would have made Jack O'Meara shake his head and smile at his daughter.

The crowd fell silent, drawing a collective breath. Ewan heard a light shuffling, like the sound of snow falling in Veridor, coming from the direction the *Horse* had flown. Then, as cheers rang out all around him, Ewan caught the difference in the air. A crisp, clean scent, like the aftermath of a great thunderstorm. He gave a shout of his own as the fresh air blew across his face, then again as a gentle warmth reached him from above and he knew that here, at least, the sun was shining onto the Earth once more.

The Director's elated voice boomed out. "Well done, indeed! In recognition of this historic moment, and in the spirit of hope made manifest, I will now release one of the most carefully guarded secrets of my office."

"What's he talking about?" Ewan asked Tree.

But Rothchild answered for her. "As we all know, the Centre was created to preserve humankind as the Mother slumbered. But until this day, only its Directors understood that we have also been preserving much more than that. Two thousand, six hundred and fourteen years ago, my founding predecessor oversaw the creation of a vast genetic repository for every species of plant and animal the people of his day could salvage. This repository, stocked with the seeds of life for the creatures of Old Earth, I officially open in hope that the light of day, so long removed from our eyes, can awaken the Mother and make these grounds the Wastes no longer!"

For a moment, there was stunned silence. "Tree," Ewan

whispered, awestruck, "did he just say there would be life on the surface again?"

"I think he did," Tree replied, her voice distant as she clenched his hand. "He never told me…Ewan, we can do it! We can restore the world!"

The gathered crowd began to clap. Slowly and uncertainly at first, then building momentum as the growing applause reassured them they'd heard correctly, until as one they roared their approval. A great pride of lions, challenging the new sun to shine brighter.

Tree gave Ewan a kiss on the cheek. "I'm sorry you can't see this."

"It's okay," Ewan said, wiping away the tears as he took another deep breath of clean air. "Like I said, I've seen it before." The memory of his last vision stirred in his mind, and he pushed away the automatic resentment that came with it. He sighed. "Gabe said the open sky would be a beacon of hope… one that would make things that much worse, in the end. He was so convinced that we're all doomed to die."

Tree gave him another kiss, harder this time. "We all are, eventually. But our perception of the world inspires us to change it, for better or worse. You've proven it to me, love, every day I've known you. Kate and Query are proving it again, right now. Even if the scrubbers were to break tomorrow, everyone here will have seen the sky as it is, waiting patiently for us. They would work to see it again."

"You're right," Ewan said with a smile, taking Dawn as Tree shifted the baby over to him. "Your mommy's a smart lady, Dawn! And we promise that we'll leave this world for you in better shape than we found it, okay?"

Dawn giggled as he bounced her, and Tree's arm slipped around his waist as they both lifted their faces to the blue sky above.

The Dawn Song

Ewan O'Meara

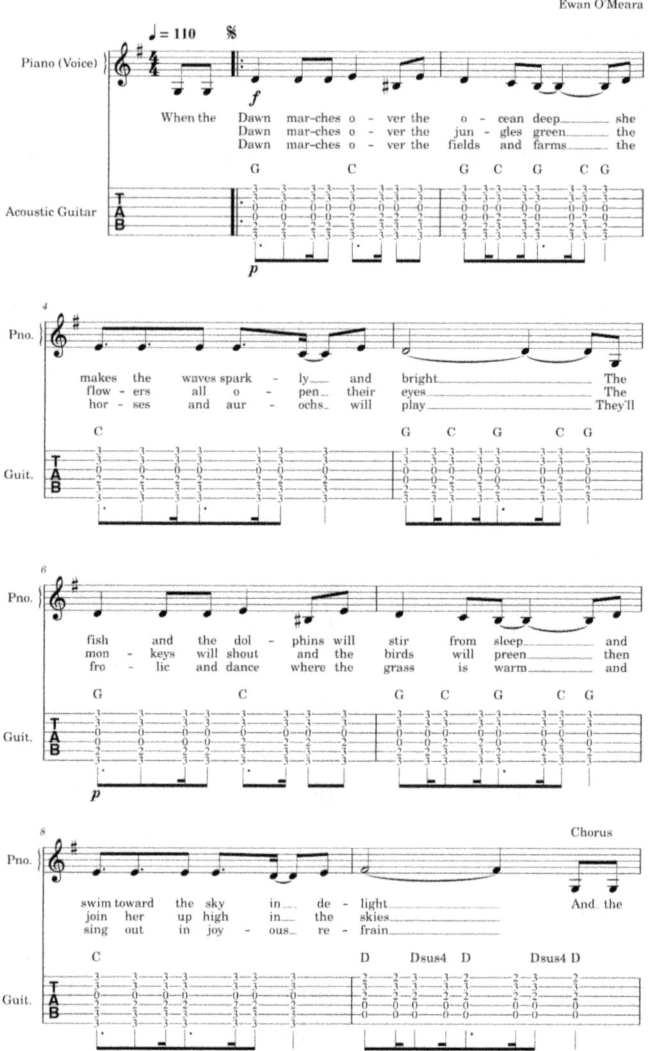

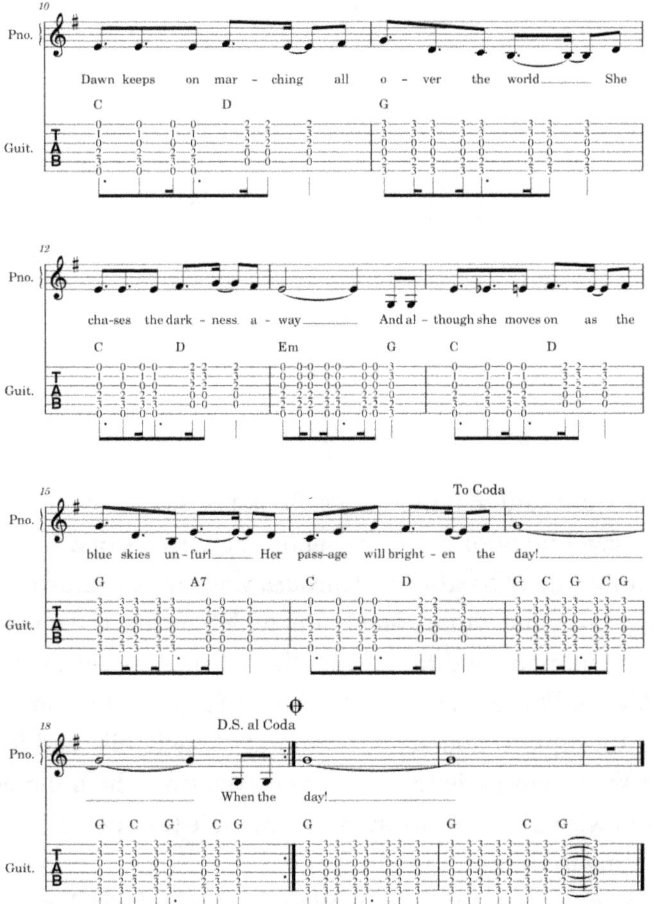
Pno.
Dawn keeps on mar - ching all o - ver the world She
C D G
Guit.
chases the dark - ness a - way And al - though she moves on as the
C D Em G C D
blue skies un - furl Her pass-age will bright - en the day!
To Coda
G A7 C D G C G C G
D.S. al Coda
When the day!
G C G C G G G C G

2

ACKNOWLEDGMENTS

I've heard it said that in a series, Book 1 is there to capture interest, while Book 2 is there set up the actual story. This is certainly true of *Sandstorm*. *Emissary* was the adventurous, daring prologue, but it's *Sandstorm* which begins the deep dive into the human condition that is the heart of the series. This book would never have seen the light of day, but for the constant support and encouragement of my family and friends. Thanks to their patience, it's also evolved from the hot mess I started with in 2015, into an immersive tale (I hope!) of adjusting to the adult world.

Thank you to my alpha readers, such as Lily Ballengee and Margaret Holz, who suffered through those chaotic first drafts. Your invaluable early feedback shaped the story while it was still young and flexible.

Thank you to my beta readers, for your insights and enthusiasm. Special thanks to my core crew of Julian Klimov, Jessica Reed, Sarah Joy Green-Hart, and my sister, Lauren (with her husband, Ben). Your reactions to the twists and turns—especially the big one—are the source of great joy for me, and I can't wait to get your thoughts on the next book in the series!

Thank you to Soraya Corcoran for continuing to map out the game worlds in stunning color, lending depth and ensuring each world has its own unique style. Thank you to Julisa Basak for taking on the cover art project; your illustrations bring Ewan's struggle to life in the best way.

Thank you to my children, Elanor and Bridget. You've heard this story so many times, but you're always up to hear the latest tweak. If only the two of you take heart from Ewan's journey, then I can count myself successful. And Elly, I still have your cartoon of "the imp-cident" in my office.

I thank my cats, especially my late daughter cat, Freya, who sat in my lap as long as you could as I put this series together. I miss you, but every time I see Cerri'dah's loving, judgmental stare in my mind, I see you and your sister, Tifa. And when I see Bach'an cavorting about, I see my late brother cat, Spartacus, loping with me through the fields of Summerland.

Most of all, I thank my wife, best friend, and critique partner, Kristina. You're my inspiration, and I'm grateful to be able to share my soul with you through our writing, from roughest draft to our ever-growing shelf of author copies. I don't even know how many little in-jokes I've scattered through these books, but I'm grateful for all the insight you've given me, especially as a mother, for this book—and I'm glad we've learned to communicate better than Ewan and Tree! I'm honored to make every journey with you.

ABOUT THE AUTHOR

E.B. Brooks lives in the southeastern USA, where he splits his time between writing, research, and homesteading. He enjoys building fictional worlds, real houses, and landscape models, but he's most at home with his wife and children, and their many, many pets.

Find out more about the Emissary Quintet at his website, ebbrooksfiction.com, and follow him on Twitter @HeroOfVeridor for official news and updates.

ALSO BY E. B. BROOKS

www.ingramcontent.com/pod-product-compliance
Lightning Source LLC
Chambersburg PA
CBHW070551310726
48982CB00011B/1539/J

* 9 7 8 1 7 3 4 7 3 9 8 4 8 *